# DAVID WEBER

Copyright © 1995 by David M. Weber

A Baen Books Original

Baen Publishing Enterprises
P.O. Box 1403
Riverdale, NY 10471

ISBN: 0-671-87642-2

Cover art by Larry Elmore
Maps by Eleanor Kostyk

First printing, February 1995
Third printing, September 1999

Distributed by Simon & Schuster
1230 Avenue of the Americas
New York, NY 10020

Printed in the United States of America

**hradani** (hrä-**dä**-ne) *n.* (1) One of the original Five Races of Man, noted for foxlike ears, great stature and physical strength, and violence of temperament. (2) A barbarian or berserker. (3) Scum, brigand. *adj.* (1) Of or pertaining to the hradani race. (2) Dangerous, bloodthirsty or cruel. (3) Treacherous, not to be trusted. (4) Incapable of civilized conduct. [Old Kontovaran: from *hra*, calm + *danahi*, fox.]

**Rage, the** (rag) *n.* Hradani term for the uncontrollable berserk bloodlust afflicting their people. Held by some scholars to be the result of black sorcery dating from the Fall of Kontovar (*q.v.*).

**Strictures of Ottovar** (**strik**-cherz uv äh-to-**vär**) *n.* Ancient code of white wizardry enforced by Council of Ottovar in pre-Fall Kontovar. The Strictures are said to have prohibited blood magic or the use of sorcery against non-wizards, and violation of its provisions was a capital offense. It is said that the wild wizard (*q.v.*) Wencit of Rum, last Lord of the Council of Ottovar prior to the Fall, still lives and attempts to enforce them with the aid of the Order of Semkirk.

—*New Manhome Encyclopedic*
*Dictionary of Norfressan Languages,*
Royal and Imperial Press:
King Kormak College, Manhome.

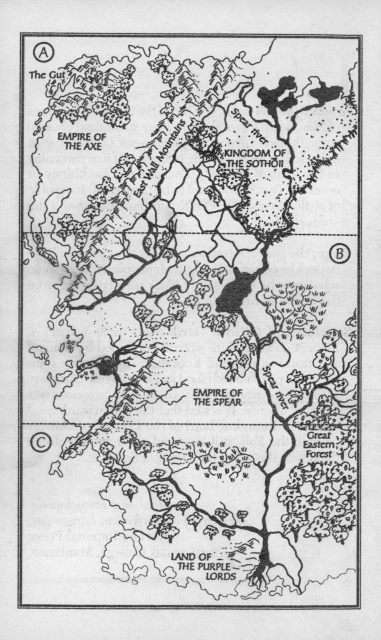

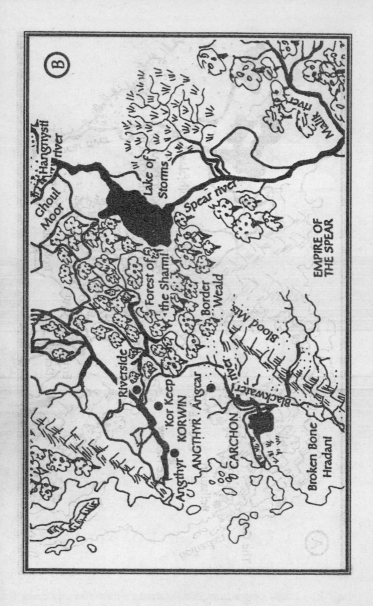

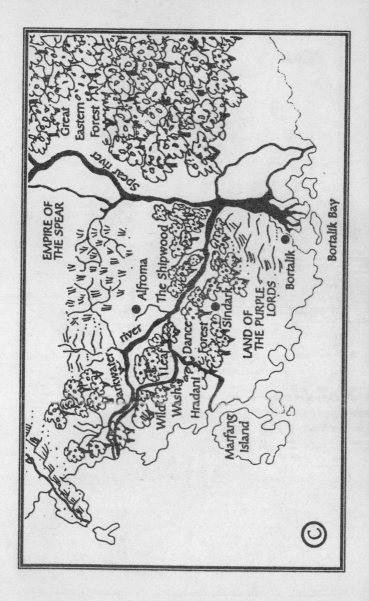

# CHAPTER ONE

He shouldn't have taken the shortcut.

Bahzell Bahnakson realized that the instant he heard the sounds drifting down the inky-dark cross corridor. He'd had to keep to the back ways used only by the palace servants—and far more numerous slaves—if he wanted to visit Brandark without the Guard's knowledge, for he was too visible to come and go openly without being seen. But he shouldn't have risked the shortcut just to avoid the more treacherous passages of the old keep.

He stood in an ill-lit hall heavy with the stink of its sparse torches (the expensive oil lamps were saved for Churnazh and his "courtiers"), and his mobile, foxlike ears strained at the faint noises. Then they flattened in recognition, and he cursed. Such sounds were none of his business, he told himself, and keeping clear of trouble was. Besides, they were far from the first screams he'd heard in Navahk . . . and there'd been nothing a prince of rival Hurgrum could do about the others, either.

1

He squeezed his dagger hilt, and his jaw clenched with the anger he dared not show his "hosts." Bahzell had never considered himself squeamish, even for a hradani, but that was before his father sent him here as an envoy. As a hostage, really, Bahzell admitted grimly. Prince Bahnak's army had crushed Navahk and its allies, yet Hurgrum was only a single city-state. She lacked the manpower to occupy her enemies' territories, though many a hradani chieftain would have let his own realm go to ruin by trying to add the others to it.

But Bahnak was no ordinary chieftain. He knew there could be no lasting peace while Churnazh lived, yet he was wise enough to know what would happen if he dispersed his strength in piecemeal garrisons, each too weak to stand alone. He could defeat Navahk and its allies in battle; to *conquer* them he needed time to bind the allies his present victories had attracted to him, and he'd bought that time by tying Churnazh and his cronies up in a tangle of treaty promises, mutual defense clauses, and contingencies a Purple Lord would have been hard put to unravel. Half a dozen mutually suspicious hradani warlords found the task all but impossible, and to make certain they kept trying rather than resorting to more direct (and traditional) means of resolution, Bahnak had insisted on an exchange of hostages. It was simply Bahzell's ill fortune that Navahk, as the most powerful of Hurgrum's opponents, was entitled to a hostage from Hurgrum's royal family.

Bahzell understood, but he wished, just this once, that he could have avoided the consequences of being Bahnak's son. Bad enough that he was a Horse Stealer, towering head and shoulders above the tallest of the Bloody Sword tribes and instantly identifiable as an outsider. Worse that Hurgrum's crushing victories had humiliated Navahk, which made him an instantly *hated* outsider. Yet both of those things were only to be expected, and Bahzell could have lived with them, if only Navahk weren't ruled by Prince Churnazh, who not only hated Prince Bahnak (and his son), but despised them as degenerate, over-civilized weaklings, as well. His cronies and hangers-on aped their prince's attitude and, predictably, each vied with the other to prove *his* contempt was deeper than any of his fellows'.

So far, Bahzell's hostage status had kept daggers out of his back and his own sword sheathed, but no hradani was truly suited to the role of diplomat, and Bahzell had come to suspect he was even less suited than most. It might have been different somewhere else, but holding himself in check when Bloody Swords tossed out insults that would have cost a fellow *Horse Stealer* blood had worn his temper thin. He wondered, sometimes, if Churnazh secretly *wanted* him to lose control, wanted to drive Bahzell into succumbing to the Rage in order to free himself from the humiliating treaties? Or was it possible Churnazh truly believed his sneer that the Rage had gone out of Hurgrum, leaving her warriors gutless as water? It was hard to be sure of anything where the Navahkan was concerned, but two things were certain as death. He hated and despised Prince Bahnak, and his contempt for the changes Bahnak had wrought in Hurgrum was boundless.

That Bahzell understood, after a fashion, for he, too, was hradani. He understood the craving for battle, the terrible hot hunger of the Rage, and he shared his people's disdain for weakness. But he had no use for blind stupidity, either, and what he *couldn't* understand was how Churnazh could continue to think Bahnak a fool. Churnazh might sneer at Hurgrum as a city of shopkeepers who'd forgotten how to be warriors, but surely even he didn't think it had been pure luck that Hurgrum had won *every* battle!

Of course, as a lad Bahzell himself had questioned some of his father's more peculiar notions. What need did a warrior have of reading and writing or arithmetic? Why worry about tradesmen and artisans or silly things like laws governing money-lending or property rights? Where was the honor in learning to hold formation instead of charging forward to carve your own glory from the enemy's ranks? And—despite himself, Bahzell smiled a little in memory, even now—surely bathing every single week would ruin a man's constitution!

But he questioned no more. Hurgrum's army hadn't simply defeated five times its own numbers; it had slaughtered them and driven their survivors from the field in a rabble, and it had done so because it fought as a disciplined unit. Because its maps were accurate and the commanders of its fast-marching contingents, or at least their aides, could read the orders their prince sent them and close in upon their enemies in coordinated attacks. And because it was uniformly trained, because its warriors *did* keep formation and were equipped with weapons of its own city's manufacture from the hands and forges of the "shopkeepers" Churnazh despised.

That was a lesson even other Horse Stealers could appreciate, which explained the new allies Hurgrum was gathering in, but since seeing Navahk, Bahzell had come to recognize an even more enduring side of his father's accomplishments. Prince Bahnak's native city had been bad enough before he came to power, yet Navahk was worse than Hurgrum had ever been. *Far* worse. It was a place of noisome streets cluttered with garbage, night soil, and small dead animals, heavy with the stench of unwashed people and waiting pestilence, all presided over by swaggering bullies in the colors of the prince who was supposed to rule his people, not plunder them himself!

But, then, Churnazh had been a common brigand before he joined the Navahkan army, rose through the ranks, and seized the throne, and he was proud of the brute strength that proved his right to rule. Strength Bahzell could appreciate; weakness was beneath contempt, and he knew his father couldn't have held his own throne if his warriors thought for one moment that he was a weakling. But in Churnazh's eyes, "strength" rested upon terror. His endless wars had made Navahk the most feared of all the Bloody Sword cities, yet Navahk herself was terrified of *him* . . . and his five sons were even worse than he.

All of which explained why the last thing a hostage from Hurgrum had any business doing was standing in this hall listening to screams and even considering intervening. Besides, whoever was screaming was only another Bloody Sword, and, with the noteworthy exception of Brandark, there wasn't a Bloody Sword worth the time to send him to Phrobus, much less risk his own life for.

Bahzell told himself that with all the hardheaded pragmatism he could summon . . . then swore vilely and started down the unlit corridor.

Crown Prince Harnak grinned as he smashed his fist into Farmah's face yet again. Her gagged scream was weaker and less satisfying than it had been, but his metal reinforced gauntlet cut fresh, bleeding gashes, and he felt a sensual thrill of power even greater than he'd felt when he raped her.

He let her slip to the floor, let her try to crawl away with her arms bound behind her, then kicked her in the ribs. The shredded chemise wadded into her mouth muffled her gurgling shriek as his boot smashed her into the stone wall, and he laughed. The bitch. Thought she was too good for a prince of the blood, did she? Well, she'd learned better now, hadn't she?

He watched her curl in a beaten ball and savored her hopeless terror. Rape was the one crime that might turn even his father's men against him, but no one would ever know who'd had this slut. When they found her body and saw all the things he'd done—and still looked forward to doing—they'd assume exactly what he wanted: that someone taken by the Rage's blood frenzy had slaughtered her like a sow, and—

An abrupt explosion of rending wood shattered his hungry anticipation and snatched him around in shock. The long abandoned sleeping chamber's locked door was thick, as stout and well built as any door in Navahk was likely to be, but its latch simply disappeared in a cloud of splinters, and the door itself slammed back against the wall so hard one iron hinge snapped. Harnak jumped back in instant panic, mind already racing for a way to bribe or threaten his way out of the consequences of discovery, but then his eyes widened as he saw who stood in the opening.

That towering figure could not be mistaken for anyone else, but it was alone, and Harnak snarled in contemptuous relief as the intruder glanced at the naked, battered girl huddled against the wall. Big he might be, but Bahzell of Hurgrum was no threat. The puling, puking coward had hidden behind his "hostage" status for over two years, swallowing insults no warrior would let pass . . . and he was armed only with a dagger, while Harnak's sword lay ready on the rotting bed. Bahzell would never raise his hand to the heir to Navahk's throne—especially if it meant matching eighteen inches of steel against forty!—and even if he carried the tale to others, no one in Navahk would dare take his word over that of a prince of the blood. Particularly if Harnak saw to it that Farmah had vanished before the Horse Stealer could get back with help. He straightened his back with an automatic, arrogant snarl, gathering his scattered wits to order the intruder out, but the words died unspoken as Bahzell's eyes moved back to him. There was something in them Harnak had never seen before . . . and Bahzell wasn't stopping in the doorway.

A ball of ice froze in Harnak's belly. He had time to feel one sudden stab of terror, to abandon his swaggering posture and leap desperately for his sword, and then an iron clamp seized him by the throat. Shouting for help would have done him no good—he'd chosen this spot so no one would hear *his* victim's screams—but he never got the chance to try, for his cry died in a wheezing gurgle as the clamp lifted his toes from the floor. He writhed and choked, beating at Bahzell's wrist with his gauntleted hands, and then another hand—not a clamp, this one, but a spiked mace—crashed into his belly.

Harnak screamed as three ribs snapped. The sound was faint and strangled . . . and dwarfed by the sound he made when a knee like a tree trunk smashed up between his legs.

His world vanished in agony so great he hardly noticed the mace crashing into his belly again. And then again and again and again. But he retained enough awareness to realize what was happening as Bahzell released his throat at last. The choking hand clasped the nape of his neck instead. Another hand caught his belt, and Crown Prince Harnak of Navahk screamed in terror . . . until he smashed face-first into the dirty little chamber's wall and the impact cut his shriek off like a knife.

He oozed down the stone, smearing it with red, and Bahzell snarled and started forward to finish the job. The Horse Stealer's muscles quivered as fury snapped and sputtered through them, but sanity still flickered, and he made himself stop. He closed his eyes and inhaled deeply, fighting back the red haze. It wasn't easy, but the killing madness ebbed without quite passing over into the Rage, and he shook himself. He opened his eyes once more and looked down, grimacing at the knuckles he'd split on his enemy's metal-studded leather jerkin, then turned to Harnak's latest victim.

She writhed away in terror, too battered and beaten

to realize he wasn't Harnak, but then she felt the gentleness of his touch and whimpered.

"There, lass. There," he murmured, bitterly aware of how useless the soothing sounds were yet making them anyway, and her frantic struggles eased. One eye opened, staring fearfully up at him, but the other was swollen shut, and the cheek below it was clearly broken.

He touched her hair gently, and disgust filled him as he recognized her cut and bloody face. Farmah. Who but Harnak—or his brothers—would rape a mere girl supposedly under his own father's protection?

He lifted her, and bleak hate filled his eyes at her pain sound when broken ribs shifted. Her hands were bound behind her, and fresh contempt snarled through him as he recalled Harnak's swaggering bluster about courage and hardihood. Courage, it seemed, required a "warrior" to bind a teenaged girl half his size to be certain she was helpless before he raped her and beat her bloody!

He eased her into a sitting position on a battered old chest against the wall. It was filthy, but the only other furnishing was the bed Harnak had raped her upon. She shuddered in terror and pain, yet she leaned forward to help as he cut the cord that had flayed her wrists raw and plucked the wad of cloth from her mouth. Returning intelligence flickered in her good eye. "Thank you, M'lord," she whispered. *"Thank you!"*

Her hand rose and squeezed his wrist with surprising strength. Or perhaps not so surprising, for she, too, was hradani, however slim and delicate she might be compared to Bahzell.

"Hush, girl. Don't be thanking me," Bahzell rumbled, and looked away from her nakedness in sudden embarrassment. He spied Harnak's discarded cloak and scooped it up, averting his eyes as he held it out to her, and her sound as she took it was trapped between a sob of pain and shame and a strange, twisted ghost of a laugh.

It snarled deep inside Bahzell, that sound, striking fresh sparks of fury. He bought a few moments to reassert control by ripping a length of cloth from Harnak's none too clean shirt and wrapping it around his bleeding knuckles, but the delay was little help, and his hand itched for his dagger once more as he glared down at Harnak. Rape. The one crime not even the Rage could excuse, even in Navahk. Hradani women had enough to endure without that, and they were too precious to abuse so, for they alone were immune to the Rage, the guardians of what little stability most hradani tribes could cling to.

"Lillinara must have sent you." Farmah's slurred words sent his ears flat once more, and he sketched an instant, instinctive warding gesture. She huddled in Harnak's cloak, shaken by pain and reaction, and used a scrap of her torn clothing to wipe at the blood trickling from her nose and split lips.

"Wish me no ill fortune, lass. No good ever came of mixing in the gods' business, and it's Phrobus' own tangle we're in now, the both of us," he muttered, and Farmah nodded in understanding.

Hradani notions of justice were harsh. They had to be for a people afflicted by the Rage, and the universal penalty for rape was castration and then to be drawn and quartered. But Harnak wasn't just Churnazh's son; he was his *eldest* son, heir to the throne, and ten years of Churnazh's rule had made it plain the law did not apply to him or his. Farmah knew that better than most, for her father and elder brother had died at the hands of an off duty Guard captain. Everyone knew Churnazh had borrowed heavily from her father, but the prince had accepted his captain's claim of the Rage and pardoned him, and somehow the debt—the money which might have meant Farmah's livelihood or means of flight—had simply vanished. Which was how she came to find herself living under Churnazh's "protection" as little more than a slave.

"Is—is he alive?" she asked weakly.

"Um." Bahzell gave the limp body a brutal kick, and it flopped onto its back without even a groan. "Aye, he's alive," he grunted, grimacing down at the ruined face and watching breath bubble in the blood from its smashed nose and lips, "but how long will he stay that way? There's the question." He knelt, and his jaw tightened as he touched an indentation in Harnak's forehead. "He's less pretty than he was, and I'm thinking he hit the wall a mite hard, but he's a head like a boulder. He might live yet, Krahana take him."

The Horse Stealer sank back on his heels, fingering his dagger. Cutting a helpless throat, even when it belonged to scum like this, went hard with him. Then again, a man had to be practical. . . .

"Chalak saw him take me," Farmah said weakly behind him, and he spat a fresh oath. Finishing Harnak might protect *him*, but if the prince's brother knew his plans for Farmah, Harnak's death would only make her hopeless situation still worse. Chalak *might* keep quiet, since Harnak's elimination would improve his own chance for power, yet he was only Churnazh's fourth son. It was unlikely Harnak's removal would profit him significantly . . . but identifying his brother's killer to their father certainly would.

The Horse Stealer stood and glared down at the motionless body while his mind raced. Killing Harnak wouldn't save Farmah, and that meant it wouldn't help *him*, either. Enough torture would loosen any tongue, and Churnazh would apply the irons himself. He'd like that, even if he hadn't lost his son. So unless Bahzell was prepared to cut the girl's throat as well as Harnak's . . .

"How badly are you hurt, lass?" he asked, turning to her at last. She looked back mutely, and he waved a hand in a gesture that mixed impatience with apology. "We're both dead if we stay, girl, whether he lives or dies. If I get you away, can you stay on your feet to run?"

"I—" Farmah looked back down at Harnak and shivered, then stiffened her shoulders and nodded as her own thoughts followed his. "I can run. Not fast, M'lord, but I can run," she said hoarsely. "Only where could I run *to?*"

"Aye, there's the question." Bahzell gave Harnak another kick, feeling her watch him in silence, and the look of trust in her one good eye made him feel even worse. He wished her no ill-fortune, but he couldn't help wishing he'd never heard her screams, and he knew too well how misplaced her trust might be against the odds they faced. But counting the odds never shortened them, and he sighed and shook himself. "I'm thinking there's just one place, lass—Hurgrum."

"*Hurgrum?*"

He smiled sourly at the shock in her voice, for if one thing was certain it was that *he* couldn't return to Hurgrum. There'd be hell enough to pay over this even if Harnak lived; if the bastard died, Churnazh was certain to outlaw Bahzell for breaking hostage bond. He might well do so even if Harnak lived—gods and demons knew he'd seemed happy enough to let others try to provoke Bahzell into something which would let him do just that! And if the Bloody Swords outlawed him and he returned to his father's court, the fragile balance holding the armies from one another's throats would come down in ruins.

"Aye, Hurgrum," he said. "But that's for you, lass, not me." He turned away from Harnak, doubts banished by action, and lifted her in his arms. "I came this way to avoid people. Let's be hoping the two of us don't meet anyone else on our way out—and that no one finds this bastard before we're gone."

# CHAPTER TWO

Bahzell moved swiftly down the ill-lit halls despite his burden. Churnazh's "palace" was a half-ruinous rabbit warren whose oldest section had been little more than a brigand's keep, built in a swampy bend of the small Navahk River as a place to lie up and count loot. Its newer sections included a few straighter, wider passages—evidence of days when Navahk's rulers had at least aspired to better things—but the present prince's notions of maintenance left much of his palace's crumbling core dangerously unsafe.

Bahzell knew that, but it was always best to know the lay of the land, and after two years, he'd learned the palace as well as any of the slaves and servants who toiled within it. Now he used that knowledge to pick a circuitous route that avoided sentries and well traveled areas, and he made it almost all the way to his assigned chambers before he heard the sound of feet.

He swore softly but with feeling, for he couldn't have

picked a worse place to meet someone. The brisk footsteps clattered down a cross passage towards the last four-way intersection before his rooms, and the bare corridor behind him offered no concealment. But at least it sounded like a single person, and he set Farmah down and drew his dagger in a whisper of steel.

The feet pattered closer. They reached the intersection, and Bahzell leapt forward—only to jerk himself up short as his intended victim jumped back with a squeak of panic.

"M-M'lord?" the middle-aged woman quavered, and, despite the situation, Bahzell grinned. Her eyes were glued to the steel gleaming in his hand, and she sounded justifiably terrified, but she wasn't running for her life. Which she would have been, if she hadn't recognized him. Churnazh's servants had the reactions of any other terrorized and abused creatures, and it had taken Bahzell months to convince them he wouldn't hurt them; now this single moment made all his efforts worthwhile.

"I'd no mind to frighten you, Tala," he said mildly as he lowered his dagger. The woman who would have been the palace's housekeeper in Hurgrum (here she was simply one slave among many, and more exposed to her "betters'" wrath than most), drew a deep breath at his pacific tone and opened her mouth . . . just as Farmah stepped waveringly out from behind him.

"*Farmah!*" Tala gasped, and leapt forward as the girl's legs began to give. Only Tala's arms kept her from collapsing, and the housekeeper gasped again as she realized how badly hurt Farmah was. Her eyes darted back to Bahzell, and he winced at the sudden, horrified accusation—the look of betrayal—in them. Yet he couldn't blame her for her automatic assumption, and the accusation vanished as quickly as it had come. The horror remained, but fury replaced the betrayal, and her ears flattened.

"Who, M'lord?" she hissed. "Who *did* this?!"

"Harnak," Farmah answered for him, resting the less injured side of her face against Tala's shoulder, and the protective arms tightened about her. Tala looked into Bahzell's eyes, searching for confirmation, and her own face tightened as he nodded. She started to speak again, then pressed her lips together and handed Farmah back to him.

She darted back to the intersection without a word and looked both ways, then beckoned him forward, and he sighed with relief as he scooped the girl back up and followed her.

Tala led the way to his chambers like a scout, then closed the outer door behind him and leaned against it to watch him deposit Farmah gently in a chair. Her expression was grim, but she showed no surprise when he shrugged out of his tunic, squirmed into a padded buckram aketon, and lifted his scale shirt from its rack. He drew it on and reached up for his sword, looping the baldric over his head and settling the hilt against his left shoulder blade, and Tala cleared her throat.

"Is he dead, M'lord?" Her voice was flat.

"He was breathing when I left him. Now?" Bahzell shrugged, and she nodded without surprise.

"I was afraid of this. He's been after her so long, and—" Tala closed her mouth and shook her head. "How can I help, M'lord?"

Bahzell shook his head quickly, his face grim. "You'd best think what you're saying, Tala. If he dies yet, or if we're caught inside the walls—"

"If you're caught, it won't matter whether I helped you or just didn't call the Guard myself." Her voice was bleak as she looked at Farmah, huddled brokenly in the chair and little more than half-conscious. "That could be me, M'lord, or my daughter, if I'd been fool enough to have one."

Bahzell frowned, but she was right. He'd already put her at risk simply by crossing her path, and he needed all the help he could get.

"Clothes first," he said, and Tala nodded, accepting his acceptance. "I've naught that would fit her, and if anyone sees that cloak—"

"I understand, M'lord. We're close enough in size my clothes would do. And then?"

"And then forget you ever saw us. I'm thinking it's the servants' way out for us."

"Can she walk?" Tala asked bluntly, and Farmah stirred.

"I can walk." Tala eyed her skeptically, and she straightened in the chair, one arm pressed to her side to cradle broken ribs. "I *can*," she repeated, "and I have to."

"But where can you— No." Tala cut herself off and shook her head. "Best I don't know any more than I must."

"Aye, for all our sakes," Bahzell agreed grimly, and began stuffing items into a leather rucksack, starting with the heavy purse his father had sent with him.

"Very well, M'lord. I'll be as quick as I can."

Tala slipped out, closing the door behind her, and Bahzell worked quickly. He could take little, and he made his choices with ruthless dispatch, watching Farmah from the corner of one eye as he packed. She listed sideways in the chair, no longer holding herself erect to prove her strength to Tala, and he didn't like the way she was favoring her right side. Something broken in there, and gods only knew what other damage she'd suffered. He admired her courage, but how far *could* she walk? And how quickly, when Churnazh's men would be after them a-horseback within hours?

He pushed the worry aside as best he could and buckled the rucksack, then took his steel-bowed arbalest from the wall. (That was one more thing for Churnazh to sneer at—what sort of a hradani relied on arrows or bolts instead of meeting his enemies hand to hand?) Bahzell had hostage right to carry his personal weapons whenever he chose, but one sight of the arbalest by any sentry would raise questions he dared not answer, and he hesitated, loath to abandon it, then whirled as the door opened silently once more.

It was Tala, clothing bundled under her arm. She paused if to speak when she saw him holding the arbalest, then shook her head and crossed quickly to Farmah and helped her up from the chair. The door of the inner bedchamber closed behind them, and Bahzell laid the arbalest aside with regret. Their chance of getting as far as the city gate unchallenged was already so slight as not to exist; adding more weight to the odds would be madness.

He shrugged to settle his armor and began to pace. No one was likely to stumble over Harnak, but every second increased the chance of his regaining consciousness and raising the alarm himself. Once that happened—

Bahzell pushed the thought aside with his worries over Farmah's strength. There was nothing he could do if it happened; best to concentrate on what to do if it didn't, and he rubbed his chin and shifted his ears slowly back and forth as he thought. The immediate problem was escaping the city, but after that he still had to get Farmah to Hurgrum somehow, and how was he to do that when he himself dared not enter Hurgrum's territory? He could think of only one way, but with Farmah's injuries and—

He turned as the bedchamber door opened once more and Farmah stepped through it. Her movements were slow and obviously painful but stronger than he'd dared hope, and Tala followed her with a worried expression.

The housekeeper had done well, Bahzell thought. It would take an observant eye to realize the plain gray gown was just too large, its hem just too short for Farmah, and the extra girth helped hide the bandages Tala had bound tight about her ribs. Its long, full sleeves hid the bruises and rope burns on the girl's arms, as well, and Tala had dressed her hair, but nothing could hide the marks on her face. The blood had been washed away, and the cuts no longer bled, yet they were raw and ugly, and her bruises, especially the ones on her broken left cheek, were dark and swelling.

Farmah felt his gaze and touched her face.

"I'm sorry, M'lord," she began wretchedly, and he felt her shame at her ugliness, her knowledge that some, at least, of those cuts would be scars for life and that anyone who saw them now would guess instantly what had happened to her, "but—"

"Hush, lass! It's no fault of yours." He glanced at Tala. "I'm thinking a hooded cloak might help," he began, "and—"

"Indeed it might, M'lord," Tala agreed, raising her arm to show him the cloak draped across it, "and I've had another thought or two, as well."

"You'd best not be getting any deeper into this," Bahzell objected, and the housekeeper snorted.

"I'm deep enough to drown already, M'lord, so save your worry for things you can change." She was old enough to be Bahzell's mother, and her tart tone was so like his old nurse's that he grinned despite his tension. It seemed Churnazh had failed to crush at least one of his slaves completely, after all.

"Better," Tala said, and folded her arms beneath her breasts. "Now, M'lord, about this plan of yours. If the pair of you try to leave together, you'll be challenged by the first guard you meet."

"Aye, that's why—"

"Please, M'lord!" Her raised hand shut his mouth with a snap. "The point is that you don't *have* to leave together. All the servants know how you creep in and out to visit

Lord Brandark." His eyes widened, and she shook her head impatiently. "Of course they do! So if they see you, they'll assume that's all you're doing and look the other way, as always. And the guards are less likely to challenge you if you're by yourself, as well. True?"

"Aye, that's true enough," he admitted slowly.

"In that case, the thing to do is for you to go out through the back ways while Farmah walks right out the front gate, M'lord."

"Are you daft?! They'll never let her pass with that face, woman! And if they do, they'll guess who marked her the moment someone finds Harnak!"

"Of course they will." Tala glared up at his towering inches and shook her head. "M'lord," she said with the patience of one addressing a small child, "they'll guess that anyway when they find her missing, so where's the sense in pretending otherwise when leaving separately gives you both the chance to pass unchallenged, at least as far as the city gate?"

"Aye," Bahzell rubbed his chin once more, "there's some sense in that. But look at her, Tala." Farmah had sagged once more, leaning against the door frame for support. She stiffened and forced herself back upright, and he shook his head gently. "It's nothing against you, Farmah, and none of your fault, but you'll not make the length of the hall without help."

"No, M'lord, she won't . . . unless I go with her." Bahzell gaped at the housekeeper, and Tala's shrug was far calmer than her eyes. "It's the only way. I'll say I'm taking her to Yanahla—she's not much of a healer, but she's better than the horse leech they keep here for the servants!"

"And if they ask what's happened to her?" Bahzell demanded.

"She fell." Tala snorted once more, bitterly, at his expression. "It won't be the first time a handsome servant wench or slave has 'fallen' in this place, M'lord. Especially a *young* one." Her voice was grim, and Bahzell's face tightened, but he shook his head once more.

"That may get you out, but it won't be getting you back in, and when they miss Farmah—"

"They'll miss me, too." Tala met his gaze with a mix of desperation and pleading. "I have no one to keep me here since my son died, and I'll try not to slow you outside the city, but—" Her voice broke, and she closed her eyes. "*Please*, M'lord. I'm . . . I'm not brave enough to run away by myself."

"It's no sure thing we'll have the chance to run," Bahzell pointed out. Her nod was sharp with fear but determined, and he winced inwardly. Fiendark knew Farmah alone was going to slow him, and if Tala was uninjured, she was no spry young maid. He started to refuse her offer, then frowned. True, two city women would be more than twice the burden of one, under normal circumstances, but these weren't normal.

He studied her intently, measuring risk and her fear against capability and the determined set of her shoulders, and realized his decision was already made. He couldn't leave her behind if she helped Farmah escape, and her aid would more than double their chance to get out of the palace. Besides, the girl would need all the nursing she could get, and if he could get the two of them to Chazdark, then *he* could—

His eyes brightened, and he nodded.

"Come along, then, if you're minded to run with us. And I'll not forget this, Tala." She opened her eyes, and he smiled crookedly. "I'm thinking my thanks won't matter much if they lay us by the heels, but if they don't, I'm minded to send Farmah to my father. She'll be safe there—and so will you."

"Thank you, M'lord," Tala whispered, and he wondered if he would ever have had the courage to trust anyone after so many years in Navahk. But then she shook herself with some of her old briskness and touched his arbalest with a faint smile. "You seemed none too happy to leave this behind, M'lord. Suppose I bundle it up in a bag of dirty linen and have one of the serving men carry it around to meet you outside the palace?"

"Can you trust them?" Bahzell asked, trying to hide his own eagerness, and her smile grew.

"Old Grumuk wanders in his mind, M'lord. He knows where the servants' way comes out—he taught it to me himself, before his wits went—but he'll ask no questions, and no one ever pays any heed to him. I think it's safe enough. I'll pass the word to him as we leave; by the time you can make your way out, he'll be waiting for you."

The creeping trip through the palace's decaying core took forever. The slaves who used the passages to sneak in and out for what little enjoyment they might find elsewhere had marked them well, once a man knew what to look for, but Bahzell had never tried them armored and armed and they'd never been built for someone his size in the first place. There were a few tight spots, especially with the sword and rucksack on his back, and two moments of near disaster as teetering stone groaned and shifted, but it was the time that truly frightened him. Likely enough Harnak would never wake again, given that dent in his skull, but if he did, or if he was found, or if Tala and Farmah had been stopped after all—

Bahzell lowered his ears in frustration and made himself concentrate on his footing and how much he hated slinking about underground at the best of times. That was a more profitable line of thought; it gave him something to curse at besides his own stupidity for mixing in something like this. Fiendark only knew what his father would have to say! The world was a hard place where people got hurt, and the best a man could do was hope to look after his own. But even as he swore at himself, he knew he couldn't have just walked away. The only thing that truly bothered him—aside from the probability that it would get him killed—was whether he'd done it to save Farmah or simply because of how much he hated Harnak. Either was reason enough, it was just that a man liked to feel certain about things like that.

He reached the last crumbling passage and brightened as he saw daylight ahead, but he also reached up to loosen his sword in its sheath before he crept the last few yards forward. If Tala had been stopped, there might already be a company and more of the Guard waiting up ahead.

There wasn't. Steel clicked as he slid the blade back home, and the aged slave squatting against a moss-grown wall looked up with a toothless grin.

"And there ye be, after all!" Old Grumuk cackled. "Indeed, an' Tala said ye would! How be ye, M'lord?"

"Fine, Grumuk. A mite muddy about the edges, but well enough else." Bahzell made his deep, rumbling voice as gentle as he could. The old man was the butt of endless blows and nasty jokes, and his senile cheerfulness could vanish into whimpering, huddled defensiveness with no warning at all.

"Aye, them tunnels uz always mucky, wasn't they, now? I mind once I was tellin' Gernuk—or were it Franuzh?" Grumuk's brow wrinkled with the effort of memory. "No matter. 'Twere one or t'other of 'em, an' I was telling him—"

He broke off, muttering to himself, and Bahzell stifled a groan. The old man could run on like this for hours, filling even the most patient (which, Bahzell admitted, did not include himself) with a maddening need to shake or beat some sense into him. But there was no longer any sense to be beaten, so he crouched and touched Grumuk's shoulder, instead. The muttering mouth snapped instantly shut, and the cloudy old eyes peered up at him.

"D'ye have summat fer me, M'lord?" he wheedled, and Bahzell shook his head regretfully.

"Not this time, granther," he apologized, "but I'm thinking it may be you have something for me?"

The old man's face fell, for Bahzell knew how he hungered for the sweetmeats a child might crave and often carried them for him, but he only shook his head. His life was filled with disappointments, and he dragged out a huge, roughly woven sack. Bahzell's eyes lit as he unwrapped the dirty clothing Tala had wadded around the arbalest and ran his fingers almost lovingly over the wooden stock and steel bow stave, and Grumuk cackled again.

"Did good fer ye, did I, M'lord?"

"Aye, old friend, that you have." Bahzell touched his shoulder again, then straightened and slung the arbalest over his right shoulder. The old man grinned up at him, and Bahzell smiled back.

"You'd best bide here a mite," he said. He turned to squint at the westering sun, then pointed at the broken stump of a drunken tower whose foundations, never too firm to begin with, were sinking slowly into the muck and sewage of the swampy river. "Sit yourself where you are, Grumuk, until the sun touches that tower yonder. Do you mind that? Will you do that for me?"

"Oh, aye, M'lord. That's not so hard. Just sit here with m' thoughts till th' tower eats th' sun. I c'n do that, M'lord," Grumuk assured him.

"Good, Grumuk. Good." Bahzell patted the old man's shoulder once more, then turned and jogged away into the shadows of the abandoned keep's walls.

The raucous stench of Navahk's streets was reassuringly normal as Bahzell strode down them. Screaming packs of naked children dashed in and out about their elders' feet, absorbed in gods knew what games or wrestling for choice bits of refuse amid the garbage, and he drew up a time or two to let them pass. He kept a close hand on his belt pouch when he did, other hand ready to clout an ear hard enough to ring for a week, but he no more blamed them for their thieving ways than he blamed the half-starved street beggars or whores who importuned him. Whores, especially, were rare in Hurgrum—or most other hradani lands—but too many women had lost their men in Navahk.

He made himself move casually, painfully aware of the armor he wore and the rucksack and arbalest on his back. Afternoon was dying into evening, thickening the crowd as the farmers who worked the plots beyond the wall streamed back to their hovels, but most he passed cringed out of his way. They were accustomed to yielding to their betters—all the more so when that better towered a foot and more above the tallest of them with five feet of blade on his back—and Bahzell was glad of it, yet his spine was taut as he waited for the first shout of challenge. Whether it came to fight or flight, he had a better chance here than he would have had in the palace . . . but not by much.

Yet no one shouted, and he was almost to the east gate when he spied two women moving slowly against the tide ahead of him. Farmah leaned heavily on the shorter, stouter housekeeper, and a tiny pocket of open space moved about them. A few people looked at them and then glanced uncomfortably away, and one or two almost reached out to help, but the combination of Farmah's battered face and the palace livery both of them wore warned off even the hardiest.

Bahzell swallowed yet another curse on Churnazh and all his get as he watched men shrink away from the women and compared it to what would have happened in

Hurgrum. But this wasn't Hurgrum. It was Navahk, and he dared not overtake them to offer his own aid, either.

It was hard, slowing his pace to the best one Farmah could manage while every nerve screamed that the pursuit *had* to be starting soon, yet he had no choice. He followed them down the narrow street, dodging as someone emptied a chamber pot out the second-floor window of one of Navahk's wretched inns. A pair of less nimble farmhands snarled curses up at the unglazed windows as the filth spattered them, but such misadventures were too common for comment here, and their curses faded when they suddenly realized they were standing in Bahzell's path. They paled and backed away quickly, and he shouldered past them as Tala and Farmah turned the last bend towards East Gate.

He hurried a little now, and his heart rose as he saw the under-captain in charge of the gate detachment glance at the women. He'd thought he remembered the gate schedule, and he was right. Under-Captain Yurgazh would never have met Prince Bahnak's standards, but at least his armor was well kept and reasonably clean. He looked almost dapper compared to the men he commanded, and he was one of the very few members of Churnazh's Guard to emerge from the war against Hurgrum with something like glory. He'd been little more than a common freesword, but he'd fought with courage, and his example had turned the men about him into one of the handfuls that held together as the pikes closed in. It took uncommon strength to hold hradani during a retreat—and even more to restrain them from final, berserk charges while they fell back—which was why Yurgazh had risen to his present rank when Churnazh recruited his depleted Guard back up to strength.

Perhaps it was because he had nothing to be ashamed of that Yurgazh was willing to show respect for the warriors who'd vanquished him. Or perhaps he simply hadn't

been long enough in Navahk's service to sink to its level.
It might even be that he'd come to know more about
the prince he served and chose to vent some of his disgust in his own, private way. But whatever his reasons,
he'd always treated Bahzell as the noble he was, and
Bahzell was betting heavily on the core of decency he
suspected Yurgazh still harbored.

He paused at the corner, watching with narrowed eyes
as Yurgazh started towards the women. Then the under-
captain stopped, and Bahzell tensed as his head rose and
one hand slipped to his sword hilt. Tala's tale of seeking
a healer for Farmah would never pass muster here, for
there were no healers in the hovels against the outer face
of the wall. Nor were palace servants allowed to leave
the city without a permit, especially so late in the day,
and two women alone, one of them obviously beaten and
both with the shoulder knot of the prince's personal service, could mean only one thing to an alert sentry.

Bahzell saw the understanding in Yurgazh's face,
even at this distance, and his jaw clenched as the under-
captain suddenly looked up. His eyes locked on Bahzell
like a lodestone on steel, and Bahzell held his breath.

But then Yurgazh released his sword. He turned his
back on the women and engaged the other two gate guards
in a discussion that seemed to require a great many pointed
gestures at ill-kept equipment, and both of them were
far too busy placating his ire to even notice the two women
who stole past them.

Bahzell made his jaw unclench, yet he allowed himself no relaxation. *He* still had to get past, and that was a
much chancier proposition when none of Churnazh's
personal guardsmen accompanied him.

He strode up to the gate, and this time Yurgazh stepped
out into the gateway. He waved one of his men forward—
one who looked even less gifted with intelligence than
most—and Bahzell let his bandaged hand rest lightly on

his belt, inches from his dagger, as the under-captain nodded respectfully to him.

"You're out late, M'lord." Yurgazh had better grammar than most of Churnazh's men, and his tone was neutral. Bahzell flicked his ears in silent agreement, and a ghost of a smile flickered in Yurgazh's eyes as they lingered briefly on the Horse Stealer's rucksack and arbalest. "Bound for a hunting party, M'lord?" he asked politely.

"Aye," Bahzell said, and it was true enough, he reflected—or would be once Harnak was found.

"I see." Yurgazh rubbed his upper lip, then shrugged. "I hate to mention this, M'lord, but you really should be accompanied by your bodyguards."

"Aye," Bahzell repeated, and something very like the Rage but lighter, more like the crackle of silk rubbed on amber, made him want to grin. "Well, Captain, I'm thinking the guards will be along soon enough."

"Oh? Then His Highness knows you're going on ahead?"

"Aye," Bahzell said yet again, then corrected himself with scrupulous accuracy. "Or that's to say he *will* know as soon as Prince Harnak thinks to tell him."

Yurgazh's eyes widened, then flicked towards the gate through which the women had vanished before they darted back to Bahzell and the bloody cloth knotted about his knuckles. A startled look that mingled alarm and respect in almost equal measure had replaced their laughter— and then the under-captain shrugged and glanced at the dull-faced guardsman beside him.

"Well, if Prince Harnak knows you're going, M'lord, I don't see how it's our business to interfere." His underling didn't—quite—nod in relief, but his fervent desire not to meddle in his prince's business was plain, and Bahzell suddenly realized why Yurgazh had brought him along. He was a witness the under-captain had done his duty by questioning Bahzell . . . and that nothing Bahzell had said or done had been suspicious enough to warrant holding him.

"In that case, I'd best be going, Captain," he said, and Yurgazh nodded and stepped back to clear the gate for him.

"Aye, so you had. And—" something in the other's suddenly softer tone brought Bahzell's eyes back to his "—good fortune in the hunt, M'lord."

# CHAPTER THREE

Tala stumbled again, and this time she lost her balance completely in the darkness. She fell hard, with a muffled cry of pain, and Bahzell bit back any word of encouragement as she struggled back up. Part of him wanted to rant at her for her clumsiness; most of him was astonished by how well she'd borne up . . . and sensed her bitter shame that she'd done no better. That was foolish of her, of course; no city woman of her age could hope to match the pace of a trained warrior of half her years, which was the very reason he'd hesitated to bring her along in the first place.

But foolish or no, he respected her determination and courage . . . which, in a strange way, was what forbade soothing words they both would know as lies. Bahzell had been trained in a school whose demands were brutally simple and in which weakness was the unforgivable sin. It wasn't enough that a man had "done his best" when defeat meant death, not just for himself but for his fellows.

If his "best" wasn't enough, he must be driven—goaded—until it was; if he couldn't be driven, then he must be discarded. Yet this woman had somehow clung to courage and self-respect despite all her world had done to her, and she knew without telling that she was slowing him. He might not fully understand his compassion, if such it was, for her, but he knew nothing he said or did could drive her to greater efforts, and he refused to shame her with platitudes that treated her as less than she was.

None of which changed her desperate need for rest. He inhaled deeply, deliberately letting her hear the weariness in the sound, and squatted to slide Farmah from his shoulder. He eased her limp body to the ground in the shadowy underbrush, and Tala sagged back on her haunches, gasping for breath and huddling in her cloak as the night's chill probed at her sweat-soaked garments.

He let her see him wipe matching sweat from his own forehead, and the gesture was less for her sake than he would have liked. Two years penned within hostile walls had taken their toll.

He shook himself and looked around. Hradani night vision was more acute than that of most of the Races of Man, and Bahzell's was superior to the average hradani's. It had *better* be, at any rate. The path they'd forced through the undergrowth seemed dismayingly obvious as he peered back down the slope, but perhaps it would be less so to mounted men pursuing them along the road they'd left a league back.

He hoped it would, anyway, and cradled his arbalest across his thighs while he glared into the darkness and made himself think.

A few he'd known would be praying to every god they could think of by now, but most hradani had little use for gods and prayers, and a distressing number of those who did gave their devotion to one or another of the dark gods. Theirs was a harsh world, and a god who rewarded his (or her) worshipers with immediate, tangible power, whatever its price, was at least something they could understand. Of all the gods, Krashnark undoubtedly boasted the largest following among hradani. Lord of devils and ambitious war he might be, but whatever the Black Swordsman's other failings, he was reputed to be a god of his word, not an innate treacher like his brothers Sharnā and Fiendark, and far less . . . hungry than his sister Krahana.

For the most part, however, the only use hradani had for deities was the laying of curses. Bahzell himself had no use at all for the dark gods, and precious little more for those of the light; black or white, no god had done his people any favors *he* knew of in the last ten or twelve centuries, and he saw little point hoping one of them might suddenly change his mind for Bahzell Bahnakson's sake. Demons, now. A good, nasty demon, suitably propitiated, could have been a help—assuming he'd had either the means or the stomach for bargaining with one of them.

He hid the motion of his arm from Tala with his body as he touched Farmah's throat. Her pulse throbbed against his fingers, more racing than he would have liked yet steadier than he'd feared. She'd done her dogged best, but she'd collapsed less than a mile from East Gate. She'd begged them to leave her and save themselves, but Bahzell had only snorted and given his rucksack to Tala so he could sling the girl over his shoulder, and her protests had died as exhaustion and pain dragged her under.

He sighed and withdrew his fingers from her throat to stroke her hair. It wasn't something he would have done if anyone could see—pity was dangerous; once revealed, it could never be hidden again, and enemies would be quick to use it against you—but his heart twisted within him as he looked down upon her. So young, he thought. So young to have suffered so much, packed so much loss into so few years. Bahzell was thirty-eight, barely into the start of young manhood for a hradani, but Farmah was less than half his age, and he bared his teeth in a snarl of self-disgust at having let consideration of political consequences stay his hand while Harnak lay helpless at his feet.

A soft sound drifted through the night, and he froze, foxlike ears swiveling to track the noise. It came again, and his spine relaxed as he realized it came from the far side of the small hill on which they crouched, not from behind them.

He reached out and grasped Tala's shoulder. The housekeeper jumped, but he'd found time to instruct her in at least the rudiments of how to conduct herself in the field, and she swallowed her gasp of surprise and kept her mouth shut as he drew her towards him.

"Horses," he breathed in her ear. Her muscles snapped tighter, and he gave a quick headshake. "Not following us; ahead, over the hill."

Tala's ear twitched, and she inhaled sharply, but her relief was far from total. He approved of her taut wariness, yet if those horse sounds meant what they might—

"Wait here," he whispered, and slipped away into the darkness.

The housekeeper watched him vanish, astonished afresh at how silently so huge a warrior moved. He was thrice her size and more, yet he'd seemed like a ghost as darkness fell, moving, despite his armor and the burden of Farmah's limp weight, with a quiet Tala couldn't even hope to match. Now he disappeared into the underbrush with no more than the soft whisper of a single branch against his scale shirt, and the night closed in about her.

Wind sighed—the coldest, loneliest sound she'd ever heard—and she shivered again, trying to imagine a warrior of Navahk who wouldn't simply keep going into the dark. No one could have blamed Lord Bahzell for abandoning them. He'd already risked far more for two women of his clan's enemies than he ever should have, yet she could no more imagine his leaving them behind than she could believe a Navahkan would have returned for them.

She settled Farmah's head in her lap, spreading her cloak to share her own warmth with that cruelly battered body, and her eyes were cold with a hate that more than matched her fear. She was glad she'd helped Lord Bahzell, whatever came of it. He was different, like Fraidahn, her long dead husband had been—like her son had been before Churnazh took him off to war and left him there, only stronger. And kinder. Gentler. It was hard for a mother to admit that, yet it was true, however he sought to hide it. But perhaps if some god had let Durgaz grow up free of Navahk . . .

She closed her eyes, hugging the dead memories of the only people she'd ever made the mistake of allowing herself to love, and moistened a cloth from Lord Bahzell's water bottle to wipe Farmah's unconscious brow.

The underbrush slowed Bahzell, but there'd been times on the Wind Plain when he would have given an arm—well, two or three fingers from his off hand—for cover to match it. He reached the crest of the hill and raised his head above the bushes, and his eyes glittered as he saw what he'd hoped for.

No wonder there was so much underbrush and the few trees were all second growth. The moon was full enough, even without the odd chink of light streaming through the shutters of the three cottages which were still occupied, for him to tell the farm below him had known better days. Half the outbuildings were abandoned, judging by their caved-in thatch, but the overgrown hills about the farm had almost certainly been logged off in

those better, pre-Churnazh days. They'd gone back to
wilderness for lack of hands to work the land, yet someone still fought to save his steading from total ruin. The
garden plots closer in to the buildings looked well maintained in the moonlight, clusters of sheep and goats dotted
the pastures . . . and a paddock held a dozen horses.

Bahzell chuckled and let his eyes sweep patiently back
and forth. Farms usually had dogs, and there was probably someone on watch, as well. Now where would *he*
have put a sentry . . . ?

His ears rose in respect as he caught the faint glint of
moonlight on steel. It wasn't on the ground after all, for
a sort of eaves-high walkway had been erected around
the roof of the tallest barn. It gave a commanding view
over the approaches to the farm, and there wasn't a single
watchman; there were two of them, each marching half
the walkway's circuit.

He settled down on his belly, resting his chin on the
hands clasped under his jaw, and pondered. Those would
be no fine saddle beasts down there, but any horse was
better than the pace Tala could manage afoot. Yet how
to lay hands on them? What would have been child's play
with two or three other Horse Stealers to help became
far more problematical on his own—especially when he
had no wish to hurt any of those farmers if he could avoid
it. Anyone who could maintain even this much prosper-
ity so close to Churnazh deserved better than to be killed
by someone running from that same Churnazh, so—

He pursed his lips with a sour snort as he watched
the sentries. It was hardly the proper way for a Horse
Stealer to go about things, but he was in a hurry. Besides,
if he was lucky, no one would ever learn of his lapse.

He rose quietly and headed back to tell Tala what he
intended.

There *were* dogs. A chorus of rumbling snarls warned

him as they came out of the dark, and he reached back to his sword hilt, ready to draw at need. But there was no need. No doubt there would have been if he'd come in across the fields, which was why he'd been careful to stick to the center of the track leading to the farm, and his open approach held them to a snarling challenge while the pack leader set up a howl to summon their master.

Bahzell stopped where he was, resting his palm on his pommel, and admired the dogs' training while he waited. It wasn't a long wait. Half a dozen sturdy hradani, all shorter than he, but well muscled from hard work and better food than most Navahkan city-dwellers ever saw, tumbled out of cottage doors. Bare steel gleamed in moonlight as they spread out about him, and Bahzell couldn't fault their cautious hostility.

"Who be ye?" a strident voice challenged. "And what d'ye want, a-botherin' decent folk in the middle o' the night?!"

"It's sorry I am to disturb you," Bahzell replied calmly. "I'm but a traveler in need of your help."

"Hey? What's that? In need o' help?" The voice barked a laugh. "You, wi' a great, whackin' sword at yer side an' a shirt o' mail on yer back, need *our* help?" The spokesman laughed again. "Ye've a wit fer a dirty, sneakin' thief—I'll say that fer ye!"

"It's no thief I am tonight," Bahzell said in that same mild voice, deliberately emphasizing his Hurgrum accent, "though I've naught against splitting a few skulls if you're caring to call me so again."

The spokesman rocked back on his heels, lowering his spear to peer at the intruder, and Bahzell gave back look for look.

"Yer not from around here, are ye?" the farmer said slowly, and it was Bahzell's turn to snort a laugh.

"You might be saying that."

"So I might." The farmer cocked his head up at Bahzell's

towering inches. "In fact, ye've the look o' one o' them Horse Stealers. Be ye so?"

"That I am. Bahzell, son of Bahnak, Prince of Hurgrum."

"Arrr! Tell us another 'un!" someone hooted, but the spokesman shook his head and held up a hand.

"Now, lads, let's not be hasty. I've heard summat o' this Bahzell. 'Tis said he's tall as a hill, like all them Horse Stealers, an' danged if this 'un isn't."

Bahzell folded his arms and looked down on them. The tallest was barely five or six inches over six feet, and he saw ears moving and eyes widening in surprise as they peered back up at him.

"But that Bahzell, he's a hostage up t' Navahk an' all," a voice objected.

"Aye, that's true," someone else agreed. "Leastways, he's s'posed t' be." A note of avarice crept into his voice. "Reckon they'd pay t' get 'im back agin, Turl?"

"Not s'much as tryin' t' lay him by the heels 'ud cost *us*, Wulgaz," the spokesman said dryly, "an' I've few enough t' work the land wi'out his spilling yer guts in the dirt."

Bahzell's teeth gleamed in a moonlit smile, and the one called Wulgaz shuffled quickly back beside his fellows.

"Mind ye, though, stranger," Turl said sharply, "there's enough o' us t' spill *yer* guts, too, if it comes t' that!"

"I'm thinking the same thing," Bahzell agreed equably, "and if it's all the same to you, I'd sooner I kept mine and you kept yours, friend."

"Would you, now?" Turl gave a gravel-voiced chuckle and grounded the butt of his spear so he could lean on it. "Well then, Lord Bahzell—if that's truly who ye be— what brings ye here?"

"Well, as to that, I'd half a mind to be stealing some

of your horses, till I spied those lads of yours up on the roof."

"Did ye, though?" Turl cocked his head the other way. "'Tis a strange way ye have o' provin' ye mean no harm!"

"Why? Because I'd a mind to take what I need? Or because I decided to buy, instead?"

"Buy?" Turl snapped upright. "D'ye mean t' say *buy*, M'lord? Cash money?"

"Aye. Mind you, I'm thinking it would have been more fun to steal them," Bahzell admitted, "but it's a bit of a hurry I'm in."

Turl gaped at him, then laughed out loud. "Well, M'lord, if its fun ye want, just go back down th' track and me an' the lads can step back inside an' let ye try agin. Course, the dogs'll be on ye quick as spit, but if that's yer notion o' fun—" He shrugged, and Bahzell joined him in his laughter.

"No, thank you kindly. It may be I'll take you up on that another day, but I've scant time for such tonight. So if you're minded to sell, I'll buy three of them from you, and tack to go with them, if you have it."

"Yer serious, ain't ye?" Turl said slowly, rubbing his chin. "'Twouldn't be ye've need t' be elsewhere, would it, M'lord?"

"It would, friend, and the sooner the better."

"Um." Turl looked at his fellows for a long, silent moment, then back at Bahzell. "Horses are hard come by in these parts, M'lord," he said bluntly, "an' harder t' replace. 'Specially when partin' wi' 'em seems like t' bring th' Black Prince an' his scum down on ye."

"Aye, I've little doubt of that," Bahzell agreed, "and I'd not be wishing that on anyone, but I've a thought on that."

"Do ye?" Turl squatted on his heels, waving the others to do the same when Bahzell followed suit. "Tell me, then, M'lord. How does an honest farmer sell his horses t' the likes o' you wi'out Black Churnazh stretchin' his neck fer his troubles?"

"As to that, friend Turl, I'm thinking there's always a way, when a man's looking hard enough." Bahzell shook his purse, letting them hear the jingle of coins, and cocked his head. "Now, as for how it works, why—"

Tala looked up nervously as hooves thudded on the dirt track. She parted the screen of branches, peering out of the clump of brush Bahzell had hidden her and Farmah in, and her ears twitched in silent relief as she recognized the huge, dark shape leading the horses.

Bahzell stopped them with a soft, soothing sound, and Tala helped Farmah to her feet. The girl had regained a little strength during Bahzell's absence, and she clung to Tala as the housekeeper half-led and half-carried her out of the brush.

"I never thought you could do it, M'lord. *Never*," Tala breathed. "How did you ever get them to agree without—?" Her eyes cut to his sword hilt, and he chuckled.

"As to that, it wasn't so hard a thing. Mind, that farmer's missed his calling, for he's one could make money selling stones to Purple Lords." He shook his head and looked at the three unprepossessing animals behind him. "My folk wouldn't be wasting pot space on two of these, and the third's no courser! I've no mind at all to hear what old Hardak or Kulgar would be saying if they knew I'd *paid* for nags like these!" He shook his head again, trying to imagine the expressions of the two captains who'd led a very young Bahzell on his first raid against the vast Sothōii herds if they could see him now. Imagination failed, and he was just as glad it did.

"But how did you talk them into it?" Tala pressed, and he shrugged.

"I'd a heavy purse, and it's a lighter one now. They

took every Navahkan coin I had, and the lot of us spent ten minutes breaking down paddock fences and scuffing the ground." He shrugged again. "If any of Churnazh's men track us back to them, why, they've proof enough how hard they tried to stop my stealing these miserable racks of—that's to say, these noble beasts." He sounded so wry Tala chuckled, despite her exhaustion and fear, and he grinned.

"There's the spirit! Now let's be getting Farmah in the saddle."

Neither woman had ever ridden a horse. Tala, at least, had ridden muleback a time or two before she fell into Churnazh's service, but Farmah had no experience at all, and she was in no fit state for lessons. She bit her lip, wide skirt bunched clumsily high, clutching at the high cantle of the saddle and trying not to flinch as the stolid horse shifted under her, and Bahzell patted her shoulder encouragingly. It wasn't hard to reach. Even mounted, her head was little higher than his.

"Don't be fretting, lass," he told her. "These are war saddles," his palm smacked leather loudly, "and you'll not fall out."

She nodded uncertainly as he buckled a strap around her waist, snapped it to rings on the saddle, and grinned at her.

"I'm thinking friend Turl—the son of Hirahim who parted with these nags—wasn't always a farmer. Not with these in his barn." He bent to adjust the stirrups to her shorter legs and went on speaking. "But however he came by them, it's grateful I am he had them. Wounded stay with the column or die in war, lass; that's why they've straps to hold a hurt man in the saddle."

She nodded nervously, and he gave her shoulder another pat and turned to Tala. The housekeeper had split her skirts down the middle and bound the shredded halves tightly about her legs; now she scrambled up into the second saddle without assistance. Fortunately, the plow horse under it was staid enough not to shy at her clumsy, if determined, style, and Bahzell nodded in approval and showed her how to adjust the straps. She had the reins in her hands, and he managed not to wince as he rearranged her grip, then tied the lead from Farmah's horse to the back of her saddle.

"But . . . what about you, M'lord?" Tala asked as she glanced at the third horse. It had no saddle, only a pack frame.

"Now wouldn't it be a cruel thing to be putting the likes of me on a horse's back?" Bahzell replied, slinging his rucksack to the frame. "I've yet to meet the beast that can carry me more than a league—or outpace me over the same distance, for that matter."

"But I thought—" Tala broke off as he looked at her, then shrugged. "They do call you 'Horse Stealers,' M'lord," she said apologetically.

"And so we are, but that's for the cooking pot."

"You *eat* them?!" Tala looked down at the huge animal under her, and Bahzell chuckled.

"Aye, but don't be saying so too loudly. You'll fret the poor beasties, and no Horse Stealer would be eating anything this bony." Tala blinked, and Bahzell lowered his ears more seriously.

"Now pay me heed, Tala. Churnazh will be after us soon—if he's not already—and I'm thinking there's no way the three of us can show them our heels." One ear flicked at Farmah, drooping in the saddle, her small store of recovered energy already spent, and Tala nodded silently.

"Well, then. When you can't outrun them, it's time to outthink them. That's why I've gone west, not east for Hurgrum as they might expect. But when they miss us on the east road, even the likes of Churnazh will think to sweep this way, as well."

He paused, ears cocked, until Tala nodded again.

"I'd a few words with Turl," he went on then, "and there's one lad as wants us caught no more than we do, not with the questions they'll be asking when they see saddles on the horses I 'stole'! From the way he tells it, there's a village—Fir Hollow, he called it—two leagues northeast of here. Do you know it?"

"Fir Hollow?" Tala repeated the name and furrowed her brow, then shook her head. "I'm afraid not, M'lord," she apologized, and Bahzell shrugged.

"No reason you should, but here's what I'm thinking. The road forks there, and the right fork—the eastern one—hooks north towards Chazdark."

"Oh!" Tala nodded sharply. "I know that town, M'lord. Fraidahn and I were there once, before—" She broke off, pushing the painful memory aside, and Bahzell squeezed her forearm.

"Good. We'll be heading cross-country a while longer, then cut back to reach the road between Fir Hollow and Chazdark, and I'll find a place for the two of you to lie close during the day. Tomorrow night, you'll be back on your way to Chazdark, and I'm thinking you'll reach it before dawn."

"We'll be on our way, M'lord?" Tala asked sharply. "What about you?"

"I'll not be with you," he said, and she sat very straight in the saddle and stared at him. He pulled a ring off his finger, and she took it, too stunned even to argue as he dug a scrap of parchment from his pouch and passed it over, as well.

"It's sorry I am to be leaving so much to you, Tala," he said quietly, "but a blind man couldn't miss the three of us together, and even ahorse, Farmah can't move fast enough. They'll run us down in a day at the best pace we can make if they spy us in the open, so we'll not get Farmah to Hurgrum without showing them another hare to chase."

"What do you mean, M'lord?" she asked tautly.

"Get off the horses when you near Chazdark. Tether them in the woods somewhere you're certain you can be describing to someone else and leave Farmah with them. Then take this—" he touched the parchment "—to the city square, and ask for a merchant called Ludahk." He repeated the name several times and made her repeat it back to him three times before he was satisfied. "Show him the parchment and the ring and tell him I sent you. Tell him where to be finding Farmah and the horses, and that I said he's to take you to my father." He held her eyes in the moonlight, face grim. "Tell him one last task pays for all—and that I'll be looking for him if it should happen he fails in it."

"W-Who is this Ludahk?" Tala asked in a tiny voice.

"Best know no more than you must. He'll not be happy to see you any road; if he thinks you know more than that he's a merchant who trades with Hurgrum—aye, and maybe does a little smuggling on the side—he might be thinking he should take his chance Churnazh can lay me by the heels and cut your throats himself."

Tala paled and swallowed hard, and Bahzell grinned at her.

"Hush, now! Ludahk knows I'm not so easy taken as that, and he'll not want the least chance that I might come hunting him, for he knows I won't come alone if I do. He'll see you safe to Hurgrum—just don't you be looking about you at anything you shouldn't be seeing. Understand?"

"Yes, M'lord." He nodded and started to turn away, but she caught his shoulder, and he turned back with ears at half-cock. "I understand, M'lord, but what I *don't* understand is why you don't come with us. If this Ludahk can get us to Hurgrum, why can't he get *you* there?"

"Well, now," Bahzell said slowly, "I'm a mite bigger and harder to hide than you are."

"That's not the reason!" she said sharply, and he shrugged.

"Well, if you'll have it out of me, I've a mind to head on west and see to it Churnazh thinks you and Farmah are with me still."

"But . . . but they'll catch you, M'lord!" she protested. "Come with us, instead. *Please*, M'lord!"

"Now that I can't," he said gently. "If Churnazh is minded to see it so, I've already broken hostage bond, and I can't be taking that home with me unless I'm wanting to start the war all over, so there's no sense in trying. And as long as they're hunting west for the three of us, they'll not be checking merchant wagons moving east, I'm thinking."

"But they'll *catch* you!" she repeated desperately.

"Ah, now. Maybe they will, and maybe they won't," he said with an outrageous twitch of his ears, "and the day a pack of Bloody Swords can catch a Horse Stealer with a fair start in the open, why that's the day they're welcome to take his ears—if they can!"

# CHAPTER FOUR

Bahzell moved quickly through brush-dotted, waist-high grass while the shadows lengthened behind him. His packhorse had given up trying to hold to a pace it found comfortable, though its eyes reproached him whenever he made one of his infrequent halts.

Bahzell grinned at the thought, amused despite the nagging sensation between his shoulder blades that said someone was on his trail. Seen in daylight, the gelding was less the nag he'd told Tala; indeed, there was a faint hint of Sothōii breeding, though untrained eyes might not have noticed, and he'd kept it because it was the best of the lot. If desperation forced him to mount, it could bear him faster—and longer—than either of the others. Not that any normal horse could carry him far, at the best of times. Despite their well-earned name, nothing short of a Sothōii courser could carry an armored Horse Stealer, and trying to steal one of the sorcery-born coursers, far less mount one, was more than any hradani's life was worth.

45

He paused, turning his back to the setting sun to squint back into the east, and gnawed his lip. He wanted Churnazh's men to follow him instead of the women, but a blind man couldn't miss the trail he'd left forging through the tall grass, and, unlike himself, the Bloody Swords were small enough to make mounted troops. Bahzell would back his own speed against anything short of Sothōii cavalry over the long haul, but a troop with enough remounts could run him down if they set their minds to it.

The thought gave added point to the itch between his shoulders, and his ears worked slowly as he studied his back trail. His stomach rumbled, but he ignored it. He'd left Tala and Farmah most of the food Turl had been able to provide, for no one had ever trained them to live off the country. He took a moment to hope they'd reached Ludahk safely, then pushed that thought aside, too. Their fate was out of his hands now, and he had his own to worry about.

He snorted at the thought, then stiffened, ears suddenly flat, as three black dots crested a hill well behind him. He strained his eyes, wishing he had a glass, but it didn't really matter. He could count them well enough, and there was only one reason for anyone to follow directly along his trail.

He looked back into the west, and his ears rose slowly. An irregular line of willows marked the meandering course of a stream a mile or so ahead, and he nodded. If those lads back there wanted to catch him, why, it would only be common courtesy to let them.

The sun had vanished, but evening light lingered along a horizon of coals and dark blue ash, and Bahzell's smile was grim as he heard approaching hooves at last.

He lay flat in the high grass with his arbalest. Few hradani were archers—their size and disposition alike were better suited to the shock of melee—but the Horse

Stealers of northern Hurgrum had become something of an exception. Their raids into the Wind Plain pitted them against the matchless Sothōii cavalry's horse archery more often than against their fellow hradani, and one of Prince Bahnak's first priorities had been to find an answer to it.

Nothing Hurgrum had could equal the combined speed and power of the Sothōii composite bow, but the Sothōii had learned to respect Horse Stealer crossbows. A Horse Stealer could use a goatsfoot to span a crossbow, or even an arbalest, which would have demanded a windlass of any human arm. They might be slower than bowmen, but they were faster than any other crossbowmen, their quarrels had enormous shock and stopping power, and a warheaded arbalest bolt could pierce even a Wind Rider's plate at close range.

More to the present point, those same crossbows, coupled with the pikes and halberds Bahnak's infantry had adopted to break mounted charges, had wreaked havoc against Navahk and Prince Churnazh's allies . . . just as Bahzell intended to do against whoever had been rash enough to overtake him.

The hooves came closer, and Bahzell rose to his knees, keeping his head below the level of the grass. It would be awkward to respan an arbalest from a prone position, even for him, but he'd chosen his position with care. His targets should be silhouetted against the still-bright western sky while he himself faded into the dimness of the eastern horizon, with time to vanish back into the grass before they even realized they were under attack. Of course, if they chose to stand, they were almost bound to spot him when he popped back up to take the second man, so there'd be no time for a third shot. But he'd take his chances against a single Bloody Sword hand-to-hand any day, and—

His thoughts broke off as the hooves stopped suddenly.

"I know you're out there," a tenor voice called, "but it's getting dark, and mistakes can happen in the dark. Why don't you come out before you shoot someone we'd both rather you didn't?"

"*Brandark?!*" Bahzell shot up out of the grass in disbelief, and the single horseman turned in his saddle.

"So there you are," he said blandly, then shook his head and waved an arm at the line of willows two hundred yards ahead. "I'm glad I went ahead and called out! I thought you were still in front of me."

"Fiendark's Furies, man!" Bahzell unloaded the arbalest and released the string with a snap while he waded through the grass. "What in the names of all the gods and demons d'you think you're doing out here?!"

"Catching up with you before any of Churnazh's patrols do," Brandark said dryly, and leaned from his saddle to clasp forearms as Bahzell reached him. "Not that it's been easy, you understand. I've just about ridden these poor horses out."

"Aye, well, that happens when the likes of you goes after a Horse Stealer, little man. You've not got the legs to catch him, any of you." Bahzell's tone was far lighter than his expression. "But why you should be wanting to is more than I can understand."

"Someone has to keep you out of trouble." Brandark dismounted, and his horse blew gratefully as his weight came off its back. Bahzell might call him "little;" few others would have, for if he was over a foot shorter than the Horse Stealer, his shoulders were just as broad. Now he straightened his embroidered jerkin and fluffed his lace cuffs with a fastidious air, and the strings of the balalaika on his back sang gently as he shrugged.

"Keep *me* out of trouble, is it? And what's to be keeping *you* out of it, I wonder? This is none of your affair, but you're like to lose that long nose of yours if you poke it into it, I'm thinking!"

"Oh, come now! It's not *that* long," Brandark protested.

"Long enough to be losing you your head," Bahzell growled.

"That would have happened soon enough if I'd stayed home," Brandark replied more soberly. "Churnazh never liked me, and he likes me less now."

Bahzell grunted in unhappy understanding, and Brandark shrugged again.

"I won't deny our friendship didn't help, but don't take all the credit. My time was running out before you ever came to Navahk." He grinned suddenly. "I think I made him uncomfortable for some reason."

"Now why would that be, I wonder?" Bahzell snorted.

"I can't imagine." Full dark had fallen as they spoke, and Brandark looked around and shuddered. "I'm city bred," he said plaintively. "Do you think we could make camp before we continue this discussion?"

Bahzell snorted again and took the lead for Brandark's packhorse without further comment. Brandark gathered up the reins of both his saddle horses and followed him toward the willows, whistling softly, and Bahzell shook his head. He had no idea how Brandark had run him down so quickly, and he wished he hadn't, but he was a bit surprised by how comforting the other's presence was. And Brandark was right; his days in Navahk would have been numbered even if Bahzell had never visited the city.

The Horse Stealer glanced over his shoulder, and his mouth twitched. Anything less like a Bloody Sword hradani than Brandark Brandarkson was impossible to imagine— a thought, Bahzell was certain, which must have occurred to Brandark the Elder on more than one occasion, for he was a hradani of the old school. More successful than many at hanging on to his plunder and making it increase, perhaps, but more than a match for any of Churnazh's bravos when it came to pure swagger and a readiness to let blood. He was more particular about his reasons for doing it, but not even Churnazh cared to push him too openly, and there must be more to the old man than met the eye, for he'd never disinherited his son.

Literacy was rare in Navahk, and Brandark was probably the only genuine scholar in Prince Churnazh's whole wretched realm. He was entirely self-taught, yet Bahzell had been stunned by the library his friend had managed to assemble. It was all bits and pieces—books were fiendishly hard to come by, even in Hurgrum—but finding it in *Navahk* had been more than simply a shock, and Bahzell often wished his father could have seen Brandark's collection.

Bahzell himself had never been a good student. Prince Bahnak had done his best to beat at least a little schooling into him, but getting him away from his arms masters had always been an uphill struggle. Yet Brandark, entirely on his own, had amassed more knowledge than any of the tutors Bahnak had paid—lavishly, by hradani standards—for their efforts to educate his sons, and he'd done it in Navahk.

It hadn't come without consequences, of course. Churnazh's contempt for Hurgrum was as nothing beside his contempt for a Bloody Sword who dabbled in the same degeneracy, and Brandark had done nothing to change his prince's mind. He fancied himself a poet, though even Bahzell knew his verse was terrible. He also considered himself a bard, and there, at least, Bahzell had to side with Churnazh. The hradani language's long, rolling cadences lent itself well to song—fortunately, since they'd been reduced to oral tradition in the centuries after the Fall and only their bards had kept any of their history alive—but Brandark couldn't have carried a melody if it had handles. He had the instrumental skills of a bard, but not the voice. Never the voice, and his efforts to prove differently were painful even to his few friends.

Coupled with his choice of songs, that voice was enough to reduce Churnazh to frothing madness. Brandark favored ditties, many of his own composition, about the prince's favorites (even he was careful to avoid any that attacked Churnazh directly), and only the tradition of bardic immunity and the fact that he'd inherited his father's ability with a sword had kept him alive this long. He'd played his dangerous game for years, and even Bahzell often wondered how much of it was real and how much an affectation specifically designed to infuriate Churnazh. Or, for that matter, if Brandark himself still knew which parts of him were genuine and which assumed.

His thoughts had carried him to where he'd left his own horse, and he picketed Brandark's pack animal in the same clump of willows and turned to help his friend with the other two. Brandark grunted his thanks, and they worked together to unsaddle them and rub them down.

"I'm thinking this isn't the very brightest thing either of us ever did," Bahzell said, breaking the companionable silence at last as they hung the saddles over a fallen tree.

"True, but no one ever said *you* were smart." Brandark seated himself on the same fallen tree and adjusted his cuffs again. Part of his image was to be the closest any hradani could come to a dandy, and he took pains with it.

"There's something in that," Bahzell agreed, busying himself with flint and steel. Brandark hauled himself off the log and began gathering wood.

"Mind you," he said over his shoulder, "you were luckier getting out of Navahk than I would have expected. I couldn't believe you'd managed it without leaving a single body behind."

"That wasn't luck, it was planning."

"Of course it was." Brandark dumped an armload of wood beside the small blaze Bahzell had kindled and returned to collect more. "And did your planning include provisions?"

"I'd enough on my mind already without that," Bahzell pointed out.

"That's what I thought. Check my pack saddle."

Bahzell opened the pack, and his stomach rumbled again—happily, this time—at its contents. He began laying out sausages, bread, and cheese beside the fire, then looked up as Brandark brought in another load of fuel.

"I'm thinking that's enough wood. We've good cover here, but let's not be building the fire up too high."

"I bow to your experience." Brandark dropped to sit cross-legged and grinned. "I always wanted an adventure, but they never seemed to come my way."

"Adventure." Bahzell's mouth twisted on the word. "There's no such thing, my lad. Or, at least, anyone who's had one would be doing his best to avoid another. What in Phrobus' name d'you think you're doing out here, Brandark?"

"I told you, keeping you out of trouble." Bahzell snorted deep in his throat, and Brandark flipped his ears at him. "From what I've seen so far, you need all the help you can get," he added, reaching for a sausage.

"I've kept my hide whole this long," Bahzell pointed out.

"So you have. But if I could find you, so can Churnazh."

"Aye, that's so," Bahzell conceded around a mouthful of cheese, then swallowed. "And if we're speaking of finding me, just how was it a soft city lad like you managed it so neatly?"

"Ah, well, I had an advantage. I knew you were running before Churnazh did—and I know how your mind, such as it is, works."

"Do you, now? And how was it you knew I was running?"

"Yurgazh told me."

"Yurgazh?!" Bahzell's ears twitched. "I'd no notion he was a friend of yours."

"He's not, but he knows I'm a friend of *yours*, and he hunted me up as soon as he got off duty." Brandark waved a hand in the firelight. "He wasn't about to say anything someone might repeat to Churnazh, but when he told me you'd gone on a 'hunting party' with one hand tied up in a bloody cloth and then mentioned that two palace women had left just before you and that one of them had been beaten, well—"

He shrugged. Bahzell bit off another chunk of cheese and nodded slowly, and Brandark cocked his head. "I don't suppose you'd care to tell me just who you bloodied your hand on?"

"Harnak," Bahzell said shortly, and Brandark lowered his sausage and stared at him. Then he pursed his lips in a silent whistle.

"I knew it had to be one of them, but Harnak? Did you leave him alive?"

"I left him that way, but I've no notion if he stayed so." Brandark's gently waving ears invited explanation, and Bahzell laughed unpleasantly. "I caught him beating Farmah and argued the point. He'd a dent the size of a hen's egg in his forehead, and no teeth to mention, when we finished."

"Well, now." Brandark stared at him a moment longer, then began to grin. "That *will* upset Churnazh, won't it?"

"A mite," Bahzell agreed. "Which brings me back to how it was you caught me up so quickly. As you say, if you can find me, there's no reason Churnazh's lads can't be doing it, too."

"Well, they won't have started until Harnak woke up— or didn't, as the case may be. And they don't know you as well as I do. I'd guess they'll have wasted a day or two thinking you really did go east."

"Aye, you'd know I'd do no such thing, wouldn't you?"

"True. I also knew you'd start out that direction, though, so I headed straight to Chazdark, then came back west. I knew I was on the right track when I reached Fir Hollow." Brandark shook his head. "I also knew you'd gotten rid of the women by then."

"Did you, now?"

"Of course. What *did* you do with them, anyway? Hide them somewhere?"

"No. I sent them on to Chazdark. There's a man I know there who'll get them safe to my father."

"Ah. I wondered about that, but as soon as that healer you spoke to told me you'd asked for supplies to care for an injured woman and then left by the west road, I knew you'd done *something* with them."

"Aren't you the clever one?" Bahzell finished his cheese and leaned back to let it settle before he started on a sausage.

"Well, not even you would be stupid enough to visit a healer openly if they were still with you. In fact, no one in Fir Hollow would have seen you at all . . . unless you meant to draw the pursuit." Brandark shook his head. "I imagine it'll work well enough against Churnazh and his lot, but it's exactly what *I* would have expected from you. Not too smart, but direct."

"It's best a man know his own limits and act accordingly," Bahzell agreed in a dangerously affable tone. Brandark laughed, and the Horse Stealer went on more seriously. "But much as it pains me to say I'm glad to see you, I'm thinking you've gotten yourself into more trouble than friendship's worth, Brandark. Aye, and your father, too, for aught I know."

"Father will be fine," Brandark assured him. "By now he's disinherited me and sent the law after me—to the east, I'm sure—for stealing three of his best horses."

"D'you think that will fool the likes of Churnazh?"

"No, not really, but Father's too tough a nut for Churnazh to crack." Bahzell grunted skeptically, and Brandark shrugged. "He'd have done something about Father years ago, even without me, if Father didn't have enough men to make him think twice. He's pulled down too many of the old families already; the ones who're left have joined forces to keep him from gutting them all, and he knows it. With his losses against Hurgrum and how restive his 'allies' have been since the war, he'll choose to let it pass."

"I'm hoping you're right, but there's still the matter of what may happen to *you* if he's laying us by the heels."

"So there is—if he lays us by the heels."

"None of which would matter if you hadn't been after poking your nose in where there was no need," Bahzell pointed out.

"Well," Brandark finished his sausage and wiped his hands, "I've always wanted to see the world. Where are you headed, anyway?"

"West," Bahzell growled.

" 'West' is a large place," Brandark remarked. "Did you have some particular part of it in mind?" Bahzell gave him a glare, and he sighed. "That's what I thought. I hope your father plans his campaigns better than you do, or Churnazh may end up ruling Hurgrum after all."

"D'you know," Bahzell said meditatively, "I'm thinking you must be even better with a sword than I'd thought. You've a true gift for making friends happy to see you."

"So I've been told. But in the meantime, it might not be amiss to think about how you'll earn your way. You can't go home, and there's little welcome for hradani elsewhere, unless you want to turn brigand."

"I've no taste for such as that," Bahzell growled, and Brandark nodded.

"In that case, we'd best make certain we stay on the

right side of the law, and that won't be easy. They don't much like hradani most places."

"Then they'd best be keeping their opinions to themselves!"

"You truly do need someone to keep you out of trouble." Brandark sighed. He thought for a moment, then shrugged. "Esgan," he said.

"Esgan?"

"The Grand Duchy of Esgan. Navahk trades with the Esganians, after a fashion. Father's sent me there now and then to dispose of the odd bit of plunder, and Esgfalas is about as far east as the big merchant caravans normally come."

"And what's that to do with us?"

"Well, if we're not going to turn brigand, then we'd best do the exact opposite and be certain we can prove we have. And our best chance to do that is to make our way to the capital and hire on as guards with one of those caravans, if they'll have us."

"Caravan guards." Bahzell shook his head in disgust, and Brandark snorted.

"It's one or the other for hradani, from all I've heard. And at least it's a trade we know, assuming we can convince anyone to hire us."

"Aye," Bahzell agreed sourly.

"And, of course," Brandark added cheerfully as he began untying his rolled sleeping blankets, "assuming we get there alive."

# CHAPTER FIVE

"*Ahhhh!* Careful, you dung-faced bitch!"

Crown Prince Harnak of Navahk snarled and clenched his fist, and the slave flinched back to the full reach of her arms as she retied the bandages. Her fingers were as nervous as her eyes, and the prince gasped again, despite her terrified care. Two smashed ribs had poked splintered ends through his skin, and getting at them to renew the dressings was a painful business.

The trembling slave finished and stepped quickly back as Harnak swung his legs off the bed and groaned up into a sitting position. His right eye remained a purple and crimson clot of swollen pain, and his lips were a split and puffy mass. Nine of his teeth had been left behind when he dragged his brutally beaten body out into the palace's more traveled hallways; his father's surgeon had removed four more that had snapped off in jagged stumps; his broken nose would never be the same again; and a huge, purple lump, skin split across its apex, disfigured his forehead.

He looked up and saw the slave staring at him, her eyes huge with fear, and shame and fury snarled within him.

"Get out, sow!" he hissed. "Get out before I have the whip to you!"

"Yes, master!"

The slave ducked her head and vanished with all the speed fear could impart, and Harnak dragged himself to his feet, no longer fighting his whimpers since there were no ears to hear them. He staggered to the window slit and leaned against the wall, panting in pain and wincing as breathing stirred his broken ribs, and his hate welled up like lava.

There was fear in that hate. More than fear, there was panic, and not just because Bahzell had wreaked such carnage upon him with nothing more than his bare hands, for there was no sign of Farmah. She and that slut Tala—and that whoreson Bahzell, curse him!—had disappeared like smoke. They were on foot, and that should have made them easy meat, despite their head start, yet none of the men Churnazh could fully trust had found a trace of them. Now he'd been forced to send out formal patrols, including men he couldn't rely upon simply to slit their throats the moment they were found, and that was bad. If Farmah told her side of the tale, if any of the Guard heard it and believed—

Harnak cut that thought off. Badly as he was hurt, he knew he'd hurt the bitch almost equally badly before Bahzell burst in on him, and she was only a slut, not a hardened warrior. She couldn't move fast or far, and the odds were good she'd kill herself trying, for she knew what would happen if she fell into his hands once more, curse her! It was all her fault! Demons knew the bitch was beautiful—or *had* been, he amended with a vicious smile—but she'd forgotten she'd become only another palace slut and refused to be schooled. The price she'd paid—so far—was little enough for refusing a prince of the blood, and his good eye closed in silent prayer to Sharnā. Let someone reliable find her, he prayed. Let them find her alive and return her to Navahk so he could finish her lesson, and her heart would be offered up still steaming as thanks when he was done. Aye, and Tala's screaming soul could go with it!

He savored that delicious possibility hungrily, but then his eye opened once more, and he glared out over the squalid city. At least the Guard was as determined to find Bahzell as Harnak could wish. His mind had been none too clear when he had awakened but he'd retained enough wit to shape his explanation. He'd played his part well, he thought, fighting the pain of his wounds out of "concern" for Farmah, driving himself to gasp out the news that Bahzell had run mad, attacking and raping the girl, beating her brutally, and then trying to kill Harnak when the prince sought to save his victim. His father and brothers had known it was a lie, but Churnazh had seized the chance with glee. He'd outlawed Bahzell within the hour, and Harnak's swollen mouth twisted in another painful, evil smile of memory.

But the smile faded, and he swore again. If only they'd taken Bahzell and the bitches quickly! With them dead, no one in Navahk would have dared disbelieve Harnak's tale or ask why Bahzell's "victim" had fled *with* her rapist. But three full days had passed without resolution, and now that very question filled the city like a plague. Churnazh's henchmen had put it about that Farmah had left *before* Bahzell—that the Horse Stealer, believing Harnak dead, had gone in pursuit to finish the only witness against him—but too many had seen her and Tala flee the palace rather than seek protection from the Guard. There were even rumors Bahzell had caught up with them in sight of the city wall—actually carried the slut off in his arms! Certainly she hadn't tried to escape him, and if she had the chance to whisper the truth to *anyone* before Harnak had her killed, it might be more deadly than any plague.

The crown prince snarled another curse and lowered himself slowly, painfully back into his bed, and hate and fear pulsed deep within him.

A low, rough-piled stone wall separated the weed-grown pasture from the road. It wasn't much of a road, even by hradani standards. Summer heat had baked its uneven surface to dusty iron; in spring or fall it would be a bottomless, sucking morass, unless Bahzell missed his guess, and he sat on the stone wall to glower at it with mixed emotions.

Leather creaked as Brandark swung down to rest his mount. The rough edges of camp life had left the Bloody Sword's finery rumpled and travel stained, and he looked more like a brigand than a scholar and would-be bard as he beat dust from his sleeves and perched on the wall at Bahzell's side.

"Well, thank the gods," he sighed.

"Oh? And what would it be you're thanking them for?" Bahzell inquired, and Brandark grinned.

"For making roads and letting us find one. Not that I'm complaining, you understand, but this business of following you cross-country without the faintest idea where I am can worry a man. What if you'd gotten lost and just led us round in circles till Churnazh's patrols found us?"

"I'm not one to 'get lost,' little man," Bahzell rumbled, "and I'll be thanking you to remember that. Besides, it was you brought your precious map along, and how could anyone be getting lost in this piddling patch of woods?" He snorted and looked back over the deserted pasturelands to the trackless wilderness behind them. "If you've a mind to get *lost*, now, let me take you up on the Wind Plain and lead you round for a week or two!"

"Thank you, but no." Brandark scrubbed at a patch of dirt on his knee, but it defied him stubbornly, and he gave up with a grimace.

"Why is it," he asked, gesturing at the road, "that I've a nagging suspicion you're none too pleased to see this?"

"I'm thinking it's because you're such an all-fired sharp-witted fellow and I'm after being so transparent." Bahzell grunted. He dug a booted toe into the dusty grass, and his ears moved slowly up and down as he frowned.

"Would you care to explain that? I'm only a city boy, and city boys *like* roads. They make us comfortable."

"Do they, now?" Bahzell's eyes glinted, then he shrugged. "It's not so complicated, Brandark. It's three days now since you caught me up; if any of Churnazh's lads had happened across my trail—or yours—I'm thinking we'd have seen them by now."

"So?"

"You *are* a city boy," Bahzell snorted. "When a man knows there's unfriendly folk looking for him, rough country's the best place to be, especially if they've no trail to follow. But roads, now. Roads are unchancy things for a man on the run. They're after going from here to there, d'you see, and they don't wiggle around while they're about it. I'm thinking Churnazh's patrols will be watching them, especially if they've had no luck elsewhere."

"You may be right," Brandark said after a moment, "but I'm afraid we don't have much choice but to follow this one." He tugged on his long nose. "The Esganians are a suspicious lot, and we're hradani. Letting them think we'd tried to sneak across their border would be a poor idea, and that means we have to cross on a road where we can collect a pass from one of their guard posts."

"Aye." Bahzell sighed and rose to stretch, then slid his arbalest off his shoulder, hooked the curved end of the goatsfoot over the string, and heaved. His mighty arm trembled with brief strain, but the steel stave bent smoothly under the lever's urging.

"I've always thought that was an especially nasty-looking weapon," Brandark remarked as the string settled over the grooved cog of the release.

"It is that," Bahzell agreed. He hung the goatsfoot back on his belt and set a quarrel on the string, and Brandark gave him a crooked smile.

"Should I assume these warlike preparations indicate a certain degree of concern on your part?"

"As to that," Bahzell said, looping back the cover of the bolt quiver at his side, "I'm thinking that if your map is good and your guess about the distance to Esgan is right—mind you, it's a Bloody Sword map and you're a city boy, so neither of them is likely—but *if* they are, then we're little more than a league or two from the border. And if I were one of Churnazh's lads—"

"—you'd be sitting up ahead waiting for us," Brandark finished.

"So I would." Bahzell nodded, and Brandark sighed. "Well, at least *they* won't have nasty things like that," he said, jutting his chin at the arbalest as he swung back up into his saddle, and Bahzell slapped the weapon fondly.

"That they won't," he agreed with a broad, square-toothed grin.

They kept as far to the side of the road's mountain-range ruts and gullies as they could. Bahzell watched his footing as he strode along beside Brandark's horse, but few words were exchanged, and his mind worked busily as he considered how *he* might have arranged things in his pursuers' place. None of Churnazh's Guard carried effete weapons like bows or crossbows, and that ruled out the simplest way to deal with embarrassing witnesses. Besides, it was likely they had orders to take him alive, if they could, and keep him so until they discovered what he'd done with Farmah. Which, unfortunately, wasn't to say they'd have any special interest in taking him in one piece.

He glanced at his friend, and his ears rose as he smiled. Brandark had put his precious balalaika on the packhorse, safely out of harm's way, and his right hand reached down to unbutton the thong across his sword hilt. It was an almost absent gesture, and his eyes never stopped sweeping their path as he reached back and untied the leads of his other horses from his saddle, as well. He might be the "city boy" he called himself, yet he knew what they were about.

Miles fell away, empty but tense, the untenanted pastures fading back into unclaimed woodland on either hand, and the rutted track curved ahead of them. It bent around a thick stand of second growth timber, and Bahzell's ears jerked suddenly up as a bird exploded from the treetops. It circled, chattering angrily down at something, then arced away with an irritated flap of its wings, and he reached up to grip Brandark's shoulder. The Bloody Sword drew rein instantly and looked down at him.

"The bird?" he asked quietly, and Bahzell nodded, narrowed eyes measuring distances and angles.

"Aye. *Something* startled it, and whatever it was, it's not coming on around the bend, now is it?"

"True." Brandark shifted in the saddle, joining his friend's survey of the terrain. The trees had closed in, turning the road into a passage a bare twenty yards wide, and he tugged on his long nose thoughtfully. "I imagine they'd like *us* to come around that bend all fat and happy," he murmured.

"So they would. The question, I'm thinking, is how patient they are."

"Well, there's one way to find out." Brandark trotted to the side of the road, and leaned out of the saddle to tie the other beasts' leads to a convenient limb. Then he

moved back to Bahzell's side, turned his mount to face
the bend once more, and rested his folded hands on his
saddle pommel.

"I make it—what? A hundred fifty yards to the bend?"

"About that," Bahzell agreed. "Maybe a mite closer
to two hundred."

"How many shots can you get off at that range?"

"Well," Bahzell plucked idly at the tuft of his right
ear, "if I get one off the instant I lay eye on them, and if
they're still after building their speed, I might make two
before one of them tries to ride me down."

"Oh, I don't think they'll do that." Brandark smiled
unpleasantly, nudging his mount with a toe, and the horse
sidestepped closer to his friend.

The sun burned down, hot and still in the windless
air, and Bahzell held the arbalest over his left forearm
while he listened to the silence. He felt no particular
temptation to mount his own horse or Brandark's second beast. Not even he could respan an arbalest handily
on horseback. Besides, a Horse Stealer's size went far to
redress the normal imbalance between a mounted man
and one on foot . . . as Navahk had learned to its cost.

Minutes trickled past. Brandark's horse stamped and
blew, puzzled by the stillness, and Bahzell reached out
his right hand to pat its shoulder, then returned it unhastily
to the arbalest. He didn't know how many men they faced,
but Churnazh must have spread his strength thin to cover
all possibilities, and he would have had no choice but to
concentrate on the roads east to Hurgrum. Six men?
Perhaps. Certainly no more than a dozen, and likely less,
or they'd not be so coy about their tactics. Of course,
even six would be more than enough if they were handled
properly, but—

A shrill whistle split the air, and a cluster of mounted
figures appeared round the bend. They advanced slowly,
walking their horses, and Bahzell grinned as he saw their

livery. Churnazh's Guard, indeed, and not a regular cavalryman—or a lance—among them.

"Two shots, I'm thinking," he murmured, and Brandark shook his head in disgust.

"It's enough to make me feel embarrassed," he murmured back. "No wonder you louts handled us so rudely."

"Now, now, don't be too harsh." Bahzell watched the riders approach. Eight of them, and Brandark was right. If they meant business, they should have taken the two of them at the charge. "There's naught but two of us, when all's said. It might be they're thinking we'd sooner surrender, being as we're so outnumbered and all."

"That's even more embarrassing," Brandark complained. "Gods, how could even Churnazh find officers that stupid?"

"He's the knack for it," Bahzell agreed, "and speaking of stupid—"

The arbalest leapt up to his shoulder, and suddenly icy eyes stared down it at the Guard captain who'd spurred his horse out in front of his men. The range was easily a hundred and twenty yards, but Bahzell saw the captain's sudden tension, the way his horse's head flared up as his hands tightened on the reins, and then the arbalest snapped.

The quarrel buzzed through the air, glittering in the sunlight with hornet speed, and the captain screamed and threw up his hands as it struck him in the chest. It ripped through his ring mail as if it were paper, exploding out his back in a grisly red spray, and his panicked horse reared wildly.

The dying hradani tumbled to the road, and his men froze for one stunned moment. Then someone shouted, and spurred heels dug deep.

The patrol came thundering up the road, but Bahzell's hands were already moving with trained, flowing speed. He never took his eyes from the accelerating horsemen, but the goatsfoot snapped into place by feel alone, and his arm jerked. The string clicked back over the cog, and he dropped the iron lever. There'd be no time for a third shot, and letting it fall saved a precious fraction of a second. Steel rasped beside him as Brandark's sword cleared the scabbard, and his friend's horse bounded forward even as the second quarrel fitted to the string and the arbalest rose once more.

Hradani—even Bloody Swords—required big horses. They needed time to gather speed, and the closest was still fifty yards clear when Bahzell spotted the rank badge he'd searched for. The arbalest steadied, the string snapped, and the dead captain's lieutenant folded forward with a bubbling shriek as the square-headed war bolt took him in the belly.

The remaining half dozen were up to a hard canter, closing on a gallop, and Brandark thundered to meet them as Bahzell dropped the arbalest and his own sword flashed free. He felt no sense of abandonment—the momentum of a cavalryman's horse was his greatest weapon, and Brandark would have been a fool to take that charge standing—and his lips drew back in an ear-flattened grin as the guardsmen split and three of them came for him. They were in too tight, jostling one another in their eagerness to get at him.

It was almost too easy for someone who'd cut his teeth against the Sothōii. Three massive horses careered towards him, intent on riding him into red ruin, his very motionlessness only urging them on. And then, when they were barely thirty feet away, he leapt suddenly to his left, and his sword flashed.

A terrible shriek of equine agony filled the world, and the right-hand horseman catapulted from the saddle as sixty inches of razor-sharp steel took his mount across the knees. He landed on his head, his shout of panic cut off with the abrupt, sickening snap of his neck, and his horse went down, screaming and twisting while blood fountained from its truncated forelegs.

Bahzell took a precious second to cut the animal's throat as he stepped across it into the road, and his eyes glittered as the other two guardsmen dragged their mounts to a sliding halt and gaped back at him. He took one hand from his sword and beckoned to them, and he could almost hear them snarl as he taunted them. His own fury rose to meet them, but he fought it down, strangling the incipient Rage, as they spurred back towards him.

The distance was too short for them to regain their previous speed, yet that made them almost more dangerous, for they wouldn't override their mark this time. They were further apart, too, opening a gap between them and wary of another feint, and he watched them come, one ear cocked to the shouts and clash of steel behind him, listening for any sound of hooves from the rear.

There was none, and he leapt forward into the opening between them as they charged down on him again. It took them by surprise. The one on his right pulled further to the side, sword poised to unleash a deadly blow, but the maneuver slowed them, bringing them in separately and not together, and Bahzell was on the off side of the one to his left. The left hand sword came over in a clumsy, cross-body slash that whistled harmlessly wide of a quick duck, and he pivoted to his own right, blade darting up to meet the more dangerous threat from that side.

Steel whined, then glanced from the shoulder of his scale mail with a sledgehammer impact, but his enemy had forgotten how tall his opponent was. He'd cut down from the saddle without guarding his own head . . . and that head bounded from his shoulders as his horse surged past Bahzell.

The Horse Stealer spun on his toes, shoulder aching from the blow his armor had turned, even as the remaining trooper's mount pivoted on its haunches and came back at him yet again. But this time there was as much fear as fury on the guardsman's face. He kept Bahzell to his right, clearing his own sword arm, yet he closed far more tentatively, and his head moved in small, quick arcs, as if he fought an urge to look over his shoulder in hopes of other aid.

But there was no aid. Bahzell faced back up the road now, and he saw one of Brandark's three foes motionless and bleeding in the roadway, the other two swirling in a twisting, furious knot as he held them both in play. His lips drew back in a grin at the sight, and the guardsman paled as he charged to meet him instead of awaiting his attack.

The horse leapt forward with a squeal as the spurs went home, but it was too late. Bahzell's size canceled out the guardsman's height advantage, and he'd sacrificed the weapon of momentum. Worse, his sword was far lighter, for no mounted man could manage a blade to match Bahzell's. What would have been a two-handed great sword for a human was little more than a bastard sword for him. The guardsman's desperate cut glanced harmlessly from the Horse Stealer's interposed blade, and Bahzell twisted at the hips, throwing his shoulders into a two-handed blow that smashed through armor—and spine—in a gout of blood.

The charging horse ran out from under the tumbling corpse, and Bahzell completed his turn and raced up the road. One of Brandark's surviving enemies pitched suddenly from his saddle, clutching at the spouting stump of an arm, and some sixth sense warned his companion. He jerked his horse aside, backing away, and swallowed hard as he realized he was all alone. His eyes darted over the sprawled bodies, and then he yanked his mount's head around, slammed in his heels, darted past Bahzell, and galloped off to the east.

Bahzell slid to a halt, chest heaving, and Brandark looked across at him from the saddle. A deep cut on the Bloody Sword's cheek dripped onto his once splendid jerkin, slashed fabric fluttered where a sword had cut his left shirtsleeve, and his eyes glittered with a fire utterly at odds with his usual dandy's role, but his tenor voice was more drawling than ever.

"Pitiful," he sighed, watching the fleeing guardsman thunder down the road in a flurry of dust. "Simply pitiful. And—" his teeth flashed in a sudden smile "—I *do* wish I could hear him explain this one to Churnazh!"

# CHAPTER SIX

The Grand Duchy of Esgan was nervous about its neighbors. Bloody Sword hradani had poured over its frontiers all too often in its seven-hundred-year history, and the posts along its eastern border were more substantial than those one might find elsewhere, with garrisons to match.

A twenty-man platoon flowed out onto the road as Bahzell and Brandark approached, and Bahzell watched speculatively while they shook themselves into order. The only humans he'd ever seen had been Sothōii cavalrymen intent on spilling his blood, and he was almost disappointed by how normal the Esganian infantry looked. They were well turned out, with better armor and weapons than even Hurgrum could provide, yet there was something just a bit sloppy about their formation, as if they knew they were mere border guards.

They were also much darker than most Sothōii . . . and smaller. The tallest was shorter than Brandark and

71

barely chest-high on Bahzell, and the Horse Stealer's ears twitched with derisive amusement as he saw them absorb that fact and draw into a tighter array.

An officer stepped to the fore, his brightly worked rank insignia gleaming, and raised an imperious hand at the two hradani.

"State your business!" His badly accented Navahkan held an edge of truculence and an even sharper one of nervousness, for in addition to their own horses, Bahzell and Brandark led no less than four more with war saddles. Two were laden with bloodstained arms and armor whose original owners no longer required them, and two badly wounded, semiconscious guardsmen were strapped into the saddles of the other two.

"Certainly." Brandark's calm Esganian was far better than the officer's Navahkan. "My companion and I wish to cross the border and travel to Esgfalas in hopes of hiring on as caravan guards."

"Caravan guards?" Even Bahzell, whose Esganian was limited at best, recognized the officer's incredulity. The man's eyes flitted back over their plunder and Churnazh's two wounded guardsmen, and he cleared his throat. "You seem a bit, ah, *well-equipped* for caravan guards, friend."

"We do?" Brandark turned in his saddle to run his own eyes back over the cavalcade. "I suppose we do, Captain, but it's all come by honestly." The officer made a strangled sound, and Brandark grinned. "We had a slight misunderstanding a few miles back, but when my companion and I were set upon without cause, we had no choice but to defend ourselves."

"Without cause?" the officer repeated politely, with a significant glance at the wounded guardsmen's livery, and Brandark shrugged.

"Well, it seemed that way to *us*, Captain. At any rate, we claim their arms and horses as lawful plunder."

"I see." The officer rubbed his chin, then shrugged.

Manifestly, the reasons for which hradani chose to slaughter one another meant nothing to him, as long as they did it on their own side of the border. "May I ask your names?"

"My name is Brandark, until recently of Navahk," Brandark replied cheerfully. "The tall fellow yonder is Bahzell Bahnakson, Prince of Hurgrum. Perhaps you've heard of him?"

"Ah, yes," the officer said. "As a matter of fact I have. Something about broken hostage bond and rape, I believe." Bahzell stiffened, but the Esganian went on in an unhurried tone. "Since, however, the tale came from an officer of Prince Churnazh's Guard—I believe that's his surcoat there, on the second horse—I saw no particular reason to believe the rape charges. As for the hostage bond, that would be between your friend, Prince Churnazh, and Hurgrum, and no concern of Esgan's. But—" he darted sharp eyes back to Brandark "—no one mentioned anything about *you*."

"I'm afraid Churnazh wasn't aware of my own travel plans when he sent word ahead," Brandark said smoothly.

"I see." The officer studied the road under his boots for several moments. "Well, under the circumstances, I see no reason to deny you entry, as long—" he looked back up "—as you're on your way *through* Esgan."

Bahzell's eyes narrowed, but Brandark only nodded. "We are, Captain."

"Good." The officer returned a crisp nod, then glanced back at the two wounded guardsmen. "Ah, may I ask exactly what you intend to do with those two?" His tone implied that it would only be polite to take them back out of sight—and onto Navahkan soil—before cutting their throats.

"Aye, Captain, you may," Bahzell said in slow, careful Esganian. "It's grateful we'd be if you'd see to their wounds till they can ride again, then send them back to Navahk."

The officer gawked at him, then shot a stunned look up at Brandark.

"As I said, Captain, I'm sure it was all a misunderstanding," the Bloody Sword said blandly. "Under the circumstances, the least we can do is send them home to explain it to Prince Churnazh."

The Esganian officer winced, then nodded with grudging respect and spared the two guardsmen a much more sympathetic look.

"I think we can do that," he said slowly, "assuming you can pay their housing and healer's bills."

"That seems reasonable." Brandark extended a handful of silver to the officer. "Would this take care of it?"

The officer glanced down and nodded, and Brandark smiled.

"In that case, Captain, we'll leave them—and their horses—with you and be on our way, if you don't mind. We wouldn't want any of their friends to turn up and have another misunderstanding right on your doorstep."

Esgan was both disturbingly like and unlike Bahzell's homeland, but it was *very* unlike Navahk. The road was almost as well maintained as Prince Bahnak's military roads, and the stone walls of the fields they passed were neatly laid and kept. Herds grazed contentedly, crops ripened as the northern summer drowsed into early fall, and there was as much traffic as he would have seen in a normal day in Hurgrum. That was a relief after the wasteland to which Churnazh had reduced his own lands, but there was a marked difference in the way these people acted. Heavy farm wagons rumbled along with the first of the harvest, but most of the traffic was afoot . . . and as wary as the farmer on muleback who paused to gawk at them, then dug in his heels and hurried along before the hradani could do anything more than glance back.

And that, Bahzell thought, was the disturbing thing.

He'd always known the other Races of Man feared his people, and he knew enough history to realize they had reason to. Yet this was the first time he'd ever encountered such sullen hostility from total strangers. Brandark seemed unaffected as he rode along at his friend's shoulder, but something inside Bahzell tightened in disgust—or perhaps it was dismay—when pedestrians shrank back against the far side of the road to avoid them and mothers actually snatched children up and turned protectively away on sight.

The hot hostility in other eyes did more than dismay, and he felt his hand steal towards his sword more than once as his hackles rose in response. Wariness, even fear, he could understand, little though he might like it; hatred and contempt were something very different.

"I told you hradani were unpopular," Brandark murmured quietly as a farmhand gestured the evil eye at them and hopped across a pasture wall rather than share the road with them, and Bahzell glanced at him in surprise. Brandark had seemed totally unaware of the Esganians' hostility, but now the Bloody Sword's twisted smile gave that appearance the lie.

"Aye, so you did, and it was in my mind I knew what you were meaning," Bahzell replied. "But this—" He waved a disgusted hand after the retreating farmhand, and Brandark's smile twisted a bit further.

"Well, it's hard to blame them," he said judiciously. "They don't know what shining, stalwart people Horse Stealers are. All they know are nasty, plundering Bloody Swords like your humble servant."

"Like Churnazh's scum, you mean," Bahzell growled.

"Ah, but those are the only hradani they know at all, and, that being the case, then *all* hradani are scum. After all, we're all the same, aren't we?"

Bahzell spat into the dust, and Brandark chuckled.

"If you think it's bad now, my friend, wait till we reach

a town!" He shook his head and brushed at his tattered, dirty shirtsleeve. "Do try to remember we're visitors—and not welcome ones—if you should feel moved to reason with anyone. I suspect lynching a pair of murdering hradani would be a whole year's entertainment for some of these folk. Why—" Brandark's eyes gleamed at Bahzell's snarl "—it might be almost as entertaining for them as cutting Churnazh into rib roasts would be for you!"

They reached the town of Waymeet late that afternoon.

It was a small town—little more than a village where a farm track crossed the main road—and it was obvious word of their coming had preceded them. None of the half dozen of the town guard who rode out to meet them were particularly well armed, and their mounts looked like hastily borrowed draft horses, but they kept their hands near their weapons as they drew up across the road and awaited the hradani.

The portly, balding man at their head was better dressed. He also wore the bronze key of a mayor on a chain around his neck, and he looked acutely uneasy as he trotted a little out in front of the others.

Bahzell stayed well back with the horses to let Brandark deal with them without the handicap of his own imposing stature or limited Esganian. The mayor relaxed a bit when the Bloody Sword addressed him in his own tongue and produced their road tokens from the border guard, but he looked unhappier than ever when Brandark announced their intention to pass the night in Waymeet.

There was little he could say about it, however, and he trotted back to his men. He led them back into town—not without a few muttered comments and baleful glances—and Brandark watched them go, then waved Bahzell forward.

"And *that*," he commented acidly, "is a man Father's

dealt with before." He shook his head. "Imagine how the others are going to react!"

Bahzell only grunted, and the two of them followed the horsemen along a road that turned to cobblestones as they reached the outlying houses.

Waymeet, Bahzell noted approvingly, was a clean, solidly built place, whatever its inhabitants might think of hradani. Half the homes were roofed with slate or shingles rather than thatch, whitewashed walls gleamed in the rich, golden light of the westering sun, and the town's single inn looked comfortable and welcoming—aside from the hostile glances of the people in its yard as he and Brandark turned into it.

Bahzell watched Brandark vanish into the inn and left his friend to arrange their lodging. He himself was a less than patient man under the best of circumstances, which these weren't, and he reminded himself to hold his temper as he led the horses towards the inn's watering trough and none of the hostlers offered to help.

He'd just shoved his own packhorse aside to make room for another when a voice spoke up.

"What the Phrobus d'you think *you're* doing?!" it snapped.

Bahzell's jaw clenched, but he concentrated on the horses and refused to turn his head. The voice had spoken in Esganian, so perhaps if he pretended he didn't understand and simply ignored it, it would go away.

"You, there! I'm talking to *you*, hradani!" the voice barked, this time in crude Navahkan. "Who told you to water your filthy animals here?!"

Bahzell's ears flattened, and he turned slowly, straightening to his full height to face the speaker. The Esganian was tall by local standards—and muscular, aside from a heavy beer belly—but his narrow face paled and he moved back half a step as he realized how enormous Bahzell truly was. He swallowed, then looked around quickly and appeared to draw courage as others in the inn yard flowed towards them.

"Is it me you're speaking to?" Bahzell rumbled in a slow, dangerously affable voice.

"Of course it is, *hradani*," the Esganian sneered. "We don't want you fouling our water with your diseased animals!"

"Well, now, if it so happened they were diseased, I wouldn't be blaming you. As they're not, you've naught to be worrying over, now do you?"

Bahzell's eyes glittered warningly, but his deep voice was even. There was no reason to tell anyone how hard it was for him to keep it so or how his hand hungered for his sword.

"D'you think I'd take a *hradani's* word for that?" the Esganian jeered. "They look diseased to *me*—after all, a hradani rode them, didn't he?"

"Friend," Bahzell said softly, "I want no trouble here. I'm but a traveler passing through your town, and I've no mind to quarrel with any man."

"Ha! We know your kind around here, *hradani*." The Esganian threw the word at him yet again, like a knife, and his teeth drew up in a vicious smile. "A 'traveler,' are you? More like brigand scum spying for more of the same!"

Bahzell drew a deep breath and squared his shoulders as the Rage stirred within him, uncoiling like a serpent, and something cold and ugly glowed in his eyes. He looked down upon his antagonist through a faint, red haze, and his sword hand tingled, but he set his teeth and fought back the sick ecstasy of his people's curse. There were over a dozen men in the inn yard by now, all watching the confrontation, and an entire town beyond them, and if only the loudmouth wore a sword, at least half the others carried dirks or daggers. To his own surprise, his time in Navahk came to his aid now, for he'd learned to endure insults in silence, yet it was hard. Hard.

He drew another breath, crushing the Rage under his heel, then deliberately turned his back and returned to the horses. A part of him prayed the loudmouth would see it as a surrender and take his petty victory and go, but he knew it wouldn't happen. Bullies didn't think that way, and another part of him was glad. A small, red flame of the Rage still flickered, and he called it sternly to heel as he reached out to draw another horse back from the trough . . . and that was when steel scraped behind him.

"Don't turn your back on *me*, you fucking hradani bast—!"

The Esganian was stepping forward as he snarled, and his eyes blazed with hard, hating cruelty as he prepared to drive his sword into Bahzell's back. But his shout broke off in a hacking grunt of anguish as Bahzell took a sideways backward step, inside the point of his sword, and a scale mail-armored elbow slammed into his belly hard enough to lift his toes from the ground.

He folded forward, wheezing in agony, and Bahzell plucked the sword from his lax hand. He dropped it into the watering trough and shook his head.

"I'm thinking that was a mistake, friend," he said softly. "Now go home before you've the making of another."

"*Son of a whore!*" The Esganian straightened with a gasp of pain, and a dirk glittered in his left hand. The hradani twisted aside, letting the blade grate off his mail shirt, and the Esganian snarled. "There's enough of us here to gut you *and* your friend!" he shouted, voice raised to set the others on Bahzell like a pack of hounds, and brought the dirk flashing back around.

A hand like a shovel snapped out and closed on his knife wrist, and he gasped—then screamed and rose on his toes as the hand twisted. His free hand flailed the air for a moment, then pounded desperately at Bahzell's armored belly, but Bahzell only smiled a cold, ugly smile and twisted harder. The roughneck went to his knees,

dropping his weapon with another, sharper scream, and
the Horse Stealer looked up. The bystanders who'd started
forward froze as his flint-hard gaze swept over them, and
his smile grew.

"I told you to go home, friend," he said in that same,
soft voice. "It was good advice, and I'm thinking you should
have heeded me."

"L-Let me *go*, you bastard!"

"Ah? It's letting you go you want me to do, is it?" Small
bones began to crack, and the Esganian writhed on his
knees. "Well, then, it's let you go I will . . . but I'm thinking—" the fingers crushed like a vise "—you'll not be
sticking any more knives in folks' backs today."

He gave one last twist, and the Esganian shrieked as
his wrist snapped back at right angles with a sharp, clear
crack that made every listener wince. Bahzell released
him, and the troublemaker crouched on his knees, cra-
dling his shattered wrist and screaming curses while the
hradani stood with his back to one of the horses and
crossed his arms across his chest. That hungry smile still
curled upon his lips, but he kept his hands well away
from any weapon, and heads turned as people looked at
one another uncertainly.

Tension hovered like lightning, poised to strike, but
Bahzell simply waited. His posture was eloquently
unthreatening, and no man there wanted to be the first
to change that, but the troublemaker staggered to his
feet, still spewing curses.

"Are you going to let this hradani bastard get *away*
with this?!" he screamed, and two others started forward,
then froze as eyes cored with icy fire swiveled to them
and Bahzell's ears went flat. One of them swallowed hard
and took a step back, and the roughneck rounded on him.

"Coward! Gutless, puking *coward!* Cowards *all* of you!
He's only a stinking *hradani*, you bastards—*kill him!* Why
don't you—"

"I think," another voice said, "that that will be enough, Falderson."

The troublemaker's mouth snapped shut, and he spun to face the inn yard gate. Two men stood there, both in the boiled leather jerkins of the town guard, and Bahzell recognized the speaker from the party who'd met them outside town. The man wore a sergeant's shoulder knot, and if there was no liking in the gaze he bent on Bahzell, there was no unthinking hatred, either.

"Arrest him!" Falderson shouted, raising his shattered wrist in his other hand. "Look what the stinking whoreson *did* to me!"

"Why are you wearing your sword belt, Falderson?" the sergeant asked instead, and the roughneck seemed to freeze. He opened his mouth, and the sergeant smiled coldly. "I see you seem to have forgotten your sword—or did you lose it somewhere? And isn't that your dirk?" A finger pointed to the weapon Falderson had dropped, and the Esganian's face went purple with shame and fury. His mouth worked soundlessly, and then he shook himself.

"I-I was *defending* myself!" he snarled. "This bastard hradani attacked me—attacked me without cause! Ask anyone, if you don't believe me!"

"I see." The sergeant looked around the hushed inn yard, but no one spoke, and his eyes narrowed as Brandark emerged from the inn. The Bloody Sword said nothing, but the crowd parted before him as he stepped to Bahzell's side. He, too, looked down at the dirk lying on the hard-packed dirt, then reached back without taking his eyes from the sergeant's. His hand vanished into the trough, then emerged with a dripping sword and dropped it beside the dirk.

"Yours, I believe?" he said quietly to Falderson in perfect Esganian, but his eyes were still on the sergeant, and the sergeant nodded slowly.

"I— I mean, he—" Falderson's gaze darted around the yard, but none of the others—not even the two who'd started forward to attack Bahzell—would meet his eyes, and his voice died into silence.

"I think we all know what you mean." The sergeant stepped forward to gather up the sword and dirk and hand them to his companion. "It's not the first time you've landed yourself in trouble, so I'll just keep these for you . . . at least until you can *hold* them again," he added meaningfully, and Falderson stared down at his shattered wrist.

"All right!" The sergeant raised his voice. "The show's over. You, Henrik—take Falderson to the healer and have that wrist set. The rest of you be about your business while I have a word with these . . . gentlemen."

Voices rose in an unhappy mutter, but the crowd began to drift away, and the sergeant walked over to the hradani. There was still no liking in his eyes, but there was a certain amusement mixed with the wariness in them.

"Falderson," he said quietly to Bahzell in passable Navahkan, "is as stupid as the day is long." He craned his neck to gaze up at the hradani and shook his head. "In fact, he's even stupider than I thought. You, sir, are the biggest damned hradani—no offense—I think I've ever seen."

"None taken," Bahzell rumbled. "And my thanks. I'm thinking it would have gotten a mite messy if you hadn't happened along."

"I didn't 'happen' along," the sergeant said. "The mayor wasn't very happy about your visit, and he asked us to keep an eye on you. Now—" he waved at the weapons his companion still held "—you can see why, I think."

"Sergeant," Brandark began, "I assure you—"

"No need to assure *me* of anything, Lord Brandark." The sergeant granted the title without irony, and Brandark cocked an eyebrow. "From all I hear, you've been here before and always avoided trouble, and it's plain as the

nose on my face your friend didn't pick this quarrel."
The sergeant's mouth quirked. "If he had, I doubt
Falderson would have gotten off with no more than broken
bones. But the fact is that Waymeet doesn't like hradani.
This is a country town, and it's not thirty years since the
entire place burned to the ground in a border raid. Country
folk have long memories, and besides—" He broke off
and shrugged, and Bahzell grunted in unhappy understanding.

"That being the case," the sergeant went on, "I think
it would be better all around if you and your friend moved
on, Lord Brandark. Meaning no disrespect, and I realize you have road tokens. More than that, I realize neither of you has any intention of making trouble. But the
point is, you don't have to *make* trouble; you *are* trouble,
and this is my town."

Bahzell's ears flattened, but he clamped his jaws on
his anger and glanced at Brandark. The Bloody Sword
looked back with a small shrug, and Bahzell snorted, then
looked back at the sergeant and nodded grimly.

"Thank you." There was a trace of embarrassment in
the man's voice, but no apology, and he glanced at the
sun. "I'd say you've another hour of light, Lord Brandark.
I'm sure the innkeeper can put up a supper for you—
tell him to put it on my tab—but I'd advise you to eat in
the saddle."

He drew himself up to a sort of attention, nodded,
and beckoned to his companion. The two guardsmen
marched out the inn gate, and Bahzell and Brandark stood
alone in the center of the silent, deserted yard.

# CHAPTER SEVEN

The gate guard gave them a sharp look as they made their way through Drover's Gate into Esgfalas. Bahzell gazed back with a certain dour bitterness but let it pass. Waymeet lay days behind, and he'd managed to conquer his fury at what had happened there, yet the all-pervasive hostility around him was worse, in its way, than anything he'd been forced to endure in Navahk. At least there he'd known his enemies had cause for their enmity.

The outright hatred had eased as they got further from the border, yet what was left was almost worse. It was a cold, smokelike thing that hovered everywhere yet lacked even the justification of border memories. It sprang not from anything he or Brandark, or even raiders, had done; it sprang from who and what they *were*.

The gate guard took his time checking their road tokens, and Bahzell folded his arms and leaned against his packhorse. The gelding blew wearily, then turned its head to

lip the hradani's ears affectionately, and Bahzell rubbed
its forehead as he studied what he could so far see of
Esgfalas.

Esgan was a human realm, and Bahzell knew the
shorter-lived, more fertile humans produced denser popu-
lations than his own folk found tolerable. But he also
knew from his tutors that Esgan was less populous than
many other human lands . . . and its capital still seemed
terrifyingly vast. The city walls were enormous, if in poorer
repair than they should have been, and the traffic passing through the gates beggared anything Bahzell had ever
seen. He couldn't even begin to guess how many people
lived within those walls, but at the very least it must be
many times the population of the city of Hurgrum, possibly greater than his father's entire princedom!

His ears twitched as they picked up the whispered
comments of the humans making their way past him.
Judging by their content, most of the speakers believed
he couldn't hear them, or that he wouldn't understand
if he did, and he chose to pretend they were right. In
fact, his Esganian was much better than it had been,
for, like most of the human tongues of central and
northern Norfressa, it was a variant of Axeman, and
Prince Bahnak had insisted all of his sons must speak
that fluently. The Empire of the Axe seldom impinged
upon the distant lands of the eastern hradani, but its
might and influence were so great no ruler could afford
*not* to speak its tongue any more than he could not
speak that of the Empire of the Spear, its single true
rival, and constant exposure to Esganian had helped
him master the differences.

Brandark finished speaking to the guard, and the two
of them made their way into the city. As always, people
tended to clear their path, pushing rudely back against
their neighbors when necessary, and Bahzell smiled sourly
as even beggars gave them a wide berth. There were

some advantages to being a brutal, murdering hradani after all, it seemed.

The sounds and smells and colors of the city made it hard to maintain his impassivity. The streets shifted with no apparent rhyme or reason from flagstone to cobbles to brick and back again, and not one of them went more than fifty yards before it bent like a serpent. He wondered how much of that was by chance and how much by design. This warren would be a nightmare for any commander, but if a defender knew the streets and an attacker didn't . . .

Some of the serpentine quality faded as they neared the center of town. The streets grew broader, too, lined with solid structures of brick, stone, and wood and no longer overhung by encroaching upper stories. Taverns and shops stood shoulder-to-shoulder with carpet stalls, cutlers, and street-side grills that gave off delicious smells, but that, too, faded as Brandark turned down a wide avenue. Houses replaced them—enormous houses, by Bahzell's standards—set in manicured grounds. He knew the smell of wealth when he met it, yet even here, the houses clustered tightly, for there simply wasn't room for spacious estates in this packed city.

Some of the well-kept homes boasted their own guards, who stood by closed entry gates, often with hands near their weapons as the hradani passed, and Bahzell wondered what he and Brandark were doing here. This was no place to find the sort of employment they sought, and the palpable suspicion of those guards left him feeling like a scout walking knowingly into an ambush, but he could only trust Brandark knew what he was about.

He pulled his attention back from the watching eyes and made himself pay more attention to the city's quality and less to its sheer size. Vast and crowded Esgfalas might be, but it was infinitely better kept than Navahk. Even the poorer streets were as clean as anything in

Hurgrum; these broad, residential avenues actually sparkled under the sun, and the gutters along their sides were deep but clean, obviously for drainage and not simply a convenient place to shove refuse. He hated the feeling of being closed in, denied long sight lines and space, yet there was a safe, solid feel to this place . . . or would have been, if the people who lived here hadn't hated him.

Brandark made another turn, and Bahzell heaved a mental sigh of relief as they left the palatial avenues behind and the buildings changed quickly back into places of business. A short quarter-hour took them into an area of huge warehouses and shouting work gangs mixed with the grating roar of wagon wheels, and he felt himself relaxing still further. A man had to watch his toes or lose them to those rumbling wheels, perhaps, but there was too much activity and energy here for anyone to waste time staring at him bitterly.

There were more foreigners, as well. He heard at least a dozen languages chattering about him, and his ears pricked in surprise as a slender, gilt-haired man crossed the street ahead of him. He'd never seen an elf, but those delicately pointed ears and angular eyebrows couldn't belong to a human, and now that he looked, he saw representatives of still other Races of Man.

He watched in fascination as a small cluster of halflings trotted busily down the street. They stood barely waist high to a human, reaching little more than to Bahzell's thigh, and delicate ivory horns gleamed on their foreheads. They attracted their own share of distrustful looks, and he snorted in understanding. The histories said there'd *been* no halflings prior to the Wizard Wars. The same wars that had brought the Fall of Kontovar and afflicted his own kind with the Rage had produced the small, horned people of the youngest Race of Man, and that was enough to make them suspect to anyone else. Nor did their reputation help, though Bahzell had always taken such tales with a grain of salt. No doubt there was some truth to them—after all, there was *some* truth even to the tales about hradani—yet he couldn't believe an entire race consisted solely of cowards and thieves. Besides, if he were such a wee, puny fellow as they, no doubt he'd be on the . . . cautious side, as well!

Brandark was watching signboards now, and suddenly he nodded and raised a hand.

"Here we are!" Bahzell suspected his friend's satisfied tone owed at least a little to their having crossed the city without incident. City boy or not, even Brandark had to find this place on the overpowering side.

"Are we, now?" he rumbled. "And where might 'here' be?"

"With any luck, the place we'll find someone to hire us. Follow me."

Brandark led the way into a brick-paved courtyard surrounded on three sides by huge, blank-faced warehouses. A score of workmen labored about them, too busy to do more than glance their way, but a quartet of guards rose from a bench beside an office door. One of them— a tall, black-haired fellow in well-worn chain mail, leather breeches, and a cavalryman's high boots—said something to his fellows and made his way across the courtyard towards the hradani with the rolling gait of a horseman. The saber scabbard at his side was as worn but well kept as his armor, and he cocked his head as he stopped in front of them.

"And what might I be able to do for you?" he growled in rough-edged Esganian. It wasn't discourtesy; Bahzell had heard the same gruffness too often to mistake a voice worn to a rasp by the habit of command.

"I'm looking for an Axeman merchant," Brandark replied.

"Aye? Would he have a name?"

"Well, yes." For the first time since Bahzell had met

him, Brandark sounded a bit embarrassed. "I'm, ah, not certain I can pronounce it properly," he apologized, "and I wouldn't care to offer insult by getting it wrong."

"Aye?" The black-haired man's dark eyes glinted with amusement. "Well, he's not here just now, whoever he might be, so you just lean back and let her rip," he said in Axeman that was much better than his Esganian.

"Very well." Brandark replied in the same language and drew a breath. "I was told to ask for . . . Kilthandahknarthos of Clan Harkanath of the Silver Caverns."

Bahzell turned his head to stare at his friend as the long, sonorous name fell from his tongue, but the black-haired man chuckled.

"Well, you didn't do so badly, at that, but it's 'knar*thas*' there at the end." He cocked his head the other way and squeezed his sword belt and rocked on his heels. "And might I ask your business with old Kilthan?"

"I'm hoping," Brandark said, "that he might have jobs for us."

"Jobs, is it?" The black-haired man sounded dubious. "What sort of job would that be?"

Brandark started to reply, but Bahzell touched his shoulder and looked down at the human.

"Your pardon, I'm sure, but I'm wondering what business of yours that might be?" he asked pleasantly, and the black-haired man nodded.

"That's fair enough. My name is Rianthus, and I command Kilthan's guardsmen. So, you see, it's my business to wonder what a pair like you—no offense—might want with my employer."

"A pair like us, hey?" Bahzell's teeth glinted. "Aye, I can see you might be thinking we'd need watching, but we'd be right fools, the both of us, to be walking slap up to you if we'd anything clever in mind, now wouldn't we?"

"The thought had crossed my mind," Rianthus agreed. "On the other hand, you might be clever enough to expect me to think just that. It wouldn't be very wise of you, but you might not know that yet, you see."

"Aye, you've a point there," Bahzell chuckled, then shrugged. "Well, if you're after commanding his guards, then I'm thinking you're the man we're most needful to see."

"Oh ho!" Rianthus nodded again, narrowed eyes glinting. "Looking to hire us your swords, are you?"

"Well, I've heard it's either guard or raid for such as us," Bahzell replied, "and I've no mind to take up brigands' ways."

"Well, that sounds honest enough," Rianthus murmured, looking the immense Horse Stealer over from head to toe, "and no question you two could be useful. Assuming you haven't taken up brigands' ways already. We've had raiders try to put a man or two inside before, but it hasn't helped 'em yet."

"And a great relief to my mind that is," Bahzell said politely, and Rianthus gave a crack of laughter.

"Aye, you'll do—if you're what you say." He looked back at Brandark. "You're the one with the name to drop, my lad, so suppose you tell me who might vouch for you?"

"I'm hoping Kilthan himself will." Brandark's reply raised the guard captain's eyebrows, and the Bloody Sword shrugged. "My father and he have, um, done business a time or two in the past." He tugged a ring off the forefinger of his left hand and held it out. "I think he'll recognize this."

"Will he, now?" Rianthus bounced the ring on his palm, then closed his fist around it with a grin. "You know, I've always suspected the old thief was just a *tad* less respectable than he claims. Wait here."

He vanished into the office, and Bahzell glanced down at his friend.

" 'Done business,' is it? And what sort of business might

your revered father have been having with an Axeman dwarf?"

"Oh, a little of this and a little of that," Brandark replied airily, then grinned. "As friend Rianthus says, old Kilthan's factors aren't above buying goods without too many questions. But aside from that small foible, he's as respectable as he claims, and honest to boot. Father always said—"

He broke off as Rianthus reappeared in the doorway and beckoned. Bahzell raised a handful of reins at him, and the captain thumped one of his men on the shoulder and pointed. The guardsman—a shorter, chunky fellow—rose with ill grace and stumped over to the hradani. He took the reins with a surly grunt and stood holding them while Brandark and Bahzell moved to join Rianthus.

The door was a close fit for Bahzell, and the ceiling beyond was worse. Navahk had been bad enough for one of his stature, but at least it had been built to fit other hradani; the warehouse office hadn't, and he fought a sense of claustrophobic enclosure as he hunched his shoulders and bent his neck to accommodate its cramped dimensions.

"Hirahim, you *are* a big one!" a deep, gravelly voice snorted. "Have a seat, man! Have a seat before you sprain something!"

Rianthus nudged Bahzell and pointed, and the Horse Stealer sank gratefully onto the chair. It was far too small, but there were no arms to get in the way, and it didn't creak too alarmingly as it took his weight.

"Better," the gravel voice said. "Now I can at least look you in the belly button, can't I?" It chuckled at its own wit, and Bahzell finally spotted its owner.

The man behind the desk had to be sitting either in a very tall chair or atop a heap of cushions, for he couldn't have stood much over four feet. He was also very nearly as broad as he was tall and bald as an egg, but a massive, forked beard streamed down his chest in compensation, and strange, topaz-colored eyes glittered in the light.

"So," he said now, turning to Brandark as the Bloody Sword found a chair of his own, "you must be young Brandarkson." He rubbed the side of his nose with a finger while his other hand spun the ring on the desk before him, and his topaz eyes narrowed. "Well, you've the look of him, and the ring's right, but what you're doing *here* has me in something of a puzzle."

"You've *met* Father?" Brandark asked, and Kilthan shrugged.

"No, I've never had that, um, privilege, but I make it my business to know what I can about those I do my business *with*. And," he added judiciously, "I've always found your father an honest sort, for a Bloody Sword hradani." He chuckled. "*Especially* for a Bloody Sword, if you'll pardon my frankness."

"I suspect Father would be amused, not insulted," Brandark replied with a smile, and Kilthan chuckled again.

"Aye, with that accent you'd almost have to be Brandarkson. Damn me, but your Axeman's better than mine!"

"Perhaps that's because it's not your native tongue, either."

"Hey? How's that?" Kilthan demanded, eyes narrower than ever.

"Well, you *were* the senior Silver Cavern delegate to the conference that asked the Empire to annex Dwarvenhame," Brandark murmured.

"So, you know that, too, do you?" Kilthan nodded, then leaned back, folding his hands on his belly. "In that case, I think we can assume you're who you say." He unfolded one hand to wag a finger at Rianthus and indicate another chair, then returned it to his belly and cocked a bushy eyebrow at Brandark. "And that being so, young Brandarkson, suppose you tell me what you're doing here and why you need a job, you and your long, tall friend?"

"Well, as to that," Brandark said, and launched into an explanation. He did it almost too well for Bahzell's peace of mind, dropping into the rhythmic cadences of a bard. At least he seemed untempted to resort to song, for which Bahzell was profoundly grateful, but he felt himself flushing as his friend enlarged on his own "nobility" in coming to Farmah's rescue. There'd been nothing "noble" about it—just an iron-headed Horse Stealer too stupid to stay out of a mess that was none of his making!

Kilthan's eyes gleamed appreciatively, and his hand crept up to cover his mouth a time or two when Bahzell flushed. But he heard the entire tale out, then nodded and leaned forward, resting his elbows on his desk to look back and forth between them with those sharp, topaz eyes.

"Well, now! That's quite a tale . . . and it matches the bits and pieces I've already heard." Bahzell's ears shifted in surprise, and Kilthan gave a crack of laughter. "Oh, yes, lads! I don't say anyone believes it, mind you—Esganians are Esganians, and the thought of hradani doing anything 'noble' isn't one they're comfortable with—but my factors stay abreast of rumors. Bad for business if they miss one and it turns out to be true, you know. But I've heard of *your* father, too, um, Prince Bahzell, and that suggests which rumor to believe in this case. If even half the tales are true, your Prince Bahnak sounds like a man who understands the business of ruling, not just looting. If Navahk and its cronies weren't in the way, I'd have factors in Hurgrum, too . . . and judging from what your people did to Churnazh two years back, I think Navahk might not be a problem so very much longer, at that.

"In the meantime, however, I can see why you've come west. And you, young Brandarkson," those disconcerting, yellow eyes cut back to Brandark, "were quite right.

Hradani who wander about without obvious employ don't fare well in other lands." He inhaled deeply, then slapped his hands on his desk.

"So! That being the case, I might just take a chance on the two of you. Mind you, you won't be lords or princes to my men, and some of them won't be any too happy to see you." His face turned much sterner. "We've our own rules, and Rianthus will tell you what they are, but one applies to everyone: no drawn steel! I doubt you two would have made it across Esgan if you were given to, ah, hastiness, but you know as well as I that someone's going to press you sooner or later, just for being what you are. Do I have your word you'll settle it without blades?"

"Well, now," Bahzell rumbled, "I'm thinking you do, so long as *they're* not after spilling blood. It's grateful I'll be for honest work, but not so grateful I'll let someone slice a piece or two from my hide without slicing a little back in trade."

"That's fair enough," Rianthus put in. Kilthan looked at him, and the captain shrugged. "If any of our lads are stupid enough to break the rules and draw against these two, we're better off without them, anyway, Kilthan."

"Hmmmm. There probably *is* something in that," Kilthan agreed after a moment, then shrugged. "Very well, do I have your words that you won't draw steel *first?*" Both hradani nodded, and Kilthan nodded back with a curiously formal air. "Done, then! Two gold kormaks a month to start with, more if you work out well. And it's a good thing you found me when you did, for I'm bound back to Manhome before the month's end." He looked back at Rianthus and jabbed a finger at Bahzell with a grin. "Get them sworn in, Rianthus—and see if we've a tent long enough for this one!"

# CHAPTER EIGHT

The next few weeks were very different, not least because Bahzell had to see much less of the locals. That would have been a vast enough relief, but Kilthandahknarthas dihna' Harkanath was far too important for anyone in Esgfalas to irritate, and Bahzell and Brandark now wore the black and orange colors of his house. The change their livery wrought in the Esganians they *were* forced to encounter was intensely satisfying, even after they discovered they owed Kilthan over a month's wages each for the bond he'd posted in their names with the Merchants Guild and Guild of Freeswords.

Not that *everything* went smoothly. As Kilthan had warned, some of their new fellows were unhappy at having hradani among them. The majority chose not to complain, particularly after they'd watched the two of them demonstrate their competence against Rianthus' arms master. Yet a few muttered balefully, especially Shergahn, the chunky ex-corporal from the army of

97

Daranfel whom Rianthus had called to hold their horses that first day, and Bahzell and Brandark both knew it was only a matter of time until more than words were exchanged.

That much they were prepared to take as it came, for it was only to be expected. They were strangers, after all, and strangers would have been tested—probably more harshly than anyone was likely to attempt here—before being accepted by any hradani unit. Neither looked forward to it, but other problems were more immediate . . . and irritating.

There was, for example, their plunder from Churnazh's guardsmen. Two hradani, one a Horse Stealer, had no need of six horses. Rianthus bought two of them, but the others were too heavy for his taste and too well bred for draft animals, so Brandark took them and the weapons to the Square of Gianthus, Esgfalas' main market, and sold them . . . for far less than their value. They were no Sothōii coursers, but they were worth far more than anyone chose to offer a hradani—even one in Kilthan's service. In the end, he had either to take what was offered or bring them home again, and he swallowed his pride and closed the deal.

Bahzell wasn't with him (which might have been as well, given how the local merchants "explained" Brandark's bargaining position to him), but he took the news more philosophically than Brandark had feared. Money, as money, had never meant much to Bahzell, and he had enough left from his father's purse for both of them to meet such needs as Kilthan left unfilled.

It was as well he did, for Brandark had acquired, at ruinous expense, a chain haubergeon of Axeman manufacture. Kilthan's guardsmen were required to supply their own equipment, but it was his custom to sell them arms and armor at cost, and though Brandark had left home well supplied with coin, he never could have afforded such armor without the merchant's canny generosity. It was dwarvish work, superior to the best hradani workmanship, and the Bloody Sword wore it with the same panache as the embroidered jerkins and lace-cuffed shirts he'd commissioned to restore his depleted wardrobe. For himself, Bahzell was content with plainer, more practical garments, and not even a merchant with Kilthan's inventory could fit *him* with armor off the rack.

Once their immediate needs had been seen to, Rianthus was at some pains to consider how best to integrate them into his command. Kilthan's caravans were rich enough to tempt any brigand, and it was Rianthus' job to see to it no one felt anything more than temptation. He commanded over two hundred men, divided into five companies, but he laughed sharply when Bahzell suggested that he seemed well supplied with troops.

"You've never seen one of old Kilthan's menageries on the move!" Kilthan maintained a sizable compound outside the city wall, and Rianthus and Bahzell watched a squad of horse archers practicing against man-sized targets from the gallop. The sun was bright in a sky already shading into a cooler, breezier blue, and the trees surrounding the compound glowed with the first, bright brush strokes of fall. "It's not just his own wagons," the captain went on sourly, "though that'd be bad enough, when all's said, but the others."

"Others?" Bahzell repeated.

"Aye." Rianthus hawked and spat into the dust. "This'll be our last caravan of the year. Kilthan never spends more than a month or two in Esgan—he leaves operations here to his factors, for the most part—but he always comes out for the final trip, because it's the richest one, and the brigands know that. They also know there won't be many more merchant trains of *anyone's* this year, so they're ready to take bigger risks for a prize fat enough to see them through the winter. That means every rag and tag merchant who can't afford enough guards of his own wants to attach himself to Kilthan's coattails, and, since the roads are open to all, we can't be shut of them. We can't force them to stay clear of us without breaking a few heads, and that would upset the Merchants Guild, so Kilthan lets them join us. He charges 'em for it, since they're riding under our house's protection, but the fee's a joke. Just enough to make the agreement formal and require them to go by our rules." The captain shrugged. "I suppose it's worth it in the long run. They'd draw brigands like a midden draws flies anyway—and not just down on themselves, either—and at least this way we can stop their doing anything *too* stupid."

He paused to snort in exasperation as two of his galloping archers narrowly avoided collision and completely missed their targets in the process, then shrugged again.

"Just our own wagons'll take up a mile and more of road. Add the other odds and sods, and we'll have over a league to cover, and precious little help from the pox-ridden incompetents the others call guardsmen."

Bahzell hid a smile at the sour disgust in Rianthus' voice. Kilthan's captain was an ex-major from the Axeman Royal and Imperial Mounted Infantry, and the standards to which he held his men were enough to make *any* ordinary freesword look "incompetent." Yet the desire to smile faded as Bahzell considered the task the captain faced. A target as long and slow as Rianthus had described would have been vulnerable with four times the men.

"D'you know," he said slowly, "I've no experience of what they call brigands in these parts, but I've met a few back home in my time, and I'm wondering what might happen if four or five chieftains should be taking it into their heads to try their hand at us together."

"It's been tried," Rianthus said grimly. "We lost thirty guards, seventeen drovers, and so many draft animals we had to abandon and burn a dozen wagons, but they didn't take a kormak home with them—and the lot who tried it never raided another merchant." He turned his head, eyes glinting at Bahzell. "You see, when someone attacks *our* caravans, we go after 'em root and branch. If we need more troops, Clan Harkanath will hire a damned army . . . and if we don't get them this year, we will the next. Or the next." He showed his teeth. "That's one reason all but the stupid ones stay clear of us."

"Is it, now?" Bahzell rubbed his chin, ears shifting slowly back and forth, then smiled. "Well, Captain, I'm thinking I can live with that."

"I thought you might." Rianthus watched the horsemen canter from the archery range, then turned to prop his elbows on the wooden rail around it and leaned back to frown thoughtfully up at the towering hradani.

"You're going to be the odd man out, I think," he went on, and nodded his head after the departing archers. "Most of our lads are mounted, but damned if I've ever seen a horse big enough for the likes of you."

"No more have I," Bahzell agreed, "and I'll not deny a man a-horse can catch me in a sprint. But I'll match your horsemen league for league on foot—aye, and leave their mounts foundered in the dust, if I've a mind to."

"I don't doubt you, but it's still made it fiendishly hard to assign you to a platoon. In the end, the only place to put you is with Hartan, I think," the captain said, and grinned at Bahzell's polite look of inquiry.

"Hartan commands Kilthan's bodyguards. They're not part of any regular company—and neither," he added wryly when Bahzell's ears cocked, "are they any sort of soft assignment. They're the lads who watch Kilthan's back, his strongboxes, and the pay chest, and if you think we work *these* fellows hard—" he waved at the archers' fading dust "—you'll soon envy them! But the point is that they never leave the column or ride sweeps, and they're the closest to infantry we have, so—" He twitched a shoulder, and Bahzell nodded.

"Aye, I can see that," he agreed, but then he fixed the captain with a quizzical eye. "I can see that, yet I can't but be wondering how the rest of your lads will feel about having such as me watch over their pay?"

"What matters is how *I* feel about it." Rianthus gave the hradani a look that boded ill for anyone who questioned his judgment—and suggested he had a shrewd notion who those individuals might be—then raised one hand in a palm up, throwing away gesture. "And while we're speaking of how I feel, I may as well tell you that one reason I agreed with Kilthan about your hire is that your—situation, shall we say?—makes you more reliable, not less. You and your friend are hradani, and you can't go home again. If you *should* be minded to play us false, finding you afterward wouldn't be so very hard, now would it?"

"You've a point there," Bahzell murmured. "Aye, you've quite a point, now I think on it. Not that I was minded to do any such thing, of course."

"Of course." Rianthus returned his grin, then pointed at the arbalest over his shoulder. "Not to change the subject, but one thing I'd like you to consider is trading that for a bow. I've seen crossbows enough to respect 'em, but they're slow, and anything we fall into is likely to be fast and sharp."

"I've neither hand nor eye for a bow," Bahzell objected, "and gaining either takes time. If it comes to that, I'm doubting there's a bow in Esgan made to my size, and gods know I'd look a right fool prancing about with one of those wee tiny bows your horse archers draw!"

"That's true, but even one lighter than the heaviest you can pull would be nasty enough—and faster."

"That's as may be." Bahzell glanced at the empty archery range, then stepped across the rail, waved politely for the other to follow, and unslung his arbalest. Rianthus raised an eyebrow, then hopped over the same rail, and his other eyebrow rose as Bahzell drew the goatsfoot from his belt and hooked it to the arbalest's string.

"You span that thing with *one hand?*"

"Well, it's faster that way, d'you see," Bahzell replied, and Rianthus folded his arms and watched with something like disbelief as the Horse Stealer cocked the weapon with a single mighty pull. He took the time to return the goatsfoot to his belt before he set a quarrel on the string, but then the arbalest rose with snake-quick speed, the string snapped, and the bolt hummed wickedly as it tore through the head of a man-shaped target over fifty yards away. Rianthus pursed his lips, but whatever he'd thought about saying died unspoken as Bahzell's flashing hands respanned the arbalest and sent a *second* quarrel through the same straw-stuffed head in less than ten seconds.

The hradani lowered the weapon and cocked his ears inquiringly at his new commander, and Rianthus let out a slow, deep breath.

"I suppose," he murmured after a moment, "that we might just let you keep that thing after all, Prince Bahzell."

They left Esgfalas on schedule to the hour, and for all Rianthus' disparaging remarks, the "rag and tag" merchants who'd attached themselves to Kilthan moved with almost the same military precision as the dwarf's own men. But Rianthus had been right about one thing: there were over three hundred wagons, and the enormous column stretched out for almost four miles.

Bahzell had never imagined such an enormous, vulnerable, toothsome target. It was enough to make any man come all over greedy, he thought, yet the size of it made sense once he'd had a look at Kilthan's maps.

The roads in Esgan might be as good as any in Hurgrum, but most merchants preferred to ship by water wherever possible. Unfortunately, the best river route of all—the mighty Spear River and its tributary, the Hangnysti, whose navigable waters ran clear from the Sothōii Wind Plain to the Purple Lords' Bortalik Bay— was out of the question for Esganians. The Hangnysti would have taken them straight to the Spear in a relatively short hop . . . except that it flowed through the lands of both the Bloody Swords and Horse Stealers alike before it crossed the Ghoul Moor. No merchant would tempt hradani with such a prize, and even hradani avoided the Ghoul Moor.

That meant all the trade to Esgan, the Kingdom of Daranfel, and the Duchy of Moretz funneled down the roads (such as they were) to Derm, capital of the Barony of Ernos, on the Saram River. The Saram was riddled with shallows and waterfalls above Derm, but from that point south river barges could ferry them down the lower Saram, Morvan, and Bellwater to the Bay of Kolvania. And, as Rianthus had said, this was one of the last (and best-guarded) caravans of the year; anyone who possibly could had made certain his goods went with it.

None of which made the lot of Kilthan's guards any easier. Rianthus had kept them training hard, but six weeks of camp living while they waited for the caravan to assemble had taken some of the edge off them, and the other merchants' guards ranged from excellent to execrable. It would take Rianthus a few days to decide which were which; until he had, he was forced to assume they were *all* useless and deploy his own men accordingly, and the constant roving patrols he maintained along the column's flanks, coupled with regular scouting forays whenever the road passed through unclaimed wilderness, took their toll. Men and horses alike grew weary and irritable, and aching muscles had a magnifying effect on even the most petty resentments.

Bahzell saw it coming. His own lot was tolerable enough—Hartan was a hard man, but one a hradani could respect, and his own assignment kept him with the column and not gallivanting about the countryside—but the mounted units were another matter, and Brandark was assigned to one of them. So was Shergahn, and the Daranfelian's bitter dislike for all hradani found fertile, weary soil, especially when he began muttering about "spies" set on to scout the caravan's weaknesses and report them to their brigand friends.

Shergahn's bigotry didn't make him or his cronies total idiots, however, and they'd decided to leave Bahzell well enough alone. None cared to try his luck unarmed against a giant who towered nine inches and then some over seven feet, and the prohibition against drawn steel precluded anything more lethal. Besides, they'd seen him at weapons drill with that monstrous sword. In fact, Rianthus—not by coincidence—had paired the worst of them off as his sparring partners to give them a closer look, and they wanted no part of it.

But Brandark was a foot and a half shorter and carried a sword of normal dimensions. Worse, his cultured grammar and dandified manner could be immensely annoying. They were also likely to provoke a fatal misjudgment, and Shergahn's contempt for any so-called warrior who wore flower-embroidered jerkins, quoted poetry, and sat by the fire strumming a balalaika while he stared dreamily into the flames was almost as boundless as Prince Churnazh's.

Bahzell sat cross-legged against a wagon wheel, fingers working on a broken harness strap while the smell of cooking stew drifted from the fires. He'd been surprised and pleased by how well Kilthan fed his men, but, then, he'd been surprised by a great many things since entering Esgan. He'd looked down on Churnazh and his Navahkans as crude barbarians, yet he'd been forced to the conclusion that *Hurgrum* was barbarian, as well. That didn't blind him to his father's achievements, but things others took for granted were still dreams for Prince Bahnak's folk. Like the lightweight tin cooking pots Kilthan's cooks used instead of the huge, clumsy iron kettles Hurgrum's field cooks lugged about, for one. And, he thought, like the wagon against which he leaned, for another.

Hradani wagons were little more than carts, often with solid wooden wheels. Kilthan's wagons were even better than those Bahzell had seen in Esganian hands; lightly but strongly built, with wheels padded in some tough, springy stuff he'd never seen before rather than rimmed in iron, and he hadn't been able to believe how well sprung they were until he'd crawled under one of them with Kilthan's chief wainwright to see the strange, fat cylinders that absorbed the shocks with his own eyes. They were a dwarvish design, and the wainwright insisted they had nothing inside them but air and plungers, yet they made Bahzell feel uneasily as if he'd stumbled across some sorcerous art . . . and more than a bit like a bumpkin over his own unease.

And those wagons and lightweight kettles were only two of the wonders about him. Discovering what his people had been denied by their long isolation filled him with anger—and a burning desire to see and learn even more.

A soft, familiar sound plucked him from his thoughts, and he looked up from his repairs as Brandark stepped into the firelight. The balalaika slung on his back chimed faintly as he swung his saddle over a wagon tongue, then he straightened wearily, kneading his posterior with both hands, and Bahzell grinned. He'd heard about the confusion in orders that had sent Brandark's platoon out on a scouting sweep . . . in the wrong direction. They'd needed three hard, extra hours in the saddle to catch back up, and the rest of their company been less than amused by how thin the absence of a third of its strength spread its remaining members.

Brandark nodded to his friend, but his long nose twitched even as he did so. He turned like a lodestone, seeking the source of that delicious aroma, gave his backside one last rub, and started for the cooking fires, when a deep, ugly voice spoke from the shadows behind him.

"So, *there* you are, you lazy bastard!" it grated. "You led the other lads a *fine* song and dance today, didn't you?"

Bahzell's hands stilled at Shergahn's growled accusation, but he made no other move. The last thing he and Brandark needed was to make this a matter of human against hradani rather than a simple case of a trouble-maker with an overlarge mouth.

Brandark paused in his beeline to the stew pot and cocked his ears.

"Should I take it you're addressing me?" he asked in a mild tone, and Shergahn barked a laugh.

"Who else would I be calling a bastard, you smooth-tongued whoreson?"

"Oh, it's you, Shergahn!" Brandark said brightly. "*Now* I understand your question."

"Which question?" Shergahn sounded a bit taken aback by the lack of anger in the hradani's voice.

"The one about bastards. I'd thought it must be some-one else asking for *you*," Brandark said, and someone chuckled.

"Ha! Think you're so damned smart, d'you?" Shergahn spat, and the Bloody Sword shook his head with a sigh.

"Only in comparison to some, Shergahn. Only in comparison to some."

Bahzell grinned, and someone closer to the fires laughed out loud at the weary melancholy that infused Brandark's tenor. A dozen others chuckled, and Shergahn spat a filthy oath. He erupted from the shadows, flinging himself at Brandark with his arms spread—and then flew forward, windmilling frantically at empty air, when the hradani stepped aside and hooked his ankles neatly from under him with a booted foot.

Brandark watched him hit hard on his belly, then shrugged and stepped over him, brushing dust from his sleeves as he resumed his journey to the food. A louder shout of laughter went up as Shergahn heaved himself to hands and knees, but there were a few ugly mutters, as well, and two of Shergahn's cronies emerged from the same shadows to help him up. He stood for a moment, shaking his head like a baffled bull, and Brandark smiled at one of the cooks and took his long iron ladle from him. He ignored Shergahn to dip up a dollop from a simmering kettle and sniff appreciatively, and his lack of concern acted on the human like a slap. He bared his teeth, exchanged glances with one of his friends, and then the two of them charged Brandark from behind.

Bahzell closed his eyes in pity. An instant later, he heard two loud thuds, followed by matched falling sounds, and opened his eyes once more.

Shergahn and friend lay like poleaxed steers, and the Daranfelian's greasy hair was thick with potatoes, carrots, gravy, and chunks of beef. His companion had less stew in his hair, but an equally large lump was rising fast, and Brandark flipped his improvised club into the air, caught it in proper dipping position, and filled it once more from the pot without even glancing at them. He raised the ladle to his nose, inhaled deeply, and glanced at the cook with an impudent twitch of his ears.

"Smells delicious," he said while the laughter started up all around the fire. "I imagine a bellyful of this should help a hungry man sleep. Why, just look what a single ladle of it did for Shergahn!"

# CHAPTER NINE

Icy rain soaked Bahzell's cloak and ran down his face, and one of the wheel horses snorted miserably beside him as the pay wagon started up another hill. The muddy road was treacherous underfoot, and raindrops drummed on the wagon's canvas covering. It was six days since Shergahn's attack on Brandark, and the rain had started yesterday, just as the road began winding its way through the hills along the border between Esgan and Moretz.

He looked up as a mounted patrol splashed by, and Brandark nodded in passing. The Bloody Sword was just as soaked and cold as Bahzell, yet he looked almost cheerful. Shergahn had never been popular, and the rest of the guards admired Brandark's style in dealing with him. Most were none too secretly pleased Rianthus had paid the troublemaker off and sent him packing, as well, and a couple had actually asked Brandark to sing for them. Which either said a great deal for how much they liked him or indicated they were all tone deaf.

Bahzell chuckled at the thought, and someone jabbed him in the back.

"You'll be laughing from a slit throat if you let your wits wander around here, m'lad!" a sharp voice said, and he turned his head to look down at his own commander.

Hartan was another dwarf, some sort of kinsman of Kilthan's. Only a dwarf could keep the various dwarven relationships straight, but Hartan hadn't gotten his job through nepotism. Few dwarves had the length of leg for a horse, and he looked a little odd on the oversized hill pony he rode, but he was as hard and tough as his people's mountains and the only person Bahzell had ever seen who could wield a battle-axe with equal adroitness on foot or mounted. He was also atypical, for a dwarf, in that he revered Tomanak, not Torframos. Bahzell had little use for any god, and he knew some of Hartan's own folk looked upon him askance for his choice of deity, but he understood it. If a man was daft enough to put his trust in gods at all, then the Sword God was a better patron for a warrior than old Stone Beard. Even a hradani could approve of Tomanak's Code—as Hartan practiced it, at least . . . except, perhaps, for that bit about always giving quarter if it was asked for.

The dwarf took people as he found them, which meant he treated anyone assigned to his outsized platoon with equally demanding impartiality. He considered his command the elite of Kilthan's private army, and all he cared about was that his men meet his own standards in weapons craft, loyalty, and courage. If they did, he would face hell itself beside them; if they didn't, he'd cut their throats himself, and his ready, if rough, approval of the hradani had gone far to ease Bahzell's acceptance into the tight-knit world of Kilthan's personal bodyguard.

Now the dwarf swept his battered axe in a one-handed arc at the steep, overgrown hillsides visible through the streaming rain, and frowned.

"This here's a nasty bit at the best of times. We're all strung out from here to Phrobus, the horses're tired, Tomanāk only knows where all the valleys and gullies in these hills come out, and our bows're all but useless in this damned rain Chemalka's decided to drop on us! If *I* was a poxy brigand, this's where *I'd* hit us, so keep sharp, you oversized lump of gristle!"

Bahzell glanced around at the terrain, then nodded.

"Aye, I will that," he agreed, and stripped off his cloak and tossed it up into the wagon. The drover handling the team's reins from his own sheltered perch caught it with a grin of mingled sympathy and rough amusement at another's misfortune, and Bahzell grinned back. The cloak was soaked through anyway, and it had covered the hilt of his sword. Now he reached back to unsnap the strap across the quillons, and Hartan bestowed a sour smile of approval upon him. He touched a heel to his pony and cantered ahead, and Bahzell heard his flinty voice issuing the same warning to the man beside the next wagon.

Rain trickled from the end of Bahzell's braid in an irritating dribble and squelched in his boots with each step, and more water found its way under his scale mail. Long, miserable miles dragged past, marked off in beating rain, splashing hooves and feet, and the noise of turning wagon wheels and creaking harness. He was cold and wet, but he'd been both those things before. With luck, he would be again, and neither of them distracted his attention from the dripping underbrush and scrub trees of the hillsides. Hartan was right, he thought. If a man wanted to hit the train at its most vulnerable, these miserable, rain-soaked hills were the best spot he was likely to find.

Someone slipped and fell on the far side of the pay wagon. Someone else laughed at the splashing thud, and the unfortunate who'd fallen swore with weary venom as he climbed back to his feet. Bahzell's mouth twitched in wry sympathy, but even as he started to turn his head and grin up at the driver, something flickered at the corner of his right eye.

His head snapped back around, ears cocked and eyes straining through the rain as he tried to pin down what had drawn his attention. A full three seconds passed, and then he realized. The sweep rider picking his way through the underbrush high above the road wasn't there anymore . . . but his horse was, and its saddle was empty.

"Man down! Right flank!"

Bahzell's hand flashed back over his left shoulder even as he bellowed the warning, and his fingers closed on the hilt of his sword as the muddy hillside suddenly vomited men.

The brigands came down the slope, howling to chill the blood, and he spared a moment to admire the skill with which they'd used the underbrush for cover. The missing sweep rider must have ridden straight into one of them without knowing. He'd no doubt paid for his inattention with his life, but Bahzell's shout of warning had come before the raiders were fully in position. They had sixty yards of tangled, mud-slippery undergrowth to cross, and bugles began to sound. Their strident signals brought Rianthus' outriders galloping through the rain to close on the column while the closest patrol wheeled towards the point of threat, and Bahzell heard hoarse breathing and splashing feet as Hartan's platoon reacted. Every other man from the train's left flank hurled himself around, over, or under the nearest wagon to slot in on the right side, deadbolts clattered and iron rang as hands wrenched open firing slits in the pay wagon's high wooden sides, and the brigands' howls took on another note—one of fury—as they found themselves facing not a spread-out file of surprised victims but a steady line. It was a thin line, with too few people in it, but it was unshaken and spined with steel.

Hartan thundered down the line on his pony. He yanked the beast to a halt as he reached Bahzell, so abruptly the beast slid on its haunches in the mud, then wheeled it to face the enemy at the hradani's right shoulder.

"Good man!" he shouted through the oncoming bellows, and then a dozen outlaws hurled themselves over the edge of the road and straight at them.

It was obvious they knew their exact target, for another score of brigands came in their wake, charging headlong for the pay wagon. Others split to either side to face off any relief force while the central force cut its way through to seize the strongboxes, but bowstrings twanged as the drover and the men detailed to the wagon itself fired through the slits in its thick sides.

A half-dozen raiders went down, yet the others kept coming, and there were too few guards to break that charge. Bahzell knew it, and he snarled as he gave himself to the Rage.

Hot, bright heat filled him like some ecstatic poison, and Hartan's pony shied in terror as a wordless howl burst from his throat. His dripping ears were flat to his skull, fire crackled in his brown eyes, his huge sword blurred in a whirring figure eight before him, and the brigand running at him gawked in sudden panic. The raider's feet skidded in mud as he tried to brake, but it was far too late. He was face-to-face with the worst nightmare of any Norfressan, a Horse Stealer hradani in the grip of the Rage, and a thunderbolt of steel split him from crown to navel.

The body tumbled away, blood and organs and shattered bone steaming in the rain, and Bahzell howled again as his sword whirled before him. His arms and blade gave him a tremendous reach, and a trio of brigands found themselves inside it. They flew back, only one of them screaming as he held the spouting stumps of his wrists up before his bulging, horrified eyes, and Bahzell stepped forward into the splendor of destruction.

An arrow whizzed past him into a raider's chest. The man screamed and twisted, trying to pull it back out, then went down without another sound as Bahzell's sword struck his head from his shoulders. Two of his fellows came at the hradani desperately, and that terrible sword smashed one of them aside even as a booted foot drove into the other's shield. The brigand lost shield and footing alike and rolled frantically, trying to get his sword up to cover himself. But Bahzell simply brought the same foot down again, and his victim's terrified shriek died with shocking suddenness as a boot heel took him in the face and smashed his skull like an egg.

A thrown hand axe whirred, and Bahzell twisted aside and lashed out again. Another brigand screamed as sixty inches of steel took him in the right thigh and his leg flew like a lopped branch. Someone else drove a desperate cut into the hradani's left side, and a rib snapped, but the blow rebounded from Bahzell's mail. His sword came around in a blood-spattering loop that claimed another head, and his howl of triumph bellowed through the rain.

The entire attack slithered in confusion as he waded into it. Few of the raiders had ever fought hradani; none had fought Horse Stealers, and the sheer carnage appalled them as he split their charge and shattered bodies flew aside in a bow wave of wreckage. A dozen were down before anyone even reached Hartan's line, and those who did reach it were shaken and staggered, already sensing failure. Bahzell heard Hartan shouting orders, the clash of steel, heaving breath, gasped curses and prayers and the screams of the wounded, and their music sang to the fury at his heart.

Other folk thought the Rage was simple bloodlust, a berserk savagery that neither knew nor cared what its target was, and so it was when it struck without warning. But when a hradani gave himself to it knowingly, it was as cold as it was hot, as rational as it was lethal. To embrace the Rage was to embrace a splendor, a glory, a denial of all restraint but not of reason. It was pure, elemental purpose, unencumbered by compassion or horror or pity, yet it was far more than mere frenzy. Bahzell knew exactly what he was doing, and he'd spotted the cluster of better armed and armored men around the single outlaw who wore composite armor. He cut his way through the others like a dire cat through jackals, closing on the raiders' leader, and the screams of the dying were the terrible anthem of his coming.

The outlaw commander shouted to his bodyguards, and all six of them charged the hradani. They were big men, for humans, and well armed. Each of them had a shield while Bahzell had none, and they used the advantage of the higher ground to build momentum, but a two-handed overhead blow whistled down as the first man reached him. It crumpled the brigand's stout, leather-faced shield like straw, and the backhand recovery took a head.

Bahzell leapt into the gap, slashing first right and then left, sending two more bodies tumbling down the muddy slope, and suddenly he was *behind* them, face-to-face with their leader. Blood oozed from a cut on his face and another on his left forearm, pain burned in his right thigh where someone had gotten through from behind, his broken rib grated with agony, but the Rage carried him forward, as untouched by pain as by pity, and his enemies moved so slowly. Everyone moved slowly, like figures in a dream. His blade came down like an earthquake of steel and smashed the outlaw chief's shield aside. A twist of the wrists sent it hurtling to the side, blocking a return blow, driving it down and to the outside almost negligently. And then another twist brought that dreadful blade flashing back to the left, cleaving armor like paper as it ripped up into the angle of the man's armpit. His victim screamed as the impact lifted him from his feet. The blow exploded up and out the top of his shoulder, slicing the limb away, ripping the pauldron from his armor in a fountain of arterial blood, and Bahzell whirled to face the others as their chieftain went down.

But there was no one to face *him*. The raiders had seen enough, and the survivors disengaged and ran as the blood-spattered, seven-foot demon came raging down the hill towards them. They scattered in terror, abandoning their prize and their wounded alike, fleeing madly through the underbrush, and Bahzell Bahnakson shook his sword above his head while the blood-chilling bellow of his triumph followed them into the driving rain.

No one wanted to come near him afterward.

He lowered his sword slowly, aware of the pain in his side, the hot blood streaking his face and runneling down his right thigh in the rain. But his cuts were shallow and his leg still worked, and he ignored his wounds as he turned upon the Rage. He fought it as he had the brigands, battering it back, driving it down, down, down into the caverns of his soul once more, and he shuddered as the cold, sick vacuum in its wake guttered deep within him.

He closed his eyes and inhaled deeply, smelling the death stench even through the fresh, wet rain, hearing the sobs and screams, and he knew exactly what he'd done. That, too, was part of the Rage's curse when a hradani called it to him, the price and consequence of its controlled and controlling fury, and shame filled him. Not for what he'd done, for it had needed doing, but for how he'd *felt* while he did it. For the exaltation, the ecstasy. Some of his folk—like Churnazh—gloried in it even after the Rage released them; Bahzell Bahnakson knew better. Knew it was the Rage that had all but destroyed his people a thousand years before . . . and that it could do so still.

He clenched his teeth and bent, despite the pain in his side, to rip a cloak from a corpse's shoulders. He wiped his blade slowly, with rock-steady hands that seemed to tremble wildly, then sheathed it, and tied a strip of cloth about his thigh to staunch the bleeding while rain thinned the blood splashed across his hands and arms and armor. He stood for another long moment, alone on the hillside among the dead and dying, then drew another deep breath, straightened, and turned to limp down the slope to the wagons.

Brandark was there. The Bloody Sword dismounted beside Hartan, handed the dwarf his reins, and walked wordlessly up the hill to meet his friend, and his eyes were dark with understanding. He reached out, clasping Bahzell's forearm, then drew him into a rough embrace and clapped his shoulders hard, and Bahzell leaned against the shorter man for a moment, then sighed.

"I'm wondering how the others will be feeling about hradani after this," he said quietly, eyes haunted with the memory of what he was as he straightened, and Brandark smiled sadly up at him.

"They'll probably be glad we're on *their* side," he replied, and reached up to rest his hand on his friend's shoulder. Hartan handed Brandark's reins to one of his men, and walked his pony forward, picking his way through the bodies towards them. He, at least, looked composed, not horrified, Bahzell saw, but then Brandark suddenly frowned and flipped a body over with his toe.

Shergahn's dead, unblinking eyes stared up into the rain, and the Bloody Sword chuckled with grim, cold humor.

"So much for turncoats and traitors going over to the brigands!" he said. "I wish I'd gotten him myself, but I forgive you—and it ought to put paid to the rest of the mutterers, don't you think?"

Bahzell nodded, staring down at the man he'd killed without even recognizing him, and Brandark gazed around at the bodies once more. He chuckled again, and the sound was lighter, with a ghost of his usual, sardonic humor.

"All the same," he murmured, "it may be just a while before Rianthus or Hartan can convince anyone to drill with you again!"

# CHAPTER TEN

There were no more attacks. In fact, some of the scouts found hastily abandoned campsites along their route, and Bahzell felt people turn to look at him whenever those reports came in. Yet the other guards, and especially Hartan's command, seemed to regard him with a sort of rough sympathy, and not the horror he'd feared.

It was odd, he thought—and he had more time to think than he would have preferred, for Kilthan's healers had never treated a hradani before. They weren't prepared for the speed with which he recovered from his minor wounds, and they'd put him on light duty rather than simply stitching him up and sending him back to his regular position as a hradani healer would have done.

And so he rode in a wagon, arbalest ready, out of the rain, and considered the strangeness of it all. Everyone "knew" hradani were murderous, uncontrollable blood-letters, and the Esganians, who'd never seen him raise even his empty hand except in self-defense, hated and

119

feared him. These men, who'd seen the full horror of the Rage, did neither. Perhaps it was only that they recognized what an asset he was to them, yet he thought not. He thought it went deeper, a recognition of the control he and Brandark exerted to hold the Rage in check that made them more willing to trust the hradani. And perhaps, just perhaps, some actually understood his shame, knew that even if they felt no horror of the thing that lived within him, *he* did.

He didn't know about that, but he knew that while some of the other merchants and their men harbored doubts, Kilthan's guard did not. If they were careful around him, they were no more so than they might have been around anyone whose temper was to be feared, and they treated him not just as a dangerous hireling but as a comrade who'd bled and fought with them. The officers cursed him as cheerfully as any of the others, the cooks grumbled over how much food it took to stoke his mountainous carcass, and his fellows included him in their coarse, rough-and-ready humor. It was the first time in two years he'd been given that sense of being among his own, and he treasured it even as he tried to push away his own guilty secret . . . that he longed to taste the Rage again and hungered for a target against which he might rightfully loose it.

The splendor of that moment, its transcendent glory and *aliveness*, haunted him. He could thrust it aside by day, but it poisoned his dreams by night, calling to him and pleading with him to unlock the chains he'd bound about it.

Yet that, at least, he understood, for this wasn't the first time he'd faced the Rage down and whipped it back to its kennel. It was the other dreams which truly disturbed him, the ones he could never quite recall when he woke sweating and gasping in his blankets. Those dreams terrified him, and he couldn't even say why, for he couldn't *remember*, however hard he tried. There were only bits and pieces, a face he couldn't quite recall, a voice he'd never heard with waking ears, and a sense of—

Of what? He didn't know, yet it haunted him like the memory of the Rage. It was as if some purpose or cause or *compulsion* walked his dreaming mind, and a fear more dreadful than any he'd ever known followed in its footsteps, for he was hradani. His people knew in their very bones and blood what it was to be used and compelled. They'd *been* used and compelled, and the terrible things done to them during the Fall of Kontovar—the horrible things they'd been driven to *do* by the black wizards who'd turned them into ravening tools—haunted his people's souls. That wizardry had left them with the Rage, and the thought of being used so again was the dark terror that horrified even their strongest, whether they would admit it or not . . . and the reason that voice he couldn't remember and had never heard struck ice into Bahzell Bahnakson's heart.

The dwarvish singer came to the end of his song, and Brandark let the last note linger, then stilled the strings with a gentle palm. There was a moment of total silence that died in applause, and he and Yahnath rose beside the fire to bow. Someone clapped harder, and Brandark slapped the stocky, bearded dwarf with the golden voice on the shoulder and grinned, trying to hide his envy even from himself as he accepted his share of the acclaim.

The moonlit night was cool, almost chill, clear, spangled with stars, and no longer soaked with rain. They were free of the hills, barely a day's journey from Hildarth, capital of the Duchy of Moretz, and the men were relaxed, less tense. The easier going, coupled with the dearth of raiders and the easing of their duties as Rianthus integrated the more reliable of the independent guard detachments into his operations, meant there was energy for songs and tales now . . . and enough singers to spare them Brandark's voice.

The Bloody Sword didn't blame them. At least they'd been polite, and they still valued his playing, but it had needed only two or three performances for them to reach the same judgment Navahk had reached. And, listening to Yahnath, he could agree with them, however much he longed not to. So he gave one last sweeping bow, slung his balalaika, adjusted his embroidered jerkin, and began picking his way towards the tent he shared with Bahzell.

Familiar, bittersweet amusement at his own foolish ambitions filled him, and he stopped for a long moment, gazing up at the brilliant moon while his throat ached with the need to praise that loveliness, express the deep, complex longing it woke within him.

And he couldn't. He knew how horrible his verse was. He longed for the rolling beauty of the written word, the cadenced purity, the exact, perfect word to express the very essence of a thought or emotion, and he produced . . . doggerel. Sometimes amusing or even witty doggerel, but doggerel, and *everyone* knew about his voice. He supposed it was funny, in a cruel way, that a barbaric hradani—and a Navahkan Bloody Sword, to boot—should spend nights staring into his lamp, begging the Singer of Light to touch him with her fire, lend him just a single spark from her glorious flame. But Chesmirsa had never answered him, any more than any god ever answered his people.

He closed his eyes in all too familiar pain, then shook himself and resumed his careful progress across the camp. There were birds and fish, he told himself, just as there were those who were meant to be bards and those who weren't. Birds drowned, and fish couldn't fly, but he knew something inside him would demand he go on trying, like a salmon perpetually hurling itself into the air in a desperate bid to become a hawk. Which was more stubborn than intelligent, perhaps, but what could one expect from a hradani? He grinned at the comfortable tartness of the thought, yet he knew his need to touch the true heart of the bard's art was far less a part of his affectations—and far more important to him—than he'd ever realized in Navahk. That might not change reality, and, after all these years, surely anyone but a hradani should be able to accept that, and yet—

His grin vanished, and his ears flicked. No one else in Kilthan's train would have recognized that sound, and even he couldn't make out the restless, muttering words from here, but he knew Hurgrumese when he heard it.

He moved more quickly, head swiveling as he scanned the moonstruck dark. None of the tents were lit, and he saw no one moving, heard only that muttering babble, all but buried in the sounds of deep, even breathing and snores. The men in this section would be going on night watch in another few hours; they needed their sleep, hence the distance between them and the wakefulness about the fire, and Brandark was glad of it as he went to his knees at the open fly of his tent.

Bahzell twisted and jerked, kicked half out of his bedroll, and sweat beaded his face. His massive hands clutched the blankets, wrestling with them as if they were constricting serpents, and Brandark's ears went flat as the terror in his friend's meaningless, fragmented mutters sank home. The Bloody Sword had known fear enough in Navahk not to despise it in another, but this was more than fear. The raw, agonized torment in it glazed his skin with ice, and he reached out to touch Bahzell's shoulder.

"*Haaahhhhhhh!*" Bahzell gasped, and a hand caught Brandark's wrist like a vise, fit to shatter any human arm, so powerful even Brandark hissed in anguish. But then the Horse Stealer's eyes flared open. Recognition flickered in their clouded depths, and his grip relaxed as quickly as it had closed.

"Brandark?" His mutter was thick, and he shook his head drunkenly. He shoved up on the elbow of the hand still gripping Brandark's wrist, scrubbing at his face with his other hand. "What?" he asked more clearly. "What is it?"

"I . . . was going to ask you that." Brandark kept his voice low and twisted his wrist gently. Bahzell looked down, ears twitching as he realized he held it, and his hand opened completely. He stared at his own fingers for a moment, then clenched them into a fist and sucked in a deep breath.

"So, it's muttering in my sleep I was, is it?" he said softly, and his jaw clenched when Brandark nodded. He opened and closed his fist a few times, then sighed and thrust himself into a sitting position. "A blooded warrior with a score of raids into the Wind Plain," he murmured in a quiet, bitter whisper, "and he's whimpering in his nightmares like a child! Pah!"

He spat in disgust, then looked up with a jerk as Brandark touched his shoulder again.

"That was no child's nightmare," the Bloody Sword said. Bahzell's eyes widened, and Brandark shrugged. "I couldn't make out exactly what you were saying, but I picked out a few words."

"Aye? And what might they have been?" Bahzell asked tautly.

"You spoke of gods, Bahzell—more than one, I think— and of wizards." Brandark's voice was harsh, and Bahzell grunted as if he'd been punched in the belly. They stared at one another in the night, and then Bahzell looked up at the moon.

"I've three hours before I go on watch, and I'm thinking it's best we go somewhere private," he said flat-voiced.

They found a place among the provision wagons, and Brandark perched on a lowered wagon tongue while Bahzell stood with a boot braced on a wheel spoke and leaned both arms on his raised knee. A silence neither wanted to break lingered, but finally Bahzell cleared his throat and straightened.

"I'm thinking," he said quietly, "that I don't like this above half, Brandark. What business does such as me have with dreams like that?"

"I suppose," Brandark said very carefully, "that the answer depends on just what sorts of dreams they are."

"Aye, so it does—or should." The Horse Stealer folded his arms, standing like a blacker, more solid chunk of night, and exhaled noisily. "The only trouble with that, Brandark my lad, is that I'm not after being able to *remember* the cursed things!"

"Then tonight wasn't the first time?" Brandark's tenor was taut.

"That it wasn't," Bahzell said grimly. "They've plagued me nightly—every night, I'm thinking—since the brigands hit us, but all I've been able to call to mind from them is bits and pieces. There's naught to get my teeth into, naught to be telling me what they mean . . . or want of me."

Brandark's hand moved in a quick, instinctive sign, and Bahzell's soft laugh was bitter in the darkness. Brandark flushed and lowered his hand. He started to speak, but Bahzell shook his head.

"No, lad. Don't fret yourself—it's more than once I've made the same sign now."

"I don't doubt it." Brandark shivered, for he, too, was hradani, then squared his shoulders. "Tell me what you do remember," he commanded.

"Little enough." Bahzell's voice was low, and he began to pace, hands clasped behind him. "There's this voice—one I'll swear I've never heard before—and it's after telling me something, asking me something . . . or maybe asking *for* something." He twitched his shoulders, ears half-flattened. "It's in my mind there's a face, as well, but it disappears like mist or smoke any time I try to lay hands on it. And there's something else beyond that, like a job waiting to be done, but I've not the least thrice-damned idea what it *is!*"

There was anguish in his voice now, and fear, and Brandark bit his lip. The last thing any hradani wanted was some sort of prophetic dream. Ancient memories of treachery and betrayed trust screamed in warning at the very thought, and Bahzell had muttered of gods and wizards while the dream was upon him, even if he couldn't recall the words to his waking mind.

The Bloody Sword made his teeth loosen on his lip and leaned an elbow on his knee, propping his chin in his palm while he tried to recall all the bits and pieces he'd ever read about such dreams. He would have liked to think it was only a nightmare—something brought on by Bahzell's Rage, perhaps—but that was unlikely if the Horse Stealer had been having them every night.

"This 'job,'" he said at last. "You've no idea at all what it is? No one's . . . telling you to do something specific?"

"I don't *know*," Bahzell half groaned. "It slips away too fast, with only broken bits left behind."

"What sort of bits?" Brandark pressed, and Bahzell paused in his pacing to furrow his brow in thought.

"I'm . . . not sure." He spoke so slowly Brandark could actually feel his painful concentration. "There's sword work and killing in it, somewhere. That much I'm certain of, but whether it's my own idea or someone else's—" The Horse Stealer shrugged, then his ears rose slowly and he cocked his head. "But now that you've pressed me, I'm thinking there *is* a wee bit more. A journey."

"A journey?" Brandark's voice sharpened. "You're supposed to go somewhere?"

"It's damned I'll be if I go *anywhere* for a sneaking, crawling dream I'm not even recalling!" Bahzell snapped, and Brandark raised a hand in quick apology.

"I didn't mean it that way. What I meant to ask was if the dream *wants* you to go somewhere?"

"Aye, that's it!" Bahzell's spine snapped straight and he planted his fists on his hips and turned to glare into the black and silver night. "The curst thing *does* want me to go somewhere."

"Where?" Brandark asked intently, and Bahzell growled in frustration.

"If I was knowing that, then I'd know what the damned thing is wanting of me when I *get* there!" he snarled, but then his rumbling voice went even deeper and his ears flattened. "And yet . . ."

He jerked his hands from his hips and began to prowl back and forth once more, pounding a fist into his palm while he stared at the grass. Brandark sat silently, letting him pace, feeling the intensity of his thought, and his stride gradually slowed. He came to a complete halt, rocking on his heels, then turned and looked sharply at the Bloody Sword.

"Wherever it is," he said flatly, "I'm on the road to it now."

"Phrobus!" Brandark whispered. "Are you certain of that?"

"Aye, that I am." Bahzell's voice was grim and stark, and Brandark swallowed. He'd never heard quite that note from his friend. It was like rock shattering into dust, and something inside him shuddered away from it in fear while silence hovered between them once more.

"What do you want to do?" he asked finally.

"I've no taste for destinies and such." Bahzell was still grim, but there was something else, as well. He'd recognized the foe, at least in part, and the elemental stubbornness of all hradanikind was rousing in defiance. "I've worries enough for a dozen men as it is, and 'destinies' and 'quests' will get a man killed quick as quick," he said harshly. "And if I spoke of gods, well, no god's done aught for our folk since the Fall, so there's no cause I can see to be doing aught for *them*."

Brandark nodded in heartfelt agreement, and square, strong teeth flashed in a fierce, moonlit grin as Bahzell returned the nod with interest.

"And if it's not some poxy god creeping round my dreams, then it's like enough some filthy wizard, and I'll see myself damned to Krahana's darkest hell before I raise hand or blade for any wizard ever born." There was a dreadful, iron tang in that, and Brandark nodded again.

"But how do you *keep* from doing what they want when you don't know what it is?" he asked slowly.

"Aye, there's the rub." Bahzell scrubbed his palms on his thighs, then shrugged. "Well, if it's on the road I am, then I'm thinking it's best I step aside."

"How?"

"By going where I'd never planned. If some cursed god or wizard's set himself on having me, then I'll just take myself somewhere he's not after expecting me to be."

"All of this means something?" Brandark asked with a trace of his normal tartness, and Bahzell chuckled nastily.

"So it does, my lad. So it does. Look you, all this time I've been heading west, with never a thought of going anywhere else. Soon or late I have to let Father know my whereabouts, but until I do, he can be telling Churnazh—aye, or anyone else who asks—he's no knowledge where I am. I've been minded to follow Kilthan clear to Manhome and see a wee bit of the Empire of the Axe before I get in touch with him again, but now I'm damned if I will."

"You can't just leave," Brandark objected, and Bahzell shook his head sharply.

"Old Kilthan's deserving better of me than that, but we've never told him we'd go clear to Manhome. No, I'm thinking I'll stay with him to Riverside. From there he'll be in the Kingdom of Angthyr, and that's an Axeman ally and safe enough for merchants, from all I hear. He'll have little need of my sword after that . . . and I'll be far enough from Navahk not to worry about steel in my back some dark night."

"In *our* backs, you mean."

Bahzell cocked his ears once more, studying his friend intently, then shook his head.

"I'm thinking you should stay clear of this," he said quietly. "It's one thing to be twisting Churnazh's nose—aye, and even to risk your neck for naught more than friendship. But this is none of your making, and it might just be your neck is the least thing you could be losing. Stay with Kilthan, Brandark. It's safer."

"Listen, I know you don't like my singing, but you don't have to go to such lengths to get rid of it."

"Leave off your jesting now! There's a time and a place for it, but not here. Not now! Against Churnazh and his lot—aye, or anything else we could feed steel till it choked—I'd take you at my side and be glad of it. But dreams and destinies . . ." Bahzell shook his head again. "Stay clear of it, Brandark. Stay clear and let it pass."

"Sorry, but I can't do that." Brandark stood and slapped his friend on the shoulder. "For all you know, I'm already caught up in it."

"Oh? And what have *your* dreams been like?" Bahzell demanded with awful irony, and the Bloody Sword laughed.

"I haven't had any—yet! But if you're busy running in the opposite direction, whatever it is might decide to pick on the single hradani who's still headed the right way, and then where would I be? If that's the case, then the safest place I could possibly be would be running right beside you."

"That," Bahzell said after a moment, "is most likely the most addlepated, clod-headed excuse for logic I've ever heard."

"Being rude won't help you. I thought it up, and I'll stick by it. You know how stubborn hradani are."

"Aye, so I do." Bahzell sighed. He gripped the smaller man by the upper arms and shook him—gently for a hradani. "You're a fool, Brandark Brandarkson. A fool to come after me from Navahk, and three times a fool if you dabble in this. It'll likely be the death of you, and not a pretty end!"

"Well, no one ever said *you* were smart," Brandark replied, "and, if the truth be known, I don't suppose anyone actually ever said *I* was."

"If they did, they lied." Bahzell gave him one last shake, then sighed again. "All right, if you're daft enough to be coming, then I suppose I'm daft enough to be glad for the company."

# CHAPTER ELEVEN

The heavy wooden chair back flew apart. The stubs of its uprights stood like broken teeth, and then they, too, flew apart as the sword thundered down between them and split the seat. Splinters hissed, and Harnak of Navahk screamed a curse as he whirled to the chest beside the ruined chair.

He drove his sword into it like an axe, then wrenched the blade free and brought it down again and again and again, cursing with every blow. He hacked until he could hack no more, then hurled the blade across the room. It leapt back from the wall, ricocheting to the floor with a whining, iron clangor, and he glared down at it, gasping while spittle ran down his chin.

But then he closed his eyes. His wrist scrubbed across his mouth and chin, and he dragged in a deep, wracking breath as the Rage faded back from the brink of explosion. It was hard for him to beat it down, for he seldom chose to do so, but this time he had no choice.

131

He mastered it at last and shook himself, glaring about his chamber at the wreckage. Even the bedposts were splintered and gouged, and he clenched his jaw, feeling the gaps of missing teeth, as he wished with all his heart those same blows had landed upon Farmah or Bahzell Bahnakson.

He swore, with more weariness than passion now, and waded through the rubble to the window. He sat in the opening's stone throat, staring hot-eyed out over the roofs of Navahk, and rubbed the permanent depression in his forehead while he made himself think.

The bitch was alive—*alive!*—and that slut Tala with her, and the pair of them were in *Hurgrum!*

The nostrils of his misshapen nose flared. How? How had two women, one a mere girl and beaten half to death into the bargain, gotten clear to Hurgrum through his father's entire Guard? It wasn't possible!

Yet that whoreson Bahzell had contrived it anyway. He'd drawn virtually all the pursuit after him, and he and that bastard Brandark—and it *had* to be Brandark, whatever the japester's father claimed!—had cut the single patrol to find them into dog meat. And while they'd done *that*, somehow the bitches had reached that sanctimonious dog-lover Bahnak's court. He'd actually taken them in, put them under his own protection in his very palace!

Harnak spat another curse, and fresh hatred rose as more spittle sprayed humiliatingly through his gap-toothed snarl. Bahnak had been careful to take no official note when Churnazh outlawed his son. He'd even restrained Farmah from accusing Harnak of the crime, for to contest the sentence Churnazh had imposed would commit him to a fresh war against Navahk. His own men would demand it—and his allies would slip away if he appeared too weak to launch it.

But, by the same token, Churnazh's allies would never support an attack on Hurgrum. If he were *attacked*, yes, they would come to his aid, for each feared the destruction of any one of them would be the opening wedge for Bahnak's conquest of them all. But they were too weakened—and frightened—by what Hurgrum had already done to carry a fresh war to Bahnak, which meant he had no *need* to refute the charges against his son. With Bahzell safely beyond Churnazh's reach, all Bahnak had to do was keep silent and let his allies—and Navahk's, curse them!—laugh.

And they *were* laughing. Harnak clenched his fists, choking on bile. Every bard in every city-state of the Bloody Swords and Horse Stealers alike seemed to be singing the tale of Bahzell Bahnakson's cunning. They'd made the puking bastard some sort of hero, and if they never mentioned Harnak's name, there was no need to. If Bahzell's father was sheltering Farmah and she was content to have it so, then Bahzell couldn't have raped her . . . and if *he* hadn't, everyone knew who must have. No one dared say so, but Harnak had seen it even in the eyes of the Guard, and he dared not show his face in public. Only the iron fist of his father's terror kept women from spitting on his shadow as he passed . . . and his father had five sons.

The crown prince glared down at his fists. He was the eldest son, his father's heir . . . while Churnazh lived. But what would happen when he died? Harnak knew his brothers. All of them, with the possible exception of that gutless wonder Arsham, had tumbled unwilling wenches, yet no one *knew* they had. Now everyone knew *he* had—yes, and believed he'd tried to kill the girl, too. Either of those crimes was more than enough to absolve any warrior of loyalty to him, and all it needed would be for one of his brothers—just one—to claim the throne to set the army of Navahk at its own throat . . . and Harnak's.

He couldn't let that happen. Yet how could he stop it?

He brooded down at his fists, the flame of his hatred smoldering down to smoking embers that would never quite die, and thought.

There were only two possibilities, he told himself at last. Either all his brothers must die, leaving no other claimant of the blood to challenge him, or else Bahzell, Farmah, and Tala must die.

Neither solution was perfect. If he had his brothers murdered, they must all die in the same hour, and his father with them, for only one person in Navahk could profit by their deaths, and Churnazh would know it. Yet even if all four of his brothers—yes, and his father, too— perished, too many who remembered how Churnazh himself had butchered his way to the throne might seek to emulate him. A crown prince rapist believed to have murdered his entire family would be too weak and tempting a target for *someone* to pass by.

But if he settled for killing Bahzell—assuming he could *find* the Sharnā-cursed bastard—and the bitches, he would have to hope his father lived for a great many years. If Bahzell died, he would become one more dead enemy, not a taunting reminder of failure, and Navahk had been taught to respect men whose enemies were all dead. And if the sluts died, then the living symbol of his crime would die, as well. Passing time would erode the certainty of his guilt, give Churnazh's countercharges the chance to sink in, but it would *take* time. It would take years, more maddening years in which he would be denied his proper place, still crown prince and never ruler.

And he *must* have all three of them, for as long as any of them breathed, their very lives would keep the tale alive. *All* of his enemies must perish to put time on his side . . . and perhaps there was a way. One not even Churnazh guessed at. Nor would he, for if he should ever suspect what allies Harnak had taken, he would rip out his son's heart with his own bare hands.

Harnak nodded, ruined face twisted in an ugly smile, and looked back out the window. The sun was well into the west. Once darkness fell, he had a call to pay.

The single horseman trotted quietly down the brush-choked valley. There was no road here, only a trail of beaten earth, and his horse's hooves fell with a dull, muffled sound. The slopes to his left cut off the moon, drowning the narrow way in darkness, and something inside him basked in the black silence even as his horse snorted and tossed an uneasy head.

A mile fell away, then another, as he threaded his way into the twisting hills. Few came here, even in daylight, for the nameless hill range had an unchancy reputation. Of the few who came, fewer still departed, and even Harnak's carefully chosen bodyguards—clanless men, outcasts who owed all they were or ever could be to him—had muttered uneasily when they realized his destination. They always did, and he'd sensed their frightened relief when he ordered them to stop and await his return. None of them knew what he did on his rides into the hills, and none cared to know, for they'd seen him come this way with prisoners tied to their saddles, and he always returned alone.

The rough trail rounded a final hill and ended against a high, blank face of stone, and his nervous horse curvetted and fought the bit, flecked with the sweat of panic, as he drew rein. He snarled and leaned forward to slam his balled fist down between its ears, and the beast squealed and went still.

Harnak grunted in satisfaction, dismounted, and tethered it to one of the stunted trees that grew in this place. He drew a golden amulet from the neck of his tunic as he approached the featureless stone slab, then spat on the ground with an odd formality and folded his arms to wait.

Seconds dribbled past, then a full minute, and then his horse whinnied fearfully and jerked against its tight-tied reins. Sullen green light glowed within the stone, growing brighter, stronger, with the livid emerald glitter of poison. The rock seemed to waver and flow, wrapped in its unnatural translucence while the venomous light threw Harnak's shadow down the valley behind him like a distorted beast, and then, sudden as a falling blade, the light vanished—and took the barren stone hillside with it.

The opening before Harnak was . . . wrong. Its angles followed a subtly perverted geometry, none of them quite square, and the carved likeness of an enormous scorpion glared down from above it. Flickering red torchlight spilled out of the bowels of the hill, and a cowled figure stood framed against the glow, arms folded in the sleeves of its robe as it bowed.

"Welcome, My Prince." The deep voice was human, not hradani, yet Harnak returned its bow with a respect he showed no other mortal.

"I thank you, Tharnatus, and beg leave to enter your house." Not even the lisping sibilance of his missing teeth hid the deference—even fear—in the prince's voice, and Tharnatus straightened.

"Not my house, My Prince," he replied, as if completing a formal exchange, "but the House of the Scorpion." He stood aside with a gesture of invitation, and Harnak bowed once more and walked past him into the hill.

The passage drove deep into the earth, its stone walls dressed and smooth, far more finely finished than anything in Churnazh's palace. Arched side passages intersected it at intervals, and the faceted chips of mosaics glittered between them in the torchlight. Things of horror ruled those mosaics. Bat-winged nightmares stormed through screaming warriors, snatching them up, snapping off heads and limbs with chitinous jaws and pincers like battle-axes. Other shapes, more obscene still, slithered through opulent temples, hungry eyes afire as they crept and flowed and oozed toward altars where maidens fought their chains in shrieking terror. And above them all, half-hinted and half-seen like some hideous cloud, stalked the huge, flame-eyed scorpion, and on its back was a manlike shape that trailed horror like waves of smoke.

The central hall led onward to a larger chamber, circular and domed with natural rock polished to mirror brightness. Torchlight danced about them like a globe of swirling blood, and double doors, carved with the same images which had haunted the mosaics, loomed before them. Tharnatus thrust them open and went to his knees, then to his belly, as the sweet stench of incense rolled out over him, and Harnak fell to the floor behind him.

The prince lay motionless, disfigured face pressing the stone, until Tharnatus rose once more. The priest gazed down at him, then touched him with a booted toe between his shoulders, the gesture of an overlord to a servant.

"Rise, My Prince," he intoned. Harnak rose and bent to kiss the hand the priest extended, then straightened as Tharnatus gestured him into the inner sanctum that proved not all gods had chosen to ignore the hradani.

The sickly-sweet incense was stronger, drifting in thin, eddying clouds, and the Scorpion of Sharná, god of demons and patron of assassins, crouched above them. The enormous sculpture towered over a stone altar, carved with blood channels and crowned with blood-encrusted iron manacles that gaped empty . . . for now, and Tharnatus and Harnak knelt side by side to press their foreheads to that hideous stone before they rose once more.

"So, My Prince!" the priest said more briskly as they completed their obeisance. "How may the House of the Scorpion aid one of its own?"

"You've heard the stories, I suppose?" Harnak knew

he sounded surly, and surliness towards a priest of Sharnā was dangerous, but his shame goaded him. Tharnatus regarded him in expressionless silence for a long moment, then let it pass. Harnak was heir to the throne of Navahk; even Sharnā's anointed could allow an occasional edge of disrespect when the Demon Lord had his pincers deep in a future ruler.

"I have, My Prince—assuming you refer to those concerning a certain palace servant and a prince of Hurgrum."

"I do." Harnak folded his arms, and his scarred and broken face was grim. "Between them, the slut and Bahzell—" he made the name a curse "—pose a threat to me and to my position. They must be eliminated."

"I see." Tharnatus gazed up at the scorpion above the altar, and his tone was thoughtful, even chiding. "You should have brought the girl here for your sport, My Prince. Had you done so, no one would ever have known. You might have enjoyed her far longer, and she could have fed the Scorpion when you were through. Now?" He shrugged, and Harnak flushed but kept his own voice level.

"I've brought the Scorpion many a feast, and I'll bring Him more. But this slut was officially a ward of the crown. I thought it best her body be found rather than vanish and raise possibly dangerous questions."

"Yet the course you followed led only to a different peril, did it not?" Harnak nodded unwilling assent at Tharnatus' raised eyebrow, and the priest continued seriously. "My prince, such pleasures are your right, both as prince and servant of the Scorpion. But it is fitting neither for you to deny your brethren *their* pleasure nor the Scorpion His due, and you must be wary. You will never be fully secure until you rule Navahk in your own right. Until then, not even He can guard you from death if your actions lead to discovery."

"Aye," Harnak agreed in a sulky tone, "yet if the

Scorpion had struck Churnazh down when first I asked, I would already wear the crown."

"You know why that was impossible," Tharnatus said sternly. "Your father's guards are too alert to guarantee the dog brothers' success, and we dare not disclose our own presence by sending a greater servant. If the dog brothers had tried and failed before the war, suspicion must have fallen upon you, and he would have had you killed. If we strike him down now, while his alliances are weak and disordered, we risk giving all of Navahk to Bahnak of Hurgrum, and Bahnak will be our mortal enemy so long as he draws breath."

Harnak bent his head once more with a guttural sound of frustrated agreement, and the priest touched his shoulder.

"Be patient, My Prince." He made his voice gentle. "Your time will come. Indeed, but for your own . . . involvement, we might attempt Churnazh now and lay the blame upon Bahnak or his son, trusting the thirst for vengeance against Hurgrum to hold the alliances together. As it is, we can but do our best within the possibilities open to us, and we shall. The Scorpion rewards His faithful well."

Harnak nodded again, less choppily, and Tharnatus slapped his arm.

"Very well, My Prince. Tell me exactly what you wish done."

"I want the sluts and Bahzell killed," Harnak said flatly. "They have to die if the tales are ever to dwindle away, and until the tales do, my chance to take the throne is small."

"Agreed." Tharnatus furrowed his brow and pursed his lips. "Yet it isn't enough that they simply die, is it, My Prince? The women—" He waved a hand in dismissal. "All we require of them is silence, but Bahzell . . . we must prove his death, not simply remove him."

Harnak's ears twitched agreement, and the priest

frowned once more. "Nor, I think, should we involve a greater servant in this. I doubt Bahnak guards the wenches as well as his own family, in which case the dog brothers can deal with them whenever we wish, perhaps even make it seem an accident. Yes," he nodded, "that would be best—an accident that points no fingers at you. And to help with that, it would be as well to wait a time, I think."

"I want them dead *now!*" Harnak snarled, but Tharnatus shook his head.

"Patience, My Prince. Patience and stealth, those are the virtues of the Scorpion. It may be unpleasant, but you must endure it for a time longer. Think, My Prince. If nothing befalls them for weeks, or even a few months, few minds will leap to the conclusion that you had them killed. If you wanted that done, would you not have acted sooner?"

Harnak grunted, then jerked his head in assent.

"So," the priest went on after a moment, "that leaves Bahzell, and in order to slay him, we first must find him. Not, I think, too difficult a task. The Scorpion's least servants can find him even in deepest wilderness, in time, yet I doubt we will require their services. A hradani in other lands should be easy enough for the dog brothers to track without the Church's aid, and if he's found a place for himself far from Navahk or Hurgrum, so much the better. He'll feel more secure, unthreatened and unwary until the dog brothers can take him. And," Tharnatus smiled unpleasantly, "he *is* an outlaw, with a price on his head. What more reasonable than that someone should return that head to Navahk to claim blood price, and so prove his death to all the world?"

"He won't die easy," Harnak growled, one hand pressing his ribs. "I'll not deny I thought him a weakling, but that's a mistake I won't make twice. In fact, I'd feel safer sending one of the greater servants after him."

"Come now, My Prince!" Tharnatus chided. "He's only one man, and any man is mortal. The dog brothers can deal with him—and the Scorpion's servants are not to be squandered on tasks others can accomplish. We may use each of them but once for each blood binding."

Harnak clenched his jaw, then sighed, for the priest was right. Sealing a demon to obedience was a risky business, even for the Church of Sharnā. A single slip could—and would—spell the grisly death of the creature's summoners, and such exercises of power were difficult to hide from those with eyes to see. Fortunately, there were few such eyes in hradani lands, where even Orr and his children were looked upon askance, but it would take only a single misstep to spell the destruction of this temple, for the hradani had not forgotten the Dark Gods' part in the Fall of Kontovar. Harnak's own cronies would cut his throat if they even suspected to whom he'd given his allegiance, but that was a risk he was willing to run. The secret power of the Scorpion had smoothed his way more than once, and the rituals that raised that power fed other, darker hungers.

"Very well, Tharnatus," he said at length. "Let it be the dog brothers. And let it be soon. I'll wait for the sluts, if I must, but I want that whoreson's head to piss on in front of my father's court!"

"And you shall have it, My Prince," the priest murmured, then raised his head and smiled as a sound echoed down the hall behind him. He and Harnak turned to the open doors, and the sounds grew louder—and terrified. Pleas for mercy and the desperate, panting sounds of struggle floated through the doors, and then two cowled priests thrust a twisting, fighting figure through them.

The girl was young, no more than fifteen or sixteen, just ripening into the curves of womanhood and clad only in a thin white robe, and her arms were bound behind her. Her ears were flat to her skull, her eyes huge with panic, as she fought the binding cords, but there was no escape, and a dozen more priests and worshipers followed into the temple.

The captive's pleas died in a strangled whimper as she saw the huge scorpion and the altar it crouched above. She stared at them, terror gurgling in the back of her throat, and then she threw back her head and shrieked in horror as her captors dragged her kicking, madly fighting body forward.

"As you see, My Prince," Tharnatus purred through her hopeless screams, "your business here tonight can be mixed with pleasure as well." He reached into his robe to withdraw the thin, razor sharp flaying knife and smiled at the crown prince of Navahk.

"Will you stay to share our worship?"

# CHAPTER TWELVE

Patchy frost glittered in shadowed hollows, but clear morning sunlight touched the city's stone walls to warm gold as Kilthan's wagons creaked and rumbled towards Derm. The road sloped steadily down to the city's colorful roofs, the Saram River swept around its western flank in a dark blue bow, gilded with silver sun-flash, and the final line of rapids and cataracts foamed white less than a league above the bustling docks. The sails of small craft dotted the Saram's broader reaches below the city, lush farmland stretched away from the river in both directions, and the mighty, snowcapped peaks of the Eastwall Mountains towered far beyond it.

The Barony of Ernos had been blessed in many ways, from the richness of its soil to the accidents of history and geography which gave it unthreatened frontiers and a ruling family noted for sagacity. The current Baroness Ernos was no exception. She'd inherited and maintained both her father's efficient and well-trained army and his longstanding alliances with the neighboring Empire of the Axe, and she used them with considerable business acumen. Her relations with Axeman merchants were good, tariffs and taxes were low, and she allowed no brigands to take root in *her* well-settled lands. All of which, coupled with her capital's location as the northernmost port on the Saram River, had conspired to turn Derm into a major trade entrepôt.

It would be too much to expect Rianthus to lower his guard anywhere, yet a palpable sense of relief had settled over the wagon train as they crossed into Ernos from Moretz. The duty schedule remained as arduous and the penalties for inattention as severe, but now the road— far better maintained than on the Moretzan side of the border—ran through rich, well-tended farmland and comfortable villages, not rough hills ideal for outlaw roosts.

Brandark was fascinated by a land where most villages lacked so much as palisades and not even larger towns had any *serious* fortifications. The chance of any Navahkan army's reaching Ernos were slight, yet he shuddered at the thought of what one would do to those defenseless towns if it ever should. But the truly remarkable thing was that none of them seemed to feel any need to protect themselves from their own neighbors. He'd known from his reading that there were places like that, yet he'd grown to adulthood in Navahk, and even now, with the evidence before him, no Navahkan could quite believe in them.

Bahzell could. He could even see in this secure land the ideal to which his father aspired. Prince Bahnak could never have been happy ruling such a peaceable realm; there was too much of the hradani warlord in him for that, and Bahzell doubted, somehow, that his father had ever fully visualized the end to which he strove. Yet that was beside the point. Bahnak looked not to the reward of his labors but to their challenge, for it was the struggle he loved. The sense of building something, content in the knowledge that the task was worth doing.

In an odd sort of way, Bahzell understood his father far better now. Prince Bahnak would die of boredom in a world bereft of intrigue or the deadly games of war and politics. Indeed, he would regard the mere notion of such a world with puzzled incomprehension and laugh at the idea that things like *altruism* had any place in his life. He was a practical man, a pragmatic builder of empire! His reforms aimed simply at making that empire stronger, more self-sufficient, better able to withstand its enemies and conquer them when the time was right. Anything else was nonsense. Bahzell couldn't have begun to count the times he'd heard his father declare that a man looked after himself and his own in this world. Those who tried to do more were bound to fail, and the sooner they did it and got out of everyone else's way, the better!

Yet that was the same prince who'd raised his sons and daughters with the notion that they owed their people something, not the reverse. It was the commander who insured that the least of his troopers got the same rations, the same care from his healers,that any of his officers might expect in the field. And it was the father who'd raised a son who couldn't turn his back on Farmah. No doubt he was heartily cursing that son for landing in such a harebrained scrape, but Bahzell could imagine exactly how he would have reacted had his son *not* taken a hand. The fact that Bahnak saw no contradiction in his own attitudes might make him less of the cold, calculating prince than he cared to think, but it also made him an even better father than Bahzell had realized.

Now the first wagons were inching through the gates of Derm amid the friendly greetings of the city guard. Bahzell strode along in his post beside the pay wagon, and he saw a few of those welcoming guards turn thoughtful when they clapped eyes on him. But Kilthan was well known here; anyone in his employ—even a murdering hradani—was automatically respectable until he proved differently, and he saw little of the instant hostility he'd met elsewhere. Wariness and curiosity, yes, but not unthinking hatred. The observation left him cheerful enough to forget, for the moment, the vague, troubling memories of the dreams which still made his nights hideous, and he found himself whistling as the cumbersome wagons wound through the streets.

Kilthan's couriers had preceded him, and his local factor was waiting. The compound the dwarf's trading house maintained just off Derm's docks was larger even than his seasonal camp outside Esgfalas, for his wagons would be left here for winter storage when he took to the river. Bahzell knew from overheard comments that Baroness Ernos paid Kilthan a handsome subsidy to make Derm the permanent base for his eastern operations, and her motive became obvious as he watched the other merchants haggle for similar facilities. Just as Kilthan's caravan served as a magnet to draw the others with him on the road, so his headquarters drew them into leasing winter space for their wagons . . . or disposing of them to local carters who would cheerfully sell them back—at a profit, no doubt—next spring.

Bahzell watched it all, making mental notes to share with his father, but then they reached the docks, and the sight of the river drove all other thoughts from his head.

The Saram had looked impressive from a distance; close at hand, it was overwhelming. Bahzell had seen the upper reaches of the Hangnysti, but they were mere creeks beside the Saram. The broad, blue river flowed past with infinite patience and slow, deep inevitability, and the thought of *that* much water in one place was daunting. He could swim—not gracefully, perhaps, but strongly—yet hradani and boats were strangers to one another, and he felt a sudden, craven longing to keep it that way.

Unfortunately, he had no choice, and he drew a deep breath and spoke sternly to his qualms as the train unraveled into its individual components. The largest string of wagons—Kilthan's—rumbled gratefully into a vast brick courtyard between high, gaunt warehouses, and work gangs were already descending upon it. Bahzell joined the six other men Hartan had told to guard the pay wagon and shook his head as he watched the bustle engulf them.

Rianthus had told him Kilthan intended to spend no more than a single day in Derm, but he hadn't quite believed it. It hadn't seemed possible to unload, sort, reorganize, and stow so much merchandise away aboard ship in so short a time; now he knew the guard captain had meant every word of it.

Teams of hostlers joined the train's drovers to unhitch the draft animals. Foremen with slates and sheafs of written orders swarmed about, shouting for their sections as they found the crates and parcels and bales whose labels matched their instructions. A full dozen local merchants circulated with their own foremen to take delivery of goods Kilthan had freighted to them from Esgun or Daranfel or Moretz, and a dozen more bustled in with new consignments bound further south or clear to the Empire. Squads of officers and senior guardsmen kept an alert eye out for pilferers, racing fingers clicked over the beads of abacuses, sputtering pens recorded transactions, fees, and bills of sale, and voices rose in a bedlam of shouted conversations, questions, answers, and orders. It was chaos, but an intricately organized chaos, and the first heaps of cargo were already being trundled off to dockside and the broad-beamed, clumsy-looking riverboats awaiting them.

"Quite, ah, *impressive*, don't you think?" a familiar tenor voice drawled. Bahzell turned his head, and Brandark grinned up at him. "Did you ever see so many people run about quite so frantically in one place in your life?"

"Not this side of a battlefield." Bahzell chuckled. "I'm thinking some of these folk might have the making of first-class generals, too. They've the knack for organization, don't they just now?"

"That they do." Brandark shook his head, ears at half-cock, then turned as his platoon commander bellowed his name and pointed at a line of carts creaking back out of the courtyard towards the docks. The Bloody Sword waved back with a vigorous nod, then glanced at his friend.

"It looks like I'm about to find out what a boat is like." He sighed, hitching up his sword belt. "I hope I don't fall off the damned thing!"

"Now, now," Bahzell soothed. "They've been sailing up and down the river for years now, and you're not so bad a fellow as all that. They'll not drop you over the side as long as you mind your manners."

"I hope not," Brandark said bleakly. "I can't swim."

He gave his sword belt a last tug and vanished into the chaos.

True to his word, Kilthan had every bit of cargo stowed by nightfall. The final consignments went aboard by torch-light, and even Bahzell, whose duties had consisted mainly of standing about and looking fierce, was exhausted by the time he plodded across the springy gangway of his assigned riverboat. He felt a bit uneasy as his boots sounded on the wooden deck and the barge seemed to tremble beneath him, but he was too tired to worry properly.

As usual, his size was a problem, especially with the limited headroom belowdecks, so he was one of those assigned berth space on deck. He would have preferred having a nice, solid bulkhead between his bedroll and the water, given his recent restless dreams, but he consoled himself with the thought that at least the air would be fresher.

The riverboat's master was a stocky, squared-off human who knew a landlubber when he saw one. He took a single look at the enormous hradani, shook his head, and pointed towards the bow.

"That's the foredeck," he said. "Get up there and stay there. Don't get in the way, and for Korthrala's sake, *don't* try to help the crew!"

"Aye, I'll be doing that," Bahzell agreed cheerfully, and the captain snorted, shook his head again, and stumped off about his own business while Bahzell ambled forward. Brandark was already there, sitting on his bedroll and gazing out at the stars and city lights reflected from the water.

"Looks nice, doesn't it?" he asked as Bahzell thumped down beside him.

"Aye—and wet." Bahzell grunted, then grinned. "Deep, too, I'm thinking."

"Oh, *thank* you!" Brandark muttered.

"You're welcome." Bahzell tugged his boots off, then stood and eeled out of his scale mail. He arranged his gear on deck and groaned in gratitude as he stretched out. "You'd best be taking that chain mail off, my lad," he murmured sleepily, eyes already drifting shut. "I'm thinking someone who can't swim's no need of an extra anchor to take him to the bottom."

He was asleep before Brandark could think of a suitable retort.

For the first night in weeks, no dream disturbed Bahzell, and he woke feeling utterly relaxed. He lay still, savoring the slowly brightening pink and salmon dawn, and a strange contentment filled him. Perhaps it was simply the consequence of undisturbed sleep, but he felt oddly satisfied, as if he were exactly where he was supposed to be. The river gurgled softly down the side of the hull, reinforcing the novelty of being afloat, and he sat up and stretched.

Others began to stir, and he sat idle, content to be so, while cooking smells drifted from the galley. The other boats of Kilthan's convoy floated ahead and astern of his own, nuzzling the docks, hatches battened down, and a peaceful sense of expectancy hovered about them. He gazed out over them, and it came to him, slowly, that for the first time in his life, he was free.

He'd never precisely resented his responsibilities as a prince of Hurgrum—not, at least, until they took him to Navahk!—but he was who he was, and they'd always been there. Now he was far from his birth land, an outcast who couldn't go home even if he wanted to, perhaps, but in command of his own fate. No doubt he'd return to Hurgrum in time, yet for now he could go where he willed, do as he chose. Up to this very moment, somehow, he hadn't quite considered that. His mind had been fixed first on getting Farmah and Tala to safety, then on keeping his own hide whole, and finally on his duties as a caravan guard. Now it was as if the simple act of boarding the riverboat had taken him beyond that, released him from some burden and freed him to explore and learn, and he suddenly realized how much he wanted to do just that.

He smiled wryly at his thoughts, drew his boots on, and stood. Brandark snored on, and he left his friend to it, rolled his own blankets, and ambled over to the forward deckhouse. It was higher than the bulwark, more comfortably placed for one of his inches to lean on, and he took advantage of that as he watched the barge master pull a watch from his pocket. The captain glanced at it and said something to his mate, and the crew began preparing to cast off. They picked their way around the snoring guardsmen wherever they could, with a consideration for the sleeping landsmen's fatigue that almost seemed to embarrass them if anyone noticed, but they couldn't avoid everyone.

One of them poked Brandark in the ribs, and the Bloody Sword snorted awake. He scrambled up and dragged his bedroll to the side to let the riverman at the mooring line he'd blocked, then stretched and ambled over to Bahzell.

"Good morning," he yawned, flopping his bedding out on the deckhouse roof and beginning to roll it up.

"And a good morning to you. I see you weren't after rolling overboard in the night after all."

"I noticed that myself." Brandark tied the bedroll and glanced somewhat uneasily at his haubergeon. He started to climb into it, then changed his mind, and Bahzell grinned.

The Bloody Sword ignored him pointedly and buckled his sword belt over his embroidered jerkin. Crewmen scampered about, untying the gaskets on the yawl-rigged barge's tan sails, and halyards started creaking aboard other boats while mooring lines splashed over the side to be hauled up by longshoremen. The first vessels moved away from the docks while canvas crept up the masts and sails were sheeted home, and Bahzell and Brandark watched in fascination as the entire convoy began to move. They understood little of what they saw, but they recognized the precision that went into making it all work.

Half the barges were away, already sweeping downriver with thin, white mustaches under their bluff bows, when a commotion awoke ashore. A brown-haired, spindle-shanked human with a flowing beard of startling white scurried past piles of cargo. He was robed in garish scarlet and green, and he grabbed people's shoulders and gesticulated wildly as he shouted at them. The hradani watched his antics with amusement, and then, just as their own mooring lines went over the side, someone pointed straight at their boat.

The robed man's head snapped around, his expression of dismay comical even at this distance, and then he whirled and raced for the dockside with remarkable speed for one of his apparently advanced years.

"Wait!" His nasal shout was thin but piercing. "Wait! I must—"

"Too late, white-beard!" the barge master bellowed back. A gap opened between the riverboat's side and the dock, and the old man shook a fist. But he didn't stop running, and Bahzell glanced at Brandark.

"I'm thinking that lackwit's going to try it," he murmured.

"Well, maybe *he* can swim," Brandark grunted, but he moved forward in Bahzell's wake as the Horse Stealer ambled towards the rail.

There was eight feet of water between the barge and the dock when the old man reached it, but he didn't even slow. He hurled himself across the gap with far more energy than prudence, then cried out in dismay as he came up short. His hands caught the bulwark, but his feet plunged into the river, and his dismayed cry became an outraged squawk as water splashed about his waist.

"Here, granther!" Bahzell leaned over the side. His hands closed on shoulders that felt surprisingly solid, and he plucked the man from the river as if he were a child. "I'm thinking that was a mite hasty of you, friend," he said as he set his dripping burden on deck.

"I had no choice!" the man snapped. He bent to glare at his soaked, garish garments, plucking at the wet cloth, and Bahzell raised a hand to hide a smile as he muttered, "My best robe. Ruined—just ruined!"

"Oh, now, it's not so bad as all that," Bahzell reassured him.

"And what do *you* know about it?" The old man—who wasn't so old as all that, Bahzell realized, despite his white beard—gave his soggy splendor a last twitch and turned to glower over his shoulder at the gales of laughter rising from the dock workers who'd watched his exploit. "Cretins!" he snarled.

Bahzell and Brandark exchanged glances, ears twitching in amusement, and then the barge master arrived.

"And just what the Phrobus d'you think *you're* doing?" he snarled.

"I told you to wait!"

"And *I* told *you* it was too late! This is a chartered vessel, not a damned excursion boat for senile idiots!"

"Senile? *Senile!?* Do you know who you're talking to, my good man?!"

"No, and I'm not your 'good man,' either. I'm the master of this vessel, and you're a damned stowaway!"

"I," the newcomer said with dreadful dignity, "am a messenger of the gods, you dolt."

"Aye, and I'm Korthrala's long lost uncle," the captain grunted, and spat derisively over the side.

"Imbecile! Ass!" The bearded man fairly danced on deck. "I'll have you know I'm Jothan Tarlnasa!"

"What's a Jothan Tarlnasa and why should I give a flying damn about one?" the captain demanded.

"I'm chairman of the philosophy department at Baron's College, you bungling incompetent! Do you think I'd have come down here in full ceremonials and set foot aboard this rat-infested scow if it weren't important?!"

"Ceremonials?" The captain eyed Tarlnasa's water-soaked splendor and barked a laugh. "Is *that* what you call 'em?"

"I'll have your papers revoked!" Tarlnasa ranted. "I'll have you barred from Derm! I'll—"

"You'll go for another swim if you don't shut your mouth,"

the captain told him, and Tarlnasa's jaw snapped shut. Not in fear, Bahzell thought, but in shock, judging by his apoplectic complexion. "Better," the captain grunted. "Now, I've no time for you—no, and no patience *with* you, either. You're on my vessel, and how you got here is your own affair. If you think the dockmaster will fault me, you're an even bigger fool than I think, and that'd take some doing! You stay out of my way if you want me to put you aboard a boat headed back up this way." Tarlnasa started to open his mouth again, but the captain shot him a dangerous look and added, "Or you can just swim back ashore right now. It's all the same to me."

Silence hovered, and then Tarlnasa sniffed. He turned his back upon the captain, and the riverman rolled his eyes at Bahzell and Brandark before he stumped back to his helmsman.

"Moron!" Tarlnasa muttered resentfully. He ran his fingers through his beard, then gave his long hair a settling tug, squared his shoulders, drew a deep breath, and looked up at Bahzell.

"Well, now that *he's* out of the way, I suppose I should get down to the reason for my visit."

"Aye, well, don't let us be stopping you," Bahzell rumbled. He started to step out of the man's way, but Tarlnasa shook his head irritably.

"No, no, *no!*" he snapped. "Gods give me patience, you're *all* idiots!"

"Idiot I may be," Bahzell said less cheerfully, "but it's in my mind you'd do better not to be calling it to my attention, friend."

"Then just listen to me, will you? You're the reason I'm here!"

"*I* am?" Bahzell's eyebrows rose, and Tarlnasa snorted. "You are, gods help us all. Why they had to pick me, and get me out of bed at this ungodly hour and send me down here to endure that loudmouthed dolt of a captain and now *this*—!" He broke off and shook his head, then folded his arms. "Attend me, Bahzell Bahnakson," he said imperiously, "for I bring you word from the gods themselves."

He raised his chin to strike a dramatic pose, and Bahzell leaned back, ears flattened, and planted his hands on his hips. Bahzell glanced at Brandark and saw the same stiffness in his friend's spine, but then the Bloody Sword made himself relax, shrugged eloquently and stepped to the side. He leaned on the bulwark, gazing back at the receding docks, and Bahzell looked back down. Tarlnasa had abandoned his theatrical pose to glare up at him in self-important impatience, as if the Horse Stealer were a none-too-bright student who ought to have sense enough to beg his mentor to illumine his ignorance. The man was an ass and a lunatic, Bahzell told himself . . . unless the gods truly *had* sent him, in which case he was something far worse. The Horse Stealer remembered his dreams, and a spike of panic stabbed him. If it was some god sending them, had they left him in peace last night because they knew this madman was coming?

"And what if I'm not so very interested in hearing what the gods' have to say?" he demanded at last.

"What?" Tarlnasa gaped at him, and the hradani shrugged.

"I don't meddle with gods," he rumbled, "and I'll thank them not to be meddling with me."

"Don't be an ass!" Tarlnasa snapped, then shook himself, recrossed his arms, and fell back into rolling periods. "You've been chosen by the gods for great deeds, Bahzell Bahnakson. A great destiny awaits you, and—"

"'Destiny,' is it?" Bahzell grunted. "You can be keeping your 'destinies'—aye, and tell whatever god sent you I said so!"

"Stop interrupting!" Tarlnasa stamped a foot and rolled his eyes heavenward, pleading for strength. "Why the gods should choose a blockhead like you is beyond me, but they have. Now be still and listen to their commands!"

"No," Bahzell said flatly. Tarlnasa goggled up at the towering Horse Stealer, and elemental hradani stubbornness glared back down at him.

"But you have to! I mean— That is—"

"That I don't." Bahzell glanced at the docks, beginning to dwindle in the distance, then back down at Tarlnasa. "We're a mite far out from shore," he said. "I'm hoping you can swim if it's needful."

"Of course I can! I was *born* in Derm, though what that has to do with anything is more than I can see. The point is that the gods have chosen me to reveal to you their plans for you. You are commanded to— Stop! What are you *doing?!* Put me *down*, you—!"

The high-pitched, nasal voice cut off in a tremendous splash as Bahzell dropped Tarlnasa overboard. The hradani leaned out across the bulwark, gazing down into the water, and watched a head of streaming brown hair break the surface in a seaweed cloud of white beard and a furious splutter.

"The shore's that way," he said genially, pointing at the riverbank while the riverboat's crew howled with laughter.

"You *idiot!*" Tarlnasa wailed. "The gods—"

"Take yourself and your poxy gods off before I'm after pushing you back under," Bahzell advised.

Tarlnasa gawked up at him, treading water as the barge pushed on downstream away from him under full sail. He seemed frozen, unable to believe what was happening, and Bahzell waved cheerfully.

"Have a nice swim, now!" he called out as the philosopher fell even further astern. Tarlnasa raised a dripping fist and shook it at the departing boat with a wordless screech, only to splutter again as he went under once more. He kicked back to the surface, spat out a mouthful of water, shouted something far less exalted than his earlier peroration, and then swam strongly for the shore while Bahzell leaned on the bulwark beside Brandark and watched him go.

"You know," Brandark said after a long, thoughtful pause, "you really ought to work on how you deal with others in social situations."

"Why?" Bahzell asked mildly as Tarlnasa dragged himself up the bank and stood knee-deep in mud, shaking both fists and screeching curses after the barge. "He made it, didn't he?"

# CHAPTER THIRTEEN

The Morvan River was a peaceful place. Golden sunlight slanted across dark blue water, ruffled here and there with white lace or streaked brown with mud where it shallowed, but the central channel was wide and deep. The trees along the banks were splashed with bright autumnal color, but the days were warmer as Kilthan's southbound convoy outran the season, and the brisk slap and gurgle of water sounded under the riverboats' bluff bows. Current and wind alike were with them, and side-mounted leeboards dug deep, providing the keel their flat bottoms lacked as they foamed along with a surprising turn of speed.

Bahzell and Brandark sat in their regular spot on the foredeck, enjoying the sun's warmth, and the Bloody Sword's clever fingers wove a gentle, pleasantly plaintive tune from his balalaika in and out around the quiet rasp of Bahzell's whetstone. The Horse Stealer sat cross-legged while he honed his sword, and his eyes were

159

hooded, despite their present tranquility, for Bahzell was uneasy. The riverborne portion of Kilthan's annual journey to Esgfalas and back was normally its safest part, but this year was different, for someone—or something—was dogging Kilthan's heels.

It hadn't seemed that way at first. The voyage from Derm to Saramfal, capital of the elvish Kingdom of Saramantha, had been without incident. Even Brandark, who still harbored a nonswimmer's doubts about this whole notion of boats, had relaxed. They'd actually learned enough to lend their weight on halyards and sheets, and Bahzell had been grateful for the peaceful interlude after his encounter with Jothan Tarlnasa.

For all his studied nonchalance with Brandark, the episode left him uneasy. The notion that the gods—*any* gods—took an interest in him was enough to make a man bilious; the idea that they had "commands" for him was downright frightening. It had taken him a full day to get the coppery fear taste out of his mouth, but he had, at length, and he'd actually begun to enjoy the voyage—until Saramfal, at least.

The elves' island capital wore the city's white walls and splendid towers on its rocky head like a spired crown. He'd known he was gawking like a country-bred lout on market day while the boats tied up in the shadow of those walls, but he hadn't been able to help it. Nor had he really cared. That first sight had been as wondrous as he'd always suspected an elvish city must be, and he'd been eager to explore it, yet once he had, Saramfal's reality had been . . . disturbing.

He knew now that the "elf" he'd seen in Esgfalas had been a half-elf, for the beauty of the homeliest Saramanthan put the other's half-human comeliness to shame. Saramfal did the same to Esgfalas, but for all its splendor, the elvish city lacked the bustling liveliness of Esgan's cruder capital. There was a sense of melancholy, a brooding disengagement, as if Saramfal's citizens had never quite connected with the world beyond their small, private kingdom. Or, he'd slowly realized, as if they hadn't *wanted* to.

The thought had come to him gradually while he watched merchants too beautiful for words and garbed in the elegance of kings bargain with stocky, bald-as-an-egg Kilthan. The dwarf was no rough provincial, yet he'd been like a fork-bearded rock thrown into a magnificent but idealized painting . . . or dream. He'd been too solid, too *real*, as if Saramantha's borders were frontiers not simply against the rest of the world but against time itself. The elves had chosen to withdraw behind the brooding wall of memory, ignoring the affairs of Norfressa, and a chill had struck deep inside as Bahzell realized why.

They remembered.

Too many of those agelessly youthful faces *remembered* the decades-long Wizard Wars of Kontovar, the slaughter and fire which had toppled a continent. Their eyes had seen the banners of the black wizards, badged with Carnadosa's golden wand, sweep over the hacked and hewn bodies of the House of Ottovar's last defenders. The Fall of Kontovar wasn't history to them; it was their own lives. It was their fathers, mothers, brothers, and sisters who'd died in battle or been dragged to the Dark Gods' altars. It was they themselves who'd boarded the refugee ships, fleeing to the wilderness of Norfressa while the last white wizards of the world spent their lives to call down fire and destruction behind them. Here on this northern continent, where all about them were engrossed in their lives, in building and planning for the future, these people carried memory as his own people carried the Rage. Not just as a thing of horror, but as a thing of shame, for not only had they failed to stop the Fall, they'd *survived* it when so much else—and so many others—perished.

Twelve centuries had passed since the Carnadosans destroyed the House of Ottovar, but the elves of Saramantha were as blasted and scarred by the horrors of that destruction as if it had happened yesterday. They *dared* not open to the world about them lest they be blasted once more, and, for the first time, Bahzell Bahnakson realized how terrible a curse immortality could be.

Yet whatever they'd chosen, the world refused to leave them entirely alone, for the work of elvish craftsmen and artists commanded enormous prices in other lands, and Saramantha had its own needs. Where those needs crossed there were always merchants to fulfill them, and with merchants came all the paraphernalia of commerce, including docks, warehouses, taverns and inns . . . and thieves.

The Saramfal Guard dealt mercilessly with any of the riffraff that spilled over into the city, but they left the Trade Quarter to its own devices—less because they condoned lawlessness than because the Quarter was so alien to them—and, over the years, the Merchants Guild had hired its own peacekeepers and evolved its own laws. By now the Quarter was a city within a city, with formal interfaces between it and Saramfal proper, and it remained a lustier, busier, far more brawling community than any elvish city.

And it was in the Quarter that the first attack had occurred.

Bahzell knew Hartan blamed himself for letting his guard down, but there'd been absolutely no sign of danger as he and his platoon's first squad escorted Kilthan toward the docks on the morning of their departure. One moment, the street was utterly normal, a congested stream of tradesmen and laborers eddying and flowing around knots of haggling hucksters and dignified merchants; the next it was a place of clashing steel and screams.

Bahzell still didn't know exactly how it had happened. They'd erupted from the very cobbles without so much as a shout, cloaks and smocks cast aside to reveal gleaming swords, and his own blade had leapt into his hands without conscious thought as three of them came straight at him.

A crowded street was a poor battlefield for someone his size. There were too many innocent bystanders fleeing for their lives while Hartan cursed his shocked men into response, and Bahzell needed space to work. It was more luck than skill that let him skewer his first attacker with a lunge so clumsy his old arms master would have beaten him senseless for trying it in practice, but it worked, and he'd dodged the sword of a second, taken a cut from a third on his scale mail, and drawn his dagger with his left hand.

He wrenched his sword free of its first victim, then brought it down, one-handed but deadly, despite the close quarters, and split a skull. Hartan's battle-axe buried itself in the third man's chest with a terrible, sodden crunch, and steel rang on steel as more of the attackers engaged the rest of the squad. Bahzell parried a blade on his dagger, slammed his sword pommel into its wielder's skull, and gutted him with the dagger as he staggered. The dying man stumbled back, blocking a fellow just long enough for Bahzell to crop his head in turn, and the bull-throated bellow of Hurgrum's war cry did almost as much as the sudden explosion of combat to scatter the crowd. The bystanders scrambled madly out of the way, and, finally, he had room to work properly.

He threw his dagger into the throat of a human who'd circled around Hartan's off side and got both hands on his sword, and the rest of the squad slotted into place on either side of him. They took him for point, forming a line about Kilthan and anchoring their flanks against a tavern wall, and bodies, limbs, and pieces of limbs flew as his blade took any target that came within his reach.

It was over in minutes, and that, too, was strange. Their attackers had conceded defeat too promptly. None of them had been able to get past Bahzell, but they hadn't even seriously tried the others. Two members of the squad had been killed in the initial attack, but no one had come even close to Kilthan or his moneybags when the attackers vanished down alleys and side streets. Fifteen bodies lay in the street, but at least that many had fled, and Bahzell had stood panting amidst the carnage, unable to understand. The squad had been outnumbered three-to-one, and surely anyone who could plan and execute that smooth an ambush in a city street should have shown more determination to reach his target!

But they hadn't, and his own puzzlement had been dwarfed by Hartan's and Rianthus' when they found the scarlet scorpion tattooed on each body's shoulder. That was the emblem of the dog brothers, and no one could understand why the Guild of Assassins should attack Kilthandahknarthas dihna' Harkanath. Kilthan had rivals in plenty but remarkably few true enemies, and Clan Harkanath had a reputation for ruthless responses to attacks on *any* of its own, much less its head. No one could think of anyone who hated—or feared—Kilthan enough to pay the fee the Guild must have demanded for a target as dangerous as he, and why dog brothers, who specialized in stealth and cunning, should try for him in something as obvious as a street brawl baffled them all.

But they had, and not just in Saramfal. Kilthan had argued the point, but the united front of Rianthus and Hartan had browbeaten him into leaving his riverboat only for specific meetings, and then only with two full squads of Hartan's men—including Bahzell. Yet they'd been attacked again in Trelith, the Kingdom of Morvan's main port, and a third time, when they made their regular detour up the Feren River to Malgas.

The Trelith attack had been a repeat of the abortive Saramfal attempt with twice the men. Fortunately, the sheer number of attackers had been harder to hide, and Hartan spotted them before Kilthan was fully into their trap. The bodyguards' commander had also had more time to plan, and his prearranged order had sent Bahzell falling back beside Kilthan to deal with any who might break through to him. But the assassins hadn't pressed the attack. Indeed, they'd broken off the instant Hartan's men formed line about Kilthan and Bahzell, yet any hope they'd given up for good had been blunted at Malgas. The attack there had been nothing less than a fire ship. Brandark had lost both eyebrows in that one, for the river barge, packed with combustibles and roaring with flame, had actually lodged against Kilthan's ship for over two minutes before the crew could boom it off, and they might never have pushed it clear without the added weight and strength of the two hradani.

Now, as the convoy headed down the last few leagues to Riverside, Bahzell felt unhappy over his plan to leave it when they reached the port. Kilthan was well beyond any likely raider attack, but leaving him now seemed poor repayment for his kindness if the dog brothers meant to have him.

"Kormak for your thoughts," a tenor voice asked.

"I'm doubting they're worth as much as all that," he rumbled.

"Call me a big spender."

Bahzell gave a wry smile, but then it faded, and he shrugged.

"I've just been casting my mind over my—our—plans. We're coming up fast on Riverside, and I'm not so easy in my mind over leaving Kilthan as I'd thought to be."

"The dog brothers?"

"Aye." Bahzell flattened his ears. "It's not a thing I can understand, Brandark, this notion of taking money to kill a man you've never met and who's done naught to you or yours. And as for any scum that would worship Sharnā into the bargain—!" The Horse Stealer spat over the side, and Brandark sat up and cradled his balalaika across his lap.

"Sometimes I think you're too much a barbarian for your own good," he said. "If you'd grown up in Navahk, you'd understand *exactly* how someone could kill for a fistful of gold—or copper, for that matter. But you really don't, do you?" He shook his head at Bahzell's blank look and sighed. "Don't let it worry you, Bahzell. You're probably better off not understanding . . . as long as you remember other folk do. But as for worshiping Sharnā—"

The Bloody Sword broke off, gazing out over the sunlit river for several long minutes, then shrugged.

"Truth to tell, I doubt many of them really 'worship' old Demon Breath. From all I've heard, a man would have to be more than just sick-minded to dabble in such as that. Oh, the dog brothers pay Sharnā lip service, at least—I suppose even assassins want a patron of some sort, and the kind of treachery and cunning Sharnā relishes is their stock in trade—and there's no doubt they maintain links to his church, but I doubt most of them would ever come any nearer a demon-raising than they could help!"

"Aye?" Bahzell raised his sword to peer down its edge, and fresh-honed steel glittered below his eye as he glanced up at his friend. "That's as may be, my lad, but if they've a mind to call such as Sharnā lord and master, then *I've* a mind to cut their gizzards out on sight."

"I doubt you'd get much argument from anyone there— except the dog brothers, of course. But I take it the attacks on Kilthan are why you're uncomfortable about leaving his service?"

Bahzell nodded again, then put his sword away. Steel

clicked as he sheathed it and tucked the whetstone into his belt pouch.

"I understand," Brandark said after a moment, "but you can only kill them when they come at him. Hartan's other fellows can do that almost as well as you, and, much as it pains me to say it, he and Rianthus between them are at least half as smart as I am, so not even my brilliance is irreplaceable to Kilthan's security."

"Ah, the modesty of the man!" Bahzell sighed, and Brandark grinned. "Still and all," the Horse Stealer went on more seriously, "you're after making sense. It's just that these are good lads, Brandark, and skipping out when they might be counting on us . . . frets me. I'll be missing them, come what may, and if aught should happen to Kilthan after we've gone—" He twitched his ears unhappily, and his eyes were dark once more.

"I know." Brandark rubbed an index finger gently down a balalaika string and frowned. "Has he said anything more about our plans?"

"Naught but what you've heard as well as me. I'm thinking he'll be sorry to see our backs, not but what he'd cut his throat sooner than admit it! But all he's said is that we'd best be looking twice before we jump. We've a place here now; if we strike out on our own, we'll lose that."

"True enough, but that'd be just as true wherever we part company with him, and if you're serious about not going further west—?"

"After that maw worm Tarlnasa?" Bahzell bared square, strong teeth. "Even allowing as how that bag of piss and wind would know Dark Gods from Light, *no* god as would choose something like that as messenger is anyone I'd want to be meeting! Oh, no, Brandark, my lad! It's happy I am no one's said aught of wizards, but I'll be taking my chances with Harnak again before I stick my neck into any god's noose!"

"Why am I not surprised?" Brandark murmured.

Bahzell glared at him, but the Bloody Sword only twitched his ears gently in thought. "Well," he said finally, "in that case, Riverside's the place for us. The further west we go, the less likely we are to find anything going east, especially with winter coming on. So if you're still determined to outrun divine interference and Kilthan is willing to let us go, I suppose we have to."

"Aye," Bahzell growled, and squinted up into the cloudless blue sky with a look that boded ill for whatever god might be stalking him.

# CHAPTER FOURTEEN

"So you're sure about this, are you?"

Kilthan's sharp topaz eyes considered the two hradani as they stood at dockside. The city of Riverside was grimy and unkempt, and it had a name as a rough place. The Kingdom of Morvan was one of the Border Kingdoms—the small states nestled along the Empire of the Axe's frontier—but it was more lawless than most. And less concerned with keeping the Axemen happy, for the Forest of Sharmi covered its southern flank. *No one* went into the Sharmi willingly, not even armies of the expansionist Empire of the Spear, which left the Morvanians with a smaller sense of dependence upon Axeman protection.

"Aye, you are," the dwarf sighed, and shook his head. "I'll be honest, you lads have worked out better than I'd expected, and Riverside is no place for a pair of hradani all on their own. I'll keep you both on—as sergeants over the winter, and with your own platoons come spring."

"We appreciate the offer." Brandark still acted as their spokesman more often than not, but Bahzell nodded in agreement. "Truly we do. But under the circumstances—" He shrugged, and Kilthan frowned up at Bahzell.

"You're remembering that idiot in Derm, aren't you?" His cocked head demanded answer, and the Horse Stealer nodded again. "Well, I don't know as I blame you, but I doubt Norfressa's big enough to outrun the gods—assuming a lunatic in a fancy bed gown would know a message from them if it bit him on the arse!"

"That's as may be, but I'm minded to try. And, truth to tell, I'd sooner whatever it is not splash on you and yours if I *can't* outrun it, Kilthan."

"Hmmmmm. You know, there might just be something in that," Kilthan agreed with a slow smile, then shook himself. "All right. You've more than pulled your weight, so here's your pay—and I've decided to absorb your bonds with the Guild." He tossed over a purse that clinked satisfyingly when Brandark caught it, and grinned at their expressions. "Don't let it get around. Hirahim knows I don't need a reputation as a curst soft touch!"

"Somehow I doubt that's going to happen," Brandark assured him.

"No more it should," Kilthan agreed, drawing an unsealed parchment letter from his tunic and handing it to Brandark as well. "You'd best take this, too. Gods know you louts will have trouble enough without me to vouch for you, but this may help." Brandark cocked his ears—his eyebrows were growing back, but remained too wispy for suitable expressiveness—and Kilthan snorted. "It's a letter of introduction. Won't do a damned bit of good if the guard decides to clap you up, and don't expect it to help much with local tradesmen, but it should carry weight with anyone from the Guild who's looking for reliable men. I perjured my immortal soul in it, but if they believe half the lies I've told, it should get you a job with some-one reputable who's headed east—assuming there *is* any-one headed east this time of year!"

"We're thanking you, Kilthan," Bahzell said softly. He reached down to clasp forearms with the dwarf. "It's a good friend you've been to us, and I'll not forget. I've written my father, as well. If any of your factors are ever after finding their way to Hurgrum, you'll find the mar-kets open to you."

"Think I didn't know that, you overgrown lump of rock?" Kilthan rose on his toes to punch the Horse Stealer in the chest. "Why else d'you think I'm sending you off with that letter? Keep your eye on the main chance and invest carefully, boy, and don't you ever forget it!"

"Aye, that would be it, of course," Bahzell agreed with a smile, and Kilthan waved both hands at them.

"All right, all right! I've things to do, and I can't be standing around all day, so be gone with you now!"

He marched briskly away, and the two hradani smiled at each other behind him. They gathered their gear and started away from dockside, only to pause as Rianthus and Hartan appeared in front of them. The human led two horses, one an excellent medium warhorse and the other a sturdy pack animal, and Hartan shook his head as he glared up at the hradani.

"Tomanāk! All this time with us, and they *still* haven't learned to think ahead," he snorted to Rianthus.

"Aye, well, no one ever said they were smart," Rianthus agreed, grinning at Brandark.

"And to what—other than a desire to perfect your rude-ness—do we owe this visit?" Brandark inquired politely.

"Well, it occurred to some of the lads that you two had to sell your horses back in Derm," Rianthus said casually, "so the lot of us went in to buy you a pair of replacements. Not as good as you could, ah, liberate from a bunch of Navahkan Bloody Swords, maybe, but passable, I think."

"Passable, is it?" Bahzell ran an appreciative eye over the horses. "Aye, you might be calling them that!"

"Here—take 'em!" Rianthus stuck out the reins, then caught Bahzell's forearm as he took them. "And watch yourselves, you two! Gods know you're not the brightest pair I've ever seen, but we're fond of you."

"Speak for yourself, high-pockets," Hartan grunted, but he, too, clasped arms with them both. Then the two captains nodded brusquely and turned back to their business, and Bahzell and Brandark walked slowly into the streets of Riverside.

They soon found Kilthan's warnings well founded. They were no longer a wealthy merchant's guards, and Riverside had its share and more of prejudice. Like most of the Border Kingdoms, Morvan was a land of mixed races, but no hradani were numbered among them, and if their people's fearsome reputation meant no one cared to push a quarrel to the point of drawn steel, neither were they welcome. There was a mysterious lack of room in the better inns, and they ended up lodging above a miserable tavern on the wrong side of the city.

Their quarters were wretched enough, but the bad side of Riverside was worse than most, and the tavern's location brought them face-to-face with half the city's would-be bravos with predictable results. Word soon got around that it was wiser to leave them in peace, however, and Bahzell hardly had to break more than an arm or two to bring it about. It took a bit more effort on Brandark's part—his balalaika and dandified air made him less elementally threatening—but after the night four burly longshoremen took flight through a second-story window, their fellows decided to leave him alone, too.

None of that was calculated to endear them to the City Guard, and the unpleasant aura of official displeasure added itself to their other problems. All in all,

Riverside was not a place either of them cared for, yet finding a way to leave was far from simple.

Their pay from Kilthan, coupled with what remained of Bahzell's original purse, was enough to carry them for a time, especially at the prices their cheerless lodgings could command, but it would never last clear through the winter. Nor would it take them very far along the road. In the long run, if they wanted to eat they needed work, and there was little of that in Riverside for hradani, even with Kilthan's letter. Not, at least, on the right side of the law, and the local underworld quickly gave up on recruiting either of them.

Had an opportunity offered, they would gladly have used that same letter to hire on with another caravan, but autumn had caught up with them once more. Norfressa looked forward to winter, and no one willingly took to the road in winter, which lent added point to the necessity of finding some means of earning their way through the icy months to come. But as days turned into a week, then into two weeks, and then into three, and the nights grew steadily colder, it began to seem they had no choice. If there was nothing for them here, they must move on soon and trust to fortune. Besides, Bahzell's dreams were back. His memories of them were as fragmented and confusing as ever, but even more disturbing, and the Horse Stealer's feet itched to be leaving.

The moonless night was windy and cold. Thin clouds, just thick enough to hide the stars without cutting the chill, pressed down on Riverside like a hand, filling the frosty shadows with a darker, more solid blackness. There were no streetlights on this side of town; only the occasional privately maintained flambeaux outside some gambling den or brothel broke the dark, and Bahzell muttered balefully to himself as he moved down the mean little street. He'd found a few days' work, of a sort, as a bouncer, but that was at an end now. He didn't know who the Krahana-cursed idiot was or why he'd tried to stick a knife in Bahzell's back, and no one ever would know now. The Guard seldom ventured into the Broken Bucket, and no one had seemed inclined to summon them when his attacker landed in the sawdust with a broken spine, but the bar's halfling owner had decided he could manage without Bahzell's services after all. So here he was, picking his way back home to Brandark with no more than a few miserable silvers in his pouch, and—

He paused in one of the many shadows, ears cocking as a sound came from in front of him, and his jaw clenched.

His ears went slowly flat in the blackness, and a vast sense of ill-use suffused him as he heard snarling male voices and a lighter, more breathless female one that tried to hide its fear. They came from an alley ahead of him, and he raised his head to glare at the low clouds.

"Why me, damn it?" he demanded. "Why in the name of all of Fiendark's Furies is it always being *me?!*"

The clouds returned no answer, and he snarled at their silence. The voices grew louder, and then there was a sudden scream of pain—a man's, not a woman's—and the male voices were abruptly uglier and far more vicious. The Horse Stealer lowered his eyes from the clouds and swore vilely. This wasn't even Navahk, and he'd spent long enough among the other Races of Man now to know rape was a far more common crime among "civilized" people than any hradani clan would tolerate. If *they* didn't want to stop it, it was certainly none of *his* business— and the woman was probably no more than one of the whores who worked these wretched streets, anyway!

He wrestled with himself, and as he did, he heard the sudden patter of light, quick feet fleeing while heavier feet thundered in pursuit. Another scream split the night— this one female—and Bahzell Bahnakson spat one last, despairing oath at his own invincible stupidity, and charged.

Someone looked up with a startled cry as the huge hradani appeared out of the night. Dim bands of light spilled through a shuttered window high in one wall, patching the alley's shadows with bleary illumination, and Bahzell swore again as he realized there were at least a dozen of them. Probably more, and three of them had hold of a kicking, scratching, hissing wildcat below the window. Cloth tore, a soprano voice spat a curse, and hoarse laughter answered it even as he turned the corner, and he wasted no time on words.

The closest man had time for one, strangled cry as an enormous hand reached for him. Then he thudded headfirst against the alley wall and oozed down it while his companions whirled in astonishment. Knives glinted, but Bahzell wore his scale mail, and he was in no mind to make this any more of a killing matter than he could help. Gods knew the authorities were more likely to hang a hradani than thank him for saving some whore's problematical virtue, he told himself bitterly, and smashed a fist into the nearest face.

His target flew backward, taking two of its fellows down with it, and someone else dashed at him. Perhaps he meant only to dart past the hradani and flee, or perhaps he hadn't realized how large Bahzell was when he started, but his feet skidded as he suddenly found himself all alone and tried too late to change his mind. Bahzell caught his right wrist and twisted, a knife rang as it fell to the paving, and the man screamed—first in pain, then in raw panic—as he was plucked off the ground by his wrist. But a scale mail-armored elbow drove up into his jaw from below, bone crunched audibly, the scream was cut off as if by an axe, and Bahzell dropped him and reached for another one.

A knife slashed the back of his hand, but the cut was shallow, and he bellowed as his other fist came down on top of the knife-wielder's head like a maul. Another body slithered to the paving, and a bass-voiced curse turned into a falsetto scream on the *far* side of the crowd. Bahzell had no time to wonder why, for a knife grated on his mail from behind, then withdrew and came up from below. The stiletto-thin blade was narrow enough to find a gap between scales, but it hung for just a second, and he reached back for a handful of cloth and heaved. His assailant cried out as he flew forward, but then he hit the alley on the back of his neck and flopped with the total inertness of a dead man, and Bahzell stepped over the body as another knife thrust at him.

He caught two more men by the fronts of their tunics, slammed their heads together, and tossed them aside as a figure tried to dash past him in the confusion. An out-thrust boot brought the would-be escapee to the ground, and a savage kick bounced him off a wall and left him curled in a sobbing knot around splintered ribs. Three of his fellows threw themselves on the hradani, swinging desperately with loaded truncheons, and Bahzell roared in fury. He caught one of them up and used him to smash the other two to the ground before he hurled his makeshift bludgeon into the alley wall. There was *another* scream and a torrent of curses from the crowd ahead of him, and the entire alley dissolved into a frantic confusion of shouts, thudding blows, and grunts of pain.

Bahzell's enemies outnumbered him, but the quarters were too close for them to mob him. They could come at him only in twos and threes, and if they had knives, he was bigger than any two of them and armored to boot, and a wild glee filled him. It wasn't the Rage, but a sort of fierce delight in paying back all the slights and insults he and Brandark had endured in Riverside, and suddenly he was roaring with laughter as he waded through them.

The last few toughs heard that bellowing laughter as their fellows flew away from the hulking titan, and they turned as one. They abandoned their plans for the night's entertainment and took to their heels, praying the alley had an open end . . . and that they could reach it before *he* reached *them*.

Bahzell heard them go and opened his left hand. The man he'd been punching with his bleeding right fist sagged bonelessly to the pavement, and he looked around quickly for the whore.

No, he corrected himself, *not* a whore. The woman with her back to the greasy alley wall was too plainly dressed for that. A whore would have shown more flesh, even on a night this cold, and she wore none of the cheap trinkets of the prostitute. He heard her fearful breathing and saw the gleam of her wide eyes, but she held a short dagger as if she knew which end was sharp. More to the point, there was blood on the blade and two dead men at her feet.

His own chest heaved, and his ears pricked in surprise as he studied her. Her clothing was drab, and her heavy skirt was badly ripped under her cheap cloak, yet it was also painfully clean. She was a small thing, even for a human, and young, but there was a lean, poised readiness about her. She looked like a peasant, but she didn't stand like one, and she was neither a half starved waif of the streets nor a fine lady.

He frowned as he tried to decide just what it was she *was*, and then she lowered the dagger with a taut smile and nodded to him.

"My thanks, friend," she said in accented Axeman. "Lillinara knows I never expected anyone to come running in a place like this—and a hradani to boot!—but . . . many thanks."

"Aye, well, I couldn't just be walking on by," he said uncomfortably in the same language.

"Most people around here could have, and would." She gave him another flickering smile and stooped to clean her dagger on a cloak. Then the blade vanished somewhere about her clothing, and she tugged at her torn skirt in a futile effort to straighten it.

"My name is Zarantha," she said, abandoning her efforts. Her accent gave her Axeman a strange, musical lilt, and she held out her hand.

"Bahzell," Bahzell muttered, bemused by her composure, and his eyebrows rose as he felt his forearm gripped in a warrior's clasp. "Bahzell Bahnakson, of the Horse Stealers."

"Horse Stealers?" It was Zarantha's turn to raise her eyebrows. "You're a long way from home, Bahzell Bahnakson."

"That I am," Bahzell agreed. She released his arm and he stood back, ankle-deep in bodies—unconscious and otherwise—and his mouth twitched in wry amusement. "And so, I'm thinking, are you, from your accent."

"True enough. I'm from Sherhan, near Alfroma in the South Weald."

"A Spearman, are you? Or should I be saying a Spearwoman?" Bahzell asked in Spearman, and she laughed out loud.

"Spearmen is what they call us, man, woman, and child," she replied in the same language. "And what does a Horse Stealer hradani know of us? You're—what, from up near Sothōii lands?"

"Well, as to that, we're thinking the Sothōii are from up near *Horse Stealer* lands," he said, and she laughed again.

"Good for you! But what, if you'll pardon my asking, are you doing in Riverside? Not that I'm ungrateful for whatever it is!"

"Naught but traveling through. And yourself?"

"I'm trying to get home."

"Home, is it?" Bahzell looked down at her, and something in the way she'd said "get home" urged him to bid her a courteous good evening and vanish. The racket they'd raised might bring the Guard down on them, even in this part of town, and even if it didn't, this Zarantha and her problems were none of his affair. But something else had control of his voice, and he cocked his head and frowned at her. "And what's to stop you from getting there, then?"

"One thing after another," she said tartly. "My family's well enough off, in a modest sort of way—we're connected to the Shâloans, one way or another—and my father sent me off to school in the Empire of the Axe. But when I started home again—"

She broke off as one of the thugs groaned and pushed up on his hands. He wavered there, then struggled to his knees, and Bahzell brought a fist down on the top of his head without even thinking about it. The man grunted and thudded back to the paving, and the hradani nodded politely to Zarantha.

"You were saying you're after being connected to the Shâloans?" She nodded back, and he frowned. "And what might a Shâloan be?"

"What?!" Zarantha blinked at him, then laughed again. It was a nice laugh, Bahzell thought, throaty and almost purring. "That's right, you wouldn't know. Well, Grand Duke Shâloan is Warden of the South Weald."

"Ah." He eyed her plain, cheap clothing again and cleared his throat. "And would the Duke know you're in difficulties?"

"I didn't say it was a *close* connection," she said wryly. "Not but what my family isn't better off than appearances might suggest. I was on my way home when my armsmen came down with a fever here in Riverside." Her face tightened, and her voice fell. "Two of them died," she said more softly, "and poor Tothas was too sick to defend even himself when my maid and I were robbed. We barely had enough left to put a roof over our heads—not that it's much of one—while we nursed him back to health."

Bahzell nodded again, slowly, tempted, despite the absurdity of what she claimed to be, to believe her. He also felt a stir of sympathy and stepped on it hard. The last thing he and Brandark needed was to get involved with an indigent noblewoman, however minor. Especially a foreign one.

"Well, it's happy I am to have been of service, Lady Zarantha," he said, "but I've a friend waiting for me, and I'd best be going, so—"

"Wait!" She held out her hand again, and Bahzell felt a sharper stab of foreboding. "If you're just traveling through, won't you help us? Tothas is still weak, and I'm sure if you—and your friend, if he's willing—help us get home, my father will see you rewarded for it!"

Bahzell's jaw clenched, and he swore at himself for not having made his escape in time.

"I've no doubt he would," he began, "but I'm thinking there's better than such as us to be helping you home. It's like enough he'd be none too happy to see you trailing a pair of hradani with you, and—"

Another thug raised a bleary head, peered about him, and began crawling down the alley, and Bahzell reached down and caught him by the cloak. He jerked the unfortunate up and bounced his head off the wall—harder than was strictly necessary in his frustration—and let him slither back.

"As I was saying—" he began again, when a loud voice spoke from behind him.

"Here, now!" it said sharply. "What's all this, then?"

Bahzell shut his mouth and turned slowly. He wore no sword—the Riverside Guard frowned on them—but he was careful to keep his hand well away from his dagger hilt, as well.

It was, perhaps, as well he had, for ten of the Guard stood in the alley mouth with torches, peering at the carnage. The sergeant at their head removed his steel cap and tucked it under his left arm to scratch his head, and more steel rasped quietly behind him as someone loosened a sword in its sheath.

"Well?" the sergeant said after a moment, gazing up at Bahzell, and the hradani opened his mouth, but Zarantha stepped past him before he could speak.

"I," she said, and Bahzell blinked at her suddenly regal tone, "am the Lady Zarantha Hûrâka, of Clan Hûrâka, sept to Shâloan of the South Weald."

"Ah?" The sergeant rocked back on his heels with a smile, but the smile faded as Zarantha faced him. She should have looked ridiculous in her cheap, drab garments, torn and streaked with the alley's filth, but she didn't. Bahzell could see only her back, but there was a dangerous tilt to her head, and the sergeant cleared his throat.

"I, uh, I see . . . My Lady," he said finally. "Ah, I don't suppose you could, um, explain what's happened here?"

"Certainly, Sergeant," she replied with that same regality. "I was on my way to my lodging when I was set upon by these . . . persons." A distasteful wave encompassed the bodies about Bahzell's feet. "No doubt they intended to rob me—or worse—and would have, but for this gentleman." A much more graceful wave indicated Bahzell, and the sergeant blinked again.

"*He* helped you?"

"He certainly did, and most efficiently, too."

"I see." The sergeant bent to roll one of the bodies onto its back, and his frown deepened. He waved a corporal forward to join him, and the corporal whistled through his teeth.

"That's Shainhard, sure as Phrobus, Sarge," he muttered, and the sergeant nodded and straightened.

"Well . . . My Lady," he said slowly, "I'm glad he did, I suppose, but I'm afraid I'm going to have to take him in for disturbing the peace."

"*Disturbing the peace*, is it?" One or two guardsmen flinched at the quiet anger in Bahzell's deep voice. "And I suppose you're thinking I should have just walked on past and let them do as they willed?"

"I didn't say that," the sergeant replied sharply, "but I've heard the reports, and this isn't the first brawl for you or your friend. I don't say they were your fault," he added as Bahzell stiffened, "for I doubt they were, but we know there's been trouble, and this looks like more, and worse, of the same. Best to get you safely in cells while we decide what happened."

"And if I'm not minded to go?" Bahzell asked in a perilously quiet voice, but the sergeant faced up to him without flinching.

"I don't think that would be very smart of you," he said flatly. "You're a stranger in town, and—no offense—you're also a hradani with no means of support. When you add that to who this lot—" he gestured at the bodies "—work for, well, there's going to be questions, like it or no."

"Questions?" Bahzell began dangerously, but Zarantha raised a hand, and the gesture was so imperious it cut him off in midbreath.

"Excuse me, Sergeant, but you're in error," she said crisply.

"I'm what?" The guardsman blinked at her.

"I said you were in error," she repeated, her voice even crisper. "You said this man has no means of support."

"Well, no more does he!"

"Yes, he does. In fact, he's been retained by Clan Hûrâka as my personal armsman, and he was acting in that capacity when I was attacked. Surely you don't question the propriety of defending his employer?"

The sergeant sucked his teeth and peered up at Bahzell, and it was all the Horse Stealer could do to keep his own mouth closed. He knew how deep was the trouble in which he stood, but his eyes narrowed as he glared down at the top of Zarantha's head, and he suddenly found himself wondering if a Riverside cell would be all that bad a place to spend the night, after all.

"Your . . . armsman," the sergeant repeated at length. "I see. And just what might you and your, ah, armsman be doing in Riverside, My Lady?"

"I was forced to stop here when one of my servants fell ill," Zarantha said coldly. "Now that he's recovered, I intend to return to my home in the South Weald. May I ask what concern that is of yours, Sergeant?"

"Well, since you ask, My Lady, I'll tell you," the guardsman said with a certain air of satisfaction. "These aren't just any street scum. This one—" he pointed at the man he and the corporal had examined "—is named Shainhard, and he's a senior lieutenant to one Molos ni'Tarth. Now, it may be none of my concern, but ni'Tarth's a nasty customer. We know he runs most of the southside drinking sties and sells protection down at the docks, and we think he's had dealings with the dog brothers. But the point, Lady Zarantha," he allowed himself to use the title with withering irony this time, "is that Shainhard is important to ni'Tarth's operations, and he doesn't look so very good right at the moment. In fact, I don't believe he's breathing anymore."

Bahzell felt his stomach sinking steadily, and the smile the sergeant gave him was a strange mix of satisfaction and sympathy.

"Now the thing is, My Lady, that ni'Tarth won't take kindly to this, not at all, at all. In fact, he'll probably try to cut your new armsman's throat—or ask his dog brother friends to do it for him. Come to that, he won't be too pleased by *your* part in this, either."

"I see." Bahzell felt an unwilling admiration for Zarantha's calm, despite what he saw coming. Her voice didn't even quaver at the mention of dog brothers, and she shrugged. "I imagine it would be better not to tempt him to be foolish, then, wouldn't it?"

"That it would, My Lady. That it *certainly* would." The sergeant beckoned to his corporal again. "Go down to the Needle Street station and bring back a couple more men and a wagon to collect the trash, Rahlath," he said.

"Aye!" The corporal trotted off, boots clattering on the uneven cobbles, and the sergeant looked back at Zarantha.

"Now, the way I see it, 'My Lady,' I really should take your armsman in—and maybe you, too, for all I know. But it's a busy night, and I've got a lot on my mind already. If it should happen that the two of you were to, ah, wander off before Corporal Rahlath gets back here, why, I'd probably be too occupied to look for you. And if you keep right on wandering fast enough, ni'Tarth might not even realize where *he* ought to look for you . . . and your 'armsman,' of course, if you take my meaning?"

"I do, Sergeant." Zarantha looked up over her shoulder at Bahzell. "I believe you said you were on your way to your friend?" she suggested.

"Aye, but—"

"In that case, I think we should be going," she interrupted, and his mouth closed with a click. The ground seemed to be slipping away beneath his feet, and try as he might, he couldn't make it hold still. "Yes, I definitely think we should be on our way," she said firmly, and he nodded.

There was nothing else he could do.

# CHAPTER FIFTEEN

Bahzell led his new employer through the deserted streets in glum silence. He'd done it again. Poked his nose into something that was none of his affair because he simply couldn't leave well enough alone, and now look what he'd landed himself in! Of all the—!

Yet for all his self-disgust, he saw no escape. He owed Zarantha something for keeping him out of jail; no doubt this ni'Tarth would have found him easy to get to there. By the same token, ni'Tarth left him no choice but to get out of Riverside, jail or no jail. Of course, none of that would have been true if he hadn't tried to help Zarantha, but he couldn't really blame *her* for that. He'd known better and done it anyway, which only made him angrier with himself. The best he could hope for now was that her family truly would be able to pay a little something for getting her home . . . which didn't seem likely. Whatever she claimed, even a hradani knew you didn't find noblewomen dressed like peasants—and *poor* peasants, at that—creeping around the stews and alleys of a place like Riverside in the middle of the night!

He growled an oath and stalked onward. At least, he told himself morosely, it gave him someplace to *go* instead of squatting in this miserable city while the money ran out, but he hated to imagine Brandark's reaction.

They reached the tavern where he and Brandark lodged, and the slatternly landlady looked up from behind the bar as he led Zarantha in. Beady eyes brightened in their harridan net of wrinkles as she saw the young woman at the hradani's side, but she put what she fondly imagined was a prim look of disapproval on her face and waved a bony finger at Bahzell.

"Here, now! This here's a decent place, it is. I'll not have ye bringin' yer fancy pieces an' gods know what pox or flux back to *my* beds!"

The Horse Stealer's foxlike ears flattened, and the landlady paled as he glared down at her. He truly couldn't have said which infuriated him more—the insult to Zarantha, the notion that he might dally with a whore, or the leering, knowing note in her voice—but any of them would have been enough tonight.

Silence hovered for a long, fragile moment before he made his fury relax and gave her a thin smile. "You were saying?" he rumbled.

The slattern swallowed nervously, but then she straightened, and defiant spite flashed in her eyes, made even stronger by the shame of her own fear as she realized he wasn't going to attack her after all.

"No need t' take that tone wi' *me*, master high an' mighty! It's me as is mistress o' this house, an' ye'll bide by my rules, or out ye goes!" She sniffed with growing confidence, for she knew how long and hard the hradani had looked before they found lodging in the first place. "Maybe ye can find someplace else as'll take yer kind, but if yer minded t' bed that hussy in *my* house, ye'll be payin' two silver extra to futter her, me lad!"

"And what," Zarantha asked, a note of amusement in her musically accented Axeman, "makes you assume that's what he has in mind?"

"Hoo! A furriner, are ye?" The landlady cackled. "Well now, missy, just what d'ye *think* I'm a-thinkin'? The shame of it, spreadin' yer legs fer the likes o' him, an' him not even human!"

Bahzell's ears went flat once more, and the slattern's vicious smile vanished as he stalked wordlessly towards her. The Horse Stealer had endured enough this night, but he reminded himself sternly that his hostess was a woman—a loathsome, disgusting woman, but a woman— and so he reached out to the thirty-gallon beer keg on the bar instead of her scrawny neck. It was half full, and beer sloshed noisily as he plucked it from its chocks.

"I'm thinking," he said softly, holding the keg out straight-armed, directly over her head, "that you're after owing this lady an apology."

The landlady looked up and blanched. The keg hung motionless above her, not even quivering, and her eyes darted back to the hradani's expressionless face and then to Zarantha.

"T-T-To be sure, I meant ye no offense, and—and I humbly begs yer pardon," she gabbled, and Bahzell allowed himself another thin smile.

"Good," he said in that same, soft voice. He replaced the keg in its chocks with neat precision and waved Zarantha towards the stairs. She inclined her head to the landlady in a gracious nod and swished up them in her torn homespun skirt, and Bahzell gave the harridan one last blood-chilling smile, patted the keg lightly, and followed her.

Brandark was still up, nursing a bottle before the tiny fire on the smoky hearth, when Bahzell and Zarantha entered the cheap room. He looked up at the opening door, and his eyes widened as he saw Zarantha. But he recovered quickly and scrambled to his feet, and her lips quirked as he twitched his lacy shirt straight and bestowed a graceful bow upon her.

"Will you stop that?" Bahzell growled. Something suspiciously like a chuckle came from Zarantha, and Brandark bobbed back up with a twinkle. Bahzell saw it and growled again, but Brandark only cocked his ears in polite inquiry.

"And who might your lovely companion be?"

"I'll 'companion' *you* one, for half a copper kormak!" Bahzell rumbled in an overtried voice.

"Now, Bahzell!" Unholy amusement danced in Brandark's eyes as he added the dried blood on Bahzell's right hand to Zarantha's general dishevelment, and he shook his head. "I apologize for my friend," he told Zarantha in his smoothest tones. "It's his hand, I think. For some reason, his brain never works too well when his hand's bloody. It seems to make him remarkably irritable for some reason, too."

"Listen, you runty, undersized, pipsqueak excuse for a hradani, I've been having about all—!"

"Now, now! Not in front of company." Brandark smiled dazzlingly. "You can abuse me all you like later," he soothed.

Bahzell made a sound midway between a growl, a sigh, and a groan, and Brandark laughed. He waggled his ears outrageously at the Horse Stealer, and, despite himself, Bahzell's lips twitched in a weary grin.

"That's better! And now if you'd introduce us?"

"Brandark Brandarkson of Navahk, be known to—" Bahzell frowned and looked at Zarantha. "What was it you were calling yourself?"

"My name is Zarantha," she said, smiling at Brandark, and the Bloody Sword's ears perked up at her accent. "Lady Zarantha Hûrâka, of Clan Hûrâka."

"Do you know," Brandark murmured, "I think you actually may be."

"Why, thank you, sir," she said with a deeper smile, and swept him a curtsy she'd never learned in the alleys of Riverside.

"But I trust you'll forgive me," he went on, "if exactly what a Spearman lady is doing in Riverside, and how we can serve her, eludes me?"

"You didn't tell me your friend was so charming," she murmured to Bahzell, and the Horse Stealer snorted.

"Aye, isn't he just?"

"Of course I am." Brandark drew the second rickety chair back from the equally unsteady table for their guest. She seated herself with a regal air, and the Bloody Sword looked expectantly back at his friend. "I assume from the state of your hand that you've been up to your old tricks. Would you care to tell me exactly what you've landed us in this time?"

Brandark took the explanation better than Bahzell had feared, though the Horse Stealer was none too sure his gales of laughter at the description of the fight in the alley were truly preferable. He sobered—some—on hearing the sergeant's warning about ni'Tarth, but he only shrugged at the revelation that he and Bahzell were now bound for the Empire of the Spear.

"Well, you said you wanted to go east," he murmured, "and you *do* have a way of, ah, *expediting* your departures, don't you?" Bahzell snorted in his throat, and the Bloody Sword chuckled. "Yes, you do. In fact, I think I feel an inspiration coming on."

"Oh, no, you don't!" Bahzell said hastily.

"Oh, but I do!" Brandark's eyes glinted at him. "I think I'll call it . . . *The Lay of Bahzell Bloody-Hand.* How does that sound?"

"Like a just enough cause for murder!"

"Nonsense! Why, I'll make you *famous*, Bahzell! Everywhere you go, folk will know of your heroic deeds and towering nobility!"

"You'd best give the idea over while you've still two hands to write with," Bahzell growled, but his own lips twitched, and Zarantha chuckled again. Then the Horse Stealer sobered. "Aye, that's well enough, Brandark, but we've landed neck-deep in trouble again, and it's me that's put us there."

"Now don't take on so. It's my fault, too. After all, I know the sorts of things you get into when I'm not there to stop you."

"*Will* you be serious?" Bahzell demanded, but Brandark only laughed, and the Horse Stealer turned his back on him to frown down at Zarantha. "I'm thinking you know you've mousetrapped me fair and square," he told her, "but I've a mind to hear a bit more about you before we're off to the South Weald."

"There's not a great deal to tell," she shrugged. "My father is Caswal of Hûrâka. Hûrâka has some claim to fame, locally at least, though it's certainly not the largest sept of Shâloan, and he wanted me properly educated."

"A Spearman noble sent his *daughter* to the Axemen for schooling?" Brandark asked with a peculiar emphasis, and Zarantha gave him a small smile.

"I see you *do* know a bit about Spearmen, Lord Brandark."

"Just Brandark, since it seems we're working for you now," the Bloody Sword said, but he continued to gaze at her intently, and she shrugged.

"As I say, Hûrâka isn't the largest sept of Shâloan, and Father's always had some . . . peculiar notions and no sons. My mother is dead, and he remarried just two years ago, so that may change, but for now I'm still his oldest child and heir. Of course, my husband would inherit the title and what lands go with it, not me, but still—"

She shrugged again, and Brandark nodded, yet a flicker of unsatisfied curiosity still glowed in his eyes.

"As for sending me to the Axemen," she went on more briskly, "pray, why should he not? There's always tension between the empires, but, as you say, I'm only a daughter. Even the most patriotic Spearman has to admit Axeman schools are better, and—" a hint of bitterness tinged her voice "—no one pays much heed to where a mere daughter is educated."

She fell silent, then gave her head a little toss. "At any rate, he sent me to Axe Hallow very quietly, I assure you. Just as I assure you he will, indeed, recompense you for any expenses you may suffer and reward you well for your assistance in getting me home."

Bahzell had the distinct impression as much was left unsaid as said, but he glanced at Brandark, and the Bloody Sword shrugged. He seemed to accept Zarantha's story at face value, but it was hard to be certain. For himself, Bahzell was inclined to believe all she'd said was true, yet that wasn't to say it was *all* the truth . . . or that she hadn't embroidered a bit about the edges.

"Well," he said at length, "if the sergeant had the right of it, we'd best be on our way quick." He bent a dubious eye on Zarantha. "Can you be staying on a horse if we put you there . . . Lady?"

She lowered her eyes demurely, but the ghost of a smile flickered about her lips.

"I think I could," she said in a meek voice, "but if you don't mind, I'd feel more comfortable on my mule. Father sent him to me, and he's a really fine mule. I have a pack mule, too, and another for my maid, Rekah, as well."

Bahzell studied the crown of her bent head, and a corner of his mind noted that her dark, shining hair was as scrupulously clean as her shabby garments had been before ni'Tarth's thugs attacked her. The thought of a father poor enough to send his eldest daughter off to foreign lands on muleback, without even a horse, caused his heart to sink, but there were worse things than mules when it came to the road. They were tough enough, with the ability to survive on forage that could never support a horse, and if he'd seldom met a mule with a disposition he cared for, they were also smarter than horses.

"Aye, well, I've no problem with that," he rumbled, "but you were saying you've still one guardsman left. D'you have a mule for him, as well?"

"Oh, no! But Tothas has an *excellent* horse," she said so reassuringly he felt an instant pang of dread. Then she raised her head and met his eyes with an earnest look. "The only problem is that, as I told you, we were robbed while he was ill. I've been able to pay our board and stable fees, but when it comes to provisions for the road—"

She raised her hands, empty palms up, and Bahzell looked at Brandark in resignation. The Bloody Sword only grinned and opened his purse to spill a scant handful of coins onto the wobbly table, and Bahzell sighed and followed suit.

They pushed their total remaining assets into a single heap, and Bahzell sat back to let Brandark count it. The Bloody Sword had a better notion of the value of foreign coins, and his fingers sorted them briskly while Zarantha sat with her hands in her lap and an anxious expression. Bahzell had an odd feeling she looked more anxious than she was, and it irritated him. He'd never seen a map of the Empire of the Spear—not one he'd trust, anyway—but it was easily half again the size of the Empire of the Axe. It was also far more sparsely settled, and the thought of crossing it with scant supplies at this time of year was hardly amusing, whatever Zarantha might think.

Bahzell finished counting and scraped the coins back into his purse, then leaned back in his chair with a thoughtful frown.

"We've enough, I think," he said after a moment. "Not much more than that, mind, but enough—assuming, that is," he added with a sharp glance at Zarantha, "that you and your servants have your own trail gear."

"We do," she assured him.

"In that case," Brandark turned his eyes to Bahzell, "we should consider where to get what we require. If this ni'Tarth is as powerful as your guardsman says, he won't need long to hear what happened. Under the circumstances, I'd just as soon get on the road quickly."

"You're minded to set out and buy what we need on the way?" Bahzell asked dubiously, and Brandark nodded.

"You and I have enough trail rations to carry us all for a day or two, and we're going to have to cross the Dreamwater when we leave Riverside. If this ni'Tarth is involved in the docks, it might be smarter to get ourselves ferried across before he puts out the word he's looking for us than to take the time to go shopping. We can buy what we need once we get over into Angthyr."

"Aye, that's true enough, but I've not the least notion where we're bound." Bahzell looked at Zarantha. "This Sherhan, now. You were saying it's near what?"

"Alfroma. That's the second largest city in the South Weald," she told him proudly.

"Well it may be, but I've no idea how to get there from here."

"Oh, that's all right. I know the way."

"Do you, now?" He gave her a grim look. "If it's all the same to you, Lady, I'm not minded to set out for a place I've no notion of how to find." He looked back at Brandark. "Would you be knowing the way?"

"No, but I know roughly where the South Weald is in relation to us, and I'm sure we can find a map in Kor Keep, if not sooner. On the other hand," it was Brandark's turn to look thoughtfully at their new employer, "I can't help wondering why your father didn't send you home by ship, My Lady. If memory serves, you could have sailed up the Sword to the Darkwater from Bortalik Bay. Surely that would have been faster, not to mention more comfortable—and safer—than traveling overland from Riverside at this time of year."

"Father doesn't like Purple Lords." For the first time, there was a truly evasive note in Zarantha's voice, but she brushed it aside and went on more briskly. "Besides, it should have been safe enough if my armsmen hadn't been taken ill," she reminded him. "There was no reason to expect that."

"I see." Brandark studied her a moment longer, then shrugged and turned back to Bahzell. "At any rate, we can get maps in Angthyr, and this Tothas probably knows the roads fairly well—"

"He does," Zarantha put in.

"—so I don't think that will be that much of a problem," Brandark continued with a flick of his ears. "At any rate, *I* don't want to hang about hunting for maps *here*. Even if this ni'Tarth didn't get us while we did it, he could probably find out which maps we'd been looking for after we'd gone. That might give him a better notion where to find us while we're still close enough for him to consider sending someone after us."

"Aye, there's that." Bahzell frowned down at the table for several silent moments, then twitched his shoulders and sighed. "In that case, I'm thinking we'd best be about it. It's coming up on dawn in an hour or two, and the ferries will be running with the sun."

"Agreed," Brandark nodded.

"Then if you'll pay our shot to the harpy downstairs—I've a notion she'd sooner see you than me, just now—let's be off."

Streetlights still burned behind them, for the sun was just rising as the ferry crept across the Dreamwater towards the

Kingdom of Angthyr's Grand Duchy of Korwin. Heavy mist pressed down on the river's cold water, but the eastern sky was a pale gold glory, bright enough to throw shadows . . . and to hurt Bahzell Bahnakson's weary eyes.

The ferry was crowded, and the boatmen were surly. They'd grumbled resentfully when Brandark pulled them away from their breakfasts, and not even the extra coins he'd slipped them when no one was looking had sweetened their dispositions. They might be making twice the legal ferry fee, but they'd stood aloof and left it to the two hradani and Zarantha's single remaining armsman to get three nervous horses and three resentful mules aboard their craft.

Overall, Bahzell had been pleasantly surprised by the quality of Zarantha's animals. Her own saddle mule had a wicked, roving eye, but all three were long-legged, big-boned, powerful animals who looked remarkably well cared for, given their owner's poverty and the wretched inn at which they'd been stabled. For its part, Tothas' mount, far from being the nag he'd feared, was an excellent medium warhorse, and its war training—and bond with Tothas—showed. Finding an animal easily worth several hundred kormaks in the hands of a retainer who served such a poverty-stricken mistress was one more puzzle for him to chew at unhappily, and Zarantha's sweet smile when he saw it told him she'd enjoyed leading him to assume the worst.

Tothas himself was a cause of some concern, however. The man wore the crossed mace and sword of the Church of Tomanāk on an amulet about his neck. He felt *solid*, somehow, yet whatever illness he'd suffered from must have been both protracted and severe. He was tall for a human, and rangy, built much along the same lines as Rianthus—indeed, but for his chestnut hair and blue eyes, he reminded Bahzell a great deal of Kilthan's captain—but his haggard face was badly wasted and his chain hauberk hung on his gaunt frame. He moved briskly, and he'd accepted his mistress' arrival with two hradani in tow with remarkable calm, but his hands trembled ever so slightly, and he'd stopped once or twice as if he were short of breath. Still, his equipment was well cared for, and he had the look of a man who knew how to use both the sword at his side and the short horsebow on his back.

The maid, Rekah, was another matter. She was taller than Zarantha, and much fairer. In fact, she was considerably prettier than her mistress, in a soft-edged sort of way. Zarantha could not be many years out of her teens, and her nose was strong and slightly hooked, her hair dark and her triangular face lively but decidedly lean, while Rekah was a bit older, with golden hair, a sweet, oval face, and a straight little nose. She was also better dressed than Zarantha, but she had a pronounced tendency to flutter, and she'd shrunk back in dismay when Bahzell followed her mistress into their poorly furnished rooms. She'd settled down when Zarantha explained, yet her initial squeak of panic seemed a poor augury. Rekah, Bahzell thought, wouldn't have produced a dagger if she'd been caught in an alley; she would have been too busy flailing about and screaming for help.

Still, it was early days yet, he told himself—then snorted at his own thought. From what little he did remember about the Empire of the Spear's geography, they'd have more than sufficient days for him to learn all the strengths and weaknesses of their small party!

The one thing that had truly bothered him was Zarantha's manner when they reached the docks. She'd been brisk and purposeful getting things organized and chivvying Rekah and Tothas through the city, but once they neared the river she'd fallen back beside her maid and become a totally different person. She'd exchanged her torn skirt and cloak for sturdy trousers, a leather cap, and an equally plain coat of Axeman cut before leaving the inn; once at dockside, she'd pulled the cap down over her ears, turned up her coat collar, and huddled down in it almost as if she were trying to hide. She'd been colorless and passive, almost timid, leaving everything in Bahzell's hands without so much as a word, and he hadn't missed how close Tothas stayed to her or the way his hand kept checking his sword hilt.

Of course, this *was* ni'Tarth's domain. That was certainly enough to account for Tothas' attitude, but Zarantha had seemed far less frightened of ni'Tarth earlier. Bahzell couldn't shake the notion that she was worried by something more than the wrath of a Riverside crime lord, however powerful, and he chewed his lip unhappily at the thought. Little though he cared for the situation he'd landed in, he found himself liking Zarantha, almost against his will, and his stubborn sense that there was more—or possibly less—to her than she'd chosen to admit bothered him more than *he* cared to admit.

Unfortunately, Brandark had found the perfect way to distract him from his worries. The Bloody Sword was following through on his threat to write his thrice-bedamned *Lay of Bahzell Bloody-Hand*. Worse, he'd chosen to set it to the tune of a well-known—and dismayingly memorable—drinking song, and he'd insisted on singing the first three verses under his breath while he and Bahzell struggled to get the animals aboard the ferry. Now he sat on the lip of the ferry's single, squat deckhouse, looking down through the open skylight at Rekah and Zarantha while he plucked out the melody on his balalaika and regaled them with his work to date.

Bahzell folded his arms, standing in the very prow of the ferry—as far from his friend as he could get—and gritted his teeth as the balalaika's spritely notes rippled through the creak of the sweeps and the sounds of rushing water. The fact that Brandark's voice was doing a better job than usual of staying with the music did nothing at all to sweeten his mood—and neither did the gurgle of female laughter that greeted the Bloody Sword's efforts.

Bahzell Bahnakson stared glumly ahead into the Dreamwater's drifting mist, and the unpleasant suspicion that this was going to be a very *long* journey filled him.

# CHAPTER SIXTEEN

It wasn't necessary to buy maps after all.

A chance remark from Brandark informed Tothas of their need shortly after the ferry set them ashore once more, and the guardsman blinked, then gave his youthful mistress a scolding look and produced his own map. Bahzell matched the Spearman's look with a glower of his own, but Zarantha—who'd regained her normal spirits as soon as the ferry vanished back into the mists—only grinned, and Brandark's smothered laughter didn't help. Bahzell had already reached the unhappy suspicion that his friend's and Zarantha's souls were entirely too much akin; now he was certain of it.

But at least he could get some idea of where he was bound, and it was even worse than he'd feared. He sat on the cold ground, opened the map across his thighs, found the scale, and located Alfroma, then tried to hide his dismay as he walked thumb and forefinger across the map. Alfroma was six hundred leagues from Riverside as the bird flew, but they were no birds, and this Sherhan place wasn't even shown.

"Could you be showing me just where Sherhan is?" he asked, and Tothas leaned over his shoulder to point to a location southeast of Alfroma. It *would* be on the far side of the city, Bahzell thought, and sat studying the map in glum silence for over ten minutes while frost melted under his backside.

The best of maps could hide unpleasant surprises, but even if this one didn't, following the roads would add another two hundred leagues, and they'd have to hunt and forage on the way. Either that or stop periodically to earn the money, somehow, for the next stage. Worse, Tothas had already assured him the roads got worse— *much* worse—once they left Angthyr.

Of course, they had sound beasts and no wagons. That would be a plus on bad roads, but this little jaunt would take them two months by his most favorable estimate. And that assumed two women and a man fresh from his sickbed could stand the sort of pace on horseback that a Horse Stealer could set on foot. Zarantha probably could; Rekah and Tothas were another matter, and the scarlet and gold leaves were already falling.

He looked up to meet Tothas' eyes, and the Spearman's expression matched his own. The others probably had no idea what they faced. Rekah certainly didn't, or she would have been far less cheerful. He suspected Zarantha had a sounder appreciation of what awaited them, whether she chose to admit it or not, but Brandark, for all his toughness, was city-bred, and he'd never made a forced march through sleet or snow in his life. Bahzell had; that was why winter campaigning had never appealed to him, and, from Tothas' face, he'd seen his own share of winter marches. Clearly, he looked forward to this one no more than Bahzell did, which raised an interesting question. If he knew what he was getting into, why hadn't he even tried to talk Zarantha out of it? Especially in his weakened condition?

Bahzell was fairly certain he wouldn't have liked the answer to that question if he'd known it. He sighed once more, then stood, handed the map back to Tothas, shouldered his arbalest, and set off through the ground fog with the others at his heels.

The fog burned away as the morning drew on, and Bahzell's heart rose as his ill-assorted party moved more briskly than he'd dared hope.

Zarantha's mule proved just as fractious as its wicked eyes suggested. It made a determined attempt to take a mouthful out of Bahzell's arm when she pushed up past Brandark to ask the Horse Stealer a question, but she controlled the abortive lunge with the ease of long practice and favored it with a description of its ancestry, personal habits, and probable fate that made both hradani cock their ears in appreciation. The mule seemed unimpressed, but though it eyed Bahzell's arm with wistful longing it also settled down, and the Horse Stealer answered Zarantha's question. She reined around and pressed with her heels to ask for a trot, and Bahzell snorted as he watched her post gracefully back to her place beside Rekah. Stay on a horse, indeed!

Tothas and Brandark changed off places at midday. The armsman rode companionably at Bahzell's shoulder, and the Horse Stealer began picking his brain about the conditions they were likely to face. The hradani didn't much care for what he learned, but that wasn't Tothas' fault. The Spearman's answers were those of a man who knew exactly what Bahzell was asking, and why. They also confirmed his own insight into the rigors stretching before them, and his every word only deepened Bahzell's puzzlement. The man was obviously of officer quality; Rianthus would have given him platoon or company command in a heartbeat. What he was doing with a penniless "noblewoman" like Zarantha baffled the hradani, but he was plainly more than a simple hireling. Even when he rode at the head of their short column with Bahzell, the corner of his eye was perpetually on Zarantha, and the answers that were so forthcoming when it came to road conditions and terrain became politely vague whenever the conversation turned towards his mistress.

It would have required someone far stupider than Bahzell to think Zarantha hadn't concealed a great deal about herself, yet the fact that Tothas was so ready to support her deception—whatever it was—reassured the Horse Stealer oddly. He couldn't have said why, except that he found himself liking Tothas even more than he liked Zarantha herself. Besides, he told himself, Zarantha might have any number of legitimate reasons for caution. Her willingness to travel at this time of year was compelling evidence her situation was grave, if not desperate, and if she'd manipulated Bahzell and Brandark into helping her, that didn't mean she had reason to trust two hradani she hadn't yet had time to learn to know.

They held to a good pace all day and continued straight past the village they reached shortly before sunset. Bahzell longed for the comfort of a roof and walls, but they had too few kormaks to squander on inns. He kept his eye out as they moved on down the high road, but it was Tothas who spotted the perfect campsite. A thicket of intermixed pine and fir provided a thick, resinous windbreak and firewood in plenty, a small stream offered fresh water, and Bahzell accepted the Spearman's suggestion with gratitude.

His new companions had borne up well and maintained a brisk pace, and there were surprisingly few rough edges to the way they made camp. Rekah might be a flutterer who'd clearly heard entirely too many romantic ballads, but she was also an excellent cook, and she took over the fire pit as soon as Brandark and Tothas finished it. Bahzell and Zarantha saw to the horses and mules, and her skill with them confirmed his suspicion that she must have been put into her first saddle before she could walk. Nor did she let the "Lady" before her name stand in the way of any task that needed doing. While Brandark and Bahzell gathered wood and Tothas tended the fire, she sat peeling potatoes and carrots for her maid without so much as a hint that it might be beneath her.

Supper was as delicious as it smelled, and no one seemed inclined to sit up afterward. They'd covered forty miles from Riverside, and all of them were fatigued, but the possibility that ni'Tarth might have sent someone after them only reinforced Bahzell's inherent caution. No one argued his decision to set watches, but Tothas started to protest when Bahzell divided the task into thirds and asked Zarantha and Rekah to take the third watch without assigning him to one . . . until a single quiet sentence from Zarantha shut his mouth with a snap. Bahzell longed to know just what she'd said, but the fast, liquid sentence was in some dialect not even Brandark recognized. Whatever it was, it worked, and Tothas wrapped himself in his blankets without another word.

The night was uneventful—aside from the usual, chaotic dream fragments that tormented Bahzell—but a quiet, horrible rasping sound pulled the Horse Stealer awake with the dawn. He rolled over and sat up, and his ears lowered in shocked sympathy as he saw its source.

Tothas sat hunched in his bedroll, coughing as if to bring his lungs up while Rekah watched anxiously and Zarantha sat beside him. The Spearman fought his bitter, convulsive coughs, strangling his sounds against a white-knuckled fist, and Zarantha held his wasted body in her arms. One hand cupped the back of his head, urging his cheek against her shoulder, and quiet agony had replaced her usual smiling deviltry. Her hands were gentle as she murmured encouragement into his ear, and tears gleamed in her eyes as she met the Horse Stealer's gaze. There was anger with the anguish in those eyes—not at Bahzell, but at whatever had wreaked such ruin on Tothas—and a silent plea, and the hradani gazed back at her in silence for a long moment. Then he nodded slowly, laid back down, and turned his back while Tothas fought his lonely battle.

The armsman coughed with wracking desperation for at least fifteen minutes before he could stop, but his face showed no sign of it when Bahzell stopped pretending to sleep twenty minutes later, and if he was a little slower as he saddled his horse the next morning, Bahzell didn't begrudge the time. He couldn't. Zarantha might play whatever role she pleased, but her devotion to her armsman disarmed his distrust. And his heart went out to Tothas' gallantry when the Spearman finally mounted as if nothing at all had happened, with a refusal to ask for quarter any hradani could respect.

They stopped in Kor Keep for supplies.

They were too poor for the gouging hradani would invite, so Bahzell and Brandark sent the humans off with their skimpy funds, and Zarantha did far better than they'd dared hope. She returned with the pack mule loaded heavily enough to fold its ears resentfully back, and managed it for barely a third of the contents of Brandark's purse. The Bloody Sword gave Bahzell one look, then handed the purse back to her and made her their official treasurer.

She'd managed to pick up a few extra blankets and enough sacked grain to eke out their animals' grazing, as well, and Bahzell actually began to feel a bit optimistic. Nothing could keep the journey from being unpleasant, but it seemed there were advantages to traveling with a poverty-stricken noblewoman. At least she seemed to have learned to pinch kormaks until they squealed!

The weather remained clear for the next few days, but the nights grew steadily chillier, and Tothas was obviously in constant pain. Yet aside from an occasional coughing fit—few, mercifully, as terrible as that first one—he neither slowed them nor once complained, and Bahzell soon realized he'd never met a braver man. The Spearman's illness was a more exhausting—and frightening—battle than the Horse Stealer had ever faced, yet Tothas fought it with unflinching courage, and Bahzell was startled by his own pride on the day he discovered he could call this man a friend.

It was easier than he'd expected when Zarantha first entrapped him. Tothas spoke seldom, but what he said made sense. More, his absolute devotion to Zarantha was the sort of loyalty hradani could appreciate, and his unwavering, uncomplaining gallantry won Brandark's heart, as well as Bahzell's.

Yet there was something more to Tothas, something in his attitude, and they were past Kor Keep on the way to the Duchy of Carchon before it dawned on the Horse Stealer what that something was. The Spearman had never looked at him and seen a hradani; he'd seen only a man, to be judged on his own merits, without prejudice or preconception.

It was the first time anyone—even Hartan—had done that since he'd left Navahk, and a small, ignoble part of him resented it, as if Tothas' acceptance were a sort of secret condescension. That shamed him when he recognized it, for Tothas never condescended. Indeed, he held others to high standards—the same ones he held himself to—and his was no hasty judgment. He'd watched both hradani for days before he decided about them; once he had, he accepted Bahzell's leadership with the same unwavering support, if not the same devotion, he gave Zarantha.

He *trusted* the two hradani, and that trust was a two-edged sword. When one was trusted, one must prove worthy of *being* trusted, and Bahzell knew Tothas' trust had transformed an arrangement forced upon him by expediency into something far more constraining. But there was a curious satisfaction in the transformation, a sense of belonging, of doing something worth the doing because those doing it with him were good people.

And they *were* good people, despite whatever secret they hid.

However rough the road, however tired Zarantha might be, Bahzell had yet to hear her first complaint, and she and Brandark had joined forces to keep his own life from becoming boring. She was actually helping the Bloody Sword refine his accursed composition. The two of them shared their labors with the others most nights, but at least Brandark let her do the singing.

Rekah was more mercurial, and she had her bad days, especially as the nights grew colder. But she did her part and a bit more, and however grumpy she might be of an evening, she was always up early, always ready for the next day, be it ever so grueling.

And then there was Tothas—a man, Bahzell had realized, who *knew* he was dying in the saddle. That was the reason he described the roads ahead so carefully. He'd chosen the hradani as his successor, the man who would see Zarantha safely home if he himself could not, for he was a man who would do his duty to the end, whatever that end was, and *that*, Bahzell realized, was what truly drew him so strongly to the Spearman.

No wonder Zarantha was so fiercely devoted to her armsman. No wonder she held him in her arms when he woke coughing and watched him with hidden hurt as they rode. She might laugh at Brandark's sallies or tease the others to hide her pain, but that, Bahzell knew, was because it would have shamed Tothas if she hadn't—and understanding how deeply she cared for her armsman touched the Horse Stealer with fear whenever he tried to guess what drove her to lead a dying man she loved into the teeth of winter.

A cold wind moaned in the leafless scrub of the lonely Carchon Hills. They were near the top of the range; tomorrow they would start down to the border between Korwin and Carchon, and Bahzell hoped they'd find warmer weather when they did. The picketed horses and mules stood silent under frost-glazed blankets, cold stars glittered pitilessly, and he shivered as he returned to the fire to build it back up. He'd been colder than this, but that didn't mean he liked it, and it was only going to get worse from here.

Flames crackled about the fresh wood, and he kept his head turned to preserve his night vision. He had no reason to anticipate trouble—they were well beyond ni'Tarth's reach, and these hills were all but unpopulated—but trouble had a way of coming without sending word ahead, and he had no mind to be fire-dazzled if it did.

He resumed his slow walk around their perimeter. Brandark had found a boulder to use as a heat reflector and slept between it and the fire with only his beaky nose poked out of his blankets. Rekah and Zarantha had pooled their bedrolls and body heat beside him, and Tothas, by common consent, had the warmest spot of all, in the low hollow with the fire itself. It was lonely, out here in the moaning night while the others slept, but Bahzell was grateful he was awake, not sleeping himself and prey to his maddening dreams. Frost squeaked under his boots as he moved still further from the fire, eyes searching the dark, and his mind was busy.

The dreams refused to release him. They besieged him night after night, until he dreaded the moment his eyes closed. Familiarity had worn the jagged edge of terror smooth, but the terror hadn't gone away. It couldn't. It was the demon he fought as Tothas fought his hacking spasms, and he was tired of it. So very, very tired. He closed his mind to the dreams, rejected them, pushed them out of memory with all his strength, yet *still* they plagued him, laughing at his efforts to outrun them. There was no mercy in them . . . and nowhere he could hide from them.

He sighed heavily, then stiffened as a boot scuffed behind him. He whirled, reaching for his sword, then relaxed.

"I was thinking you were asleep," he said.

"I was." Tothas' voice was raspy, as if he hovered on the brink of one of his coughing fits, but his face was calm in the starlight. He'd wrapped a blanket over his cloak, and he stepped past the hradani to sit on another boulder, drawing the blanket tighter about him, and shivered.

"A bitter night," he said quietly. "Not much good for sleeping anyway, I suppose."

"Aye, but not so bitter as we'll be seeing soon enough," Bahzell replied in a tone of quiet grimness.

"No, not that bitter." Tothas gazed at the toes of his boots for a long, silent moment, then raised his eyes once more. "You're troubled by your dreams, Bahzell," he said in the soft voice of a man making a simple statement, and the hradani stiffened, ears half-flat, and looked down at him. A minute passed, then two, and Tothas only gazed back up at him and waited.

"Aye." Bahzell cleared his throat. "Aye, I am that. I'd hoped you'd not notice."

"I don't think Rekah or Lady Zarantha have. I'm not sure about My Lady—she sees things others miss—but I don't sleep so well these days." Tothas allowed himself a small smile. Not bitter or resentful, but one of what might almost have been wry amusement. "I've heard you muttering in your sleep. I don't speak your language, but I know trouble when I hear it, and I thought—"

He shrugged, but his invitation hovered, and Bahzell sighed and sat beside him. He placed himself to cut the wind that tugged at Tothas' blanket without even realizing he had and rubbed his chin in thought, then sighed again.

"Aye, it's trouble you've heard. No, let's be honest; it's fear," he admitted, and it was amazingly easy to confess it to this man.

"Why?" Tothas asked simply, and Bahzell told him. He told him everything, even things he'd never told Brandark. Of course, Brandark was hradani. He'd understood the terror those dreams held without telling, but there were depths of fear Bahzell had never been able to expose to his friend. Not in so many words. Not with the honesty with which he revealed it to Tothas there in the windy blackness.

The Spearman heard him out without comment, other than a thoughtful frown as Bahzell described Jothan Tarlnasa's appearance at Derm and a smothered chuckle at the way Tarlnasa had left the barge. But when the hradani ran out of words at last and sat staring down at his empty fists, Tothas cleared his throat and laid a hand on Bahzell's knee.

"I understand your fear, Bahzell," he said. "I don't suppose I would have if you hadn't explained it—you and Brandark are the first hradani I've ever met, and we in the South Weald know little about your people. The West Weald and Border Weald run up against the Broken Bone hradani; they may know more, but all most Spearmen know of them are the old tales of the Fall, and I've never heard them from the hradani side. What was done to you—what you call the Rage—" He shook his head, and his hand tightened on Bahzell's knee. Then he released it with a pat and rose.

"We all lost in the Fall," he said, standing with his back to the Horse Stealer, his voice frayed by the wind.

"We were all betrayed, yet none, I think, so badly as you. So, yes, I understand your fear. But—" he turned back "—perhaps there's no need for it. Dreams need not be evidence of fresh betrayal, and the fact that this Tarlnasa fellow is undoubtedly an idiot doesn't make him a liar. It may truly be the gods speaking to you."

"Aye." Bahzell rose to stare out into the night beside him. "I've thought on that. I'll not deny it was in my mind at first that it was some poxy wizard, but my folk remember a thing or two about wizards. Old wives' tales maybe, but we've not forgotten what was done to us, and I'm thinking this thing's lasted too long for such as that. Aye, and it's grown no weaker, and it should have, with the leagues I've put behind me since it started. I suppose it's grateful I should be if it's not, but that's not the way of it. The Dark Gods have brought naught but ruin to my folk, and as for the Gods of Light—"

He clenched his jaw, staring into the dark until his eyes ached, then looked down at the Spearman, and his voice was harsh and ugly.

"I've no use for gods, Tothas. Those of the Dark may torment my folk, but at least they're honest about it! And what have the precious '*good*' gods ever done for me or mine? Did they help us? Or did they leave us to rot when the other Races of Man turned their backs to us for things we never chose to do? Evil—aye, that I can be understanding, but where's the use in gods that prate of how '*good*' they are yet do naught at all, at all, for those as need it, and why should I be giving a fart in Phrobus' face for them?!"

Silence stretched out between them once more, and then Tothas sighed.

"A hard question," he said, "and one I can't answer. I'm no priest, only a warrior. I know what I believe, but I'm not you, not a hradani."

The sorrow in his voice shamed Bahzell somehow. The

Horse Stealer bit his lip and laid a hand on his friend's shoulder.

"Tell me what you believe," he said so softly it surprised him.

"I believe there are gods worth following," Tothas said simply. "I don't understand all that happens in the world, but I know evil could never flourish without the Races of Man. It's *us*, Bahzell—we're the ones who turn to the Dark or the Light, choose which we'll serve. Good people may do terrible things through fear or foolishness or stupidity—even spite—but what if there *were* no 'good' people? What if there were never *anyone* to take a stand, to say, 'No, this is evil, and I will not allow it!'?"

"And who's been saying that for my folk?" It should have come out bitter and filled with hate, but somehow it didn't.

"No one." Tothas sighed. "But perhaps that's the reason for your dreams—had you thought of that? You say you've no use for gods, Bahzell. Aren't there *any* you could think worthy of your service?"

"None." Bahzell grunted. He cocked his head, looking down at the Spearman, and his tone softened once more. "You're after being a good man, Tothas." The Spearman flushed and started to shake his head, but the hradani's voice stopped him. "Don't be shaking your head at me—and don't think it's in my mind to flatter you. You're no saint, and a dead pain in the arse a saint would be in the field, I'm thinking! But you've guts, and loyalty, and a readiness to understand, and those are things even a murdering hradani can value. But—" Bahzell's deep voice rumbled even softer, gentle yet unflinching "—I'm knowing how sick you are, what it is that loyalty's costing you. So tell me, Tothas—what god is it *you* serve, and why?"

"I serve the Gods of Light." Tothas' voice accepted the reference to his illness without a quaver, and he shrugged. "Oh, I'm sure others serve them better, but I do the best I can—when I'm not feeling sorry for myself." He smiled up at the towering hradani. "I thank Orr for wisdom, when it can get through my thick skull, and Silendros for beauty, when I have the eyes to see it. When I've time for it, I sit on a hill somewhere out in the plains of the South Weald and look at the trees and grass and the summer sky and thank Toragan for them. But I'm a warrior, Bahzell. It's my trade, the thing I do best, and its Tomanak I follow. The Sword God can be hard, but He's just, and He stands for the things *I'd* like to stand for. For skill in battle, for honor and courage in defeat, for decency in victory, and loyalty."

"But *why?*" Bahzell pressed. "Oh, aye, I can respect those things, but why turn to a god for them? Why thank a god for wisdom when it comes out of your own head? Or for beauty, when it's your own eyes that have the seeing of it? Or for guts and loyalty, when those things come from in *here*—" his huge hand brushed Tothas' chest "—and not from out there?" The same hand rose and gestured at the skies.

"You follow them, yet not one of them's reached down to you and said, 'This is a good man, who's been after doing all I ask of him, and I take his illness from him.' Not *one* of them, Tothas, and *still* you follow!" He shook his head. "That's a thing no hradani would be understanding. It's not my folk's way to ask others for aught. We've learned the hard way that it won't be given, that there's no one and naught to count on but our own selves when all's said and done. What we have, we build or take for ourselves, and spit on 'gods' who've no time for such as us. A man looks after his own in this world, Tothas, and it's lucky he is if he can do it, for no one else will!"

Tothas smiled.

"That sounds to me like a man who's angry at what he hears himself saying."

"Whether I'm liking it or hating it won't change what *is*," Bahzell shot back. "It's the way of the world, and no one knows it better than hradani, for we've seen it too often. Aye, we've had a bellyful of it!"

The Spearman looked up at him for another long moment, then cocked his head.

"Why are you here, Bahzell?" he asked softly.

"Eh?" Bahzell blinked down at the human.

"Why are you here?" Tothas repeated. "In a world where a man looks after his own and Phrobus take the hindmost, why did you save Lady Zarantha in Riverside and why are you still here? Why didn't you leave us to fend for ourselves once we left the city?"

"Because I've a head of solid rock," Bahzell said bitterly, and Tothas' laugh was soft.

"I believe that. Oh, yes, I believe that, my friend! But if you believe that's the *only* reason, you know yourself less well than you think."

"Now don't you be thinking I'm aught but what I am," Bahzell said uneasily. "Stupid, aye, and one who's yet to learn to think before he acts—that I'll grant you! And maybe I've a wee bit of guts, and a notion my word should be meaning something when I give it, but I'm no knight in shining armor. No, and I've no least desire to *be* one, either!"

"'A knight in shining armor'?" There was a smile in Tothas' voice, and he slapped the hradani on the elbow. "No, you're certainly not *that*, Bahzell Bahnakson! The gods only know all that you may be, but I don't think even they could see you as that!"

"Aye, and don't you be forgetting it!" Bahzell snorted.

"I won't," Tothas reassured him. He gathered his blanket about him and shivered, then turned back towards the fire. "But while I'm remembering you aren't, you might ask yourself whoever said you should be? Or why in Tomanāk's name the gods should need one?"

Bahzell stared after him, ears at half-cock, and the Spearman chuckled as he picked his way back to his bedroll through the windy cold.

# CHAPTER SEVENTEEN

The rain started at dawn; by midday the racing spatter of drops had become a steady, bone-chilling downpour.

Bahzell slogged through it, head bent against the wind while his cloak snapped about his knees like a living thing, and a weary litany of curses rolled through his mind at what the icy rain was doing to Tothas. The armsman rode in the center of the column, huddled deep in his cloak, and Zarantha and Rekah both rode upwind of him in a vain effort to shield him. It was a sign of his distress that he didn't even notice what they were trying to do, and the Horse Stealer gritted his teeth every time one of those terrible, strangling coughs twisted the Spearman.

The sloping road was ankle-deep in watery mud that wore away at their strength and spirits, and the storm cut the already short day still shorter. Bahzell had started searching for a suitable campsite before midafternoon, but the hillsides were clothed in scrub, without sheltering trees. Even without the soaking rain, firewood would have been hard to find, and the thought of subjecting Tothas to a fireless camp in such weather tightened Bahzell's belly. But it was evening now; the light was going fast, they *had* to stop soon, and he was almost desperate when a flicker of movement caught the corner of his eye.

He turned his head quickly, but whatever it was had vanished into a barren hillside. His raised hand halted the column, and he reached up under his cloak; it was an awkward way to draw a sword, but he managed it, and Brandark walked his horse up beside him.

"What?" Even the Bloody Sword's tenor was worn and creaky, and Bahzell nodded at the hill.

"I'm thinking I saw something yonder."

"What?" Brandark repeated with a bit more interest.

"Now that's what I'm none too sure of," the Horse Stealer admitted. "But whatever it was, it up and disappeared."

"Up there?" Brandark eyed the rocky, water-running slope skeptically.

"Aye." Bahzell studied the hillside for another moment, then shrugged. "Wait here," he said shortly, and started up the slope.

It was hard going, and he couldn't have told Brandark why he was bothering, yet something poked at the corner of his brain. Chill water ran knee-deep as he waded up a gully towards the point where the movement had disappeared, and he was almost there when he heard a deep, angry squall.

He rocked back on his heels as a tawny shape flowed out of the very ground. It was a dire cat—not the enormous predator that ruled the Eastwall Mountains, but the smaller cousin that roamed their foothills—and Bahzell's ears flattened as black lips wrinkled back from four-inch ivory fangs and the cat squalled again, furious at his intrusion.

But dire cats were as intelligent as they were deadly, and the beast let out yet a third squall—this one of pure frustration—as it digested Bahzell's size and the menace of his sword. It hunkered down on the rock, tail lashing as if to pounce, then hissed in disgust and vanished into the rain in a single, prodigious leap.

Bahzell released the deep, tense breath he hadn't realized he was holding, but even as he exhaled a suspicion as to why the cat had been so angry touched him. His eyes narrowed, and he moved forward again more eagerly.

There! An out-thrust shoulder of rock had hidden it from below, but a narrow slit pierced the hillside. It was tall enough even for Bahzell, though it would be a tight fit for his shoulders, and he edged into it. He felt his way for several yards, rubbing against the rock, muscles taut and sword ready. No dire cat would have abandoned a regular lair without a fight, sword or no sword, but Bahzell wasn't about to assume anything, and if the cat had a mate—

It didn't. Another ten feet, and gray light beckoned. The rock opened up, and he inched further forward, then came to a stop and smiled broadly.

It was a cave, and large enough for all their mounts, at that. Runoff cascaded from an open cleft in the high roof into a churning pool which must have an underground outlet, since it hadn't risen to flow out through the cave entrance. There was no fuel here, but he'd gathered a heavy load of kindling as soon as the rain started. The packhorse had tossed its head in protest when he'd added the wood to its load and covered it with a cloak, but it would be enough to dry whatever fuel he and Brandark could gather from the scrub at the base of the hill. All they had to do was get the beasts up here. That didn't promise to be easy, but Bahzell Bahnakson would cheerfully have tackled a far more difficult task to get out of the rain.

He sheathed his sword and started back to tell the others.

Something woke him, and, for a change, it wasn't a dream. He sat up, straining his ears as he wondered what it *had* been, but he detected no danger.

Red and yellow light flowed over rock walls as the small fire crackled cheerfully, and the smell of horses and mules mingled with the smoke. The combined body heat of animals and people had helped the fire warm the cave, and his bedroll was almost dry. Taken all together, he was more comfortable than he'd had any right to expect after such a day, and he'd tumbled into his blankets in weary gratitude. But he was oddly wide awake now, and he stretched.

Brandark sat cross-legged by the cave entrance, sheathed sword on his thighs. The rain must have eased, for the water no longer chattered and hissed into the pool. It fell gently, almost musically, soft enough for Brandark to hear Bahzell stir and turn his head.

"What are you doing up?" he asked quietly as the Horse Stealer rose.

"I've no idea," Bahzell replied, equally quietly. He yawned and stretched again, then shrugged and parked himself beside Brandark. "But it's up I am, so if you're minded to turn in—?"

"It's my watch," Brandark disagreed with a little headshake.

"In that case, I'll just be keeping you company for a bit—unless you've some objection?"

Brandark chuckled and shook his head again, and Bahzell looked over his shoulder to survey the others. Tothas looked much better than he had when they half-carried him into the cave, and Zarantha and Rekah were curled up like kittens under the blankets they shared. The soft, steady sound of breathing carried through the musical patter of water and the crackle of the fire, and an odd sense of safety—of comfort—seemed to fill the cave.

He turned back to join Brandark in watching the cave's narrow stone throat, and a companionable silence enveloped them. They'd have to move on in the morning, and the fact that the rain had eased for now was no guarantee tomorrow wouldn't be still worse, but all that mattered just now was the peace of the moment, and he savored it almost sensually.

He didn't know how long he'd sat there when he heard the abrupt scuff of a boot on stone. He stiffened, ears rising, and felt Brandark tense beside him, but neither said anything. They just sat there, staring down the narrow passageway, and the boot scuffed again. And then, suddenly, a small, slender, brown-haired woman in a rain-beaded cloak turned a bend and stopped dead.

Bahzell's ears went straight up in astonishment as the woman found herself face-to-face with two hradani and simply stood there. She didn't yelp in panic, didn't turn to flee—didn't even stiffen in surprise. She only gazed at them with grave brown eyes, then shrugged and walked calmly forward.

"Good evening," she said in a soft, husky contralto, and Bahzell blinked. He turned a look of disbelief on Brandark, and the same expression looked back at him. Then the two of them turned as one to the newcomer, and Bahzell cleared his throat.

"Ah, and a good evening to yourself."

"Would you mind dreadfully if I shared your cave?" she asked in that same calm voice, as unruffled as if things like this happened to her every day. "It's rather wet outside," she added with a small smile, and Bahzell shook his head in bemusement. "Thank you," she said, and untied her cloak.

She must, the Horse Stealer thought, be insane. She had to have seen the light of their fire before she ever started up the entry passage, but not only had she walked slap up to them and refused to turn a hair when she found a pair of hradani, she wasn't even armed—not with so much as a dagger!

She seemed totally unconcerned as she stepped forward, draped her cloak near the fire, and unslung the small harp case she'd worn on her back beneath it. She settled down beside the fire and cocked her head as she regarded them with those huge brown eyes.

"Something smells good," she announced.

"Ah, help yourself," Brandark invited, and gestured at the covered pot of beans and salt pork left over from supper.

"Thank you," she said again, and reached into her belt pouch. The knife she produced would have been as useless for self-defense as the fork and spoon that came with it, but gems glittered in their handles, and Bahzell's eyes narrowed. Those eating utensils would have been at home on a duke's table; no one in his right mind flashed something that valuable before two unknown warriors of *any* stripe, much less two with the reputation of hradani. He watched her select a tin bowl and ladle food into it, then cleared his throat.

"Don't be taking me wrongly," he said carefully, "but are you after being in the habit of walking up to strange camps like this?"

"Like what?"

"Like what?!" Bahzell blinked and glanced at Brankdark again. "What I mean to be saying, ah, Lady, is that, well, not everyone's exactly— I mean—"

He broke off in unaccustomed confusion, and she smiled at him. It was quite a lovely smile, he thought, watching it light her triangular, spritelike face, and felt himself smile back for no good reason.

"Thank you for your concern, but I'll be all right. I'm only a wandering bard, after all. No one would hurt me."

"Begging your pardon," Brandark said, "but I wouldn't count on that. What my friend means is that one of these days you're likely to run into someone who *will* hurt you— or worse."

"Well, you two won't, will you?" Amusement flickered in her grave eyes, and the hradani found themselves shaking their heads in unison. "There, you see?" She swallowed a mouthful of food and sighed. "Ummm! Delicious. I miss good, simple cooking like this."

"Uh, yes," Brandark said helplessly. Someone should lock this lunatic up in a nice, safe cage, but her simple confidence in her own safety was a shield that baffled him. He knew she was insane, and so did Bahzell, but how did they tell *her* that?

She smiled at them and returned to her food with slow, obvious relish. She cleaned the bowl of the last morsel, chasing the final bean around and around it with almost childish delight, then sighed once more.

"Oh, that was *nice!*" She closed her eyes as if to savor some special treat, then opened them with another smile. "Thank you for your generosity."

"It was only a bowl of beans," Brandark protested, and she shrugged.

"Perhaps. But it was all you had, and you shared it with a stranger. How can I repay you?"

"Brandark's the right of it," Bahzell said uncomfortably. "It was naught but a bowl of beans, and it's welcome to it you were."

"Oh, I insist on paying *something*," she said with yet another of those lovely smiles, and reached for her harp. "If you won't accept anything else, perhaps I could sing for my supper?"

Eyebrows arched above brilliant eyes, and the hradani

nodded like puppets as she uncased her harp. A corner of Bahzell's brain said something very strange was happening, but the thought was tiny, lost and unimportant.

She drew out her harp, and air hissed between Brandark's teeth. The strings shone silver in a frame of midnight ebony, and faceted gems flashed back the fire from the tuning pegs. The forearm was a woman, draped in a flowing, archaic gown, mouth open in song, and the Bloody Sword blinked as the bard tucked the instrument against her shoulder, for the carved face matched her own. He started to speak, but then her fingers stroked the strings and he froze, mouth hanging open, as music filled the cave.

No one could wring that rich, rippling purity from a harp that small! It wasn't the sound of a single harp at all—he *knew* it wasn't. Viols and lutes sounded in the background, laughing dulcimers wove in and out between the harp notes, bassoons and oboes crooned to violins and the deep, sweet voice of cellos, and he knew it couldn't happen even as it did. But then she opened her mouth, and he forgot the music, forgot the smell of horses and smoke and wet cloth and the rock he sat upon. He forgot everything, for there *was* nothing—nothing but that voice.

He could never remember it clearly later. That was the cruelest curse and the greatest blessing of all, for if he *had* been able to remember, his love of music would have died forever. Who could be content with the mud pies of children playing in a ditch when he'd seen the work of Saramantha's greatest sculptors? If he were able to remember—really *remember*—that voice, he would hunger only to hear it once more, and its perfection would turn all other voices, all other music to dust and ashes in his mouth.

Yet if he could never recall it clearly, he would always know he'd heard it once. That for a single night, in a smelly winter cave, he'd experienced all the splendor after which he'd fumbled for so many years. Not death itself could take that from him, and he knew he would hear its echo in every other song.

She sang words they'd never heard, in a language they'd never known, and it didn't matter. They sat motionless, two barbarian hradani, lost in a beauty beyond imagining, and she took them with her. She swept them away into another place, where time was irrelevant and there was no world, no reality, no meaning but the music of her harp, the majesty of her voice, and the glow of her huge brown eyes. They soared with her, flew on her wings, tasted things for which there were no words in any language, and then, as gently as she'd borne them aloft, she returned them to their own world, and the greatest magic of all was that she did not break their hearts. That they returned unscarred, content to be who and what they were, for it would have been so easy—so unthinkably easy—to surrender all they'd ever been for the chance to become two more notes in that glorious sound.

Her voice died, her hand stilled the strings, and Brandark Brandarkson went to his knees before her.

"My Lady," he whispered, and tears fogged his voice and soaked his face.

"Don't be silly, Brandark." Her voice was no longer a weapon to break men's hearts but laughing and tender, and her slender hand brushed his head. She gripped an ear and tugged, and he looked up, his own eyes suddenly laughing through his tears, and she nodded. "Better," she said. "Now stand up, Brandark. You've never come to me on your knees before; I see no reason to begin now."

He smiled and rose, and Bahzell blinked like a man waking from sleep.

"Who—?" he began, but then words failed him. He could only stare at Brandark, and the Bloody Sword touched his shoulder.

"Chesmirsa," he said very, very softly. "The Singer of Light."

Bahzell's eyes flew wide, and he jerked upright. He towered two feet and more taller than the woman by the fire, but she'd put aside her mortality. He was less than a child before her, and fear and confusion boiled through him.

"I—" His voice died, and she smiled once more.

"Sit, Bahzell." It was a request when she could have commanded, and he sank back onto the rock while he stared at her. She nodded to Brandark, and the Bloody Sword sat beside him once more, eyes fixed upon the goddess' face. "Thank you," she said softly. She laid her harp in her lap and leaned forward across it, still a slender, brown-haired woman and yet infinitely more, and her gentle eyes were compassionate. "I know how confused you are—both of you—and I suppose I was wicked to sneak up on you, but would you *really* have preferred a flash of light and a roll of thunder?" All the merriment of a universe danced in her dimpled smile, and they felt themselves smiling back. "Besides," she added, "to be greeted as a mortal and offered the kindness of mortals—that, my friends, is a gift whose value you cannot begin to imagine."

"But . . . but why?" Brandark asked, and the silver, rippling magic of her laugh went through them like a sword.

"Because of your friend, Brandark—and you. You were the only reason I *could* come here, and I have a message for you, but it's Bahzell's stubbornness that brings me to deliver it here and now."

"My stubbornness?" Bahzell rumbled, and she nodded.

"Your stubbornness. Your elemental, pigheaded, stiff-necked, iron-pated, wonderful hradani stubbornness."

"I'm not after understanding," he said with unwonted uncertainty.

"Of course not; you've been fighting for months *not* to understand."

"The dreams?" His voice was suddenly sharper, and she nodded again.

"The dreams." A touch of sternness gilded her reply. "You've been doing the equivalent of jamming your fingers in your ears and drumming your heels on the floor long enough, Bahzell."

"Is that what I've been doing, now?" he asked more challengingly. Brandark touched his arm, but the Horse Stealer's eyes were fixed on Chesmirsa's face, and she cocked her head.

"Of course it is. Come now, Bahzell, would we send you dreams you couldn't understand if we had a choice?"

"I've no way of knowing," he said flatly. "I'm naught but a hradani, Lady. We've no experience with how or what gods send to folk they care about."

Brandark inhaled sharply, yet the goddess didn't even wince. Sorrow dimmed her glorious eyes for just a moment, but not anger, and she sighed.

"I know how you feel about us, Bahzell Bahnakson," she said gently, "and who are we to blame you? If you were less of what you are your anger with us would be less, as well . . . and the time to send a hradani dreams would not have come."

"My anger, is it?" Bahzell rose once more, meeting her gaze on his own two feet, and his eyes glittered. He felt her presence, knew she was veiling her power, that if she'd loosed it upon him he could never have stood before it, but he felt no awe. Respect and wonder, yes, but not awe. His people had suffered too much—been *left* to suffer too much—for that.

"Yes, your anger. And your fear, Bahzell." His eyes flashed, and she raised a graceful hand. "Not of us, but lest we 'betray' your people once again by turning our backs upon them. But I tell you this, Bahzell Bahnakson, and I do not lie; what happened to your people was none of our doing, and its wounds cut deeper than even you can imagine. We've labored for a millennium to undo it, whether you knew it or not, but the final healing must be yours. *You* must take the final step—you and all your people. No one else can take it for you."

"Words, Lady," Bahzell said stubbornly. "All I hear are words."

"No, Bahzell. All you've heard so far have been *my* words, and this task isn't mine. It was laid upon my brother Tomanāk—and upon you."

"Upon *me?!*"

"You. It will be no easy task, Bahzell Bahnakson, and it will bring you pain beyond your dreams, for my brother's province is war and justice, and those are hard masters for man or god. But this is the task for which you were born, the proper challenge for your strength and courage and stubbornness, and there will be joy with the pain. Yet it's also a burden no one can compel you to shoulder, one no unwilling back could bear even had we the right to demand your obedience."

"Lady," the Horse Stealer spoke slowly, each word forged of iron, "I'll bow down to no one, god, demon, or devil. What I do, I'll do because I *choose* to do it, and for no other reason."

"I know. *We* know," Chesmirsa said. "Nor is it my task to ask you to accept this burden. I ask you only to consider it, only to be willing to hear so that you *can* choose when the time comes. Is that so much for anyone to ask?"

Bahzell met her eyes levelly, then shook his head, almost against his will.

"Thank you," she said softly, and her eyes told him she knew how hard it had been to make even that concession. "But as the choice must be your own, so must the decision to hear. You will be troubled by no more dreams, Bahzell Bahnakson, but think well and hard upon what I've told you. When the time comes that you're ready to hear, then hear you shall. And if you never decide you're ready, then we will leave you in the peace you desire."

Bahzell recognized an oath when he heard one, and he bent his head in acknowledgment. The goddess gazed at him for one more moment, then turned her eyes to Brandark, and her face lightened.

"And so to you." The Bloody Sword looked up once more, his eyes bright, and she smiled. "Ah, Brandark! Brandark! What *shall* I do with you?"

"Do with me, Lady?" he asked hesitantly, and her smile became an urchin's grin.

"Alas, Brandark, you have the soul of a poet, but the other tools—!" He felt himself blush, yet her eyes lit a bubble of laughter in his heart even as she shook her head at him.

"I do my best, My Lady," he said humbly, and she nodded.

"That you do, and always have. But the truth, Brandark, is that you were never meant for the task you thought. You are too much my brother's, too apt to other tasks. You will never be a bard."

"Never?" Brandark Brandarkson had never dreamed he could feel such sorrow—or that so much joy could wrap itself about the hurt—and his goddess smiled upon him.

"Never," she said firmly. "Music you will have always, and my blessing on your joy in it, but another career awaits you. One that will demand all you have and are, and which will fill you with a joy you never knew to seek. I promise you that, and—" her eyes danced at him "—I think you'll find it one to suit a poet's soul. Live it well, Brandark."

"I'll . . . try, My Lady," he whispered, and she touched his head once more. Then she returned her harp to its case and slung it upon her back. She shook out her plain, everyday cloak and draped it across her shoulders, and smiled at them.

"You are not quite what we expected, either of you. And yet each of you is precisely what you must be. It's only that you're so much more than we dared hope, my children. Farewell."

She vanished. One instant she was there; the next she was gone, and the hradani shook themselves. The gray light of dawn glimmered in the hole in the cave's roof, and Bahzell frowned as he tried to calculate how many hours must have sped past in what had seemed so few minutes. Yet the fire still burned, the horses and mules still drowsed in their corner of the cave, and their three companions slept on, untouched by all that had happened. He should have been exhausted from a sleepless night, but he felt rested and restored, and he looked at his friend.

Brandark looked back, his eyes huge with bemused sorrow and joy. And as they looked into one another's eyes, the Bloody Sword felt unseen fingers tug gently at his ear once more while a husky contralto voice ran around the cave like the laughter of the first day of creation.

"Remember, Brandark," it said softly. "You may have another task, but you *do* have a poet's soul, and that means a part of you will always be mine. Live your life well, Brandark Brandarkson. Take joy of it, and remember I will be with you to its end . . . and beyond."

# CHAPTER EIGHTEEN

A south wind blew misty rain into Bahzell's eyes as the gray walls of Angcar rose before him. It was two hours till gate-closing, but lanterns already glimmered from the battlements, and he blinked away water, looked back over his shoulder, and bit his lip. All of them, including those who'd slept through Chesmirsa's visit, had felt invigorated and renewed when they left the cave. But they'd no sooner set out once more than the gray, persistent rain had returned, and flooded valleys and mud-treacherous slopes had taken toll of their mounts and slowed them badly. The rain looked like blowing itself out at last, but Tothas was hunched in the saddle, his face pinched and gray, and his harsh, rasping cough came all too often. Short of funds or no, they had to get him under a roof, Bahzell thought grimly, and increased his pace toward Carchon's capital.

They'd fallen into the habit of letting Tothas act as their spokesman in the towns they passed, for he was less threatening than a hradani, but he was folded forward over his saddle pommel in a fresh, wracking spasm when they finally reached the gates. Bahzell stood beside his horse, one hand on the beast's neck, hiding his anxiety as best he could while he watched the armsman cough, and Brandark trotted ahead to state their business.

The guards, already surly over pulling gate duty on such a miserable day, looked less than pleased to see a hradani, but Bahzell had little worry to spare them. The rain was far worse on Tothas than the dry cold had been. Finding the cave had been greater fortune than they had any right to expect, and what would happen to the Spearman if they met the same weather in deep wilderness frightened the Horse Stealer.

The thought touched him with strangely bitter frustration, and he stroked the neck of Tothas' horse again while he grappled with it. He had a notion finding that cave had been something more than a stroke of simple luck, and there was a certain seductiveness to the idea of being able to call upon a god for aid. Only, if a man got into the habit of counting on some poxy god to save his neck, what did he do the day the god was busy elsewhere or got bored and decided to do something else? Besides, there was something bribe-like about the way that cave had popped up. It was like a bait, a bit of cheese enticing him into the trap.

He snorted in the rain. The dreams had stopped, as promised, but he wasn't certain that was an improvement. He'd always believed knowing the truth was best, that it meant a man didn't have to wonder or torment himself with hopes, but he'd learned better. Bad enough to *suspect* a god was after him; having it confirmed was much, much worse. This business about destinies, and tasks, and "pain beyond your dreams"—!

He watched Brandark speaking with the gate guards and shook his head stubbornly. Pain didn't frighten him.

He relished it no more than the next man, but any hradani knew pain was part of life. Yet he'd meant what he'd said. What he did, he would do because *he* chose to do it, not because someone or something commanded him to, and he still saw no reason any man—especially a hradani—should go about trusting gods. He couldn't deny Chesmirsa's impact upon him, how much he'd . . . well, liked her. But the goddess of music and bards damned well *ought* to be likable, charming, and all those other things! And all that talk of him and Brandark being "more" than she'd hoped—! *Best be keeping your hand on your purse when you hear such from someone who's wanting something from you, my lad,* he told himself sourly.

He pulled himself from his thoughts and glanced at Zarantha, and her momentarily unguarded eyes echoed his own fears for Tothas. She felt the hradani's gaze and looked back at him, and a spark of anger for what she was doing to her armsman burned within him, but her expression's sick self-loathing silenced any outburst, and he looked away once more as Brandark trotted back.

The Bloody Sword was as soaked as any of them, his finery bedraggled and mud-spattered, but meeting his goddess seemed to have honed his elemental insouciance, and there was still something jaunty about the way he drew rein. "I don't think they were glad to see a hradani, but they'll let us in. The sergeant was even kind enough to direct me to an inn with reasonable rates—remind me to mention his name to be sure he gets his rake-off."

"I'll be doing that, if it's after being decent. And if we can get Tothas into a warm bed."

"I'm—I'm all—" Tothas broke off in another spasm of coughing, and Bahzell grunted.

"Oh, save your strength, man!" he snapped. "We're all knowing you've guts enough for three men—now show you've the wit to go with them!"

Tothas coughed yet again, then shook himself weakly
and nodded. The Horse Stealer clapped him on the shoulder and looked back to Brandark. "All right, my lad. You're
the one has the name and address, so—" He made a shooing gesture, and Brandark turned his horse with a damp
grin and led the way.

The Laughing God was on the poor side of town,
and its weathered walls looked none too splendid.
Bahzell suspected Hirahim Lightfoot would have been
less than pleased to discover he was the inn's patron,
yet it turned out to be much better than first appearances suggested.

Brandark went off to examine the stables while Bahzell
accompanied Zarantha and Rekah inside, and the Horse
Stealer's eyes flitted about the taproom as they awaited
their host. The miserable weather had swelled its custom, but the place was clean enough, and its patrons
seemed unwontedly well behaved. Rough clothing and
general shabbiness proclaimed their lack of affluence,
yet there was no rowdiness, and no one gave the two
overworked barmaids trouble. Which might have something to do with the stocky, powerfully built human who
stood with both elbows on the bar and watched the crowd.
He was two feet shorter than Bahzell, with an eagle's-
beak nose in the face of someone it would be wiser not
to cross, and his eyes considered the hradani warily, then
flipped to where Tothas leaned on Zarantha's shoulder.
His hard gaze softened as it rested on the armsman, then
tracked back to Bahzell, and he nodded to the hradani
before he returned his attention to the crowd.

One patron looked up and paled, then rose quickly,
paid his shot, and departed hastily, but no one else
seemed worried by Bahzell's sudden arrival. Either that,
or they had a great deal of faith in the man at the bar,
and Bahzell was inclined to agree with them. That was

a fighting man over there, and an unlikely character to play bouncer in a place such as this, he thought—until he saw the owner. The landlord had lost a leg at the knee somewhere, but that nose could only belong to the bouncer's brother.

The landlord stopped short as he saw the hradani towering in his taproom, but a glance at Bahzell's companions seemed to reassure him. His shoulders relaxed, and he wiped his hands on the towel draped over his shoulder and stumped forward on his peg leg.

"What can I do for you?" he asked in rough Spearman.

"We're hoping you've room for us," Bahzell rumbled back.

"That depends on how much room you need. We're not the largest inn in Angcar, and I've let most of the private rooms already."

"As to that, it's two rooms we're needing—one for the ladies, and one for myself and my two friends." The landlord raised an eyebrow, and Bahzell twitched his ears. "We've one more man. He's seeing to our animals."

"I see." The landlord thought for a moment, then nodded. "We can manage that. I've two adjoining rooms left on the second floor, but they're not the cheapest ones, mind! They'll run you a silver kormak a night each, but I'll throw in stable space and fodder for your animals at no extra charge."

Bahzell winced, but he felt Tothas sagging despite his most gallant efforts and glanced at Zarantha. She nodded almost imperceptibly, and he looked back down at the landlord.

"Done. And if we can be getting a hot meal for our friend—?" He flicked an ear sideways at Tothas, and the landlord nodded.

"We can manage that, too, and maybe a little better." He shouted over his shoulder, and a youngster with that same beaky nose appeared like magic. "See these people to seven and eight and tell Matha they need hot food. And see there's a warming pan for the bed linen in both rooms!"

The youngster dashed off, and the landlord turned back to Bahzell.

"There's washrooms at the back: one for men and one for women. All the hot water you need for a copper each—and a bargain at the price for someone your size, I think!" He chuckled, and Bahzell gave him a weary grin. "If you're inclined to get your friend into a tub to soak, my people will have his bed warmed and waiting by the time he comes out to dry."

"I'm thanking you." Sincerity softened Bahzell's voice, but the landlord only shrugged and stumped back off, and the hradani took Tothas' weight from Zarantha's shoulder.

"I'm thinking—" he began, then broke off as the door flew open. Brandark's arms were heaped with enough baggage to weigh down even a hradani, and the women hurried over to relieve him of sufficient for him to see over the rest.

"I'm thinking," Bahzell resumed, "that now Brandark's here, he can be seeing you to our rooms while I get Tothas neck-deep in hot water."

"By all means," Zarantha said briskly. She opened one of the bags she'd taken from Brandark and withdrew a small bottle and a horn spoon. "And give him two spoonfuls of this—it'll ease the coughing."

Bahzell stuffed the medication into his belt pouch with a nod and turned away to half lead and half carry Tothas to the washrooms.

Hirahim, Bahzell thought a few hours later, might not be as irked as he'd first thought to find this inn named after him. Its rooms were expensive for its neighborhood, but the food was excellent, and the staff had seen to their needs with rare dispatch. Tothas had stayed awake long enough to consume an enormous bowl of thick, hot soup before they tucked him between the warmed sheets of his bed, and his breathing had been far easier as he dozed off.

Bahzell and Brandark, immeasurably refreshed by their own hot baths, had left Zarantha and Rekah watching over him and repaired, at Zarantha's insistence, to the taproom after supper.

"You two have done your share and more," she'd half scolded when Bahzell questioned the wisdom of wasting their scant funds on drink. "We can spend a few coppers on you. So go! Get out of here! Just don't get into any brawls and break anything we'll have to pay for!"

The hradani had departed with alacrity, and they'd soon discovered that The Laughing God's cellars matched its kitchen. The local wines were too thick and sweet, but they couldn't really afford wine anyway, whatever Zarantha might say, and the ale was excellent.

Now they sat before the hearth, listening to the pop of burning wood and the sizzling spit as an occasional raindrop came down the flue, and nursed two of The Laughing God's biggest tankards. The other patrons had made room for them with a bit more haste than dignity, but they'd calmed down since, and Bahzell stretched his boots towards the fire while he savored his ale . . . and the surprised faces about him. Brandark's finery had astounded everyone, and some of those who'd prudently withdrawn from his vicinity had been lured back when he uncased his balalaika and began strumming.

It hadn't taken long for someone a little braver than the others to ask for a song, and the Bloody Sword had obliged with a smile, though he'd asked—with uncommon tact, Bahzell thought—for someone else to provide the voice. By now he was in a huddle with two locals, fingering silent chords while one of them played something softly on a penny whistle. His head nodded as he followed the melody, and Bahzell suspected the trio would soon be shouting for someone to sing along with their joint efforts.

The bouncer had kept an eye on them at first. Not hostilely, simply with a trace of wariness, but he, too, had relaxed when Brandark began to play. Taken all in all, it was the warmest reception two hradani were likely to find anywhere outside their native lands.

It was being a good night for The Laughing God, too— due, perhaps, to the attraction of two "tame" hradani, Bahzell thought sardonically. Few had left, and enough newcomers had filtered in to fill the taproom. The landlord had assigned two more servants to help the harried barmaids and stood behind the bar in person, eyes smiling as he watched the briskness of his business. More people wandered in by twos or threes, finding room to sit where they could, and Bahzell raised his own tankard for a refill.

One of the barmaids swung past on her way back to the bar and thunked it down on her already crowded tray, and he looked back at Brandark. The Bloody Sword was nodding vigorously now, one of the locals was beckoning to a deep-voiced fellow who'd already favored them with two songs, and—

*"Watch yourself, hradani!"*

The shout cracked across the taproom, and surprise jerked Bahzell's head around. He caught movement from the corner of his eye even as he turned, and pure instinct sent him lunging to his feet and away from it.

The same shout had stopped the man who'd walked up behind the Horse Stealer. But only for a second; even as Bahzell moved, the stranger raised a clenched fist to his lips and blew.

Something hummed past Bahzell's ear on a *pffffft!* of expelled breath. It spanged off a polished copper pot above the hearth, and the hradani snarled. He was

vaguely aware of other movement—of Brandark cata-
pulting from his chair, the bouncer reaching back over
the bar towards his brother, a wave of confusion and
consternation—but his eyes were on the man who'd
tried to kill him. The stranger's clenched fist opened,
throwing the small, hollow tube it had held into the
fire, and his other hand went up under his cloak.

A shortsword gleamed as he drew it, and Bahzell
snatched out his dagger, but a wave of bodies erupted
from the crowd before he could move. At least ten of
them, foaming up from the tables and benches to join a
concerted rush, and all of them were armed.

Bahzell cursed and stepped back. His foot hooked
under the trestle bench he'd been seated upon, and his
lead attacker ducked frantically as its heavy wooden seat
exploded upward. *He* managed to evade it, but three others
went down, tangling their fellows, and Bahzell's ears were
flat to his skull as he went for the leader.

He didn't know who these people were, but each
of them carried a shortsword—the longest weapon a
man could expect to conceal under a tunic or smock—
in one hand and a knife in the other, and they knew
what to do with them. Neither hradani had expected
trouble, and their armor and swords had been left in
their room, but Bahzell's dagger was as long as most
human shortswords . . . and he, too, knew what he
was doing.

His would-be killer came at him in a strange, circling stance Bahzell had never seen before, sword
advanced and knife held back at his hip, and the
hradani's empty left hand spread wide. He had no time
for subtlety against so many enemies, and he took a
chance and lunged.

The sword darted out as he'd expected, engaging his
dagger, and the knife drove forward for his belly, but his
left hand struck like a serpent. Fingers of steel clamped

the man's wrist. They yanked him close, a tree-like knee rammed up between his legs, and Bahzell's dagger slipped free of his sword as he convulsed in agony. The blade twisted in, driving up under his arm, and blood sprayed from his mouth as he went down with a gurgling scream.

Steel clashed to Bahzell's left as he kicked the dying man aside. Brandark had reacted almost as quickly as his friend, tossing his balalaika to one of his fellow musicians with one hand while the other went to his own dagger. The local caught the instrument in sheer reflex, then yelled in panic and scrambled for safety as the killers stormed forward.

Customers scattered like quail, and someone shrieked and folded forward as Brandark opened his belly. The horrible sound died with chilling suddenness as the Bloody Sword drove his dagger into the nape of his victim's neck like an ice pick, but three more attackers vaulted over the trio Bahzell's bench had felled, and the Horse Stealer sprang back to get his back to the hearth.

Brandark fell in beside him, as if summoned by telepathy, and a third would-be killer fell to writhe and scream in the sawdust as Bahzell ducked and hooked a vicious upward thrust into his groin. A sword hissed at the Horse Stealer's face, and he was just too slow to dodge. It opened his cheek from eye to chin, but the man behind it paid with his life. He went down, momentarily entangling the man beside him, and Bahzell roared as he caught the encumbered man by the throat and drove his dagger up under his sternum.

A wild, fierce war cry split the air beyond the attackers, and steel flashed in the lamplight as the bouncer brought down the broadsword his brother had tossed him from under the bar. It caught a man between neck and shoulder, and the dead man went down shrieking, but Bahzell had no time to see more than that. The innocent bystanders had disappeared through windows and doors or under tables; the taproom was clear now, and he'd been wrong about the numbers. At least a dozen men were still trying to kill him, and the world dissolved into a boil of confusion as they very nearly succeeded.

Steel clashed, someone's blood soaked his right arm to the elbow, he heard Brandark gasp at his side, the bouncer's shrill war cries echoed in his ears, and even through that howling bedlam he heard the sharp, musical snap of a bowstring. A slash got through to his left arm, but he sensed it coming and managed to avoid the worst of it. It opened his forearm from wrist to elbow, but the messy cut was shallow, and even as the sword went back for another thrust, he brought his boot heel down on its wielder's instep. Bone crunched, the attacker screamed and faltered, and Bahzell slashed his throat.

Someone else disappeared from in front of him, and the bouncer leapt through the gap. He slotted into place between the two hradani, his broadsword trailing gory spray as he hacked down yet another attacker. The bowstring twanged again, and then, as suddenly as it had begun, it was over.

Bahzell braced his shoulders against the mantel, feeling the fire's heat against his back, and breath rasped in his lungs as his eyes darted about in search of fresh threats. But there were none. Sixteen bodies lay leaking blood into the sawdust, and he lowered his dagger slowly.

The bouncer sighed beside him and lowered his own weapon, and the Horse Stealer gave him a quick look of thanks, then stepped past him as Brandark sat down very carefully. His left leg was soaked with blood, and Bahzell knelt to rip his trouser leg open, then sagged in relief. The cut was ugly, but it was in the meaty part of the thigh, just below the hip, and it hadn't gotten deep enough to sever muscles or tendons.

The Horse Stealer reached out to rip a bandage from a dead man's tunic, but the bouncer shouldered him aside.

"See to yourself, hradani," he said gruffly, and Bahzell slumped back on his heels and looked bemusedly down at his own bleeding arm.

Feet pattered down the stairs, and then strong, slender hands were ripping his sleeve apart. It was Zarantha, with Tothas' quiver over her shoulder. The Spearman's strung horsebow lay beside her in the sawdust as she muttered under her breath and probed the cut carefully, and Rekah came more slowly downstairs behind her with Tothas' saber clutched in both hands.

He hissed in pain as Zarantha turned his arm to get better access, then looked away while she wound a clean cloth—gods only knew where she'd gotten it—and knotted it tight. Four of the bodies, he noted with curious detachment, had arrows in their backs or chests. He started to comment on the fact, but Zarantha gripped his chin and turned his head to examine his freely bleeding cheek.

"I thought," she said between gritted teeth as she wiped blood from the wound, "that I told you two *not* to get into any brawls!"

# CHAPTER NINETEEN

The landlord astonished Bahzell. He summoned the Guard, but, despite the carnage, he didn't even consider turning his unchancy guests out.

Some of that might have been because of the bouncer. The brothers had a brisk discussion while they awaited the Guard's arrival, and it turned even brisker when the bouncer bent and ripped open a dead man's smock to bare his left shoulder. Bahzell watched them bend over the corpse while Zarantha set neat, painful stitches in his gashed cheek, then touched her gently on the shoulder and crossed the sawdust to them.

"My thanks, friend," he rumbled to the bouncer, and the man shrugged.

"It's my job to keep people from being murdered in the taproom."

"Aye, that may well be, but I'm thinking it was more than your job to get involved against those odds for folk you don't know." Bahzell clasped his forearm. "My name

241

is Bahzell Bahnakson, of Hurgrum, and if there's ever aught I or anyone from Hurgrum can be doing for you, be pleased to let me know it."

"I may just do that, friend Bahzell," the bouncer said with a tight smile, "and while we're naming names, I'm Talamar Ratherson, and this—" he jabbed a thumb at the landlord "—is my brother Alwith."

"It's pleased I am to know you both." Bahzell clasped Alwith's arm in turn, and the landlord gripped back, but there was a worried light in his eyes.

"I'd say you've an enemy somewhere," Talamar went on, pointing to the body, and Bahzell's ears flattened as he saw the scarlet scorpion tattoo.

"Aye, it seems I have that," he said softly, and his mind raced. Dog brothers set on to assassinate Kilthan might make some sort of sense, despite the risk, but why should they try to kill *him* now that he was no longer even in the dwarf's employ? Unless . . .

"What's this?" Brandark had hobbled over and stood beside him, glowering down at the tattoo.

"Now, I'm thinking you're a clever enough lad to know that as well as I," Bahzell murmured, kneading his wounded left arm, and his face was grim.

"But why—?" Brandark paused with a frown. "Phrobus take it, were they after *you* the whole time?"

"If you can be finding another reason for all this—" Bahzell waved at the carnage "—it's more than happy I'll be to hear it."

"Um." Brandark pulled on his nose in thought, then shook his head. "It does make a sort of sense, you know. Everyone assumed they were after Kilthan, but you were with him each time they tried an ambush, and that fireship in Malgas would have fried your tripes right along with his."

"Aye, so I was, and so it would. And I'm thinking, Brandark my lad, that there's only one reason to be sending dog brothers after me."

"Harnak," Brandark agreed grimly.

"Or Churnazh. Either of 'em would piss on my grave and be glad to do it. But how would one of them be knowing how to set dog brothers on me?"

"A point," Brandark murmured. "Definitely a point. Not even Churnazh would let Sharnā's get into Navahk—not when they might be used against *him*."

"True." Bahzell stopped kneading his arm and glanced sideways at his friend. "Would you be thinking what I am? That that sick bastard Harnak might be a bit sicker even than we'd thought?"

"I don't like it, but it makes sense." Brandark sighed. "Wonderful. Hundreds of leagues yet to go, and dog brothers on our track!"

"Well, as to that, we may just end up costing them enough they decide to give over," Bahzell rumbled with a bleak smile. "Sixteen here, fifteen in Saramfal . . . that's after being a lot of dead men, Brandark. How many funerals d'you think Harnak has gold enough to pay for?"

"I wouldn't count on that, friend." Talamar traced the sign of the War God's mace, and the hradani winced at the reminder. "Tomanāk knows no decent man has any use for such as this," Talamar's toe prodded the body, "but this I will say: once the dog brothers take a man's gold, they do the job. They have to, if they want their reputation to stand."

"They do it if they *can*," Bahzell corrected grimly, "and I'm thinking this time they've bitten off a mite more than they'll like chewing." He shook himself and looked at Alwith. "But be that as it may, we'd no notion of bringing trouble like this down on your house. It's in my mind we should be gone before we bring you more grief."

The landlord looked like he wanted to agree but shook his head firmly, and his brother echoed the refusal.

"You've paid your shot," Talamar said. "You're under the protection of our roof, and your friend's too sick to be out on a night like this. Besides, Tomanāk wouldn't like it if we threw you out."

"I'm not talking of throwing out," Bahzell objected, "but of leaving of our own will." He liked the thought of taking Tothas back out into the wet no more than Talamar did, yet this was his trouble, not the Angcarans'. There was no reason for them to mix in it—and he owed Talamar for saving his life. It would be poor gratitude to get him killed in thanks, and Talamar's repeated references to Tomanāk only made it worse, for it felt like another "bribe," and this was no empty cave. It was something that could cost lives.

"It doesn't matter," Talamar said firmly. "The Sword God knows only one way to deal with scum like this, and it would dishonor us to let you face them alone with both of you hurt and a sick man on your hands to boot."

"Talamar's right." Alwith still looked unhappy, but his voice was just as firm, and Bahzell studied both brothers' faces.

It made no sense. He and Brandark had learned only too well how most of the world regarded hradani, and they'd brought the Assassins Guild down on The Laughing God. It was only Norfram's own luck neither brother nor any of their patrons had been killed. Talamar's warning had already saved his life—not to mention how the Angcaran had fought at his side—which was more than ample repayment for the cost of their food and lodging, and Bahzell was *offering* to leave. Yet they were arguing with him, the both of them, and they actually sounded as if they meant it.

"Well, then," he said finally, his deep voice soft, "if you're daft enough to mean that, there's naught for me to do but thank you once again."

The City Guard wasn't happy when it finally arrived, for Angcar was an orderly place. The city fathers frowned on battles in a public inn at the best of times, and sixteen dead was a dismaying body count, even when the Guard didn't find two hradani in the midst of the carnage.

By the time it arrived in the person of one Captain Deskhan, however, the patrons who hadn't taken to their heels had reemerged from under the tables. The musician who'd caught up Brandark's balalaika had returned it, and he and the Bloody Sword sat in a corner, with the Angcaran keeping time on a small hand drum while the hradani plucked out a melody. Alwith had ordered ale all round on the house, and the witnesses were prepared to wax vehement in the hradani's defense. In fact, four or five of them illustrated every gory moment of the encounter in graphic pantomime, and the baffled Deskhan had no choice but to accept that whatever had happened, the hradani hadn't started it.

He departed at last with a wagonload of dead assassins and a grudging verdict of self-defense, and Talamar stood in the inn door and waved farewell with a cheeriness that astonished Bahzell.

"I'm thinking that's an unhappy man yonder. How likely is it he'll be after making trouble for you out of this?"

"Oh, not very." Talamar shrugged. "He doesn't like it, but he'll cool off once you folk leave. Besides, he's as little liking for dog brothers as the next man, and he can use this tale to astonish people for years."

The Angcaran cocked his head and grinned. "For that matter, so can Alwith and I. We'll have more custom than we can handle for days—maybe weeks—once word of this gets around!"

"And welcome to it," Bahzell rumbled. "But, d'you know, I'm still wondering how you spotted them at the start like that?"

"I didn't." Talamar closed the door and headed back to the taproom beside him. "To be honest, I was keeping an eye on *you*." He shrugged with another grin. "The two of you seemed like peaceable fellows, but if someone got drunk enough, he might have taken it into his head to pick a quarrel with you. As for the dog brothers," his grin became a frown, "they came in in ones and twos, so gradually I never noticed, and I should have, since they were all strangers. But there was something odd about the way that first fellow held his hand when he headed over your way, and I've seen those little blowguns before."

"D'you think he really believed he could kill me with such as that and not be found out?"

"Bahzell, if he'd hit you with that dart, you'd never have known a thing about it," Talamar said grimly. "Didn't you see it?"

"Not clear," the hradani rumbled, "and your Guard captain was after taking it with him when he left."

"It was tipped with mindanwe sap. A scratch of that, and you're gone in seconds. All anyone would think would be that your heart had burst—which it *would* have— and once you were down, he'd've bent over you to 'help' and picked the dart back out while he pretended to 'examine' you."

A shiver rippled up Bahzell's spine. Poison. The most loathsome weapon of a coward, but an effective one.

"Begging your pardon, and don't take this wrongly, but it sounds as if you've experience of such," he murmured.

"I do. Alwith and I served in a troop of freeswords up in Ferenmoss some years back. That civil war is a nightmare, but at least it offers steady work for mercenaries. Only our troop must have been a bit too good, because someone on the other side set the dog brothers on us. We lost half our officers in less than two weeks, and Alwith and I caught the bastard who killed our captain with one of those damned blowguns. He was a good man, Captain Vakhan, and any time I can get sword into the same kind of scum who murdered him—"

Talamar broke off with yet another shrug, almost an apologetic one, and Bahzell touched his shoulder.

"I'm sorry for your captain, but grateful you saw this coming."

"I suppose some good comes of almost anything," the Angcaran sighed, then gave himself a brisk shake. "In the meantime, I've put out the word, and a dozen mercs will be dropping by shortly. They're good men—most of them were with us in Ferenmoss—and they've settled in to pass the winter here. When they hear about dog brothers in Angcar, they'll be only too happy to spend a night or two drinking our ale, so you and your people get what sleep you can."

"Aye, we'll be doing that," Bahzell agreed, and beckoned to Brandark to follow as he started up the stairs.

They did get some sleep, but not immediately. Zarantha was still up—not surprisingly—and insisted on rechecking the work she'd done on their wounds. And then, of course, Bahzell had to tell her what had happened and as much as they'd been able to guess about why. He did *not* mention any nocturnal visits by goddesses, but that was hardly relevant anyway.

Zarantha heard him out with remarkable calm, but her dark eyes were haunted when he finished. Rekah sat quietly beside Tothas' bed, her oval face white, yet she said nothing, and Bahzell touched Zarantha's knee gently.

"Lass," he said, abandoning the "My Ladies" he usually remembered to use, "you've bought into more trouble with us than we'd any notion, either of us. I'm knowing you've need of help to get home, but it's in my mind you might best be considering whether it's *our* help you need."

"Because of the dog brothers?"

"Of course because of the dog brothers! I've told you

why Harnak wants me dead—aye, and his father, too—
and a pair of hradani aren't after being the hardest targets to spot. We're like to bring them down on you again,
and—" He paused, then sighed. "Lass, d'you think
Brandark and I don't know you've troubles of your own?
We're not wishful to make them worse."

"After the way I trapped you into this?" Zarantha
blinked damply, and Bahzell shrugged.

"As for that, I've no one to blame but myself for mixing in your troubles in the first place, and it was you kept
me out of jail and away from ni'Tarth's daggers. Aye, and
so far as that goes, the dog brothers would've been more
than pleased to have me penned up in a cell like a sheep
on slaughtering day!"

"No one to blame but yourself," Zarantha murmured.
She swiped a hand across her eyes and smiled at him.
"You're not nearly so hard a man as you'd have people
think, are you, Bahzell Bahnakson? First that girl in
Navahk, then me. And do you think I haven't seen the
way you watch after Tothas?"

He looked away uncomfortably, and it was her turn
to pat *his* knee.

"Tell me this, Bahzell. If I were able to find someone
else to see us the rest of the way home, what would you
and Brandark do?"

"Well, we couldn't be staying here, for if one thing's
sure it's that the dog brothers know our whereabouts."

"So you'd be moving on anyway?"

"Aye, that we would."

"In that case, if you're still willing, I'd rather move on
with you. As you say, I've troubles of my own, and—"

She broke off, almost against her will, and shook her
head. The Horse Stealer looked closely at her, recognizing her temptation to tell him whatever she'd so far concealed, but he recognized her decision not to, as well.
He felt disappointed, yet not truly resentful. Whatever

it was, he'd already accepted its seriousness, and her willingness to continue in company with two hradani marked for death by the Assassins Guild only reinforced his sense of her desperation.

"All right, then," he sighed. "If that's the way of it, then we'll be staying with you, and I'm only hoping it's not a choice we'll both regret."

It was, he'd already accepted its seriousness, and her will migrate to continue his company with two human married for death by the Assassins Guild only reflected of his sense of his deprivation.

"All right, then," he sighed. "We'll take the worst of it, then we'll be sharing with you, and I'm only hoping it's not a choice we'll both regret."

# CHAPTER TWENTY

They stayed three days at The Laughing God without further incident. The Guard dropped by at odd times on no set schedule, Talamar's mercenary friends made the taproom their permanent headquarters, and if business was down, Alwith was almost cheerful when Bahzell apologized for it.

"Talamar's right," the landlord said, "once they're not worried about getting caught in the middle, they'll be spilling out the windows while they tell each other how brave they were. Half of 'em will be convinced *they* fought the dog brothers off while your lot just watched!"

It was windy and cold when they finally set out again—with the brothers Ratherson's invitation to return in, um, more peaceable times—but it was also clear and dry, and the rest had done Tothas good. He was in far less pain, and his coughs, when they came, were ghosts of his previous terrible spasms. Even their animals seemed more cheerful; indeed, Zarantha had to stop her mule from biting Bahzell three times the first day out.

But clear weather or no, all of them felt wariness tingling in their blood like an extra layer of frost, and Tothas was no longer excused watch duty. He and the women between them took the first watch each night, before the full cold set in. Bahzell had the second watch, and when Tothas turned in at last, it was to find the hradani had gotten up early and tucked a heated stone into his blankets to take the chill off them.

It was as well he did, for the last leaves had vanished. By this time, Bahzell knew, Hurgrum was covered in snow; this far south, it was merely cold. Bitterly cold—far colder than he'd expected. Tothas assured him it was an unseasonal cold snap that would ease—for a time, at least—soon, but that was scant comfort as he watched his breath plume and felt the ground like iron under his feet.

Almost as worrisome as the weather, the road started getting worse from the moment they left Angcar; by the time they approached Angthyr's border with the Empire of the Spear, it was no more than dirt. The upper inch or so was frozen, but Bahzell felt it give under his weight in low spots, and the slight, stiff flexing promised unfrozen water below. If they got the warmer weather Tothas predicted, it was going to turn into a bottomless bog.

The thought filled him with gloom, yet it was but one of many things he had to feel gloomy over. He no longer wore himself out with worry in his dreams; now he got to do it while he was awake, because he knew what the dreams had been *about*. And as if gods with missions weren't enough, the dog brothers were after him, as well. Nor had Zarantha's worries—whatever the Phrobus they were!—lightened. He'd suggested, once, that when they crossed into the empire she might find shelter while she sent word ahead to her father. After all, she'd be on her own ground then, no longer among foreigners, even if she was still a long way from home, but she'd answered with a single, almost spastic headshake. A grim shadow in Tothas' eyes had echoed her refusal, and Bahzell and Brandark had decided to concentrate on more immediate problems—like the weather, visiting gods, and the imminence of dog brother attack—and let the rest of the future take care of itself.

They crossed the Blackwater River into the Border Weald just after dawn on the fourth day out of Angcar. There was no bridge, but flat ferry-rafts winched their way across it on heavy cables, and icy, slate-gray water gurgled under a dull, pewter sky.

Zarantha was huddled deep into her coat once more. She made the crossing in silence and busied herself helping unload the ferry when they reached the small village on the empire's bank, but Rekah simply walked off the raft. She tapped her toe and frowned at her mistress, pretty face eloquent with impatience, and Bahzell blinked in surprise when Tothas snapped a brusque order for Zarantha to "Get a move on, there!"

Her armsman watched her for a moment, then snorted and produced a document for the officer commanding the handful of soldiers who manned the border station at the ferry landing.

"That wench is as lazy as the day is long!" he sighed as the officer unfolded the parchment. "Unfortunately, she's also my niece. I'm grateful My Lady saw fit to hire her on for the trip, but I'm going to have a few words with my brother when I get her home, let me tell you! I'd've taken a stick to her long ago if she were *my* daughter!"

The border guard grinned and turned the document to catch the light. His lips moved as he spelled his way slowly through it, then looked up at Tothas.

"That'd be this Mahrisa your passport lists?"

"Aye, that's her. My second brother's oldest girl, drat her!"

"And she's maid to Lady Rekahna?"

"Just as it says, and I'm Lady Rekahna's armsman."

"And you're on your way home to Howacimb?"

"Frethigar, actually. It's a little place south of Howacimb."

"I see." The officer rubbed his upper lip with a gloved finger, then handed the parchment back. "This all seems in order, but—" he gestured to the two hradani "—who might these two be?"

"I picked them up in Kolvania." Tothas shrugged. "Gods know it's a bad time of year for one man alone with two women to watch after, but Lady Rekahna's father's not so plump in the pocket as I'd like these days." He shrugged again. "I had to make do with what I could find."

"Um." The officer rocked back to study the hradani, and Bahzell concentrated on looking fierce but blank. No one had warned him about this—a point he intended to discuss with Zarantha at some length—but it had occurred to him that it would be much better if he couldn't speak Spearman.

"The little one's a sharp dresser for a hradani—reminds me of a pimp I used to know—but the big 'un looks a little slow," the officer said at last.

"I didn't hire him for his brains." Tothas turned his head, hiding his face from the guards, to grin wickedly at Bahzell. "If I had, I'd've gotten a mighty poor bargain!"

"Are you sure you want to travel with them? They've no papers, so you'll have to vouch for them, since they're in your employ. If they cause any trouble, you'll be the one liable for damages—or worse."

"Oh, they'll be all right. They came downriver to Kolva Keep with some Axeman merchant; *he* hadn't had any trouble out of them, and they've behaved so far. Besides, neither of them speaks a word of Spearman. Even their Axeman is pretty terrible, and I doubt they'll risk anything that might cause me to cut 'em adrift where they can't even talk to people. They're stupid, but they're not *that* stupid."

Bahzell maintained his blank expression, but his ears twitched, and his eyes slid sideways to meet an equally fulminating glance from Brandark.

"Well, just remember—you're responsible for them, so keep 'em in order," the officer grunted. He gave the hradani another long, hard look, then waved his men back into the warmth of their guard post, and Bahzell looked down at Tothas while Brandark and Zarantha led the last two mules off the ferry.

"Stupid, is it, now?" Brandark murmured in Axeman.

"I had to say *something*," Tothas murmured back in the same language. "And at least it kept him from asking *you* any questions."

"Aye, it did that," Bahzell admitted as the Spearman swung up onto his horse, "and the two of us kept him from looking very close at 'Lady Rekahna's' maid, now didn't we just?"

"True," Tothas agreed. He watched Brandark help "Lady Rekahna" into her saddle while Zarantha scrambled up onto her own mule with far less than her usual grace, then glanced back down at Bahzell, and his grin had vanished. "And truth to tell, my friend, that was the most important thing of all."

The Horse Stealer simply nodded and led off down the road once more, but a corner of his mind wondered just where—and when—Tothas had gotten that "passport." It hadn't occurred to Bahzell that such documentation would be needed, but Zarantha had clearly known. More, she'd felt compelled to hide behind false papers, and he suspected procuring them had been expensive. The way the officer had labored to read them suggested he was barely literate, yet she couldn't have counted on that, and even a total illiterate might have recognized a poor forgery. So why—and how—had an "indigent" noblewoman secured a *good* forgery?

He strode along the frozen road, and the foothills of

the North Blood Mountains rose slowly before him as he chewed that thought in silence.

They made another forty miles before the cold snap broke as Tothas had promised. And, just as Bahzell had feared, the road turned promptly into thick, clinging soup. The weather, though warmer, was still chill, and it was also damper, which aggravated Tothas' cough once more . . . and gave the Horse Stealer one more worry to cope with.

The road rose as they slogged on into the foothills of the Blood Mountains, but if the drainage improved, the steady climb compensated for that, and winding turns added long, weary miles to their journey. They'd passed an occasional village or prosperous-looking steading between the river and the hills; now they moved through lonely wilderness, and as Bahzell peered out into each frosty, fog-drenched morning, he understood exactly why that was. Only a madman would live in such a place if he could help it.

And then the rain started again. Cold and slow, falling with infinitely patient, soaking malice. They kept Tothas as warm and dry as they could, and the armsman no longer tried to pretend he didn't need it. He husbanded his strength whenever he could—and felt the rough side of Zarantha's tongue anytime he forgot to—yet his face took on that wan, pinched look once more, and his gloved hands shook on his reins. But at least there was no sign of assassins (who, Bahzell thought, probably had better sense than to be out in such weather), and seven days after crossing the Blackwater, they finally emerged on the far side of the hills.

The Horse Stealer stood at the head of their soaked, mud-spattered party and peered down the final slope. Evening was coming on fast, there was a hint of sleet in the rain, the beasts steamed in the icy wet, and he could feel the sagging weariness of his friends, but his ears twitched under his hood as lights glimmered ahead. It looked like a good-sized village or small town, and he touched Tothas on the knee, then pointed at the lights.

"Would you be knowing what that might be?" Even his deep, rumbling voice was hoarse with fatigue, and the Spearman blinked for a moment before his mind churned back to life.

"I think—" He pursed his lips, then nodded wearily. "That would be Dunsahnta," he said wearily. "We passed through it when we took My Lady north."

"What sort of place is it after being?"

"It's a village—good sized, but much like any other." Tothas frowned. "There's an inn, and Baron Dunsahnta has a keep of sorts to the northeast, I think." He shrugged. "He wasn't home when we came through."

"Did you stay at the inn?" Bahzell pressed. Tothas blinked again, and the Horse Stealer sighed. "Tothas, it's a right dummy I'd be—aye, nigh on as stupid as you were after telling that border guard—not to've guessed you and Lady Zarantha are hiding. So tell me—d'you think there's any down there as might remember her from your last trip through?"

Tothas flushed, but then he shook his head. "I doubt it. We didn't stop on the way north. We came through in the morning and kept right on going."

"Ah." Bahzell patted his knee again and slogged back to Zarantha. Her mule looked as weary as the hradani felt—it didn't even try a nip—and sleety water crusted Zarantha's coat. "You've the purse, such as it is," he rumbled. "Will it stretch enough to get Tothas under a roof?"

"Where are we?" Zarantha countered, and nodded when Bahzell repeated what Tothas had told him. "Yes, I remember the place. And he's right, we didn't stop." She bit her lip for a moment, then nodded again, more firmly. "Yes. We can cover two or even three days' lodging, I think."

"Good." Bahzell sighed, and led off into the gloom once more.

# CHAPTER TWENTY-ONE

Dunsahnta did, indeed, boast an inn, but The Brown Horse was a poor exchange for The Laughing God, and the pudgy, nervous little landlord looked acutely unhappy when he found a dripping wet Horse Stealer on his doorstep.

At least Tothas was able to speak for them this time, and the innkeeper seemed to take courage from the armsman's accent. He continued to eye Bahzell askance—especially when Brandark came in from the stables as well—but he finally admitted he had available rooms. Zarantha was back in her persona as "Lady Rekahna's" maid, and Tothas scolded her for her sloth as he paid the landlord, then chivvied her up the stairs while Bahzell and Brandark followed as impassively and menacingly as possible.

The rooms were bigger than The Laughing God's, but no fires had been laid, there were no hot baths, and meals cost two coppers apiece. Yet they were out of the rain,

259

though it occurred to Bahzell, as he considered their rooms, that the landlord had hardly given them his best chambers. They were on the second floor, off a stubby, blind hallway, with the smaller room squeezed into an awkward space between the inn's upper storerooms and the attached stables.

Bahzell assigned that one to Zarantha and Rekah the instant he saw it. The only way to it led past the room he and Brandark shared with Tothas, and, for all its short-comings, The Brown Horse offered stout doors. With their own door open and the hradani taking watch and watch about, no one could get to Zarantha or Rekah unchallenged.

Tothas nodded approval of Bahzell's arrangements, and this time he raised no argument over leaving the guard duty to the hradani. Indeed, he crawled into one of the beds the instant he finished supper, and Bahzell looked at Brandark and pointed to the other.

"I'll be waking you in four hours," he rumbled, "so you'd best not lie awake thinking of more verses for your curst song!"

Morning came noisily. None of The Brown Horse's servants had ever heard of tiptoes, and Bahzell groaned in protest as a waiter barged in with a can of hot water. The servant dropped it beside the wash basin with an appalling bang, then trooped out like an entire company of heavy infantry, and the Horse Stealer sat up with another groan.

"My, aren't *we* grumpy in the morning?" Brandark sat with his chair tipped back on two legs. "You really should cultivate a sunnier disposition," he went on in a severe tone. "I know! I finished two fresh verses to *Bahzell Bloody-Hand* last night! Why don't I sing them f— *ummpphh!*"

The thrown pillow hit hard enough to knock his chair

over with a crash, and Tothas shoved up on an elbow and dragged hair out of his eyes.

"*Must* you two be so cheerful this early?" He cocked his head at Brandark, then glanced at Bahzell as the Bloody Sword dragged the pillow out of his face. "What's he doing on the floor?"

"Penance," Bahzell growled, and threw back his own blankets.

He stretched enormously, crossed to the washstand, and poured hot water into the basin, then frowned. There was no steam, and he shoved a finger into the basin and sighed. The "hot" water was barely lukewarm.

He grimaced, but it was all there was, and at least his people's lack of facial hair meant that, unlike Tothas, he wouldn't have to shave with it. He washed his face, rinsed and emptied the basin into the chamber pot, then checked the clothing he'd hung before the fire overnight. It was dry, and he climbed into it with only a trace of wistfulness for The Laughing God's baths.

Brandark followed him to the basin, and Bahzell peered out the window. The rain had pulled back to blowing spatters, but a raw, gusting wind shook leafless branches like swords. It looked thoroughly miserable out there, and he hoped Zarantha was right about how long they could stay here, poor service or no.

A maid walked past their open door with another can of so-called hot water as if his thoughts of Zarantha had summoned her. She knocked much more gently than Bahzell would have anticipated and stood waiting a moment, then knocked again, harder. And then again, harder still.

Bahzell's ears cocked as the maid knocked yet a fourth time. He knew how light a sleeper Zarantha was, and he stepped into the hall with a frown.

The maid looked back over her shoulder and squeaked as she saw him. She couldn't have been more than fourteen, and this was her first sight of him, and she pressed her back against the closed door, hugging the water can before her like some sort of shield, her eyes huge.

"Oh, be still, girl!" he rumbled in her language, and wiggled his ears at her. "I gave over eating little girls for breakfast years ago!"

She jerked and tried to press her back *through* the door for just an instant, then smiled timidly at the rough humor in his voice.

"That's better," he encouraged. "Now what's the to-do?"

"The lady won't answer the door, sir," the maid said in a tiny voice, obviously still more than a little uncertain about him.

"She won't, hey?" Bahzell waved her aside and knocked himself. No one answered, and his amusement at the maid's reaction vanished. He pounded again, loud enough to wake the dead, and Brandark came out into the hall behind him.

"What's going on?"

"If I was knowing that, I wouldn't be after pounding on this damned door!" Bahzell hammered so hard the door leapt against the bar, but still no one answered. "Fetch the landlord, Brandark. I'm not liking this one tiny bit!"

The Bloody Sword jerked a nod and thundered down the stairs while Tothas took his place in the hall. The Spearman took one look at Bahzell, then at the door, and his face went paper-white. He shoved the hradani aside and beat on the door with both fists.

"My Lady!" he shouted. "Lady Zarantha!" Silence answered, and he looked desperately up at Bahzell. "Break it down!"

"So I'm thinking myself, but best we get the landlord up here first."

"No! She might—she might be *dying* in there!"

"Calm now, Tothas," Bahzell said as gently as his own fear allowed, and drew Tothas back from the door with

compassionately implacable strength, despite the armsman's struggles. "No one got past us last night, you've
my word for that, but if aught's wrong with Zarantha,
then it must be so with Rekah, as well, for they're neither of them answering. And if that's so, I'm thinking
there's no point in haste."

Tothas gave one more futile wrench against his grip,
eyes full of agony in his wasted face, then slumped and
patted the Horse Stealer's wrist.

"Aye," he whispered. "Aye, you're right. Would to
Tomanāk you weren't, but you are."

He sagged against the wall, hands scrubbing his face,
and Bahzell turned as Brandark clattered back with the
landlord. The pudgy little man looked both indignant and
frightened in his ridiculous nightgown, and he was badly
out of breath from the ruthless haste with which the
Bloody Sword had dragged him from his bed.

"What's the meaning of this?!" he tried to snap, but it came
out in a nervous quaver, and Bahzell frowned down at him.

"Little man," he said, "we've people behind yonder
door, and they're not after answering." The landlord jerked
as if he'd been struck. His eyes darted to the door, and
he paled, then swallowed.

"M-Maybe they're just a asleep," he stuttered.

"Then it's the soundest sleep *I've* ever heard of," Bahzell
rumbled.

"Well, I can't help that! What do you want *me* to do
about it?"

"Just you stand right there," the Horse Stealer told
him grimly. "I'm after opening this door, one way or
another, and I'm wanting you to know why I've done
it when I do."

"You mean—?" The landlord stiffened as the hradani
backed up four paces. "No, *wait!* You can't just—!"

Bahzell ignored him and charged. The human-sized
hall was too cramped for him to build much speed,

but, as Harnak had learned in Navahk, the door that could stop Bahzell Bahnakson was a very rare door indeed. The crash shook the inn to its foundations, the bar ripped its brackets from the wall with an ear-piercing screech, and the door itself flew clear across the room.

The Horse Stealer stumbled two more paces forward to regain his balance, but his eyes were already sweeping the room, and a snarl rose in his throat. The single small window hung wide to the rain, and the furnishings were smashed and splintered, as if a madman had run amok with an axe. One bed was empty, but a bloody oval face hung over the side of the other slashed and tattered mattress in a tangle of golden hair.

The hradani crossed the room in one enormous stride, and his hands were gentle as he touched Rekah's throat. Her neck was ringed in brutal purple bruises too long and thin to have come from any mortal hand, and blood streaked the bedpost where her attacker had slammed her face into it again and again while he choked her, but a faint pulse fluttered against his fingertips.

"Fetch a healer!" he snapped over his shoulder. Tothas sagged in the doorway like a man who'd taken his death wound, and the petrified landlord gawked past the armsman. "Phrobus take you, fetch a healer before I gut your lard-swollen belly!" Bahzell roared, and the man vanished with a squeal.

The maid disappeared on his heels, and Brandark caught Tothas, easing him down to sit on the floor, horrified eyes locked on the empty bed.

"How?" The Bloody Sword's tenor voice was hard with fury. "In the names of all the gods and demons *how?* And why didn't we *hear* something?!"

Bahzell only shook his head, but Tothas shoved himself up from the floor. "Sorcery," he groaned, crossing to Rekah like an old, old man. He touched her bloody face with trembling fingers, and his voice was riven and harrowed. "Sorcery—black, black sorcery!" he whispered, going back to his knees beside the maid, then laid his face on the bed and wept.

The healer was a stout, gray-haired matron with a gentle face, and she hissed in horror when she saw the room. She looked ridiculous with her clothing all askew and her hair all wild under the cloak she'd snatched over her head, but her hands were gently deft as she examined Rekah. She peered into the maid's eyes and moved her head with infinite care, then sighed in relief.

"Eh, it's bad!" she murmured. "Mortal bad, but her neck's unbroken, praise Kontifrio." She muttered to herself as she checked for other wounds and broken bones, then rounded on Tothas and the two hradani. "And which of you treated her so?!" she snapped furiously, but Bahzell shook his head.

"No, mother. I'll swear whatever oath you're wishing, we'd no hand in it. The door was barred from inside; we broke it down to find her."

"What?!" The healer stared at him, then looked at the wrecked door and went almost as pale as the innkeeper had. "Lillinara preserve us!" she whispered, tracing the full-moon circle of the Mother with her right hand, then shook herself and glared back up at the Horse Stealer.

"Well, that's as may be, but this lass is bad hurt—bad! She's a crack in her skull like someone hit her with an axe, and it's the gods' own mercy she's still alive. Out— out, all of you! I've work to do, so clear my way!"

Bahzell nodded and drew Tothas gently away. The landlord was nowhere in sight. His servants had copied his example, and Brandark dived into his personal pack for a carefully wrapped bottle of brandy as the three of them returned to their own room. Tothas coughed and tried to pull away when Brandark forced a huge swallow down him, but something like intelligence returned to his eyes, and Bahzell cleared his throat.

"Now, Tothas," he said in a soft voice, "I'm thinking it's time you told us what Lady Zarantha never did."

"Why?" Tothas' voice was hopeless, and he rocked in his chair, arms folded across his chest. "Oh, My Lady!"

"Hush, now, man!" Bahzell's voice was harsh, and Tothas looked up. "There's no body in yonder room, only Rekah. I'm thinking whoever—or whatever—it was left her for dead, and never a sound did it make while it was about it. If it was minded to kill Zarantha, why not kill her then and there? No, Tothas, she's alive, or was, and if we're to get her back, we've time for naught but the truth!"

"Alive?" Tothas blinked, and the horror retreated—a little—as his face recovered some of its normal determination. "Aye," he said softly. "She would be. She is! They won't kill her here—they'll take her home for that!"

"Who, man? *Who?!*"

"I don't know—not for certain." Tothas shook himself again, harder. "You're right. Tomanāk knows we should have told you sooner, but My Lady was afraid that—" He drew a deep breath, then stood and faced the two hradani.

"I ask you to believe," he said in a deep, formal voice, "that we kept it from you out of no distrust. It was My Lady's decision, and she meant it for the best—for you, as well as for her."

"Meant what?" Brandark asked flatly.

"My Lady . . . misled you. She is, indeed, the Lady Zarantha Hûrâka, and her father *is* Caswal of Hûrâka, but few know them by that name. Hûrâka is an all but dead clan—she, her father, and her sisters are its only members—but Lord Caswal is also lord of Clan Jashân, and most know him as Caswal of Jashân, Duke Jashân."

"*Duke?!*" Brandark blurted.

"Aye, the highest noble of the South Weald after Grand Duke Shâloan himself."

"Phrobus!" the Bloody Sword whispered, and Bahzell's eyes went flint hard as he stared into Tothas' face.

"Are you after telling me the second noble of the South Weald sent his oldest daughter *overland* to the Empire of the Axe with naught but a single maid and three armsmen?!"

"No. Oh, he sent her overland, but we had an escort of sixty men for the trip. Rekah and I—and Arthan and Erdan, Isvaria keep them—stayed with her in Axe Hallow when the others returned home."

"And what were you doing there?"

"My Lady is a mage," Tothas said simply. Bahzell heard Brandark gasp and sat down abruptly, his ears flat in shock.

There'd been a time when "mage" and "wizard" meant one and the same thing, but those days were long past. Bahzell had never met a mage—so far as he knew, there'd never *been* any of hradani blood—yet he'd heard of them. They were said to have appeared only since the Fall, men and women gifted with strange powers of the mind. Some said they could heal with a touch, read thoughts a hundred leagues away, vanish in the blink of an eye, or any of a thousand other strange abilities, but they were trusted as much as wizards were hated, for they were sworn to use their powers only to help, never to harm except in self-defense. More, they were mortal enemies of black sorcery, pledged before their patron deity Semkirk to fight it wherever they found it.

"A mage," Bahzell said finally, very softly, and Tothas nodded.

"Aye, and there was the problem, for we've never had a Spearman mage that lived to come into his powers. You see, when a mage's powers first wake, he suffers something called a 'mage crisis.' I don't know much about it—

it's only been in the last few years we even knew what to watch for—but no one has ever survived it in the empire. Or, if they have, someone else killed them."

"Why?" Brandark asked, and Tothas turned to him.

"Because of the Oath of the Magi. Only the Axeman mage academies know how to train a mage. Give them their due, they've always offered the training to anyone, be they Axeman or not, but they require mage oath as the price of their help. Oh," he waved a hand as both hradani stiffened, "My Lady had no objection! For the most part it's no more than an oath never to abuse their powers—d'you think My Lady would refuse *that?*" He glared fiercely at his listeners, and Bahzell shook his head.

"But it's also a promise to seek out and destroy black sorcery. No mage can match a wizard unaided. None of them have more than three or four—at most six—of the mage talents, and they can draw only on their own energy, not steal it from the world about them. But *every* mage can sense wizardry, and a *group* of them has the power to do something about it."

"Which wouldn't make them so popular with wizards," Bahzell murmured, eyes dark as he recalled the wreckage of Zarantha's room.

"Exactly," Tothas said grimly. "My Lady and her father believe that's the true reason no Spearman mage has ever survived mage crisis. It's not that severe for most magi, or so I'm told. The more talents a mage has—and the more powerful they are—the more severe the crisis, but surely at least *one* mage should have survived in a thousand years!"

"Unless someone was after helping them to die."

"Exactly," Tothas repeated. "So when My Lord Duke's daughter showed early signs of talent, he was terrified for her. He *had* to send her to the Axemen—and quickly and in secret—if he wanted her to live."

"And Lady Zarantha? How was she feeling about it?"

"She wanted it, Bahzell. She wanted it with all her heart and soul, and not just for the power of it. She wanted to come home, build our own mage academy under Duke Jashân's protection. If we've been so poisoned by black sorcery that it can reach out and kill the talented while they're still helpless, we *need* our own magi. Her father begged her to stay with the Axemen where she'd be safe, but she— Well, she's a mind of her own."

"But why overland? Why not by ship?" Brandark asked.

"My Lady had a . . . a *feeling*." Tothas shook his head. "One of her talents is something called 'precognition.' I don't understand how it works, and it's one of her weaker talents, erratic and hard to control. But it's let her see the future a time or two, and she dared not pass through the Lands of the Purple Lords. She thought *that* was the source of the wizardry, and the Purple Lords control all shipping from Bortalik Bay to Robanwar in the East Weald. If she'd gone by ship—"

Bahzell nodded. If one of the half-elven Purple Lords *was* killing magi, the last thing Zarantha could have done was pass through their hands.

"But was she going to try to sneak home with no more than three armsmen?" Brandark asked.

"No. We were to come down through the Axemen's South Province and meet our escort in Kolvania. Fifty men should have been there at least a month before we arrived, but no one had heard of them when we got there. We waited another week, and then My Lady got another 'feeling' and we took ship to Riverside. I think she was already considering hiding her identity and trying to get home unrecognized, but then the dog brothers killed Arthan and Erdan."

"*Dog brothers?!*" both hradani exclaimed, and Tothas nodded miserably.

"I know she told you it was illness, but it was poison, and wicked stuff. They ate before me—I was waiting upon

My Lady and came to supper late—and that saved my own life, for the symptoms came on them first. It was too late for them, but My Lady's a healer. I don't know how she kept me alive—I was out of my head and raving—but she and Rekah got us into that miserable place you met us in, and the two of them nursed me through the worst of it."

"And the dog brothers missed you?" Brandark said skeptically.

"Aye. My Lady's a powerful mage, with three major talents and two minor, and one of the minors lets her confuse the eye. She hid our going, then made certain no one looked closely at her whenever she left the inn. Rekah and I stayed hidden while she made her way about town, searching for a way to get home. I didn't like it, but the strain of hiding more than one person is wicked, and she wouldn't let me come with her."

"So why didn't she just 'confuse the eye' all the way home?"

"It only *confuses* the eye. It won't work if there's no one else to direct it to, and out on the high road—" Tothas shrugged again, unhappily, and looked at Bahzell. "That was why that scum cornered her in the alley, Bahzell. She was alone on the street when they spied her."

The Horse Stealer nodded, and Tothas sucked in another deep breath.

"After that—with ni'Tarth hunting her as well as the dog brothers—she dared not stay in Riverside. She'd used a name no one would recognize, but if ni'Tarth was part of the Assassins Guild, they were bound to realize who she truly was when he set them on her."

"But why didn't she just tell us the truth?" Brandark asked.

"My Lady's no telepath, no thought-hearer. She's an empath. She could sense your feelings, knew you for honest and honorable men, but she couldn't hear your thoughts, and we'd been in hiding for over three *months*. She'd . . . forgotten how to trust, I think, and when we knew we *could* trust you, she'd thought better of it. There's a trick some wizards have—Phrobus, for all I know *all* of them have it!—that lets them pluck thoughts from unguarded minds. They can't do it to a mage, and Rekah and I were taught a way to block against it in Axe Hallow, but there was no time to teach that to you. All it would have taken would be one wizard to see her identity in your mind, and—"

"And it's dead we'd all have been," Bahzell said grimly.

"Dead, indeed," Tothas agreed.

"And when she found the dog brothers were after *us?*" Brandark asked.

"What could she do but go on? Tomanāk knows I'd die for her—I've been her personal armsman since she was a babe—but I'm not likely to live out the journey," Tothas said, and Bahzell's eyes softened. "She knows it as well as I, but she dared not leave me behind, nor would I have let her. Yet she *needed* you two, needed your guts and loyalty as much as your swords. And at least we knew the dog brothers hadn't realized who she was, or they would have killed her first, while she was unguarded upstairs, before trying for Bahzell."

"Aye, that's sense, but why the forged passport, Tothas? Why not be telling that border guard captain the truth and ask an escort home?"

"Because My Lady's asked after our escort in every village we've passed through, and no one she's asked yet ever saw them. That means they never got this far, that whatever happened to them is still ahead somewhere. I *knew* those men, Bahzell. I'd've taken Sword Oath nothing could stop them—not all of them—but something did, and there's no reason to think it wouldn't have stopped another fifty men. Aye, or a hundred for all I know!"

Bahzell nodded and leaned back in his too-small chair,

ankles crossed and ears lowered in thought, and Tothas watched him in taut silence. He and Brandark could almost feel the intensity with which the Horse Stealer's mind worked, and, finally, Bahzell gave a slow nod and straightened.

"All right, Tothas. You've told it, and I'm thinking Lady Zarantha had the right of it all along. Yet something's happened to her now, and it's in my mind that means something was after changing here in Dunsahnta."

"Here?" Brandark asked. "Why not somewhere back along the road?"

"Because whatever could take her from a locked room—aye, and half-kill Rekah in the way of it, without our hearing a sound—could have done the same thing in the night on a lonely road. No, something *here* gave her away."

"But what?" Tothas asked hopelessly.

"Well, as to that, I've no certain knowledge, but were either of you after watching that greasy little landlord when he first arrived?"

Bahzell eyed his companions keenly, and they shook their heads.

"I was," he said grimly, "and it was white as snow he went, even before that door came down."

"You think he set them on us?" Brandark asked in an ugly voice, and Bahzell shrugged.

"It might be, and it might not, but what I *am* thinking is that he'd guessed what had happened from the start. And for that, he had to be knowing *something*."

"Ah?" Brandark murmured evilly, and Bahzell nodded.

"Ah, indeed," he agreed, and stood. He dragged on his aketon and scale mail and reached for his sword, and his face was bleak. "If yonder wee toad is after knowing a single thing, I'll have it out of him one way or another, and when I've done, it may just be we'll know where to start looking."

"But what can we do against sorcery?" Tothas asked, and Brandark smiled at him.

"Tothas, we're hradani. We *know* what wizards can do, but none of us would ever have made it to Norfressa without learning a trick or two."

"Wizardry?"

"No wizardry," Bahzell grunted, "but there's precious little a wizard can be doing with a foot of steel in his guts, and no wizard ever born can control a hradani who's given himself to the Rage. That was their mistake, d'you see, when they made us what we are. The only way they can stop us is to kill us, and a hradani, Tothas," his eyes burned, and his voice was very, very soft, "takes a lot of killing with a wizard in reach of his blade."

# CHAPTER TWENTY-TWO

Mail jingled and weapons harness creaked as Bahzell led Brandark and Tothas downstairs. The taproom was a wasteland of empty chairs and crooked tables, smelling of stale drink and smoke, and the two servants who should have been putting last night's clutter to rights huddled in a corner, whispering urgently to one another.

Their whispers chopped off with knife-sharp suddenness as the armed and armored trio appeared. The servants exchanged furtive, frightened glances, then one of them reached for his broom while the other cleared his throat, picked up a heavy tray of dirty tankards, and started to sidle out.

"Not so fast, my lad," a deep voice rumbled, and a tree-trunk arm blocked his way. Bahzell smiled, and the servant froze and licked his lips.

"M-M-M'lord?" he quavered.

"It's a word with your master I want. Where might I be finding him?"

"I-I'm sure I w-wouldn't know, M'lord."

"Wouldn't you, now?" Bahzell watched the man's shoulders tighten. "I'd not like to think you a liar, so just you give me your best guess, and it's grateful I'll be."

The servant swallowed and darted an agonized look of appeal over his shoulder, but his fellow was busy sweeping up sawdust—a task which obviously occupied him to the exclusion of all else.

The man with the tray looked back up at Bahzell. The hradani made no threatening gestures, but his eyes were cold, and someone his size required no theatrics. The servant swallowed again, then slumped.

"I-In the kitchen, M'lord."

"There, now. You *did* have a notion, didn't you? And it's grateful I am." Bahzell looked at Brandark. "Brandark, my lad, why don't you find a seat and keep these fine fellows company for a bit."

"Certainly." The Bloody Sword bowed to the servants and settled into a chair just inside the doorway.

"Don't be long," he called after his departing friends. "I left my balalaika upstairs, and I can't entertain properly without it."

The Brown Horse's kitchens were none too clean, and Bahzell's nose wrinkled at the smell of rancid grease and over-ripe garbage as he thrust the swinging door open.

The landlord was in the middle of the kitchen, talking excitedly to another servant. This one was just fastening his cloak when Bahzell and Tothas entered, and he and his master froze like rabbits.

The Horse Stealer hooked his thumbs in his belt and rocked gently, his smile almost genial, and the landlord's face twitched.

"Ah, that will be all, Lamach," he said, and the servant started for a rear door, only to freeze again as Bahzell cleared his throat. He looked back over his shoulder, and the hradani cocked his head at him.

"Now don't you run off on our account, Lamach. You'd be after making me think you don't like us."

He crooked a beckoning finger, and Lamach swallowed, but his feet moved as if against his will, carrying him back to the towering hradani.

"That's a good lad!" Bahzell looked at Tothas. "Why don't you take Lamach outside there, Tothas? It's only a word or two I need with his master, and if the two of you see to it we're bothered by naught, why, Lamach can be on his way as soon as we've done. Unless, of course, there's some reason his master should be reconsidering his errand."

Tothas nodded curtly and waved Lamach out into the hall. The doors swung shut, and Bahzell turned back to the pudgy, white-faced, sweating landlord, and folded his arms across his massive chest.

"Now don't you worry, friend," he soothed. "I've no doubt you've been told all manner of tales about my folk, and dreadful they must have been, but you've my word they weren't true. Why, we're almost as civilized as your own folk these days, and as one civilized man to another, I'd not harm a hair on your head. Still," his voice stayed just as soothing, but his eyes glittered, "I'm bound to admit there *are* things can cause any of us to backslide a mite. Like lies. Why, I've seen one of my folk rip both a man's arms off for a lie. Dreadful sorry he was for it afterward, but—"

He shrugged, and the landlord whimpered. Bahzell let him sweat for a long, frightened minute, then went on in a harder voice.

"It's in my mind you know more about this than you're wishful to admit, friend."

"N-N-No!" the landlord gasped.

"Ah!" Bahzell cocked his ears. "Was that a *lie* I heard?"

He unfolded his arms, and the landlord flinched in terror, but the hradani merely scratched his chin thoughtfully. "No," he said after a moment, "no, it's certain I am you'd not lie, but you'd best speak more clearly, friend. For a moment there I was thinking you'd said 'No'."

"I-I-I—" the pudgy man stuttered, and Bahzell frowned.

"Look you here, now," he said in a sterner voice. "You were after pissing yourself even before Brandark fetched you upstairs this morning. You *knew* something was wrong—aye, and you'd more than a suspicion *what*, too, I'm thinking—before ever that door went down. Come to that, I can't but wonder just where you were sending Lamach in such a hurry. It's enough to make a man think you meant to warn someone I might be hunting him. Now, I'm naught but a hradani, but to my mind a man as knows what's happened to my friends and won't tell me, he's not so good a friend to me. And if he's not my *friend*, well—"

He shrugged, and the landlord sank to his knees on the greasy floor, round belly shaking like pudding, and clasped his hands before him.

"Please!" he whispered. "Oh, *please!* I-I don't *know* anything—truly I don't! A-And if I were . . . were to say anything that *wasn't* true, or . . . or if I *don't* tell him you're . . . you're asking questions—"

His voice broke piteously, but Bahzell only gazed down with flinty eyes, and something inside the landlord shriveled under their dreadful promise.

"There's a lass half-dead upstairs," Bahzell said softly. "A good lass—not perfect, maybe, but a good person. If it should happen you'd aught to do with that, I just might take it into my head to carve out your liver and fry it in front of you." The Horse Stealer's voice was infinitely more terrifying for its matter-of-fact sincerity, and the innkeeper shuddered.

"That's bad enough, I'm thinking," the hradani went on, "but there's worse, for Lady Zarantha *isn't* upstairs. Now, it's possible she's dead, but there's no way I can know until I find her, and find her I will, one way or another. Alive or dead, I *will* find her, and if it should happen when I do that I'm after learning you *did* know something and kept it from me, or warned those as have her I was coming, I'll be back." The landlord looked up in dull terror, and Bahzell bared his teeth and spoke very, very softly.

"You'd best be remembering every tale you ever heard about my folk, friend, because this I promise you. If Lady Zarantha dies and you've kept aught back from me, you'll wish you'd died with her—however it was—before you do."

"—so that's the whole of it, so far as he knows," Bahzell told his friends grimly. The healer was still upstairs with Rekah, and they sat before the cold taproom hearth while he spoke quietly. "Mind, it's not so certain I am he's told me *all* he knows, but I'm thinking what he has said is true enough."

"Yes, and it makes sense, too," Brandark muttered. The Bloody Sword's dagger glittered as he carved patterns in the tabletop, and his ears were half-flattened. "Gods! No wonder the poor bastard's scared to death. Black wizards less than a league away, and he can't even tell the authorities because one of them *is* the authorities!"

Tothas nodded, wasted face shocked, for despite all that had happened since he first set out for Axe Hollow with Zarantha, the possibility that wizards had infiltrated the Empire had been only a suspicion before.

"Aye, well, I was listening hard to all he said," Bahzell said, "and I'm thinking Baron Dunsahnta himself's not so powerful a wizard as all that."

"But the landlord claims he's their leader!" Tothas objected.

"So he does, but think. The baron's magistrate and land-lord in one. That's making him king frog in a tiny pond; if you were after being one of the tadpoles in his puddle, wouldn't you think he *had* to be the one in charge?"

The Spearman nodded after a moment, and Bahzell shrugged.

"Well, then, think on this. It's death to dabble in black sorcery and blood magic, so if you were after being a black wizard and you were wishful to move into an area, who would you look to recruit first of all?"

"The most powerful noble in it," Tothas said flatly. "Aye, they'd almost have to bring him in on their side—or kill him and put one of their own in his place."

"So they would. And I'm wondering about something else, as well. If magi can sense black wizards, can a wizard sense a mage?"

Tothas screwed his forehead up in thought, then shook his head.

"No. Oh, they can sense the mage *talent*, if it's strong enough, but only if it's used, and—"

"And she was probably using it," Brandark said grimly. Tothas frowned at him, and the Bloody Sword's ears twitched. "Think, man. You say she can 'confuse the eye' into not noticing her, and she was pretending to be Rekah's maid. Don't you think she'd have been reinforcing that any way she could?"

Tothas drew a deep breath and nodded unwillingly.

"That was in my own mind," Bahzell murmured. He drummed on the table for a long, silent moment while Brandark carved a fresh design, then glanced sideways at Tothas. "You were saying something this morning—something about their taking her 'home' to kill." Tothas nodded, and Bahzell frowned. "How sure would you be of that? And why would they do it?"

"I can't be positive, but if they know *who* she is, not just what, it's what they'll do. Oh, they'll kill her out of hand sooner than let her go, but if they can get her home and kill her on her own ground, they will."

"Why?" Bahzell repeated.

"Because she's heir to Jashân," the armsman said, as if that explained everything.

"And?" Brandark asked, and sighed at Tothas' look of disbelief. "Tothas, what our people remember about wizards is how to *kill* them, not how they do whatever they do, and *we* didn't spend years in Axe Hallow learning about them."

"Oh." The Spearman digested that for a moment, then shrugged. "Well, it has to do with the nature of blood magic. Mind you, My Lady knows far more about it than I do, but from what I've been told, no wizard produces his own power. Mage talent draws on the power of the mage's own mind, but a wizard uses the energy that—well, that holds everything *together*, if you see what I mean."

Both hradani looked blank, and he sighed.

"The magi say there's power in everything, even a rock, but especially in living things. The white wizards—when there were any—were sworn never to use the energy of living things, especially people, unless someone chose to let them, and even then they were bound never to kill or injure the . . . the donor. Are you with me so far?"

"Yessssss," Brandark said slowly. "Or I *think* I am, anyway."

"All right, then. The trouble is, very few wizards can use the energy of *un*living things without years of study. It's harder to work with for some reason. But life energy, now, that's easy to work with, especially at the moment of death. When a living thing dies, its energy—its life force—flows back out to merge with all the energy about it, and if a wizard seizes it when it does, he can use it however he wants. That's why blood wizards seem so powerful. They may actually be weak—compared to other wizards, anyway—but they have a stronger energy source to work with, you see."

Both hradani nodded this time, and Tothas leaned over the table.

"Remember I got all this in bits and pieces, so I may have some of it wrong, but from what I understand, the more intelligent a creature, the greater its energy. That's why the most powerful blood rituals use people, not animals. And, by the same token, a younger person has more energy than someone who's old and closer to death . . . and a mage has more than almost anyone else."

Bahzell's mouth tightened, and Tothas nodded.

"But that's not all," he said more harshly, no longer discussing theory but returning to the mistress he loved. "Some people, well, they 'resonate' with the life force around them."

"'Resonate'?" Brandark repeated carefully, and Tothas nodded again.

"That's the word Master Kreska used the one time he discussed it with me. You see, when someone follows another person, then a tiny bit of *his* energy is tied up with that person's. It's . . . well, it's like a burning glass. Whenever you give allegiance to someone, that person is a focus for you, almost a *part* of you, and if you give allegiance willingly—because you trust or love them, not just because you must—the bond is stronger. D'you follow?"

Brandark and Bahzell nodded dubiously, and Tothas sighed.

"Well, when you're a ruler—or a ruler's heir—you're the focus of a great many people's energy. And when you're a ruler like Duke Jashân—or Lady Zarantha—most of those people love and trust you. So if they can get her back onto Jashân land, back into range of all that energy, and *then* kill her—"

He broke off, biting his lip, and Bahzell squeezed his shoulder.

"All right," the Horse Stealer said quietly. "From what you've said, I'm thinking you're right. She's alive so far, and they'll be looking for a way to get her home, and that means we've still time to find her first."

"Where do we start?" Brandark asked.

"Well, as to that, I'm minded to pay a little call on the baron," Bahzell rumbled. "I've fair pumped that landlord dry, and from all he's said, Dunsahnta can't have above two score armsmen, and his 'keep's' scarce more than a fortified manor house. Now wouldn't it be a strange thing if such as we couldn't get into a place like that if it so happened we'd a mind to?"

Neither of his companions seemed to find anything to object to in that statement, and he smiled.

"Now, it may be we'll find Lady Zarantha clapped up in there somewhere, but, truth to tell, I'm thinking they'll have started her off to the South Weald as soon as ever they could. They've no way to know what we'll do, so they'll try to get her home quick enough to outrun anything we *might* do."

Tothas nodded unhappily, but Bahzell squeezed his shoulder again.

"Buck up, man. Unless they've some magical beastie to use for it, they've no choice but to move her by horse, wagon, or afoot. Just let me sniff out the way they've gone, and I'll run them to ground before they make it." Brandark nodded sharply, endorsing the Horse Stealer's promise, and Bahzell's eyes gleamed at Zarantha's armsman.

"And, d'you know, Tothas, if I can but have a word with this Baron Dunsahnta—aye, or with one or two of his guardsmen—I'll know exactly where to look for her."

# CHAPTER TWENTY-THREE

A nail-paring moon floated in racing cloud wrack as Brandark and Tothas swung down from their horses under the leafless trees. Bahzell tied Zarantha's mule to a branch and stood looking out from the woods at their objective, then turned his head as the other two stepped up beside him.

"You were right—it *isn't* much of a keep," Brandark murmured.

Bahzell grunted and returned his attention to Baron Dunsahnta's home. Dunsahnta had never been a rich holding, despite its position on the main road north. The current baron's father had won his title for service in the Spearman army that pushed the Empire's borders up to the Blackwater River, but he'd never had the money to build a proper seat for his barony. Instead, he'd taken over the single fortified manor in the area and expanded it. In fairness to him, his military instincts had been sound, and his "keep" would have been a much nastier proposition if his son had maintained it properly.

The first baron had laid out an extended perimeter of earthen ramparts with angled bastions to let archers sweep the wall between them, and a deep ditch had been dug at the foot of the wall. He'd clearly never intended to hold that much wall solely with his own retainers; he'd built it to cover the entire population of Dunsahnta Village and all of his other subjects in time of war, and he would have expected them to help man the defenses.

His son, however, had let the earthworks crumble. Parts of them had eroded and slipped down into the ditch at their foot, providing breaches and bridges in one, and no one had brushed back the approaches in years. Some of the saplings out there were taller than Bahzell, and what should have been a clear killing zone for archery was waist high in undergrowth. It seemed the current baron had more important charges on his purse than sheltering his people against attack.

Still, he hadn't totally neglected his security. The inner stone wall about the manor house proper was high enough, and sound, and Bahzell's night vision made out two guards at the main gate. Lanterns gleamed at the wall's corners, as well. He couldn't be certain whether there were any guards up there, though it seemed likely. But there was a smaller gate—not quite a sally port, but something similar—in an angle of the wall. It was drenched in shadow, hidden from anyone who might be standing atop the wall, and even his eyes saw no guard anywhere near it.

"There," he said finally, pointing at the side gate.

"There?" Tothas sounded doubtful. "That's a long way to go without being spotted, and you don't really expect it to be unlocked, do you?"

"I can't know till I've looked, now can I? And as for 'a long way to go'—" Bahzell snorted. "I've crossed barer ground than yon against *Sothōii* sentries, Tothas! Against these lads, and with all that lovely brush, it's after being no challenge at all, at all."

"*You've* crossed?" Brandark asked sharply. "I don't like the sound of that, Bahzell! You weren't thinking of leaving us behind, were you?"

"So I was—and am." Brandark started to protest, but Bahzell's raised hand cut him off. "Hush, now! How's a city boy like you to know his arse from his elbow when it comes to skulking in the shrubbery? Aye, and Tothas here's naught but a great, thundering cavalryman! No, lads. This is a job for someone who knows how to move quick and quiet in the grass."

Tothas started a protest, but he bit it back when Bahzell looked down at him. It would take only one of his harsh, strangling coughs to give them all away, and they both knew it, but Brandark was less easily silenced.

"Quick and quiet you may be, but there's only one of you and forty of them. At least an extra pair of eyes could watch your back!"

"So they could, but it's more useful the pair of you will be out here. It may just be I'll be leaving a mite faster than I came, and if I am, there's like enough to be someone following after. If there is, I'm thinking two men on horseback will seem at least a dozen in the dark."

"Humpf!" Brandark brooded up at his friend, then sighed. "All right. All right! I don't believe for a minute that's your real reason, but go ahead. Hog all the fun!"

The grounds inside the earthworks weren't quite as overgrown as those outside. Parts of the area, particularly around the manor's front entrance, were actually landscaped, but less attention had been paid to its flanks, and Bahzell flowed from clump to clump of brush like winter fog.

He worked his way towards the side gate, but the sliver of moon broke from the clouds again as he started to slip out of the last underbrush. He dropped instantly back with a mental curse, but his curse became something else a moment later, for the faint moonlight glimmered on the dull steel of a helmet in the inner wall's shadows. The Horse Stealer went flatter than ever, and his eyes narrowed as the man under that helmet stirred. Had he been seen after all? But the lone guard only stamped his feet against the chill, then flapped his arms across his chest, and Bahzell's momentary worry faded into satisfaction. The gateway was equipped with a portcullis, but it was raised and the entry was protected only by a light, almost ornamental iron lattice. A flagstoned path led from the gate into a formal garden that had reverted to tangled wilderness, but if there was a guard out here, people still used that gate. And if they used it, it might just be unlocked after all.

Yet that guard was a problem. His sword didn't worry Bahzell—not taken by surprise out of the dark—but if he had time for a single shout, the hradani might as well not have come. Still, this was a problem he'd dealt with before, and against guards far more alert than this fellow seemed.

The hradani cocked an eye at the moon. A nice, thick patch of cloud was coming up fast, and he drew his dagger. He'd left his arbalest with Brandark, for it was only in tales that men obliged by dying silently with arrows in their guts. If you wanted to be quiet, you needed a knife at close quarters, and he'd coated the blade in lampblack against any betraying gleam.

He held the weapon at his side, but his attention never wavered from the guard. A tiny corner of his mind supposed he should feel sympathy for the stranger he was about to kill, but he didn't. If that fellow's friends had done their jobs, they wouldn't have a Horse Stealer in the shrubbery thirty feet from the wall. Besides, if the innkeeper knew of their baron's activities, *they* surely did, and anyone who served wizards deserved whatever came his way.

The cloud swept towards the moon, and Bahzell waited with the motionless patience he'd learned the hard way. Then the moonlight dimmed, and the hradani was on the move. He didn't wait for the light to go completely; he moved while it was still dimming and the guard's eyes would be adjusting to the change, and for all his size and bulk, he made no more sound than the wind.

The hapless guardsman had no warning at all. One instant all was still, as cold and boring as it had been all night; in the next, a hand of iron clamped over his mouth and wrenched his head back as if he were a child. He had one instant to see the glitter of brown eyes, the loom of half-flattened, foxlike ears, and then a dagger drove up under his chin and into his brain.

Bahzell lowered the corpse to the ground and crouched above it, ears cocked for any sound, then straightened and peered through the lattice. It had two leaves, meeting in the middle, and he detected no sign of life in the ill-lit courtyard beyond. So far, so good, but the iron gate bars were leprous with rust, and his hand was cautious as he reached for the latch handle.

He turned it gently, and hissed a curse at pinch-penny landlords as metal squealed. The sound seemed loud enough to wake the dead, but he gritted his teeth and hoped the wind would hide it. Besides, he reminded himself, noises always seemed louder to the fellow trying to creep in than to a sentry.

Hinges creaked less shrilly than the latch as he eased the gate open, and he pulled the dead guard to his feet. He leaned the body back in the angle of the wall and propped it there. It didn't look much like an alert sentry to him—then again, the fellow hadn't *been* an alert sentry, so perhaps no one would notice a change if they glanced his way.

The Horse Stealer shrugged and slipped through the opening. He drew the gate gently closed behind him, gritting his teeth once more as hinges squeaked, but he didn't latch it. The latch mechanism was too damned noisy for that; besides, he might be in a hurry when he came back this way.

Few windows were lit, and most of those that were glowed only dimly. Either the baron's servants were expected to get along with poor illumination, or else most of them had gone to bed, leaving only night lights behind them. Bahzell reminded himself to assume it was the former—which, given the state of the grounds, seemed likely, anyway—and turned to the one wing whose many-paned windows gleamed brightly. He worked his way silently along the wall towards it, hugging the shadows, and his keen ears were cocked for any noise while his eyes swept back and forth.

He reached the well-lit wing and allowed himself a sigh of relief, but the truly hard part was just beginning. He couldn't go about peering through windows to find what he sought. Leaving aside what it would do to his night vision, he'd silhouette himself against them. Even the baron's men might notice a seven-and-a-half-foot hradani under those circumstances, which meant he had to get inside and take his chances on who he met.

The ground-floor windows were little more than slits, precisely to make life difficult for intruders, but the second-floor windows were wider. Of course, they were also closed, and half of them were shuttered as well, but Bahzell picked a glass-paned door that was neither lit nor shuttered. It gave onto a small balcony, and he wondered fleetingly how comforting a prayer might have been just now for a man with any use for gods as he sheathed his dagger and jumped up to catch a balustrade that would have been beyond the reach of any human.

He worked his hands up the carved stone uprights and grunted as he got a knee over the balcony's lip and rolled over the railing. It was awkward in mail, especially with his sword on his back, and he made far more noise than he liked, but no one raised a shout of alarm.

He flattened against the wall beside the door, waiting a moment to be sure no one had seen him, then tried the latch. It was locked, of course, and the crack between it and its frame was too narrow to get his dagger through. He muttered a quiet malediction, tugged off his gloves, and dug his dagger point into the soft lead that sealed the pane beside the latch in place.

It was nerve-wracking work, yet he made himself work slowly. His hands were cold, but his fingers needed their ungloved nimbleness, and he bared his teeth as the first diamond-shaped pane fell into his palm. He laid it aside and went back to work, and an adjoining pane came away quickly. With both of them out and the supporting lattice between them cut, he could reach through to grip the next pane from both sides, and within five minutes he had a gap large enough to get his entire forearm through.

He examined the latch by touch and found the deadbolt. The door popped obediently open, and he slipped inside and drew it shut once more.

The smell of leather and ink told him he was in a library. Light gleamed under a door across from him, and he picked his careful way towards it, skirting the half-seen tables and chairs which furnished the room.

The door was unlocked. He eased it open a tiny crack and peered out on a hallway as richly furnished as the outer keep was poorly maintained. No one was visible in the only direction he could see, but there was a mirror on the facing wall, and he froze instantly, holding the door exactly where it was.

The guardsman in the hall was unarmored, but he wore a broadsword at his side as he stood with his back to a closed door at the end of the passage, and he looked far more alert than the gate guard had been.

The Horse Stealer mouthed another silent curse, then paused. A guard implied something—or someone—to guard. It was remotely possible Zarantha was behind that door; if she wasn't, then the sentry was likely there to protect the baron's own privacy, and—

His thoughts chopped off, and his lips drew back in a snarl as a high, shrill scream echoed through the thick door. His muscles twitched, but he made himself stand a moment longer. If that was the baron, and if the baron was a wizard, there was but one way to face him. The thought sickened Bahzell, yet it was the only way—he'd known that before ever setting out tonight.

He drew a deep breath, stepped back from the door, closed his eyes, and reached deliberately deep within himself.

He felt the bright, instant flare, the shock of a barrier going down, a door opening . . . a monster rousing. Jaw muscles lumped and sweat dotted his forehead, but he fought the monster. He'd never attempted anything quite like this, for he'd been afraid to. The Rage was too potent. He dared not free it often, lest it grow too terrible to control, and that had always precluded experiments. Yet tonight he needed it, and he let it wake but slowly, rationing out the chain of his will link by single link, strangling the need to roar his challenge as the fierce exultation swept through him.

The massive hradani trembled with the physical echo of the struggle against his demon. Beads of sweat merged into a solid sheet, breath hissed between his teeth in sharp, sibilant spits of air, and a guttural sound—too soft to be a snarl yet too savage to be anything else—shivered in his throat. It was a slow, agonizing process, this controlled waking of the Rage, but he fought his way through it, clinging to the purpose which had brought him here, and then, suddenly, his shoulders relaxed and his eyes flared open once more.

They were different, those eyes. Both brighter and darker, hard as polished stone, and his lips drew back as another shriek of pain floated down the corridor.

The Rage boiled within him like fixed, focused purpose, and he sheathed his dagger and flexed his fingers, then toed the library door open.

He made no move to step through it as it swung gently, silently wide. His thoughts were crystal clear, gilded in the Rage's fire yet colder than ice, and he simply stood watching in the mirror as the guard at the head of the hall looked up. The sentry frowned and opened his mouth, but another scream—more desperate than the others—came through the door at his back, and he grimaced.

Not the time for a prudent guard to be disturbing his master, Bahzell thought through the glitter of the Rage, and his ears flattened as the sentry drew his sword and started down the hall. He *was* better than the gate guard had been, and his head turned in slow, small arcs, as if he sensed some unseen danger. But he couldn't quite bring himself to raise the alarm over no more than a door that had opened of itself. Perhaps, he thought, the baron had failed to close it securely and some gust of wind through the library windows had pushed it open. Unlikely though that seemed, it was far more likely than that someone had crept past all the outer guards, scaled to a second-floor room undetected, and then opened the door without even stepping through it!

Yet even as his mind sought some harmless reason, his sword was out and his eyes were wary. He reached the door and stood listening, unaware Bahzell could see him in the mirror. He reached out and gripped the door in his free hand, drawing it further back to step around it, and as the door moved, Bahzell, too, reached out. His long arm darted around the door with the blinding, pitiless speed of the Rage. He ignored the sentry's sword; his hand went for the other man's throat like a striking serpent.

The guard's eyes flared in panic. He sucked in air to shout even as he tried to leap back, but that enormous hand didn't encircle his neck. It gripped the *front* of his throat between thumb and fisted fingers, and his still-born shout died in an agonized gurgle as Bahzell twisted his hand. A trachea crushed, ripped, tore, and then the Horse Stealer stepped out into the hall, and his other hand caught the guard's sword hand as the strangling sentry tried frantically to strike at him.

The guardsman's free hand beat at Bahzell, but the hradani's grip was an iron manacle upon his sword hand. He couldn't even open his fingers to drop the weapon, and Bahzell Bahnakson's cold, merciless smile was the last thing his bulging eyes ever saw as his crushed wind-pipe strangled him to death.

Bahzell held the body until it stopped twitching, dragged it back into the library, and lowered it to the carpet. Steel rasped as he drew his own sword, and then he went down the hall with the deadly tread of a dire cat.

The carved door was locked, and Bahzell raised a booted foot. He drove it forward, and the door crashed open as its lock disintegrated.

It wasn't a woman who'd been screaming; it was a boy—naked, no more than twelve, bound to a stone table, his chest already a bloody ruin of oozing cuts—and a silk clad man leapt back with a startled cry as his door flew wide.

"*What in Carnad—?!*" he snapped, whirling towards the intrusion, but the oath died in his throat and his eyes went huge. He stared at Bahzell in disbelief, then dropped his razor-edged knife, and his hands flickered.

Something tore at Bahzell, twisting deep in his brain, but he barely felt its pain, and the wordless snarl of a hunting beast quivered in his throat. He bounded through the door and kicked it shut behind him, and Baron

Dunsahnta paled as his spell of compulsion failed. He spat a phrase in High Kontovaran, hands moving again, but the force of Bahzell's Rage filled the very air. The baron had never encountered its like—never imagined anything like it—and the terrible power of the curse of the hradani lashed at him. Not even a full adept could have adjusted for its impact, for the way it twisted and reverberated in the energy fields about him, and the baron was little more than a journeyman. The bolt of power which should have struck Bahzell down flashed up from the baron's hands in a dazzling burst of light that accomplished absolutely nothing, and then that huge sword whistled at him.

Baron Dunsahnta screamed as the flat of the blade crashed into his left arm. Bone splintered, hurling him to the floor, and a boot slammed down on his right elbow. He shrieked again as more bone broke, then wailed in terror as a hand gripped his robe and snatched him up. Brown eyes, harder than stone and colder than death itself, stared into his, and he writhed in agony and strangling panic as the mouth below those eyes smiled.

"Now then," a voice that was inhuman in every sense of the word said coldly, almost caressingly, "I'm thinking it's time we had a little chat."

# CHAPTER TWENTY-FOUR

Brandark stared out into the night, trying to hide his concern. Bahzell had been gone too long, but he'd heard no alarms, and one thing was certain: his friend would never be taken quietly, whatever happened. So—

"And a good evening to you, Brandark," a deep voice said, and the Bloody Sword leapt a full foot into the air. His sword was in his hand by the time he landed, and he whirled with a curse.

"Fiendark seize you, don't *do* that!" he gasped at the huge shadow which had filtered from the night and heard Tothas' soft, sibilant endorsement, but both of them crowded forward to seize the Horse Stealer's shoulders— only to pause as they saw the small, cloth-wrapped body he held.

Bahzell ignored them and bent over the boy in his arms. The youngster shook like a terrified leaf, and his eyes were huge with fear and pain, but a smile trembled on his mouth when the hradani nodded to him.

"There now, didn't I say we'd be making it out?" The boy managed a tiny answering nod. "So I did, and now we'll take you where it's safe. You've my word."

The boy closed his eyes and pressed his face into the Horse Stealer's armored chest, and Bahzell's huge, gentle hands held him close.

"My Lady?" Tothas demanded, and slumped as Bahzell shook his head.

"Buck up, man. We'd never much hope of finding her here, but now I've a notion where I should be looking."

"You do?" Tothas looked back up eagerly, and the hradani nodded.

"Aye. But first we've a lad to get safe back to The Brown Horse, and then it's time we were making some plans."

The landlord was less than pleased to see them back— until he recognized his own nephew in Bahzell's arms. The healer was still there, watching over Rekah, and the innkeeper snatched the boy up and hurried upstairs with him while Bahzell turned to his friends once more in the taproom.

"You know where to find My Lady?" Tothas demanded urgently.

"In a manner of speaking." Bahzell swallowed a huge gulp of ale, and only Brandark recognized the dark core of sickness, the remembered hunger of the Rage, in his eyes. "Look you, Tothas, we knew they'd not waste time, and so they haven't. Lady Zarantha is on her way to Jashân, but they daren't risk the roads lest someone see them, so it's cross-country they've taken her."

Tothas stared at him, mouth working with fear for his mistress, then nodded sharply.

"How many of them?" Brandark asked, and Bahzell frowned.

"Aye, well, there's the bad news. They've two wizards

with 'em, and ten of the baron's men, which would be bad enough, I'm thinking, but there's ten dog brothers, as well."

"*Dog* brothers?" Brandark repeated, and cursed at Bahzell's nod. "Phrobus take it, will we *never* be done with those scum?"

"Not just yet, any road," Bahzell replied, "and they're to meet with still more men along the way."

"Where?" Tothas asked sharply.

"As to that, the baron didn't know. But where they *started* from's another thing, and even a blind Horse Stealer could follow a score of horses!"

"Then let's be on our way!"

"Wait, now." Bahzell's powerful hand pushed the Spearman gently back into his chair, and he shook his head. "Think, man. Even such as I need light to see by. And—" his voice deepened, and his grip on Tothas' shoulder tightened "—it's not 'we' must be on our way, but only Brandark and me."

"*What?!*" Tothas' face went white, and he shook his head violently. "She's my *lady*, Bahzell! I've watched over her since she could walk!"

"Aye, and you'll die in a week in weather like this." Tothas flinched, but the hradani went on with brutal honesty. "Or, worse, you'll slow us. I know you'd die for her, but out there in the cold and wet, with no roof and like as not no fire, it's die for *nothing* you would. Leave this to us."

Tothas stared at him, mouth tragic, then closed his eyes while tears trickled down his wasted face, and Bahzell squeezed his shoulder hard.

"Will you trust us with her life, sword brother?" he asked softly, and the armsman nodded brokenly.

"As with my own honor," he whispered.

"Thank you." Bahzell squeezed his shoulder once more, then sat back and smiled sadly. "And before you come all over useless feeling, Tothas, it's in my mind you'll have enough on your plate as it is."

"What?" Tothas blinked in confusion, and Bahzell shook his head.

"There's Rekah upstairs. She'll need you—aye, and the boy, too. It's marked for more of the baron's blood magic he was, and I'm thinking there's some would be happier if neither he nor Rekah told what happened to them."

"The baron?" Brandark asked sharply, and, despite himself, Tothas shivered at Bahzell's smile.

"Oh, no, not the baron," the Horse Stealer said. Brandark grunted in approval, and Bahzell went on. "But it's naught but a matter of time before one of his men gets up the guts to poke his head into his chambers and find him. There's not many will weep for him, and both his wizard friends are away with Lady Zarantha, but this village will be like a hornet's nest come morning. And that, Tothas, is where I'm thinking you come in."

"How?" Tothas asked, but his voice said he already knew.

"You're a Spearman—and a senior armsman to a Spearman duke. Would the nearest army post send a company or two this way if you asked?"

"Yes." There was no doubt in Tothas' reply, and Bahzell nodded.

"Then we'd best ask someone—the healer, I'm thinking, and not our landlord—who you can trust to be taking word to the army. And until help comes, we'll trust you to keep Rekah and the boy alive to talk when it *does* come. Aye, and while I'm thinking on it, you'd best send word to Duke Jashân, as well. If it's home they're headed, it just might be couriers on the highway can beat them there. But only to Jashân, mind! From the way the baron talked, I've a feeling there's hands in this closer to home."

"I'll do it." Tothas nodded grimly. "Trust me for that and get her back safe. And . . . tell her I love her."

"Ah, don't be daft, man!" Bahzell laughed sadly. "If she needs to be told after all these years, then she's not half so bright as I thought her."

"Tell her anyway," Tothas said with a small, sad smile. "And Tomanāk bless and guide you both."

"Aye, well, thank you," Bahzell said, and glanced wryly at Brandark.

Dawn bled in the east as two hradani picked their way across a field of wheat stubble. They were uncommonly well provided with riding beasts and pack animals, especially when only one of them was mounted. If they were able to find—and rescue—Zarantha, she'd need her mule, and Bahzell's packhorse, the pack mule, and Rekah's mule all carried pack saddles. Brandark thought his friend had been a little unreasonable to insist on loading the pack animals so lightly, but he hadn't argued. They had to take them along, anyway—just as they'd had to take along Tothas' warhorse.

Any villager would recognize the horse as a stranger, and Tothas had decided his best chance for the next few days was to lie hidden in the inn. His horse's presence would betray his own, and taking it along would not only give any who strayed across their tracks the idea that they'd taken *him* along but also provide Brandark with a war-trained change of mounts.

They'd taken Rekah's mule for much the same reasons. Only the healer and the staff of The Brown Horse knew how badly the maid had actually been hurt, and the innkeeper had grown a backbone when Bahzell restored his nephew to him. He was still terrified, but he had the boy's life to worry about now—and a chance to be free of the terror which had haunted his village. He'd agreed to hide both Rekah and Tothas, as well as the boy, while the healer's son—a square, solid young man whose bovine features disguised a ready wit—took word to the nearest garrison.

So now Bahzell and Brandark crossed the field to a narrow track well back from the main road. The twisting band of mud, little used and completely overgrown in places, snaked through desolate winter woodland, but its surface was pocked with the marks of shod hooves and dotted with occasional droppings. The dung was spongy, but not broken down as a heavy rain would have left it. That meant it could be no more than forty-eight hours old, and Bahzell squatted on his heels and studied the hoofprints carefully while Brandark sat his horse beside him and tried not to fidget.

"What are you doing?" the Bloody Sword asked finally.

"Even such as you should know any hoof is after leaving its own mark, city boy, and I've a mind to be sure I'll know 'em when I see them again." Brandark's ears shifted in question, and Bahzell shrugged. "It's like enough we'll lose them somewhere. If it happens we do, don't you think it would be helpful to know what we're looking for when it comes time to be casting about for them?"

Brandark stared at the churned mud and shook his head dubiously. "You can actually recognize individual prints in that mess?"

"D'you recognize notes in a song?" Bahzell asked in reply. Brandark nodded, and the Horse Stealer shrugged. "Well, I'll not say I've all of them straight already, but I'll be having them all tucked away in here—" he tapped his temple "—by the time we've put a mile or two behind us."

"How far ahead are they?"

"As to that," Bahzell frowned and rubbed his chin, ears half-lowered, "they've a full day's start on us, and from all the baron said, they'll have moved like Phrobus himself was on their trail, to start at least, and they've at least two mounts each from these tracks." He shook his head slowly. "I'd not be surprised if they're near thirty leagues in front of us, but they've the better part of four hundred leagues to go in a straight line, and it's no straight line they'll move in. Not if they're minded to avoid the roads. And I'm doubting they'll find fresh mounts once these tire."

"Why?"

"Because they'd no notion Zarantha was after walking into their hands. Close to home, they'll have folk ready to remount them without question, but once out of their own front yard they'll have to buy fresh as they go— assuming they find someplace with more than plowhorses to sell in the middle of all this nothing—and there's too many of them to do that without raising questions. No, once they've settled in to run cross-country they'll have naught but the horses under 'em to do it with, and a strange thing it will be if we can't make up a bit on them every day then." He shook his head again. "It's in my mind we'll catch them up, Brandark, but we'll not do it all in a jump."

Brandark chewed his lip unhappily. "I don't like leaving her in their hands that long."

"No more do I." Bahzell's face turned grim, and his ears went tight to his skull. "They'll be after keeping her alive as long as they've a hope of getting her home to Jashân, but that's not to say they'll treat her well." The Horse Stealer's jaw tightened, and then he shook himself. "Well, we'll not accomplish much while we stand about talking, so—"

He adjusted his sword baldric, and then Brandark blinked as he vanished up the narrow slot of the trail in the ground-devouring lope of the Horse Stealer hradani.

Brandark had heard of how rapidly Horse Stealers could

cover ground and hadn't believed it. But for the first time since leaving Navahk, Bahzell was truly in a hurry, with neither injured women, merchant wagons, nor sick armsmen to slow him, and Brandark had no choice but to believe. He pressed with his heels, urging his horse to a trot, yet he had to ask for a mud-spattering canter, with the long line of horses and mules thudding along behind him, before he could catch up and drop back to a trot. No wonder the infantry of Hurgrum had seemed so baffling to Navahk's cavalry!

Bahzell turned his head and flashed a grin over his shoulder, then turned his eyes back to the trail before him and loped on into the sunrise with the horses and mules bounding along behind him.

# CHAPTER TWENTY-FIVE

Cold wind blew into Brandark Brandarkson's face. It was the sixth evening of their pursuit, and Tothas' horse moved wearily under him as the western horizon ate the sun. Shadows stretched inky black with the onset of evening, but Bahzell jogged steadily on like some tireless, questing hound, and Brandark wrapped his cloak about himself and shivered.

Their quarry had, indeed, kept to wild country. They'd also hooked further east than Brandark had anticipated before turning south, and their twisting path had kept them off ridge lines and avoided open stretches. The hradani had made up ground, as Bahzell had predicted, but less than he'd hoped. Their targets were pushing even harder than he'd feared, almost as if they knew—not suspected, but *knew*—someone was behind them. They were even riding on after nightfall, which took toll of their mounts but meant they regained an hour or two each evening when darkness forced Bahzell to halt.

A stronger gust flapped Brandark's cloak, and he glowered at the clouds in the east. Rain was bad enough—two days back, a storm had all but obliterated the trail; how Bahzell had held to it was more than Brandark could even guess—but this wind smelled of snow. A blanket of that would hide any trail, even from a Horse Stealer, and—

Bahzell's hand flew up. Brandark drew rein, and the other animals shuffled to a grateful halt behind him, breath steaming as they blew. Even Zarantha's mule hung its head without its normal fractiousness, and Brandark frowned as Bahzell swerved off the trail and moved along the flank of a hill. He climbed the slope and knelt to examine something, then stood, put his hands on his hips, and turned slowly. He looked back into the west and then peered into the rapidly darkening east for several minutes, cloak blowing on the wind, before he shook his head and walked back to Brandark.

"What?" Brandark's voice sounded harsh and unnatural to his own ears after the long silence of the afternoon, and Bahzell shrugged.

"There's a spot yonder we can camp." He jabbed a thumb back over his shoulder, but there was an odd note in his voice. Brandark cocked his head, and Bahzell shrugged again. "I'm thinking something new's been added. We're not the only ones following those bastards."

"We're not?" Brandark's ears pricked, and Bahzell grunted.

"That we're not, though who else it may be has me puzzled."

The Horse Stealer scratched his chin for a moment, then turned back the way he'd come, and Brandark dismounted and followed him, leading Tothas' horse. Zarantha's mule pricked its ears and snorted to the other animals as it realized they were headed for a stopping place. Bahzell's packhorse seemed inclined to lag, but the mule's sharp nip drove it on while Brandark followed the Horse Stealer into a hollow cut from the hillside by a spring-fed, ice-crusted stream. A small stand of scrubby trees offered fuel, the slope to the east broke the wind, and the spring bubbled out of the hill with enough energy that it hadn't yet frozen. It was a perfect campsite, but Brandark's ears flattened as he saw where someone had buried the ashes of a small fire.

He started to speak, then stopped himself and let Tothas' horse stand ground-hitched while he dug out the picket pins and began driving them into the ground. Bahzell dragged a boot toe through the earth covering the fire, then thrust his ungloved hand into the ashes, grunted, and rose once more, and Brandark looked up from his picket pins in question.

"Cold," the Horse Stealer said, beginning to remove saddles from their weary animals. "Last night, at least, I'm thinking."

"Was it theirs?"

"That it wasn't. They're after building bigger fires. Besides, there's been only one horse here."

"Just one, hey?" Brandark chewed on that while he finished driving in the picket pins, and Bahzell nodded as he led the first horse over.

"Just the one. And whoever he may be, he's an eye for the land—aye, and one fine horse under him, too."

"What makes you so sure?"

"I've spied his tracks twice today, and there's a fine, long stride on him. That's a horse bred to cover ground, and he's Sothōii war shoes on his feet."

"*Sothōii?!*" Brandark looked up sharply, and Bahzell frowned.

"Aye, and what he's doing so far south is more than I can say. But whatever it is, the fellow on his back seems all-fired interested in the same folk *we're* following. He's a Sothōii's own eye for the trail, too—and I'd not be so very surprised if he's not having a shrewd notion where they're bound."

"Why do you say that?"

"Because he's on them like a lodestone on steel." Bahzell led a second horse over and paused, frowning as he patted the beast's shoulder. "It's not just their trail he's following, Brandark. He's swung wide of it, not simply come down it as we have, and it's in my mind he's cut across more than one loop of it to make up time on them. Either he's a fiendishly good nose for shortcuts, or else he's after knowing where they're headed."

"But how could he know? And why should anyone else follow them?"

"As for that, you've as good a chance of guessing as I do." Both hradani busied themselves removing pack saddles from the mules in the windy dark, but Bahzell's ears shifted in thought as he worked. "No, I've no notion why he's following them," he said at last, "but he is. It's certain I am of that, yet that's what has me puzzled. I'm thinking they're no more than a day ahead of us now, and that fire of his is a day old, at least. So if he's following, why not catch them up and be done with it?"

"Maybe he has and we just don't know it yet," Brandark suggested as he ladled out grain for the animals, but Bahzell shook his head.

"No. If he camped here last night, then he could have caught them up yesterday, so why didn't he? Why be waiting?"

"Maybe he doesn't want to take on twenty men by himself."

"Aye, there's something in that," Bahzell agreed, but he sounded dissatisfied. Brandark frowned in question, and he shrugged. "This lad moves like a Sothōii, and unless I'm badly mistaken, it's a Sothōii warhorse he's riding. Not a courser, no, but still Sothōii. And if you put a Sothōii

on horseback with a bow against such as we're following—" He shrugged.

"Against twenty men?" Brandark said skeptically.

"Or twice that." Brandark blinked in disbelief, and
Bahzell smiled coldly. "If our lad *is* Sothōii, this country
is just the sort he'd like. He'd be on 'em before they
knew it, empty a dozen saddles in a minute, then break
off, and that horse of his would ride any three of theirs
under if they tried to run him down after. Two or three
passes, and he'd have them cut to pieces, and there's not
a way in the world they could be stopping him."

"Not even with wizards to help them?"

"Well, now," Bahzell murmured, "there *is* that, isn't
there? But I'm thinking not even a wizard could have
stopped him from taking two or three before he died,
and we've seen no bodies at all, at all. Which makes me
wonder, Brandark, if he's not knowing *exactly* what it is
he's after?"

"Um." Brandark frowned. "D'you think we've picked
up an ally?"

Bahzell snorted. "Oh, he's on their trail, right enough,
but we've no notion of *why*, and any Sothōii's likely to
be putting an arrow in our gizzards the instant he sees a
pair of hradani. And even if he's not, he's ahead of us.
It's likely enough he knows what it is he's following, but
how's he to know who's following *him*?"

"You *do* have a gift for seeing the bright side, don't
you?" Brandark grumbled, and Bahzell laughed and
headed for the trees with his axe.

A palm-sized fire flickered at the heart of the hollow,
and Bahzell sat at the depression's upper end, just his
head rising above the crest of the low hill while Brandark
slept behind him. His sword lay at his side, and he grimaced and wrapped his cloak a bit tighter as a few dry
pellets of snow whipped at him on the teeth of the wind.

Snow, he thought. Just what they needed. But at least the clouds were thinner than he'd feared—he could actually see a lighter patch where the moon ought to be—and so far the snow was no more than spits. It wouldn't be too bad if it held to flurries, yet Zarantha's captors were keeping to a more rapid pace than he'd expected. He and Brandark had closed the gap, but they were beginning to feel the pace themselves.

Bahzell had only a vague notion of exactly where they were—somewhere in the Middle Weald, he thought. They'd crossed what passed for a Spearman highroad yesterday, which might have been the one between Midrancimb and Boracimb. If it *had* been, then they were little more than two hundred leagues from Alfroma, and if Zarantha's captors were able to keep pushing this hard, the hradani must catch them up soon or risk never catching them at all.

He chewed that thought unhappily, and his mind turned as if by association to the mystery horseman. Bahzell had spent too much time on the Wind Plain not to recognize a Sothōii warhorse's stride when he saw one, but whoever was riding it *wasn't* Sothōii. The more he thought about it, the more certain of that he was, and not just because a Sothōii warrior had no business this far south. No, he *rode* like a Sothōii, and he *tracked* like one, but he didn't *think* like one—not even one who knew he was on the trail of wizards.

The Sothōii horsebow was a deadly weapon in expert hands, and any Sothōii warrior was, by definition, expert. He was also both canny and patient as the grass itself. If a Sothōii knew what he was up against—and the evidence said this rider did—he'd scout the enemy, establish exactly who among them were the wizards and be certain his first two arrows went into them, then take the others one by one. It might take him a while, but he could have them all. If anyone knew that, a Horse Stealer did, and that was exactly why Bahzell was so convinced this fellow was something else.

Yet what sort of something else baffled him, and one thing he didn't need was fresh puzzles. He had enough trouble trying to understand what in the names of all the gods and demons a pair of *hradani* were doing chasing wizards through winter weather in the middle of the Empire of the Spear without wondering why someone else was doing the same thing!

He swore under his breath and shifted position. Brandark, he knew, was in this because of him. Oh, the Bloody Sword had his own reasons for helping Zarantha, but he wouldn't have been here in the first place if he hadn't followed Bahzell out of Navahk—and if Bahzell hadn't dragged Zarantha into his life in Riverside. But why was *Bahzell* in it? He knew what drove him to see Zarantha safe *now*, yet try as he might, he couldn't lay hands on how his life had gotten so tangled to begin with. Each step of the road made sense in and of itself, but why the Phrobus had he set out on it in the *first* place?

As he'd told Tothas, he was no knight in shining armor— the very thought made him ill—nor did his friendship for Tothas and Rekah and Zarantha have anything in common with the revoltingly noble heroes who infested the romantic ballads. And it wasn't nobility that had driven him to help Farmah in Navahk, either. It had been anger and disgust and perhaps, little though he cared to admit it, pity—and look where it had landed him!

His mind flickered back against his will to a firelit cave and the ripple of music, and he growled another curse. Whatever the Lady might say, *he* wasn't out here in the dark for any thrice-damned gods! He was out here because he'd been fool enough to stick his nose into other people's troubles . . . and because he was too softheaded—and hearted—to leave people he liked to their fates. The fact that he'd given his friendship and loyalty to strangers might prove he was stupid, yet at least he understood it. And at least it had been his own decision, his own choice. But as for anything more than that, any notion he had some sort of "destiny" or "task"—

His thoughts broke off, and his head snapped up. Something had changed—something he couldn't see or hear, yet something that sparkled down his nerves and drove his ears flat to his skull. He snatched at his sword hilt, and steel rasped as he surged to his feet, but his shout to Brandark died stillborn as an impossibly deep voice spoke from behind him. A mountain might have spoken so, had some spell given it life, and its deep, resounding music sang in his bones and blood.

"Good evening, Bahzell Bahnakson," it said. "I understand you've met my sister."

# CHAPTER TWENTY-SIX

Bahzell spun around, sword raised, and his eyes went huge.

A man—or what *looked* like a man—stood in the hollow behind him, arms folded across his chest. He was at least ten feet tall, dark haired and dark eyed, with a strong, triangular face that shouted his kinship to the only deity Bahzell had ever seen. A light mace hung at his belt, a sword hilt showed at his left shoulder, and he wore chain mail under a green tabard. No special light of divinity shone about him . . . but he didn't need one.

Tomanāk Orfro, God of War and Judge of Princes, second in power only to his father Orr, stood there in the dark, brown hair stirring on the sharp breeze, and Bahzell lowered his sword almost mechanically. Stillness hovered, broken only by the sigh of the wind, and Tomanāk's sheer presence gripped Bahzell like an iron fist. Something deep inside urged him to his knees, but something deeper and even stronger kept him on his feet.

He bent slowly, eyes never leaving the god, and lifted his baldric from the ground. He sheathed his blade and looped the baldric back over his shoulder, settling the sword on his back, and gave the War God look for look in stubborn silence.

Tomanāk's eyes gleamed. "Shall we stand here all night?" Amusement danced in that earthquake-deep voice. "Or shall we discuss why I'm here?"

"I'm thinking I know why you're here, and it's no part of it I want." Bahzell was astounded by how level his own voice sounded—and by his own temerity—but Tomanāk only smiled.

"You've made that plain enough," he said wryly. "Of all the mortals I've ever tried to contact, your skull must be the thickest."

"Must it, now?" A sort of lunatic hilarity flickered inside Bahzell, and he folded his arms across his own chest and snorted. "I'm thinking that should be giving you a hint," he said, and Tomanāk laughed out loud.

It was a terrible sound—and a wonderful one. It sang in the bones of the earth and rang from the clouds, bright and delighted yet dreadful, its merriment undergirt with bugles, thundering hooves, and clashing steel. It shook Bahzell to the bone like a fierce summer wind, yet there was no menace in it.

"Bahzell, Bahzell!" Tomanāk shook his head, laughter still dancing in his eyes. "How many mortals do you think would dare say that to *me*?"

"As to that, I've no way of knowing, I'm sure. But it might be more of my folk would do it than you'd think."

"I doubt that." Tomanāk's nostrils flared as if to scent the wind. "No, I doubt that. Reject me, yes, but tell *me* to go away once they're face-to-face with me? Not even your people are that bold, Bahzell."

Bahzell simply raised his eyebrows, and Tomanāk shrugged.

"Well, not *most* of them." Bahzell said nothing, and the War God nodded. "And that, my friend, is what makes you so important."

"Important, is it?" Bahzell's lips thinned. "Twelve hundred years my folk have suffered and died, with never a bit of help from you or yours. Just what might be making *me* so all-fired 'important' to the likes of you?"

"Nothing . . . except what you are. I need you, Bahzell." It seemed impossible for that mountainous voice to soften, but it did.

"Ah, now! Isn't that just what I might have expected?" Bahzell bared his teeth. "You've no time to be helping them as need it, but let someone have something *you* want, and you plague him with nightmares and hunt him across half a continent! Well, it's little I know—and less I'm *wishful* to know—of gods. But this I *do* know: I've seen naught at all, at all, to make me want to bow down and worship you. And, meaning no disrespect, I'd as soon have naught at all to do with you, if you take my meaning."

"Oh, I understand you, Bahzell—perhaps better than you think." Tomanāk shook his head once more. "But are you so certain it's what you truly mean? Didn't Chesmirsa tell you the decision to hear me must be your own?"

"So she did. But, meaning no disrespect again, it's in my mind I'm not so wishful as all that to speak to you, so why should I believe her?" Tomanāk frowned, but Bahzell met his eyes steadily—and hoped the god didn't realize just how hard that was. "My folk have had promises enough to choke on, and never a bit of good has it done us."

"I see." Tomanāk studied him a moment, then smiled sadly. "Do you know the real reason you're so angry with me, Bahzell?"

"Angry?" It was Bahzell's turn to frown and shake his head. "It's not *angry* I am, but a man's too little time in this world to waste it on 'gods' that do naught when they're needed most!" He glared up, a corner of his soul shocked by his own effrontery. This was a *god*, a being who could crush him with a thought, but fear was the smallest part of what he felt.

"And that," Tomanāk's earth-shaking voice was gentle, "is why you're angry. Because we've 'done nothing' for your people."

"Because you've done naught *at all*," Bahzell returned hotly. "I'm but a man, but I'm thinking I know what to think of a *man* who saw someone hurt and did naught to help! If you're after being so all-fired concerned about 'good' and 'evil,' then why not *do* something about it and be done with it?!"

"So that's what you want of me?" Tomanāk rumbled. "To reach down my hand and root out all evil, destroy it wherever I find it?" Bahzell scowled in answer, and the god shook his head. "Even if I could, I wouldn't, but I can't. If I stretch out my hand, then the Gods of Darkness will do the same."

"Will they now?" Bahzell snorted with scathing irony. "And here was I, thinking as how they'd already done just that!"

"Then you thought wrongly," Tomanāk said sternly. "Neither they nor we may tamper directly with the world of mortals, lest we destroy it utterly." Bahzell's lips drew back, and Tomanāk frowned. "You think you know a great deal about evil, Bahzell Bahnakson, and so you do—by mortal standards. But it was I who cast Phrobus down, and the evil *I* have seen makes all any mortal can do but a shadow, an echo, of itself. If I fought that evil in your world, power-to-power and hand-to-hand, we would grind an entire universe to dust."

"So where's the use in you, then?" Bahzell demanded.

"Without us, there would be nothing to stop the Gods of Darkness. If we clash directly, we would destroy your world; without the fear of that, the Dark Gods wouldn't hesitate to meddle. They would do as they willed—not just with some mortals, but with *all* of you—and nothing could stop them."

"Aye? And what's after making us so curst important to the both of you? It's long enough you've been squabbling over us, the way tales tell it!"

"I could say we'd be just as angry to see evil take a single mortal as an entire world," Tomanāk's deep voice rumbled, "and that would be true. But it wouldn't be the entire truth. On the other hand, you couldn't understand the *entire* truth." Bahzell bristled, and Tomanāk smiled sadly. "As you yourself said, meaning no disrespect, but the totality is a bit much even for gods to keep straight. Think of it this way, Bahzell. Yours is but one of more universes than you can imagine, and across all those universes, 'good' and 'evil' are eternally at war. Each universe is much like a single city in the total kingdom of existence; if one side triumphs there, then the weight of that universe—that city—is added to its armies. It grows a little stronger; its enemy grows a little weaker. In the end—if there *is* an end—the side which controls enough 'cities' will defeat the other. Remember, I'm offering you only an analogy, but it's close enough to serve."

"So we're naught but sword fodder, are we?" Bahzell curled a lip. "Well, that's something hradani can understand clear enough!"

"You are *not* simple 'sword fodder.'" Tomanāk's eyes flashed, and there was an edge of strained patience in the grumbling thunder of his voice. "Oh, that's what the Dark Gods would make you, and that gives them an edge. They don't *care* what happens to mortals, either individually or as a group; the Gods of Light do care, and that limits what we may do." Bahzell frowned, and Tomanāk's sigh seemed to shake the world. "Your father cares what happens to his people, Bahzell; Churnazh doesn't. Which of them is more free to do as he wills, when he wills, without thinking of others?"

Bahzell's ears cocked. Then he nodded, almost against his will, and Tomanāk shrugged.

"We think well of your father. He's a hard man, and a bit too tempted by expedience at times, but he cares about the people he rules, not simply his power. Yet just as he can work only by degrees, we can't sweep away evil in a moment. And, to give you truth for truth, the Dark Gods won an immense victory in the Fall of Kontovar. What happened to your people is only a part of the evil stemming from that victory, yet it wasn't total. Their servants paid too high a price for it, too many of the free folk escaped to Norfressa, and the war goes on."

"And now you're wanting *me* to sign on for it," Bahzell said shrewdly. Tomanāk considered him for a moment, then nodded, and Bahzell snorted. "Well, I'm thinking it'll be a cold day in Krashnark's Hell first!"

"After railing at *me* for doing nothing?" Tomanāk uncrossed his arms and rested his huge right hand on the haft of his mace.

"As to that, *you're* the god," Bahzell shot back. "I'm naught but what you see. Oh, no question but I'm stupid enough to land myself in messes like this one, yet it's damned I'll be if I join up in a war I never made! Stupid hradani may be, but not so stupid as to be forgetting what happened the *last* time we fought for gods or wizards!"

"You truly are stubborn, aren't you?"

"Aye. It's a lesson my folk were overlong in learning, but learn it we did. I've no notion how long twelve hundred years are to a god, but they've been mortal long and hard for us, and never a sign of you have we seen. You talk of wars, and struggles, and eternity, and that's as may be, but we've no use for 'eternity' when it's all we can do to be keeping our families alive from day to day! No, Tomanāk," Bahzell straightened, and his eyes flashed, "it's no use bidding me to bow down to worship you, for I'll not do it."

"I haven't asked you to—and that's not what I want of you."

Bahzell's jaw dropped. He gaped up at the god, and Tomanāk smiled.

"Don't misunderstand," he said. "Worship *is* a source of power, but it's a *passive* sort of power. Belief is something we can draw upon when we face another god or some task only a god can perform, but it's not very useful in the mortal world. Or, at least, not by itself. Did you think I wanted you to sit around in a temple and tell me how wonderful I am? To bribe me with incense and gifts? To get down on your knees and ask me to solve all your problems? Oh, no, Bahzell Bahnakson! I've too many 'worshipers' who do that already—and even if it was what I wanted from you, you'd be a poor hand at it!"

Bahzell shook himself, and, for the first time, an unwilling grin twitched at the corners of his mouth.

"So I would. And if we're both after agreeing to that, then why should I stand freezing my arse in this wind while you jaw away at me?" he demanded impudently, and Tomanāk laughed once more, then sobered.

"I don't want your worship, Bahzell, but I *do* want you to follow me."

"Ah? And where's the difference, if you don't mind my asking?"

"If I minded, I wouldn't be arguing with a rock-headed hradani while he freezes his arse off!" Bahzell blinked at the tartness in the god's deep voice, but Tomanāk went on more seriously. "I said worship was a passive sort of power, and it is. In many ways, it's most useful to the Dark Gods, because they're prone to meddle so much more openly than we. They can't act directly, but they can use their worshipers as proxies and lend them some of their own power. Even worse, perhaps, they can use other creatures—servants in the same army, drawn from universes where that army has already triumphed—to act for them for a price, and their worshipers provide that price to them. Mortals call those servants demons and devils, though there are far more—and worse—that mortals have never given names to. We spend a great deal of the 'passive' power of *our* worshipers blocking the intrusion of those more terrible servants, but powerful as their lesser servants may be in mortal terms, they're so weak by other standards as to be . . . call it faint. They're difficult to see in the shadows, and they creep past us. Once they reach your world, we can no longer deal with them directly without imperiling that world's very existence. Do you understand that much?"

"No," Bahzell said frankly, "but I've little choice but to be taking your word. Yet even if I do, what's that to me?"

"This," Tomanāk said very seriously. "Because we may not act directly against them—or against mortals who give themselves to evil—we need *followers*, not just worshipers. We require people—warriors—to fight against the Dark, not just people who sit about and ask *us* to."

Bahzell looked unconvinced, and Tomanāk cocked his head.

"Do you worship your father, Bahzell?" The hradani gawked at him for a moment, then snorted derisively at the very thought, and Tomanāk smiled again. "Of course you don't, but you *do* follow him. You share his beliefs and values and act accordingly. Well, I ask no more of you than that."

"Aye, with you telling me what to be thinking and doing!"

"No, with your own heart and mind telling you what to think and do. Puppets are useless, Bahzell, and if I simply commanded and you simply obeyed, then a puppet would be all you were. I am the god and patron of warriors, Bahzell Bahnakson. Loyalty, yes, as you would give any captain—that much I ask of you. But not unthinking worship. Not the surrender of your will to mine. Subservience is what the Dark Gods crave, for warriors who never question will do terrible things and claim they were 'only following orders.' If I stripped your will from you, you would become no more than a slave . . . and I would become no better than Phrobus."

"Would I, now?" Bahzell murmured. He tugged on the end of his nose, considering the god's words, then frowned. "It may be there's something in that," he said finally, slowly, not noticing the change in his own voice, "but true or no, it only tells what you want of me. So tell me this: why should *I* be following you? What's after being in it for *me?*"

For the first time, Tomanāk actually looked nonplused, and Bahzell crossed his arms once more and gazed up at him.

"I've heard your oath," he said derisively. "How your 'followers' are after swearing always to give quarter if it's asked for and never to rape or loot or pillage!"

"But you already don't do those things!" Tomanāk said almost plaintively. "I never asked my followers not to claim legitimate prizes of war, only that they not plunder the helpless and innocent while they're about it. And aside from a few, ah, acquisitions on raids against the Sothōii, you've never looted or pillaged in your life. As for rape—!" Tomanāk threw up his hands as if to indicate the winter-barren wilderness about them and how Bahzell had come to be here, but the hradani shook his head stubbornly.

"That's as may be, but I've never promised I wouldn't," he shot back. Tomanāk refolded his arms with another of those world-shaking sighs, and Bahzell shifted uneasily under his stern gaze, like a little boy who knows perfectly well he's raised a pointless objection out of sheer petulance, but then he shook himself and glared back up at the god.

"Aye, well, that's as may be," he repeated, "but it's often enough now I've seen what *else* serving such as you can cost. Zarantha, now. She swore Mage Oath to Semkirk, and never a bit of good it did her when Baron Dunsahnta and his scummy friends took her. No, nor Rekah, now I think on it. And what of Tothas? He's after being a good man—a better man than *me*, I'm thinking—and it's yourself he 'follows.' But did you save him and his men in Riverside? Did you once reach down your hand to him when he was after coughing his lungs up?"

Silence hovered for a long, fragile moment before Tomanāk spoke once more.

"Tothas," he said, "is *not* a better man than you are. Oh, he's a good man, and one I value highly, but he lacks something you have." Bahzell's ears twitched in disbelief, and the War God smiled crookedly. "Do you really think Tothas would *argue* with me this way, Bahzell? By all the Powers of Light, I haven't met a mortal as stubborn as *you* in millennia! You ignore my dreams, force me to resort to dolts like that idiot in Derm—even *argue* with my sister and me face-to-face! Can't you get it through your thick skull that it's your very stubbornness, your refusal to do anything *you* don't believe is right, that makes you so important?!"

"As to that, I've no way to know. How could I?" Bahzell shot back. "But is it only a man's value makes him worth helping? Tothas may be less iron-pated than I, but that's not making him one bit less worthy!"

"No, it doesn't, but Tothas never asked me for healing." Bahzell blinked in fresh disbelief, and the god cocked his head. "There would have been little I could have done for him if he *had* asked," he admitted, "just as I can't crook my finger and put Zarantha safe home in her bed. I've already explained why I dare not meddle directly, and it would have taken direct intervention to save Tothas from the dog brothers' original attack. Nor, for the same reasons, can I make the attack as if it never happened. No god—Light or Dark—dares change the past. You can have no idea of all the possible consequences if we once started doing that, but a little thought should suggest at least some of them to you."

He held Bahzell's eyes until the hradani was forced to nod once more, then went on.

"By the same token, Tothas is an excellent example—a small one, perhaps, on the scale of universes, but nonetheless worthy—of how mortals can accomplish things even gods cannot. Zarantha's done all mortal healing can do for him. Without the healing talent, not even she could have saved him; as it is, you and she between you did just that. She arrested the poison and began his healing; when you compelled him to remain in Dunsahnta, you gave him the time and rest he needs to complete his recovery. But all Tothas ever asked me for were the very things you yourself told him he already had: the heart and courage to endure what he must to fulfill his sworn word to his lady."

"But you should have done *more* than that, whether he asked or no!" Bahzell cried, shaken by a sudden, terrible anger, and Tomanāk sighed.

"I should have, and had he encountered one of my champions, perhaps I could have. I *can* heal, through my priests or champions. Those are my swords in the mortal world, but my priesthood is smaller than most, Bahzell, and I give you fair warning—few of my champions die in bed. I can strengthen and aid them, but they're made for the shock of battle, and warriors fall in battle."

"So that's what you're wanting of me," Bahzell said bitterly. "You're after making me one of your 'champions.' Would Tothas have been my price, then? His healing for my service?"

"No," Tomanāk said more sternly than ever. "Had you been my champion, then, yes, you might have healed him, but I buy no man's service! If you would follow me, then follow me because you believe it's *right*, not for what it can buy you or others. The Dark Gods bribe and corrupt; the only reward *I* offer is the knowledge that you've chosen to do what you believed to be right!"

The anger in that boulder-crushing voice could have annihilated Bahzell on the spot, yet it wasn't directed at him. It seemed to split and flow about him, and he stood unshaken in the eye of the hurricane until the final echoes rumbled into silence.

"Then just what *is* it you're offering me?" he asked finally. "If it's so all-fired wonderful I am, where's the need to recruit me for what I'd do of my own stubbornness?"

"I'm trying to offer you my help!" Tomanāk said with pronounced asperity. "I can't interfere directly in mortal affairs, but I *can* strengthen and aid mortals against the Dark Gods' servants . . . if they'll *let* me! Your head may be solid stone, Bahzell, but even you must realize by now that you're as made for battle as a sword—and that you've no stomach for fighting on the wrong side! By my Mace, just what do you think you're *doing* out here chasing twenty-odd men and a pair of wizards?!" He glared down, eyes flashing like bare swords in the dawn, and his voice shook the clouds. "Well, if you want to fight on the *right* side, do it under my banner. I'll show you foes worthy of all the steel in you, and give you a keener edge than you ever knew you could have."

"Humpf." Bahzell lowered his gaze from the god's flashing eyes and chewed his lip. He sensed the power in that plea, and deep inside he knew how much more compelling it could have been. That Tomanāk truly sought to convince, not to command or usurp his will. But too much had come at him too quickly this night. He knew himself too well to believe he had the makings of some god-chosen champion, and all of a hradani's bone-deep distrust for the promises of those who would use them questioned every word the god had said. That elemental core of stubbornness dug in its heels and hunched its head obstinately against the force of Tomanāk's appeal, and, at last, he shook his head.

"No." It took more strength than he'd ever suspected he had to get the word out, but he raised his eyes once more to the god's face. "I'm not saying you'd lie to me, but it's in my mind that I can't *know* that. And even if I knew every word was true, it's not a thing for a man to be saying aye or nay to all in one night." Tomanāk said nothing, and Bahzell raised his right hand, palm cupped as if to hold something.

"It's not much the world's left my people, but this much we have; when we give our word, it means something, so I'll not swear any oath before I'm sure in my own mind of what I'm doing."

"Of course not," Tomanāk said quietly. "Nor would I ask you to. I ask only that you keep an open mind—that you *do* think about it before you say no."

"And you'll not plague my dreams in the meantime?" Bahzell demanded.

"No, I won't 'plague your dreams,'" Tomanāk promised with a smile.

"Well, then." Bahzell looked up at the towering War God and nodded briskly, and Tomanāk's smile grew even broader.

"Such a cavalier dismissal," he murmured, and, for the third time, his laugh shook the earth beneath Bahzell's feet. Then he faded from view—slowly, not with the suddenness of his sister's departure in the cave—and his deep voice spoke silently in the back of Bahzell's brain.

"Very well, I'll go, Bahzell. But I'll be back," it said.

# CHAPTER TWENTY-SEVEN

Incense drifted once more about Crown Prince Harnak, and he forced himself not to pace. It was hard. Harnak was always nervous when High Priest Tharnatus summoned him; even the Scorpion's messengers could stumble and betray themselves—or Harnak. But this summons had been no less curt for the polite formulae in which it was couched, and the prince gnawed his lower lip with his remaining teeth while he waited.

A foot sounded behind him, and he turned quickly from the altar. He flushed at the evidence of his anxiety, but Tharnatus smiled.

"I thank you for coming so promptly, My Prince, especially on so bitter a night."

Harnak simply nodded, though "bitter" was a weak word for the night beyond the temple. The snow had been belly-deep on his horse, and he'd passed two drifts high as a mounted man's head. Only Tharnatus could have gotten him out on such a night, and the thought of how the priest must relish the power to do just that touched him with resentment.

Tharnatus' eyes gleamed as if he'd read the prince's thoughts, but he only waved for Harnak to sit in one of the front pews and folded his own hands in the sleeves of his robe as he faced him.

"I would not have requested your presence, My Prince, had the matter been less than urgent. I understand things remain . . . difficult at court?"

"You understand aright." Harnak didn't—quite—snarl, and Tharnatus smiled gently. "Those bitches are practically members of Bahnak's own family by now, and he's using the damned bards to keep the tale alive." Harnak's molars ground together. "Even my brothers have taken to laughing behind my back, curse them, and the winter only makes it worse! With so much time indoors and nothing to do but drink and listen to tales—"

He clenched his fists, and Tharnatus nodded in grave sympathy.

"I regret hearing that, My Prince—and even more that I must tell you the dog brothers have . . . encountered difficulties."

"Difficulties?" Harnak's head snapped up, and Tharnatus shrugged.

"The Guild has never been the most reliable of the Scorpion's servants, My Prince. True, I believed they should have sufficed for this simple a task, but the Guild Master has written to inform me otherwise. To date, the dog brothers have lost upward of forty men trying to kill Bahzell."

"*Forty?!*" Harnak repeated. The priest nodded, and the prince swallowed. How could even Bahzell have—?

"In fairness to the dog brothers," Tharnatus said gravely, "Bahzell seems to have had far more luck than he should have. Apparently he took service with an Axeman merchant as far as Morvan, and the other guards shielded him from the Guild's initial attacks. He has left that protection since, yet he seems unusually difficult to track. Even the Scorpion's lesser servants can find him only with difficulty in the wilderness, and the dog brothers seem able to find him only when he enters their net in a town or city. They almost had him twice in Morvan itself—once in a tavern where he was working as a bouncer—" Harnak's eyes glowed, even in his disappointment, at the thought of Bahzell's finding himself so reduced "—and again in an alley. Unfortunately, he survived both attacks, as well as a third in Angthyr. By now, he knows the Guild has marked him, which will only make him harder to kill. The Guild Master hasn't abandoned all hope, but it seems we set them a more difficult task than we realized, My Prince."

The priest's voice trailed off suggestively. Harnak looked at him, but Tharnatus only looked back impassively.

"And?" the prince prompted harshly when he could stand the silence no longer, and Tharnatus surprised him. The priest pursed his lips and rocked slightly on his toes for several moments, then shrugged.

"There are more ways than the dog brothers to our goal, My Prince."

"Such as?" Harnak made himself speak calmly, but disbelief and hope warred in him. Could it be after all that Tharnatus meant to suggest—?

"It seems Bahzell is more important than we guessed," the priest said at last. "You need not know all of them— indeed, not even I know them all—but his death has become important to the Scorpion for many reasons. The entire Church has been mobilized against him, with all its resources, and we have the aid of certain servants of Carnadosa in this, as well."

"We do?" Harnak sat back in astonishment. The dark churches seldom cooperated. That, little though any of them cared to admit it, was their greatest weakness; they, like their deities, were too jealous of their own power and individual strategies to join forces as their enemies did, and mutual suspicion worked against them when they did. What in Sharnā's name could make that whoreson Bahzell important enough to produce such cooperation?!

"We do," Tharnatus confirmed calmly. "Yet we can count on little from them, at least for the immediate future, for their own power is even weaker than our own in the Empire of the Spear."

"The Empire of the Spear?" Harnak blinked again. "*Bahzell* is in the Empire of the Spear?" Tharnatus nodded, and Harnak's eyebrows rose. "Why?"

"I'm not certain, My Prince," the priest admitted. "Something, I suspect, to do with the Carnadosans, since they've offered us their assistance, but not even they seem to know precisely where he is at the moment. The dog brothers have also lost track of him, I fear, though he must surface again somewhere. In the meantime, however, the time has come for us to make an end of him, and it is for that reason I requested you to visit me tonight."

"What can I do?" Harnak's earlier resentment had vanished at the thought of bringing Bahzell down once and for all, and Tharnatus smiled.

"The Scorpion has decided to commit a greater servant to the task." His smile turned as hungry as Harnak's, but there was fear in it, as well, and the prince understood why even before the priest continued. "Since Bahzell first transgressed against the Scorpion in Navahk, it is only fitting his death should come from here, and the great dark of the moon falls four nights hence. On that night, we shall summon one of the greater servants and bind it to Bahzell's destruction, and we look to you to provide the sacrifice."

"Of course," Harnak said instantly. "Tell me what you require."

"As this will be one of the more powerful of the greater servants, My Prince, the ritual requires a sacrifice of special value. I shall need a virgin of childbearing age, fit and strong. It would be best if she has been handfasted so that we may bind her betrothed through her, as well. Ah, and intelligence is important. Can you find such in the time we have?"

"Um." Harnak rubbed the permanent dent in his forehead in the nervous gesture he'd acquired, and frowned. "I think so. It won't be easy—we can't use peasant scum for this, and the girl I'm thinking of comes of a powerful family. I may need the Church's help to take her without trace."

"Are you certain of her virginity?"

"Who can be certain?" Harnak chuckled coarsely, but the priest didn't join him, and his look banished the amusement from Harnak's face. "I believe she is," he said more defensively, "but I can hardly ask her!"

"No, I suppose not." Tharnatus frowned and rubbed his chin, then sighed. "Very well, the Church will help take her, but it would be best to choose two, just in case. This sacrifice *must* go to the knife virgin; best to be on the safe side, and we can always make use of the other later."

"Of course," Harnak agreed.

"Good! But after the binding, My Prince, the Scorpion has a special task for you, as well."

"For me?" Harnak's voice was more cautious, and Tharnatus nodded.

"For you. The servant may fail. It seems unlikely, yet something seems to have protected Bahzell so far. But even if something has, it will be no aid—whatever it may be—against a blade consecrated in the sacrifice's blood. Yet there must be a hand to wield the blade, and you, as the follower of the Scorpion most personally affronted by Bahzell, must bear it."

"I must bear it?" Harnak stared at Tharnatus in horror.

"You, My Prince. It is your destiny, for you and Bahzell have become counterweights in a struggle even greater than that between Navahk and Hurgrum. Both of you are princes, and the war to which you are called has greater implications than even I had realized. You stand in the Scorpion's own stead in that war, and it is only through you that His greatest power may be unleashed."

"But you said Bahzell is in the Empire of the Spear!" Harnak protested desperately.

"So he is. As soon as the ritual has been completed, you must depart for the Empire to seek him."

"In winter?" Harnak was aghast at the very idea—and even more so at the thought of facing Bahzell sword-to-sword, cursed blade or not. "The journey would take weeks—months!—in this weather. How could I justify it to my father, and who knows where he might be by the time I got there?"

"The Scorpion requires this service of you," Tharnatus said sternly. Harnak swallowed audibly, and the priest softened his rebuke with a smile. "Come, My Prince! There are answers to all your concerns."

"There are?"

"Indeed. You will justify the journey to your father by telling him you've heard Bahzell is bound for the Lands of the Purple Lords, there to take ship up the Spear come spring to return to Hurgrum. The dog brothers will see to it that a 'traveler' with word to that effect arrives in the city within the next few days, and Churnazh will be as eager as we to see to it that Bahzell never does any such thing. Bahnak has grown stronger over the fall and winter; by spring he might even be ready to take the field against Navahk once more—or so Churnazh will fear, and he knows as well as we how the tales weaken your position as his heir. Your desire to deal with Bahzell once and for all will make perfect sense to him, will it not?"

Harnak nodded against his will, and Tharnatus shrugged.

"Under the circumstances, I believe he will not only

allow you to go but to take a sizable retinue with you, as well. You will then take ship at Krelik and sail down the Spear. With luck, you should reach the Empire before Bahzell resurfaces."

"Take ship at *Krelik?!*" Shock startled Harnak to his feet. The thought of trekking overland down the course of the Saram in Bahzell's wake had been bad enough, but this was insane! "How can I possibly reach Krelik?" he demanded in a slightly calmer voice under the weight of Tharnatus' reproving eyes. "Surely you don't think the other Horse Stealers will grant me safe passage through their lands? None of them would dare offend Bahnak so!"

"You'll avoid Horse Stealer lands," Tharnatus said. "And, no," he went on when Harnak opened his mouth once more, "I'm not so great a fool as to suggest crossing the Wind Plain. You'll go south, around the Horse Stealers."

"Across Troll Garth and the Ghoul Moor?" Harnak swallowed again, harder, and his voice was faint. Trolls were far from intelligent and tended to lair up in the winter, but they were also nine feet of perpetually hungry killing machine. If one of them scented fresh meat in winter, an entire pack would materialize out of the very ground, and as for the *Ghoul Moor*—!

"Across Troll Garth and the Ghoul Moor," Tharnatus confirmed. "The Scorpion will protect you, although," he added thoughtfully, "it would certainly be wiser not to travel at night."

"Tharnatus, I—" Harnak began, but a raised hand silenced him.

"The Scorpion requires this service," the priest repeated, and Harnak sank back down into the pew while sweat beaded his brow. There was no recourse from that cold, inflexible demand, for if the Scorpion gave much, He could also demand much . . . and those of His servants who denied His demands would envy the sacrifices upon His altars before they died.

"Do not fear, My Prince," Tharnatus said more gently. "The Scorpion's sting shall be above you, and His pincers shall go on either hand. No creature of the Dark will dare defy his power." He squeezed Harnak's shoulder. "If there were more time, He would not send you into peril, even with His protection. Surely you must realize your value to Him, the hidden sting waiting at the heart of Navahk to destroy what His enemies like Bahnak would achieve here? But the upper Spear is frozen already; within weeks, the ice will reach as far south as the Lake of Storms, and should the greater servant fail, you must reach Bahzell and slay him quickly. The Horse Stealer *must* die, My Prince, both for your sake and the Scorpion's, and His greater servants are but His pincers. *You* will be His sting, armed with His own power and mightier than any servant. He will see to it you reach Bahzell unharmed."

"Of course." Harnak summoned a smile. Even he knew how weak it was, but Tharnatus squeezed his shoulder again and nodded in approval.

"Good, My Prince! And remember the ritual to come. Yours may be a cold road, but at least we shall start you upon it warm and well fed."

# CHAPTER TWENTY-EIGHT

White flakes curtsied before Bahzell's nose, then shot upward as a fist of wind snatched them away and plucked at his snow-clotted hood. He and Brandark had followed their targets into the fringes of the Darkwater Marshes, the vast stretch of hilly swamps stretching east from the river of the same name to the River of the Spear. The winter cold had hardened the ground and made their journey easier, for which he was grateful, but the clouds had thickened steadily through the three days since his . . . interview with Tomanāk, and now the iron-gray sky pressed down upon him like a bowl. It was only early afternoon, but the light was dim, and despite the occasional, moaning gusts, the air held a strange, furry stillness a northern hradani knew too well. The heavens were about to deluge them with snow, and he felt the relentless pressure of time, like a dire cat's hot, damp breath on his neck.

But the tracks of Zarantha's captors were clear enough for now—not that it was much comfort—and his breath steamed in a quiet, fervent curse as he knelt to examine the ground once more. Their enemies had snaked along ridge lines and hilltops through the swamp in a twisting, snakelike progress that slowed their pace still further, and the hradani had made up even more distance on them. But a second trail merged with the one they'd followed for so long, and the riders they were tracking had halted and dismounted here for some time before the newcomers joined them. The frozen surface soil had been kicked up in icy, snow-dusted clots, and Bahzell rose and shook his head as Brandark drew rein beside him.

"Well?"

"I'm thinking they've some way of sending word ahead of them after all," Bahzell growled. "It's clear enough they drew up here to wait on someone, and whoever it was never found them without knowing just where to be doing it."

"How many, do you think?" Brandark asked, and Bahzell shook his head.

"I couldn't be saying, not for certain, but it's surprised I'll be if they haven't doubled their strength."

"Phrobus!" Brandark swore, and Bahzell nodded, then scratched his chin.

"Still and all, Brandark, it might be worse." His friend looked at him incredulously, and he shrugged. "There may be more of them, my lad, but they waited here long enough for us to be making up time. We're no more than an hour—two at the outside—behind now."

"Wonderful. When we catch them, you can take the twenty on the right while I take the twenty on the left . . . and hope those poxy wizards don't turn us into cucumbers for our pains!"

"As to that, I'm thinking we'd best take whatever chance

we get and hope," Bahzell returned with a wave at the lazily spiraling flakes. "If we *don't* hit them soon, we'll have snow enough to hide an army's tracks. They're easy enough to follow now, but if snow once hides the trail and they're after changing direction, we'll be needing hours to find 'em again—if we ever do."

"Better and better." Brandark straightened in the saddle, sweeping the horizon through the slowly thickening veil of flakes, then sighed in glum agreement and looked back at the Horse Stealer.

"Any more sign of our friend?"

"Not since morning," Bahzell replied, "but he was bound southwest, so I'm thinking he's looped out around them again. He's up ahead somewhere, waiting for them, though how he's after doing it is more than I can guess."

"Why should he make any more sense than the rest of this?" Brandark demanded, waving an arm at the hills and low-growing scrub that dotted the snowy, half-frozen marsh.

"Aye, you've a point there." Bahzell stood absently picking clots of ice from his packhorse's mane while he gazed ahead at the tracks before him. He and Brandark were within striking distance at last, but there were too many unknowns for him to be happy about it. Zarantha's wizard captors had at least forty men with them now, and even if the hradani somehow took them totally by surprise, those were steep odds. Then there was the mystery rider who wasn't a Sothōii, whatever he was mounted on. Tomanāk only knew what *he* was up to.

He snorted at his own choice of phrase. If Tomanāk was so all-fired anxious to secure his service, then why couldn't he at least make himself useful by providing some of the information Bahzell lacked?

"Among other reasons," a deep voice said in the recesses of his brain, "because you haven't asked me."

"Will you *stop* that?!" Bahzell snapped, and Brandark looked up in surprise, then swallowed and edged his horse carefully away. Bahzell saw him go, and the Bloody Sword's painfully neutral expression made him still angrier. This wasn't Tomanak's first communication since that night in the hollow, and Brandark had reacted far less calmly the first time Bahzell stopped dead to argue with empty air. It hadn't taken him long to deduce who the Horse Stealer was really speaking to, yet he'd been very, very careful never to say a word about it. Bahzell supposed that was better than having his friend decide he was mad, but it didn't feel that way.

"If you don't want answers," the deep, infuriatingly reasonable voice seemed to vibrate in his bones, "you shouldn't ask questions."

Bahzell drew a deep breath, exhaled half of it and held the rest, propped his hands on his hips, and glared up at the clouds.

"I wasn't asking you a thing," he said slowly and distinctly, "and it was in my mind as how you'd said you'd not plague me until I was after being ready to hear you?"

"I also said I'd be back," Tomanak's silent voice pointed out, "and you *did* ask me a question, whether you realized it or not. As for being ready to hear, if you *weren't* ready, you wouldn't be able to."

"D'you mean to say that any time one of your 'champions' is after even mentioning your name you come yammer in his ear?" Bahzell demanded, and a deep, echoing chuckle rolled through him.

"Not normally, no," the god said after a moment. "Most mortal minds aren't up to sustaining this sort of contact for long. Magi can handle more of it, but too much would burn out even one of them."

"Well, isn't that reassuring!" Bahzell snorted, and Tomanak chuckled again.

"Oh, you're in no danger yet, Bahzell. You have quite

a strong mind, actually, and I wouldn't be here if I were likely to damage it."

"Now there's a comforting thought." Bahzell glowered up at the clouds a moment longer, then shrugged. "Well, if you're here, why not be making yourself useful and tell me what's happening up ahead?"

"I said your refusal to ask me was only one of the reasons," Tomanāk reminded him. "There are others."

"Such as?"

"First, it would be entirely too close to direct meddling; it's not the sort of thing even a god can do too often, so we save it for really important matters. Then, too, there are things you *shouldn't* know. If I were to tell you everything, you'd come to rely on that and make your decisions based solely on what I told you. After a time, you'd be the very thing you're so determined to avoid: a puppet, controlled by the information I provided."

"Um." Bahzell chewed his lip for a moment, then nodded reluctantly.

"What I can and will do for my champions," Tomanāk went on, "is strengthen them when they need it. Their decisions are their own to make. They know my Code and their own hearts, but it's the exercise of their own wills and their reliance on their own courage which *makes* them champions. A warrior who's led by the hand and protected from all danger becomes a shell. If I make them less than the best they can be I betray them . . . and leave them unsuited to the tasks for which I need them, like a blade that's lost its temper."

Bahzell nodded again, less reluctantly, then sighed.

"All right, that much I can see. But if that's the case, then I'll be thanking you not to gab away at me with no warning at all, at all."

"That may be a bit difficult," Tomanāk said almost apologetically. "A part of my attention is attuned to you at all times, and when you have questions that may affect your ultimate decision, I owe you answers—or the reasons why there aren't any. I realize what I'm asking of you, and you deserve the fullest explanation I can give you while you think things over. So until you make up your mind one way or the other, I'm afraid I'll be 'gabbing away' at you any time you think a question at me."

"But I'm not *wanting* you to!" Bahzell pointed out.

"Perhaps not, but I'm the god of justice as well as war, Bahzell, and it would be unjust not to explain whatever I can. If you don't want to hear from me, then don't think about me."

"Oh, that's a *fine* piece of advice! And just how is it I'm to *stop* thinking about you when you're wanting to turn my life inside out?!"

"By making a decision, one way or the other," Tomanak returned with a sort of implacable gentleness. "Until then—"

Bahzell had the strong impression of an unseen shrug, and then the voice in his mind was gone and there was only the wind moaning about him as it gathered strength and the snow fell more thickly. He growled under his breath, and a vast sense of ill-use filled him—one that was made even more infuriating by his own nagging feeling that he was childish to feel it. Maddening as the sudden, unexpected inner conversations might be, Tomanak was right; anyone who asked a man for his allegiance owed that man the fullest explanation he could give of what that entailed. It was just Bahzell's cursed luck that a god could explain—or not, as the case might be—*anything*.

He growled again and shook himself. Discussions with gods might be very impressive, he thought grumpily, but they seemed to offer far less guidance than all the tales insisted. It was still up to him and Brandark to deal with the scum ahead of them, and he looked around for his friend.

The Bloody Sword had fallen back beside the pack animals, sitting his horse with a sort of studied nonchalance to emphasize his disinterest in Bahzell's one-sided conversation. The Horse Stealer smiled sourly and walked across to him.

"I'm thinking we'd best be hitting them this afternoon," he said, resuming the discussion Tomanāk had interrupted. "It's not the odds I'd choose, but they'll not get better just for our wishing, and it's in my mind we might use the snow against them. If it's after coming down as heavy as it looks to, we can likely use it for cover and keep 'em from realizing there's naught but the two of us."

Brandark's expression was unhappy as he contemplated the odds, yet he couldn't fault Bahzell's reasoning. If two warriors were mad enough to attack forty, they'd best wring every possible advantage from surprise and confusion, and few things were more surprising or confusing than an ambush out of a snowstorm.

"Agreed," he said after a moment, "and I thin—"

He broke off in midword, staring past Bahzell's shoulder, then gasped an oath. The Horse Stealer wasted no time asking what he'd seen. He only reached up and ripped his cloak loose with one hand even as he spun on his toes. He flung the garment away like a huge, dark hat, billowing on a sudden gust of wind, while his other hand went back over his shoulder. One instant he was speaking to Brandark; the next, five feet of sword flared from its sheath and gleamed dully in the pewter light as he fell into a guard stance.

A mounted rider sat his horse ten yards away. Neither of the hradani nor any of their animals had as much as noticed his arrival; he was simply *there*, as if he'd oozed up out of the herringbones of snow and stems of dead grass, and Bahzell's ears went flat and the nape of his neck prickled. Snow or no snow, no one could have crept up that close—not on a horse—without his noticing!

Zarantha's mule stamped, steel rasped, and saddle leather creaked behind him as Brandark drew his own sword, and the background moan and sigh of the wind only made the stillness seem more hushed.

Bahzell watched the rider, poised to attack, and the horseman cocked his head to gaze back. He was tall for a human—almost as tall as Brandark—and he sat his saddle as if he'd been born in it. The raised hood of his snow-stippled Sothōii-style poncho shadowed his face and hid his features, but he wore a longsword, not a sabre, and there was neither a quiver at his saddle nor a bow on his back. The stranger let the silence linger for a long, breathless moment, then touched his mount with his heels. The horse walked slowly closer, and the Horse Stealer's ears folded even tighter to his skull. That winter-shaggy warhorse was no courser, but only a Sothōii—or someone with a prince's purse—could own its equal. The hradani held his breath as the rider drew up again, well within the reach of Bahzell's sword, and rested both gloved hands on the pommel of his saddle.

"Impressive," he said dryly. His voice was deep for a human's, though far lighter than Bahzell's own subterranean bass. "Very impressive. But there's no need for all this martial ardor, I assure you."

"Do you, now?" Bahzell rumbled back.

"Of course I do, Bahzell Bahnakson."

The Horse Stealer gritted his teeth in pure frustration. Dreams, magi, wizards, gods, missions—his life had become entirely too full of portents and omens without mysterious horsemen materializing out of the very ground to call him by name, and there was a hard, dangerous edge to his voice when he spoke again.

"Suppose you let me be making my own mind up about that. And while you're being so free with *my* name, who might *you* be?"

The stranger chuckled. The pure amusement of the

sound flicked the hradani like a whip, and he felt the first, hot flicker of the Rage. He ground his heel down upon it, but it was hard in his present mood. He'd served as the butt of the universe's bad jokes long enough, and he growled deep in his throat as the newcomer reached up and drew back the hood of his poncho.

The horseman was older than Bahzell had assumed from his voice and the way he sat his horse. His neatly trimmed beard and hair were whiter than the snow about them, and his lean face was dark and weathered. There were surprisingly few wrinkles to go with that silver hair, yet something about his features suggested an ancient hardiness that went far beyond mere age. The Horse Stealer noted the Sothoii-style leather sweatband that held back his hair, the strong straight nose, the square jaw whose stubborn jut not even the beard could disguise, but they hardly registered, for they were dominated and eclipsed by the horseman's eyes. Strange eyes, that called no color their own but flickered and shifted even as he watched, dancing like wildfire in the dull winter light. They had neither pupil nor white, those eyes, only the unearthly flowing fire that filled the sockets under craggy white eyebrows.

Bahzell stared at them, shaken and half-mesmerized. An alarm bell seemed to toll deep inside him, battering at the fascination which held him motionless, and he heard Brandark hiss behind him.

"I think Brandark recognizes me, Bahzell," the stranger said in that same, dryly amused tone.

"That's as may be, but *I* don't," Bahzell shot back, shaking off the impact of those fiery eyes with an effort, "and I've had a hard enough day without riddle games in the snow."

He took a half-step forward, sword ready. The horseman only smiled, as if at a child in a tantrum, and Bahzell felt the Rage flare at his core once more at the other's amusement, but Brandark spoke suddenly from behind him.

"I wouldn't do anything hasty, Bahzell," the Bloody Sword said in a very careful tone. "Not unless you really want to spend a few years as a toad."

"What?" Bahzell's ears twitched, but his attention was so focused on the stranger that his friend's words hardly registered.

"That sort of thing happens to people who attack wizards," Brandark said, and a bolt of sheer fury lashed through the Horse Stealer at the word "wizards." The Rage slipped the frayed leash of his will, and he lunged forward with a murderous snarl. The tip of his sword thrust straight for the stranger's chest, but the horseman didn't even move. He only gazed at the hradani, and his eldritch eyes flashed like twin suns.

Something Bahzell had no words to describe slammed into him. It struck like a hammer fit to shatter a world, yet there was a delicacy to it, as well—almost a gentleness, like a man snatching a hummingbird from midair without so much as ruffling its feathers—and unaccustomed panic sparkled at his heart as it did the impossible and froze a hradani in the grip of the Rage. He found himself utterly unable to move, his murderous lunge arrested a foot from its target, and the stranger shook his head apologetically.

"Excuse me. I know you've had a difficult time of late, and I really shouldn't let my questionable sense of humor get the better of me. But I've been looking forward to this moment for a very long time, Bahzell, and I just couldn't resist."

Bahzell stood motionless, and fresh shock rippled through him as he realized the Rage had vanished. Somehow the stranger had banished it as if it had never come, and that was the strangest thing of all.

The horseman moved his mount aside, out of the line of Bahzell's lunge but still where the hradani could see him, and he bowed from the saddle.

"Again, I ask your pardon for my behavior," he said gravely. "And in answer to your question, Bahzell, my name is Wencit. Wencit of Rūm." This time he made a tiny gesture with one hand, and whatever had held Bahzell fled. He staggered forward with the force of his interrupted attack, but a fresh paralysis—this one of sheer disbelief—held him as tightly as the vanished spell. He gawked at the man on the horse, jaw dropping, stunned as even Tomanāk's appearance out of the night had not left him, and lowered his sword very, very slowly.

Wencit of Rūm. It couldn't be. Yet, at the same time, it *had* to be. Only one man had eyes like that, and he'd been a fool not to realize it, but even as he thought that, he knew why he hadn't. A man didn't expect to meet a figure out of legend in a snowstorm a hundred leagues from anywhere.

"Wencit of Rūm?" he repeated in a dazed tone, and the horseman nodded. "*The* Wencit of Rūm?" Bahzell persisted with the numbness of his shock.

"So far as I know, there's only one of me," Wencit said gravely. Bahzell darted a look at Brandark, and the astonishment on the Bloody Sword's face was almost deeper than his own. Of course. Brandark was a scholar who'd always wanted to be a bard. No doubt he knew all the tales of the Fall and the part Wencit of Rūm, lord of the last White Council of Wizards, had played in saving what he could from the wreck of Kontovar. But that had been twelve *centuries* ago—surely the man couldn't still be alive!

But he was a wizard, Bahzell reminded himself. A *wild* wizard. Possibly the most powerful single wizard who'd ever lived. Who knew what he could or couldn't be?

"Well," the Horse Stealer said finally, sheathing his sword with mechanical precision. "Wencit of Rūm." He shook himself like a dog shaking water from its coat. "It's not so very fond of wizards my folk are, but then, most of them aren't so very fond of *us*, either." He smiled crookedly and folded his arms across his chest. "And what, if I might be asking, brings Wencit of Rūm out in all this?" He flicked his ears at the thickening snow, and there was an edge of darkness in Wencit's answering smile.

"Very much what brings you." The wizard dismounted and stroked his mount's neck while the horse lipped his white hair affectionately.

"Ah?"

"Ah, indeed. There's no White Council now, Bahzell, but I do what I can to stop the abuse of the art. I've come to rely heavily on the magi's aid for that, and the Axe Hallow mage academy got word to me when Zarantha didn't reach home on schedule."

He shrugged, and Bahzell nodded.

"Aye, she'd be important to you, and the magi, wouldn't she now?"

"If you're referring to her plans to found a Spearman mage academy, the answer is yes. But if you're suggesting her mage talent is all that makes her important to us, you're wrong." Wencit spoke almost mildly, but there was a hint of steel in his voice, and Bahzell nodded again, accepting the rebuke, if that was what it had been.

"Fair enough," he said slowly, "but I'm just the tiniest bit confused. You've been glued to their trail like a lodestone for days now, and I'm thinking the likes of you could deal with the wizards who have her."

"And you want to know why I haven't." Wencit made the question a statement, and Bahzell nodded yet again. "It's not quite as simple as you may think, Bahzell. Oh, you're right, I could deal with either of them—or both together—easily enough, but not with the men they have with them. Not without violating the Strictures, at any rate."

"The Strictures?" Bahzell's arched eyebrow invited further explanation, but it was Brandark who answered him.

"The Strictures of Ottovar, Bahzell," the Bloody Sword said, dismounting from his own horse to stand beside his friend. "They were the laws of wizardry in Kontovar, the rules the White Council was formed to enforce."

"Among other things," Wencit amended with a nod.

"And what might the Strictures be?" Bahzell asked.

"Exactly what Brandark said: the laws of wizardry. Or of *white* wizardry, at any rate. They were written by Ottovar the Great and Gwynytha the Wise when they ended the wizard wars of their own time and founded Ottovar's empire. In simple terms, they were designed to protect those who don't have power from casual abuse by those who do."

"And you're still after following them all these years later?"

"If I don't, who will?" That steely edge was back in Wencit's voice, and his wildfire gaze bored into Bahzell's eyes. "Does time alone define right or wrong? And even if it did, by what right could I demand other wizards obey them—or hold them accountable when they don't—if I violated them myself?"

"Aye, there's that," Bahzell agreed slowly, rubbing his chin with one hand, then gave the wizard a sharp look. "Still and all, I can't but think you've hunted us out to do more than tell us what it is you *can't* be doing."

"True." Wencit smiled almost impishly and gave his horse's neck another pat, then leaned back against his saddle and surveyed the two hradani. "Under the Strictures, I may use sorcery against nonwizards only in direct self-defense, and even then I can't kill them if anything short of killing will keep me alive. Wizards—especially dark wizards—are another matter. Them I can challenge to arcane combat, but somehow I doubt their henchmen could refrain from sticking a knife in my back while I do it."

"Ah," Bahzell said again, and exchanged glances with

Brandark before he looked back at Wencit. "I'm hoping you won't take this wrongly," he said politely, "but I'm thinking I see where you're headed, and twenty-to-one might be just a mite heavy odds for us to be keeping off your back while you satisfy your principles, Wencit."

"I know," Wencit said cheerfully, "but with the right help, you won't be facing twenty-to-one odds."

"And here I was thinking you'd just said you couldn't use sorcery against nonwizards."

"Oh, but I won't use a single spell on *them*," Wencit said, and something in his smile was as cold as the falling snow.

# CHAPTER TWENTY-NINE

The sentry huddled in the lee of a patch of scrub, hugging himself under his cloak while cataracts of white roared past. Storms this fierce were rare in these southern plains, and he stamped his feet and peered uselessly into the whirling snow devils. Visibility was as much as thirty yards between wind gusts, but such intervals were rare, and he swore balefully. Posting guards was pointless on a night like this, but there'd been no use arguing, and he swore again, this time at himself for ever having taken service with the Church of Carnadosa.

Black wizards were perilous paymasters at any time, for the same penalties applied to a black wizard's hirelings as to himself. That meant the money was good, of course, yet his employers were being less open than usual this time, and the presence of assassins made him almost as uneasy as his ignorance of what was on their track. Carnadosa and Sharna were never comfortable allies, and anything that could bring their followers into alliance was bound to be risky.

The sentry knew he was only a hired sword to the Church, yet this was the first time his masters had refused to explain *anything*. They'd simply sent him and twenty others out to meet two of their number—and the dog brothers—in the middle of this howling wilderness, and the palpable anxiety which possessed the people they'd met was enough to make anyone nervous. Whatever was back there, it had inspired the travelers to push their horses dangerously close to collapse and post guards even in the heart of a blizzard, and the sentry was uncomfortably certain it was all somehow due to the presence of their prisoner. He didn't know who she was, either, and he didn't want to. The senior of his employers—a priest of Carnadosa, as well as a wizard—had her under some sort of compulsion that turned her into a walking corpse, something that moved pliantly and obediently and ate whatever was put into its mouth, yet the sentry had seen her eyes—once—and there was nothing dead about them. They burned with fury and a sort of desperate horror that set his nerves on edge and made him wish he'd never taken the money.

But he had, and wizards were bad masters to betray or desert . . . even if there'd been anywhere to desert *to* in this godsforsaken wasteland. No, he was stuck, and—

He never completed the thought. A towering, snow-shrouded form blended silently from the swirling whiteness behind him, a hand yanked his head back, a dagger drove up under his chin into his brain, and he never even realized he was dead.

Bahzell let the corpse slither down and wiped his dagger on its cloak. He resheathed the blade and drew his sword as two horses appeared out of the roaring, white-streaked darkness like a pair of ghosts, and he felt the hair stir on the back of his neck once more. Wencit of Rūm had a pedigree not even hradani could question, but that made him no less uncanny, and no hradani could ever be comfortable in *any* wizard's web. The notion that there was still at least one white wizard in the world would take getting used to, and even now Bahzell couldn't quite believe that he and Brandark had actually agreed to let him enwrap them in his magic. On the other hand, Wencit had guided them to their enemies' camp as unerringly as if the night had been clear and still, not this snowy maelstrom, and if his spells did what he'd claimed they would—

The Horse Stealer's thoughts broke off as his companions reached him and drew rein. Wencit rose in the stirrups, thrusting his head above the low-growing trees' cover and peering into the roaring wind as if he could actually see. He stayed there for several minutes, turning his head to sweep his gaze back and forth across something visible only to him, then settled back and wiped snow from his beard. He tucked up the skirt of his poncho to clear his well-worn sword hilt, and Bahzell told himself it was only the cold that made him shiver as those wildfire eyes moved back to him.

"There are four more sentries!" Wencit had to shout to make himself heard above the gale. "The closest is about fifty yards that way!" He gestured off to the left, then shrugged. "I imagine they'll take to their heels when they realize what's happening, but watch your backs!"

Both hradani nodded grimly, and Brandark drew his own sword. Wencit didn't, but then, if all went well, the wizard would have no use for steel tonight.

If all went well.

"Remember! So far I haven't done anything to draw attention to myself, but the instant the spell goes up, the wizards at least will know I'm here! Leave them to me, but get to Zarantha as quick as you can!"

Bahzell nodded again. The wizards might prefer to use Zarantha's death to raise power, but if their main goal was to prevent the creation of Spearmen magi, their hirelings would have orders to kill her to prevent her rescue.

"Ready?" Wencit demanded. Two more nods answered, though a corner of Bahzell's mind shouted at him to get the hell out of this. Too much of their plan depended on a man they'd met only hours before, and whatever his reputation, Wencit *was* a wizard. But this was no time for second thoughts, and he stepped out around the edge of the scrubby trees into the teeth of the wind.

Brandark followed at his shoulder, and they moved confidently forward despite the howling near invisibility. They were all but blind, but Wencit had briefed them well. Bahzell had felt acutely uneasy when the wizard produced the polished stone he called a "gramerhain" and peered into it. The heart-sized crystal had flared and flickered even more brightly than Wencit's eyes, blinding the hradani if they glanced at it too closely, but Wencit had stared intently into it for long, studious moments. Then he'd put it away and drawn an impossibly detailed diagram of the enemy's camp in the snow. The wind should have blotted it out in a moment, but it hadn't, and he'd taken them patiently through it again and again, until they knew it as intimately as the backs of their own hands. Bahzell might be uncomfortable with the way the information for that diagram had been obtained, yet he had to admit there seemed to be advantages to having a wizard on his side.

Assuming of course that Wencit truly *was* on his side.

He shook his head sharply, castigating himself for his doubts, but Fiendark take it, the man was a *wizard*. Twelve centuries of instant, instinctive hatred couldn't be set aside in an instant, and—

The nagging undercurrent of thought broke off, and he touched Brandark on the knee as the ground began to angle downward before them. They stood at the lip of the deep, sheltered hollow their enemies had selected for their camp, and it was time.

Bahzell looked up at his friend for just a moment, seeing

the echo of his own doubts on the Bloody Sword's face, then grinned crookedly, shrugged, and squeezed Brandark's knee once. The Bloody Sword nodded back, and Bahzell got both hands on the hilt of his sword, drew a deep breath, and hurled himself down the slope with a bull-throated bellow.

Hooves thudded beside him as Brandark spurred forward, and the Bloody Sword's high, fierce yell answered his own war cry. Their voices should have been lost without a trace on such a night, but they weren't. They couldn't be, for they were answered and echoed from all sides, and suddenly there weren't just two hradani charging down the slope. There were thirty of them, mounted and afoot alike, bellowing their fury, and even though he'd known it was supposed to happen, superstitious dread stirred deep inside Bahzell Bahnakson.

He felt the cold and wind, the snow on his face and the hilt in his hands and the wild, fierce pounding of his heart, and exhilaration filled him, banishing his dread, as he gave himself to the Rage and the phantom warriors charged at his side. His and Brandark's own war cries had triggered the spell Wencit had woven, and a strange, wild sense of creation—of having snapped the others into existence by his own will—sparkled through him. And, in a sense, he *had* created them, even more than Wencit. The wizard could have settled for simple duplicates of Brandark and himself, but his spell was subtler than that. He'd plucked images of remembered warriors from the hradani's memories, breathing life into them, and the verisimilitude of his illusion was stunning. The bellowing, immaterial figures actually left footprints in the snow, and the sheer multiplicity of warriors—each with his own face, his own weapons and armor and voice—left no room for question. This was a *real* attack, and shouts of panic and the scream of startled horses split the night as Bahzell bounded through the last swirling snow curtain into the sheltered hollow.

Forty men rolled out of their blankets, snatching for weapons, leaping to their feet in horror as the horde of hradani erupted into their midst. There was no time to don armor; those who'd shed their mail for the night were forced to let it lie, and their vulnerability filled them with its own panic.

A man dodged frantically, scrambling to evade Bahzell, but there was no time for that, either. The Horse Stealer's massive blade whistled, and his victim went down, screaming as his guts spilled out in a cloud of steam. Brandark thundered past, leaning from the saddle, longsword sweeping like a scythe. A raised blade sought desperately to block the stroke, but its wielder's arm flew in a spray of blood, and he shrieked as the Bloody Sword rode him down. The shrieks cut off with sickening suddenness under trained, iron-shod hooves, and the warhorse pivoted, spurning the body as Brandark reined it around to split the skull of a fleeing foe. Another enemy, this one braver, helmetless but clad in chain mail, leapt to engage Bahzell, and the Horse Stealer smashed him into bloody ruin with a single mighty stroke.

Steel clashed all around him, and even through the Rage and the fury of battle a corner of his mind marveled at the depth of Wencit's illusion. His phantom allies couldn't actually harm anyone—that would have been against the Strictures—but that was the *only* thing they couldn't do. The men who engaged them "felt" and "heard" their own blows go home against armor or shield. They knew—didn't just think, but *knew*—they were locked in mortal combat with real enemies, and Bahzell and Brandark rampaged through them like dire cats. The hradani were the only ones in that entire mad melee who knew the truth. They were unhampered by any confusion as to who could kill them and who couldn't, and they forged straight for the knot of figures beside the fire.

Two unarmed men leapt to their feet in almost comical

disbelief, but they were wizards. Even through the cacophony of shouts and shrieks and clashing steel, Bahzell heard one of them scream a curse as he recognized the illusory horde for what it was. The man's head darted from side to side, seeking the real attackers he knew had to be present, and his hand went up as Bahzell crashed through his panicked retainers. Light flashed on his palm, and the Horse Stealer felt something tug at him even as he kicked a guardsman in the belly and lopped his head as he went down. But the wizard behind that spell was no Wencit of Rūm. The elemental fury of the Rage brushed his spell aside, and both wizards stumbled back as Bahzell vaulted over the body of his latest victim towards them.

Steel glinted as one of their men whirled towards a slender, blanket-wrapped figure beside the fire. Zarantha didn't stir as the blade went up. She simply lay there, watching it rise, seeing it sweep down. She fought desperately against the spell which held her motionless, but there was no escape. She couldn't even scream—and then a gory thunderbolt swept up beneath the descending blade. It smashed the death stroke aside, and the man who'd tried to kill her screamed as Bahzell cut his legs from under him.

Bahzell straddled Zarantha's motionless body. Two more guards came at him, and he snarled with the terrible glory of the Rage as he smashed them back. Brandark's horse reared, trampling another victim, forehooves crashing down like the War God's mace, and the Bloody Sword lashed out with a backhand blow that flung a body aside in a gout of blood. All around them, men threw aside weapons, turned their backs, fled madly into the snow. Half a dozen of them thought of their horses and ran desperately for the picket line, but Brandark was on their heels. He rode two of them down and scattered the rest, and Bahzell hacked aside the last guardsman foolhardy enough to come at him.

The Horse Stealer whirled on the wizards, blade hissing as he drove a furious slash at the nearer one, but their retainers' deaths had bought them a few precious seconds. Sparks showered and flashed as Bahzell's blade slammed into an unseen barrier and rebounded, and the wizard behind that barrier spat a curse and raised both hands—not at the hradani, this time, but at Zarantha.

Bahzell flung himself between those hands and their target. He had no idea if his Rage would protect another from a spell, or even guard *him* against death magic, but it was the only defense he could give Zarantha. He went to his knees, snarling up at the wizard, covering her with his own body, and the wizard bared his teeth in triumph as he brought both hands down in a convulsive, throwing gesture.

Light glared and hissed between his clenched fists, spitting towards Bahzell like evil green lightning, but it never struck. Something flashed in its path—a brilliant blue disk, brighter even than the lightning—and the hissing light-snake shattered like glass.

The wizard staggered back in disbelief, then jerked his head around as another horseman rode slowly forward. The rider's eyes flamed brighter than the camp's fire, and the sword in his hand glittered with the same blue light that had shielded Bahzell and Zarantha. The surviving dog brothers vanished into the howling snow and the last guardsmen yelped in panic and cast down their weapons at the sight, and the wizard who'd tried to kill Zarantha seemed to shrink in on himself. He and his fellow stood rooted to the ground, faces whiter than the blizzard, and Wencit stopped his horse. He dismounted with slow, graceful precision, and sheathed his sword, never taking his wildfire gaze from his enemies.

"My name," he didn't raise his voice, but it carried crisp and clear and coldly formal through the howl of the wind in a dialect unheard in Norfressa in centuries, "is Wencit of Rūm, and by my paramount authority as Lord of the Council of Ottovar I judge thee guilty of offense against the Strictures. Wouldst thou defend thyselves, or must I slay thee where thou standest?"

One of the wizards whimpered, but the Carnadosan priest who'd tried to kill Zarantha was made of sterner stuff. He wasted no time on words; his right hand darted to his belt, snatching out a short, thick wand, and brought it up in a darting arc at Wencit.

The wild wizard raised his own hand almost negligently, and the wand exploded in a shower of smoking fragments. The wizard howled and seized his right wrist in his left hand, shaking it frantically as a curl of flame rose from his palm, and Wencit nodded.

"So be it." His voice held an executioner's dispassion, and he pointed a finger at his writhing foe. "As thou hast chosen, so shalt thou answer."

A spear of light—the same wildfire light as his eyes— leapt from his finger, and the priest screamed as it struck his chest. His spine arched, convulsing in agony, and the wildfire crawled up inside him. It spewed from his shrieking mouth in a tide of brilliance, glaring and pulsing with the rhythm of his wildly racing heart, and then he collapsed in upon himself like a figure of straw in the heart of a furnace. Smoke poured up from his crumpling body in a stinking tide, whipped and shredded by the wind, and when it cleared only a smoldering heap of ash remained.

The second wizard fell to his knees, mouth working soundlessly as he raised his hands in piteous supplication, but Wencit's face was colder than the storm. His hand swung, his finger pointed, a second shaft of light lanced out from it, and his victim shrieked like a soul in hell as he blazed.

Bahzell crouched on his knees, still shielding Zarantha, and even through the Rage he felt a stab of pure, atavistic terror as he stared at Wencit. Wind roared across the hollow, roofing it in a boiling cauldron of white, and the wild wizard loomed against it like a figure out of Kontovar's most terrifying myths. He lowered his hand slowly while the smoke of his enemies streamed up to whip away on the gale, and his words carried with that same, impossible clarity through the blizzard's bellow.

"By their works I knew them, by the Strictures I judged, and by my oath I acted," he said softly, and turned away at last.

# CHAPTER THIRTY

There was no dawn. The storm howled on, roaring like an enraged giant, and Bahzell sat beside the fire and watched their prisoners.

There were eleven of them: six Carnadosan guardsmen and five dog brothers. One assassin would die soon; all four of his fellows and two of the guardsmen were wounded, and cold hatred urged the Horse Stealer to cut all their throats. But the aftertaste of the Rage was poison on his tongue, copper-bright with too much blood, too much exaltation in its shedding. Even if it hadn't been, these men had surrendered; if he killed them now, it would be in cold blood—murder, not battle—and Bahzell Bahnakson was no dog brother.

Thirteen bodies lay piled beyond the fire's warmth, frozen and stiff. The dead wizards' remaining henchmen had fled into the shrieking blizzard, most without cloaks, some without even boots. Few would survive the storm, and bleak satisfaction filled Bahzell at the thought as he looked at Zarantha.

She lay across the fire from him, closed eyes like bruised wounds in her stark, white face as she slept with her head on Wencit's thigh. Her captors had been careful not to abuse her physically, for they'd wanted her strong and fit for sacrifice, and she was tough, Zarantha of Jashân. Yet the horror of what she'd endured—of riding obediently to what she knew was hideous death, a prisoner in her own body—had marked her . . . and the compulsion that had held her so had survived her captors' deaths.

Wencit's face had been grim as he bent over her, and Bahzell had knelt behind her, supporting her shoulders against his knee as the wizard's eyes flamed and the cleansing fire of his wizardry burned deep inside her. Bahzell had felt Zarantha's terrible shudders as that sorcery warred with the noisome, clinging shroud about her soul, heard her teeth-clenched groan of agony as the compulsion frayed and tore under the power of Wencit's will, and he'd gathered her in his arms as she sobbed explosively against his mailed chest when the spell broke. He'd smoothed her black hair, murmured to her, held her like a child, and she'd clung to him, burying her face against him.

That had been almost enough to send him raging amidst the prisoners, murder or no, but it hadn't. He'd only held her, and thought no less of her as she wept, for hradani knew the horror of helplessness in the hands of wizards.

She'd mastered her tears more quickly than he would have believed possible. She'd drawn the discipline of the magi about her and pushed herself back to smile at him, her white cheeks wet.

"And so I owe you my life again, Bahzell Bahnakson," she'd said, voice wavering with the aftershock of her tearing sobs. "Oh, Bahzell, Bahzell! What god sent you and Brandark to me, and how can I ever prove worthy of you?"

"Hush, lass," he'd growled, and patted her roughly,

awkward and uncomfortable as a stripling before the glow in her eyes. "You've no call to be 'worthy' of such as us!"

"Oh, but I do—both of you." She'd reached out a hand to Brandark, and the Bloody Sword had squeezed it gently. "I lied to you, and tricked you into this, and still you came for me."

"Huh!" Brandark had snorted. "It was no more than a leisurely jog for longshanks here! Now, *I*, on the other hand—!"

Zarantha had answered with a gurgle of tearful laughter, but she'd shaken her head until Bahzell cupped her face in one huge hand and turned it back to him.

"Lass, you never lied. Less than the full truth, aye, but were you thinking the two of us stupid enough not to be guessing you'd reason for it?" Her lips had trembled, and he'd touched her hair once more. "Tothas told us what it was, and I'll not fault your thinking—no, nor your judgment, either."

"*Tothas!*" she'd gasped, her eyes darting suddenly about, wide with fresh, sudden dread as she noted her armsman's absence. "Is he—?!"

"Tothas is well," Bahzell had said firmly. "He'd not the strength for a run like this, so we left him safe enough in Dunsahnta to watch over Rekah. It's half mad with worry over you he was, but he'd sense enough to know this was best left to us, and he sent his love with us."

"Rekah is alive?!" Incredulous joy had flickered in her shadowed eyes. "They told me she was dead!"

"Aye, well, as to that, I've no doubt they thought she was, but she was alive enough when last we saw her, and I'm thinking we left her in the hands of a healer who's kept her so."

"So you did, and so she is," Wencit had said. Bahzell turned his head, eyebrows raised, and the wild wizard smiled. "I try to keep abreast of things," he'd explained gruffly, "and Tothas and Rekah are just fine. In fact, the commander of Dunsahnta's military district arrived there four days ago, and he's been cleaning out the late baron's friends ever since."

Zarantha had closed her eyes and sagged against Bahzell once more. "You answer my prayers yet again," she'd murmured. "Dear friend, I can never repay you for all you've done."

"No, and there's no cause you should," he'd said, letting her rest in his arms. "I told you before, lass; a man looks after his own in this world."

Bahzell's mind returned to the present, and he looked back at Zarantha. He hadn't wanted to relinquish her to Wencit when she dozed off, but however little he knew of sorcery, he'd recognized Wencit's expression. The wild wizard was worried, and Bahzell had sensed a sort of unseen probing, as if Wencit's mind delved deep inside Zarantha's, seeking for wounds yet unhealed. Now he cleared his throat, and the wizard looked up at him.

"I'm thinking you're not so satisfied about her as you'd like," the hradani said, and Wencit sighed.

"Not yet. In time, she'll recover fully, I think, but she'll need care—and watching—till she heals."

"Ah?" Bahzell cocked his ears.

"They raped her, Bahzell. Not physically, but inside her mind, and she's a mage." Wencit shook his head, face tight with anger. "She *knew* what they were doing, which made it still worse. She's . . . open to them. Vulnerable. And if they get the chance to strike her again, it won't be to control, but to kill."

"Can you be stopping them?" the Horse Stealer demanded flatly.

"I can, but I'll have to keep her under my eye to shield her. And all I can really do about the damage is hold it where it is—keep it from growing any worse—until we get her someplace safe and familiar, where I can use past associations to help her rebuild her defenses. That means either a mage academy or Jashân itself, and getting her to either of those places won't be easy."

"Why not?" Brandark asked across the fire.

"Carnadosa has more followers in Norfressa than most people dream is possible," Wencit replied. "They dare not draw attention to themselves, but they're always with us. The Dark Gods promise their followers a great deal, and the lust for power cuts deep . . . especially in wizards." He smiled bleakly at the two hradani. "For those who can, the need—the hunger—to wield the art is too terrible to resist. In a sense, it's our own Rage. It drives us with a power and passion I doubt anyone but a hradani could truly understand."

Bahzell sat motionless for a long moment, then nodded slowly. He'd never considered it in those terms, yet it made sense, and Wencit nodded back as he saw the understanding on the Horse Stealer's face.

"Ottovar and Gwynytha understood that when they forged the Strictures," the wild wizard said. "A wizard *must* use his powers, for there's a glory—a splendor—in the art no one can resist. You can kill a wizard, but you can no more forbid him the use of the art than you could forbid the winter, so Ottovar and Gwynytha channeled and confined it, instead. They created a code to prevent the abuse of the art, yet by its very nature that code is eternally in conflict with temptations every wizard faces. The mere fact that it forbids them the unbridled use of their powers would make many resent and hate it, but there's more to it than that, for the study of sorcery is a perilous one, and the restrictions of the Strictures make it more so."

"Why?" Brandark asked.

"Because a wizard becomes a nexus of power when he plies his art. What he can accomplish depends directly upon the amount of energy he applies to the task, and he must place himself at the focus of the energies he wields. It requires years of study to develop the technique and strength of will to handle truly powerful concentrations, especially of the types of energy the Strictures allow a wizard to tap. If a wizard's attention wavers at a critical moment, the power will turn on him in an eyeblink, but blood magic and black sorcery are far easier to manipulate than the wizardry the Strictures allow. A white wizard must stretch to the limits of his ability to command the power for complex, high-level applications; a black wizard requires less strength of will because the *nature* of the power he uses makes it easier to control. That's why the dark art is so seductive, and it gives black wizards certain advantages. They deny the Strictures and pervert the art, and most of them are weaker than white wizards in the sense that they seldom fully develop their potential. They can achieve less with a given amount of power because their technique is more, well, *lazy*. Yet because the energy they tap is more susceptible to control, they can hold their own against inherently more powerful wizards bound by the Strictures—and if a white wizard resorts to expediency to match them, he becomes the very thing he fights, just as a warrior who breaks Tomanāk's Code reduces himself to the level of a Churnazh or Harnak."

Bahzell's eyes narrowed at the fresh evidence that Wencit knew all too much about him, but Brandark leaned towards the wizard, eyes intent. "I've always wondered what wizardry truly is. You talk about kinds of energy and power, about 'blood magic' and 'black wizards.' How does what you do truly differ from what *they* do?"

"It doesn't," Wencit said simply, and smiled as both hradani stiffened. "How does a sword in your hand differ from the same sword in the hand of a Harnak?" he challenged. Brandark frowned, and Wencit snorted. "The art is a tool, my friends; the use to which it's put determines whether it's 'white' or 'black.'"

"Even blood magic?" Brandark challenged in turn.

"Even blood magic, though blood magic is by far the

easiest to pervert. Wizardry—any wizardry—is simply the application of energy, and everything has its own energy. You do, Bahzell does, this rock I'm sitting on does. Indeed, if you could but perceive it, the entire universe is composed *solely* of energy. What you think of as 'solid matter' is a blaze of energy, bound up in shape and form and substance."

Bahzell frowned skeptically, then remembered who was speaking. If anyone living knew what sorcery was, Wencit of Rūm was that anyone.

"The problem," the wizard went on, "is that not all energy is equally accessible. For example, the energy latent in nonliving matter is hard to lay hands on or bend to your will. It's . . . call it *raw* energy. It's unregulated and dangerous, apt to backlash through a wizard if his concentration falters, so he learns specific manipulations, carefully limited ways to use it. But living creatures, especially intelligent ones, act like lenses. Their energy *content* is no different from any other energy, but it's channeled and focused. It resonates in time with the wizard's, which makes it far easier to grasp. There's power in life, my friends, in blood, and some of the most delicate workings of the art permitted under the Strictures were made possible only by the willing surrender of that focused power into the wizard's hands.

"But the Strictures require that that surrender *be* willing, and what you think of as blood magic isn't. That's what makes it 'evil,' just as a sword used to strike down the helpless is 'evil.' Which, unfortunately, doesn't make it any less potent for anyone willing to seize it by force."

"I'm thinking I'm not so very fond of anyone who dabbles in power such as that, be it willingly given or no," Bahzell rumbled.

"Which is why the Strictures' limitations are so specific," Wencit replied. "And why the only sentence for violating those limits is death."

Silence hovered, broken only by the background howl of the wind, for long, still moments. Then Brandark frowned.

"But there's a third sort of power, isn't there?" Wencit looked at him, and the Bloody Sword shrugged. "I mean, all the tales refer to you as a 'wild wizard.' Doesn't that mean there's some sort of energy that only you or wizards like you can tap?"

"No. It only means we tap it in a different way." Brandark looked as perplexed as Bahzell felt, and Wencit smiled crookedly. "Wild wizardry's hard come by—someday I may tell you the price it carries—but it uses the same energy. The difference—" the wildfire eyes glittered and danced at them "—is that a wild wizard can use all the energy of *any* object."

It was Bahzell's turn to frown, but then his eyes widened and his ears pricked forward. "You mean—?"

"Precisely." Wencit nodded. "Most wizards are what we call 'wand wizards.' They can't really touch the energy of the universe directly. They require techniques—call them tools—to manipulate it. A wild wizard doesn't 'manipulate' it at all; he simply channels it. In theory, a wild wizard could seize the total energy of every ounce of matter in an entire universe and focus it all upon a single task, a single objective."

"Gods!" Brandark breathed, staring at Wencit in something very like horror.

"I said 'in theory,'" Wencit reminded him gently. "In fact, no mortal could channel a fraction of such energy. For that matter, I doubt a *god* could survive channeling all of it! But even the minute portion of it a wild wizard can touch is far greater than the most powerful wand wizard can wield. It . . . changes him, of course. These—" he gestured at his glowing eyes "—are only the most obvious of those changes; others are far deeper and more subtle. Yet it's that ability to draw on an effectively infinite reservoir of power that makes wild wizards so feared by other wizards. No wand wizard can match it, and the younger and stronger a wild wizard, the more of it his body can endure."

"That being the case," Bahzell said dryly, gesturing to where Wencit had slain the two black wizards, "I'm thinking it's not so strange those two weren't so very happy to be seeing you."

"I imagine you're right," Wencit agreed with a cold, thin smile, then shook himself. "But the nature of the art is of less immediate importance than its consequences," he said more briskly. "And the consequences are that there are a great many more black wizards than there are of me, and at this moment, quite a few of them are no doubt working to determine exactly where I am. My touch is quite distinctive, I'm afraid. Even if it weren't, they'd almost have to suspect who was behind what happened to 'those two,' as you put it. They won't be eager to match themselves against me, but they don't really have to. They're like spiders, weaving webs of influence in the dark, where no one can see. Even with the aid of the magi, I can't hope to find all the Baron Dunsahntas they've enmeshed, but they've swords in plenty to send after me if they can track me. More than that, the presence of dog brothers in their train suggests the cooperation of Sharnā, and if his church takes an active hand—"

Wencit shrugged, and Bahzell shivered. Wizard or no, the thought of meeting one of Sharnā's demons was a frightening one.

"So what is it you're thinking to do?" he asked after a moment.

"I have to keep Zarantha close to guard her and, eventually, get her to safety. For the moment, I'm maintaining a glamour—think of it as a spell of evasion that turns their scrying attempts aside. As long as I hold the glamour,

I and anyone with me become a blank spot, something they can't quite 'see.'"

"So you're safe from detection," Brandark said.

"No, they just can't see me," Wencit corrected, and the Bloody Sword scratched his chin in evident confusion. "They can't see *anything* where I am, Brandark. All they have to do is look long and hard enough to find the blank spot in their scrying spells, and they'll know I'm inside it."

Bahzell grunted in unhappy understanding. They couldn't move on in this weather, especially not with Zarantha so weakened and exhausted. They had to wait for the storm to break, and it was only too likely that the dead wizards' allies knew precisely where to find them this moment. If those allies simply had to spot the blind spot in their vision, tracking it would be almost as easy as tracking a target they could see clearly, and if they knew Wencit was in it, they'd throw everything they had at it the moment they could. But—

"Tell me," he rumbled slowly, "would they be knowing that you know they can be following after this blank spot?"

"Of course."

"Well, that being the case, would they be so very surprised if you *didn't* hold your glamour?" Wencit crooked an eyebrow, and the Horse Stealer shrugged. "What I'm wondering is whether or not they'd be smelling something if you chose to trust in speed, not stealth, and simply ran for it."

"I don't know." Wencit pursed his lips, then shrugged. "Probably not—not, at least, if I ran in a direction that made sense to them."

"Ah." Bahzell nodded in satisfaction, and Brandark shot him a speculative glance.

"I know that tone, Bahzell. You're up to something."

"Aye, that I am," the Horse Stealer admitted. "It's in

my mind that we might be giving them something they can see clear enough and let them chase after that."

"Like what?" Brandark demanded, and Bahzell looked at the wizard.

"Suppose you were casting another of your illusions, Wencit—not of hradani, this time, but of all of us—and sent it straight off towards Jashân while the lot of us were actually heading off north under your glamour? By the time they were catching up with the illusion, why, we'd be so far away a single 'blank spot' would be a mortal hard thing to be finding in so much space."

"It wouldn't work," Wencit disagreed with a headshake. "Oh, the plan's good enough, but an illusion requires a focus. I couldn't project one that complex more than a league or two from me without something to tie it to, and that's not far enough to do us much good."

"What sort of focus would you be needing?" Bahzell asked intently.

"Almost anything would do in a pinch, but a living mind is best. An illusion feeds on itself, in a way; if someone at its heart can see it about him, his perception of it becomes part of the spell and helps maintain and reinforce it for other observers."

"Does it now?" Bahzell murmured, and Brandark straightened with a jerk.

"Bahzell—!" he began sharply, but the Horse Stealer silenced him with a raised hand, never taking his own eyes from Wencit.

"Suppose you were using *me* for this focus of yours. I'm thinking I could be leading them a merry chase while you and Brandark saw Zarantha home."

"No!" Brandark ignored the look Bahzell gave him and shook his head fiercely. "You're not sneaking off without me, Bahzell!"

"Oh, hush, now! Where's the point in risking more than one when there's no need at all, at all, to be doing it?"

"If you're bound and determined to be the hero in some stupid ballad, then I'll be damned if I let you hog all the glory for yourself!" Brandark shot back in something much more like his normal tone. "And what sort of bard would miss the chance to write the ballad from the inside, anyway?"

Bahzell started to reply, but Wencit cut him off.

"It's a generous offer, Bahzell, but I don't think you realize what you'd be letting yourself in for. You've trouble enough without borrowing mine, and not just from dog brothers."

"Do I, now?" The Horse Stealer cocked his ears at the wizard. "And just what else might it be that's following after me?"

"I can't say for certain." Wencit paused, and he seemed to select his words with care when he continued. "You're in a . . . pivotal position just now. I realize you haven't decided to accept an, ah, offer you were recently made, but certain other powers know it was offered. They're determined that you *won't* accept it, and I expect them to take rather drastic steps to insure you don't."

"D'you know," Bahzell said almost meditatively, "I'm thinking you're knowing entirely too much about me for my peace of mind, Wencit of Rūm."

"I'm a wizard. Wizards are supposed to know too much for other people's peace of mind."

"Are they, indeed? D'you suppose that might be one reason they're after being so popular with other folk?"

"No doubt. But that doesn't change facts, and the facts are that even without me or Zarantha along, you're going to draw entirely too many enemies after you, wherever you go. There's no point adding my troubles to yours."

"I'll grant you that, but that's not to be saying there's reason to be adding *my* troubles to *yours*, either. If they're after knowing we're together, then all we'll do by staying so is to bring both our enemies down on all of us," Bahzell argued. "I've given my word to see Zarantha safe home, and I'll not be doing that if they're pulling us all down and taking her back again. No, Wencit," he shook his head. "Best to give them a target they can be seeing while you get her back to her father, and I'm thinking they'll find me a mite hard to catch—aye, or to be doing aught with if they *do* run me down!"

"You," Wencit said testily, "have a skull of solid rock!"

"It's been said before, and no doubt with reason, but that's not to say I'm wrong, is it now?" The Horse Stealer held the wizard's glowing eyes steadily, and it was Wencit who looked away with an angry jerk of his head.

"Right or wrong, you're not sneaking off without me," Brandark repeated. Bahzell glared at him, and the Bloody Sword glared right back. "If Wencit is going to rely on stealth to avoid enemies, then he won't need anyone to watch his back in a fight, and *you* will."

"Brandark, I'm not wishful to see you dead," Bahzell replied quietly, "and from all Wencit's saying, this is my trouble, not yours."

"I've had a little hand in getting you into it," Brandark shot back. "Remember the cave? If I hadn't been with you, you still might not even know what's going on, in which case these bastards wouldn't be chasing you. Besides, you need looking after. If I let you wander off without my guidance to keep you out of trouble, I'd never sleep soundly again."

Bahzell opened his mouth, then shut it with a sigh as he recognized the fundamental hradani stubbornness in Brandark's expression. The Bloody Sword snorted with an edge of triumph, then looked back at Wencit.

"And as for you," he said, "it's time you stopped thinking of reasons we shouldn't do it and started considering how to do it most effectively." Wencit blinked at the asperity of his tone, and Brandark snorted again. "For one thing, how long will you need to get enough of a start to make it impossible for them to find you?"

"I can't make it 'impossible,'" Wencit said mildly after a short pause. "All I can do is make it difficult." Brandark frowned, and the wizard smiled briefly. "I take your meaning, though. Give me two or three days of clear travel, and I can make the target area so wide it would take a special miracle for them to spot me."

"All right, then." Brandark gave a satisfied nod. "Cast your illusion using us as the focus, but set it to vanish or dissipate or whatever the Phrobus it does after three days. When it does, they'll realize we've split up, but they can't be certain exactly when or where we did it. They'll have to divide their efforts to look for both of us—and when they do, they'll probably split back into factions. The ones who want you and Zarantha will pull out to hunt for you and leave us alone, and the ones who want Bahzell and me will go on chasing us and leave *you* alone."

He gazed at his companions with an air of triumph, and Bahzell and Wencit blinked at one another as they realized he was right. The best they could hope for was to divide their enemies' attention, and Brandark's suggestion was clearly their best chance to do just that. Silence lingered about the campfire, broken only by the background howl of the storm, and then Wencit sighed.

"All right. I don't like it, but I'll do it."

# CHAPTER THIRTY-ONE

The treeline along the southern horizon had first appeared early that morning; by the time Bahzell and Brandark stopped at midday, it was clearly defined and far darker.

"Think we'll make the woods by nightfall?" Brandark asked as he dismounted and stood rubbing his posterior.

"Aye." Bahzell was rummaging in a pack saddle, but he looked up to squint at the trees. Wencit had provided them (by means Bahzell preferred not to consider too deeply) with the finest maps he'd ever seen. Unless his reading of them was sadly mistaken, that was the Shipwood, straddling the Spearmen's border with the Purple Lords, and he was relieved to see it. Four days had passed since they parted from Wencit and Zarantha, and he'd been privately certain they'd never make it this far without being overtaken by *someone*.

It helped that the snow had melted so quickly after the blizzard. Indeed, Bahzell's northern-bred weather instincts were a bit affronted by how rapidly it had vanished, not that he meant to complain. The hard freeze had lasted long enough for them to get free of the marshes, and if the soggy, mucky sod of the plains made less than pleasant hiking, it was infinitely preferable to horse belly-deep snow.

He found the cheese and dried meat he'd hunted for and let the saddle flap fall. Brandark had already unslung the big skin of beer they'd liberated from their enemies, and the two of them hunkered down to eat while they watched their animals browse on the muddy, winter-killed grass.

It had been an eerie sensation, those first three days, to see Wencit and Zarantha riding alongside them. Knowing they weren't really there at all had made Bahzell uneasy at first, but his initial discomfort had faded into fascination with the sheer perfection of the illusion. The false warriors Wencit had conjured up for the attack on the wizards' camp had been exquisitely detailed, but he hadn't had time to pay those details much heed. This time he did, and his instinctive hatred for wizardry had turned into something very like awe as he studied them.

Wencit, he'd decided, was as much artist as wizard. The false Zarantha and Wencit never spoke to either hradani, but they carried on conversations of their own, and every nuance of tone and gesture was perfect. The immaterial images had left illusory hoofprints in the snow until it melted, and cast shadows at precisely the right angle as the sun moved. They cared for their equally unreal horses at each halt, ate from nonexistent plates beside the campfire, even developed fresh travel stains as they splashed across the muddy plains. Wencit had explained that Bahzell's and Brandark's perceptions were part of the spell, feeding back into the illusion to maintain its integrity and update its details, yet even so it had been difficult at times to remember that Zarantha and the wizard weren't really with them.

Until yesterday morning, that was, when the spell abruptly died.

Bahzell had been looking straight at "Wencit" when it happened, and the wizard's sudden disappearance had hit him like a fist. He'd known it was coming, but the illusion had been so real, so solid. It was as if the *real* Wencit had been snuffed from existence, and the Horse Stealer had felt an icy chill. It had been almost like an omen, a premonition of disaster poised to strike their distant companions, and the thought had been hard to throw off. He'd managed it finally by remembering the real Zarantha's tearful farewell and her fierce demand that he and Brandark promise to visit her in Jashân before returning home. He'd used that memory like a talisman, proof that the phantom Zarantha who'd vanished with Wencit *hadn't* been the real one, yet he still caught himself worrying about her at odd moments.

Like now. He snorted at himself and shook the worry away. There was nothing he could do if she *was* in trouble, and anyone with Wencit of Rūm to look after her had more help than most mortals could imagine asking for. Besides, he and Brandark had their own worries.

He cocked an eye at the sun while he chewed iron-hard jerky. They should make the trees with an hour of daylight to spare, he thought, and he'd be glad to get under their cover. He felt naked out here, more exposed than he'd ever felt on the Wind Plain, for the Sothōii didn't use wizards to hunt for hradani raiders. Still, if Brandark's plan had worked, any ill-intentioned wizards were probably bending their efforts on finding Wencit and Zarantha by now, which meant the two hradani had only their own enemies to deal with.

And it was just possible that they'd reduced those enemies' numbers a bit. Not likely, but possible. They'd left their prisoners the more exhausted of the captured horses—more out of kindness to the beasts than to their riders, Bahzell admitted—and supplies for two or three weeks, and he'd taken time to issue a blunt warning to the senior of the four surviving dog brothers.

"I'm not after being a patient man," he'd said in a flat, cold voice, "and by rights I should be cutting your throat, for we're both knowing what would happen if the boot was on the other foot." He'd seen the fear flickering behind the assassin's eyes and snorted. "Don't be brooding on it, for I'll not do it. Instead, I've a message for your precious guild."

He'd paused, frowning at the assassin until the man could endure the silence no longer and swallowed hard. "A message?" he'd asked, and Bahzell had nodded.

"Aye, a message. By my count, you've spent nigh on sixty men in trying to take my ears, and not a bit of luck have you had. Well, I'm minded to call it even if you are, but call off your hounds while you can, dog brother. You'll find your gold hard earned before you bring *me* down—and I'll not be so reasonable if it should happen I see another of your kind on my heels." He'd smiled coldly. "So far I've done naught but defend myself, but if it should happen you're minded to keep up the hunt, then I'll be having a little hunt of my own—aye, and a mortal lot of other Horse Stealers with me. I'm thinking your guild won't be so very happy at all, at all, if that happens."

He'd given the suddenly pale assassin one more glare, then stalked away, and now he grinned with wry humor at the memory. His warning might not do a bit of good, he admitted, biting off another rocky lump of jerky, but it had certainly made *him* feel better.

They made even better time than Bahzell had estimated. He and Brandark still had three good hours of daylight when they reached the Shipwood and plunged into it, and they were just as glad they did. The shade of the forest's towering trees had choked out the underbrush that could make second-growth woodland a trackless tangle, but it was dark and empty, cold and unwelcoming in its winter bareness.

After so long in open grassland, they felt hemmed in and confined as they picked their way through it. Bahzell led the way, wading ankle deep through wet drifts of fallen leaves, and the trees seemed to brood down on him from all sides. He was an invader here, and they disapproved of his presence.

He tried to brush the thought aside by reminding himself how he'd looked forward to getting under cover, yet he was unhappily aware of his own sudden, contrary longing for the long, clear sight lines of the plains. He might have felt naked and exposed out there, but he'd also felt comfortably certain no one could creep up on them unseen. Now he felt the nape of his neck crawl, as if something were waiting to pounce, and he cursed his nerves.

He looked up uneasily. It was dark under the trees, even in leafless winter, but the sky beyond the web of overhead limbs was still clear and blue. Yet the prickle on the back of his neck only intensified, and he stopped dead, turning in place to scan the wet, silent woods.

"What?" Brandark's soft question felt shockingly loud in the quiet, and Bahzell twitched his ears.

"I'm none too sure," he replied quietly, "but something—"

He broke off, ears going flat to his skull, as wind roared suddenly in the branches above him. The day had been still, without so much as a breeze, and he heard Brandark curse behind him as a fist of air smote the forest. One moment all was still; the next a sucking gale snatched at the trees like angry hands. Limbs creaked and groaned, crying out against the sudden violence, and the afternoon light was abruptly quenched. It didn't fade. It wasn't cut off by moving clouds. It simply died, plunging the forest into inky blackness, and a long, savage roll of thunder smashed through the roar of the unnatural wind.

Bahzell staggered as the tumult crashed about him. Small, broken branches pelted them, and Brandark's horse screamed in panic. The pack animals and remounts caught its fear, lunging against their leads and squealing in terror, and Bahzell leapt in among them to calm them. Brandark fought his horse back under control, then dismounted, clinging to its reins with one hand while he lent Bahzell as much aid as he could with the others, but the shriek of the wind battered at them all. Two of the horses broke free and thundered madly away, then a third, and the wind howl went on and on and on and *on*.

Fresh thunder crashed, louder even than before. A glare like a hundred lightning bolts lit the forest in lurid light, and Brandark shouted something. Bahzell turned his head, but the Bloody Sword wasn't looking at him; he was staring up, ears flat, lips drawn back in a snarl. Bahzell followed his gaze upward—and froze as thunder smashed the heavens yet again.

There was more than thunder in that wind-sick darkness. There was something huge and black, riding the maelstrom on batlike wings. He couldn't see it clearly, but what little he *could* see was the stuff of nightmares. The glare of lightning leapt back from ebon hide and scale and bony plates, and the hideous shape swept back around, circling like a hawk in search of prey.

Thunder crashed in a final, shattering spasm, more terrible than any that had come before, and then, as suddenly as a slamming door, it died. The wind eased—a little—and both pack mules broke their leads and galloped frantically into the blackness.

*"BAHZELL!"* The deafening bellow was louder than the thunder had been. It split the darkness like an axe, huge and inhuman, a hissing, cackling sound mortal ears had never been meant to hear. *"BAHZELL!"* it shrieked again, and Brandark snatched his eyes back down from the heavens to stare at his friend.

Neither spoke. They simply turned as one, dragging their remaining horses with them, and fled while that hideous voice howled across the sky.

The vast, inhuman bellow roared Bahzell's name once more, and unaccustomed panic gripped him. The packhorse he led squealed, lunging against the lead rein in terror as it caught on a low-hanging branch, and he swore as he jerked the leather free. The forest was darker than the pits of Krahana, trees loomed like the rough-barked legs of monsters intent on tripping him up, and *still* that guttural voice shrieked his name. Brandark's horse went to its knees, and Bahzell slithered to a halt, waiting while the Bloody Sword wrenched the beast back up lest they lose track of one another in the blackness.

Something crashed behind them, like a dozen city gates splintering under a score of rams, and his name hooted and gibbered at them out of the darkness. They redoubled their pace, running blindly, bouncing off trees, stumbling over uneven ground, and the crashing, splintering sounds pursued them. Bahzell could picture the monster ripping entire trees out by the roots, throwing them aside as it rampaged through the forest in pursuit. He heard Brandark's desperate panting beside him as his friend gasped for breath, knew they could run no faster, but the sounds of shattering wood were overtaking them quickly, and he swore savagely. They couldn't outrun something that could batter whole trees from its path, and the thought of being pulled down from behind while he ran like a panicked rabbit was too much to endure.

The ground angled suddenly upward, and he staggered

as the abrupt slope surprised him. He scrubbed sweat from his eyes, chest heaving, and saw a hill like a bare, black knob. A long-ago fire had created a clearing about it, and he turned his head as Brandark slithered to a stop beside him.

"We won't . . . find . . a better spot!" the Bloody Sword gasped, and Bahzell nodded grimly. At least if they faced whatever it was out here it couldn't drop trees on them—unless it brought a trunk or two with it.

"Keep going!" he panted back, but Brandark shook his head. He was already leading the two horses he still had towards the top of the hill, and he actually managed a grin as he looked back over his shoulder.

"No point!" he shouted. "D'you honestly think I can outrun *that?!*"

Bahzell swore again, but his friend was probably right—and there was no time to argue. He followed Brandark up the hill, and the two of them tethered their remaining horses to the burned out snag of a mammoth oak. Bahzell took time to make sure the knot was secure—partly because he'd need the packhorse's supplies in the improbable event that he survived, but mainly because it was something to do besides simply stand there—then drew his sword. He walked to the very crest of the hill and stood gazing back the way he'd come, and bright, sharp fear filled his mouth. He knew his capabilities; he also knew this was a foe no man could fight and win.

Brandark scrambled up beside him, his own sword in hand, and wind whined about their ears. A faint, corpse-green glow lit the sky above them, and they stood silhouetted against it, listening to the crash of toppling trees as the bat-winged horror stormed towards them. Bahzell's starving lungs sucked in enormous gulps of air after his long, stumbling run, and then he stiffened as an enormous oak toppled in a smash of splintered limbs and shattered trunk. That tree had to be sixty feet tall, but it crashed to earth and bounced, and a monstrous form—all spider legs and bat wings and huge, fanged, pincer-armed head—stalked down its broken length like a dream of Hell taken flesh.

"*BAHZELL!*" it howled, and started up the slope.

It was an obscene mix of insect and bat, moving with the darting vitality of a lizard, and foot-long fangs clashed as it snapped its jaws and screamed his name. He remembered Tomanāk's description of demons as something so weak they were hard for the gods to "see" and knew in that moment that he never wanted to meet anything the gods could see clearly. The thing's breath hissed and bubbled, strands of emerald spittle drooled from its teeth and pincers, and the stench of an open grave blew to them from it.

"Ah, Bahzell," Brandark's tenor was unnaturally clear, almost calm, through the wind and the noise of wood splitting in talons of night-black horn, "I realize you've been having something of a religious crisis lately, and I'd never dream of pushing you one way or another. But if you *have* been considering accepting Tomanāk's offer, well, this might be a very good time for it."

Bahzell gritted his teeth, eyes fixed on the approaching demon. The Rage glittered within him, already reaching out to claim him, yet Brandark's words echoed through it, and he felt a sudden, terrible suspicion. Had Tomanāk known this would happen? Worse, had he *arranged* for it to trap Bahzell into his service? Twelve hundred years of distrust shouted that the god had done just that, but only for an instant. Just long enough for him to recognize it . . . and reject it instantly. Tomanāk was the god of justice, and justice could be hard, but it didn't lie— and neither did its patron.

More than that, there was no need for Tomanāk to entrap him. Not now. For Tomanāk had been right; Bahzell had only thought he knew what evil was. Now he saw its very embodiment flowing up the muddy slope towards him and realized the War God had known him better than he'd known himself. Bahzell Bahnakson could not look upon such horror and vileness, couldn't picture it stalking someone *else*, and not fight it. His terror flashed like spits of lightning, and the oncoming demon turned his bowels to water as no mortal foe ever had. He wanted desperately to turn and flee once more, and it wasn't the Rage that stopped him and stiffened his spine. It was outrage stronger even than his fear. The recognition of evil . . . and the knowledge, the acceptance, that it was what he'd been born and bred to fight.

"All right!" he howled to the wind. "If it's wanting me you are, then have me you can!"

He raised his sword in both hands, and the steel flashed like a mirror as a bolt of savage blue lightning split the darkness. He felt it strike the five-foot blade, run down it, flare up his arms and stutter in his heart, and his lips drew back in the snarl of the Rage.

"Bahzell, no!" Brandark screamed. "I didn't mean *alone*, you idiot!"

The Bloody Sword clutched at his friend's harness, but too late. Bahzell launched himself down the slope at the armored monstrosity that shrieked his name, and a new war cry ripped from his throat in answer.

"*Tomanāk!*" he bellowed, and the demon reared up on four legs, fanning its bat wings and howling in fury at the sound of that name. Two forelimbs spread wide, reaching out, and for all his towering inches, Bahzell was a pygmy as he charged straight into its grasp.

Brandark shouted a despairing curse and floundered down the hill in Bahzell's wake, then bounced back with a bone-shaking crash as he ran full tilt into an unseen barrier. He staggered back upright, smashing at the invisible wall with his sword and all the fury of his own Rage, but it refused to yield. He couldn't pass it, couldn't follow. He could only watch in sick horror as his best friend hurled himself at his titanic foe.

*"BAHZELL!"* the demon thundered yet again, lashing out with talonlike claws thicker than Bahzell's arm, but the Horse Stealer twisted impossibly, still hurtling forward. A slime-dripping claw grated along his mail, ripping away a shower of iron scales, and his sword whistled down in a two-handed blow. It struck like a steel avalanche, and eye-tearing blue light flashed as it sheared through segmented bony armor and flesh. Viscous blood spouted, and the monster shrieked and snatched the wounded limb back as if from the heart of a fire, but its other forelimb slashed in to strike Bahzell from behind.

The impact hurled him from his feet. He hit hard, bouncing through the muddy ash of the ancient forest fire, slithering on his belly, but somehow he retained his sword. He twisted around, slowing his headlong sprawl, and rolled back to his knees, and he was under the demon. Its belly loomed above him, plated in thick black scales, and the monster tossed its head, searching for its prey while it howled.

There was no more fear in Bahzell Bahnakson. The Rage was upon him, and something else came with it. A terrible something, equally bright yet hotter—a focused purpose, a total concentration, that melded with the Rage. It fanned the Rage, fueled it, wrapped it about him and drove him to his feet.

Brandark slid down the invisible wall, and his eyes were huge as Bahzell lunged upright under the demon's belly. The Horse Stealer glowed in the darkness, glittering with a blinding blue corona. A stab of brilliance flashed along his blade as he thrust straight upward, and the demon shrieked as three feet of flaming steel punched through its scales.

The monster hurled itself backward with a bubbling, head-lashing howl and curled its wounded forelimb against its body, twisting back and forth while thick, stinking blood pulsed from its belly. It stood that way for one endless second, staring at the hradani mite who'd dared set steel to its flesh, and Bahzell snarled into its faceted, insect eyes.

"Come on, then!" he bellowed, and the demon's head swept down in a murderous arc. Its pincers plowed leaf mold and earth as they ripped back up in a stroke fit to disembowel a titan, and Bahzell stepped straight into them. He brought his blade down to meet them in a howling half-circle of light, and the splintering sound of that impact shook the forest.

Nothing mortal could have withstood the force of the demon's attack, and Bahzell flew backward. He crashed into the oak it had torn to splinters and bounced from the riven trunk, but his explosive grunt of anguish was lost in the monster's scream as its pincer split. Not even Bahzell's stupendous blow could shear it off, but the slick black horn tore and cracked, dangling uselessly, and the Horse Stealer staggered back to his feet.

"*Tomanāk!*" he bellowed once more, slashing out in a perfectly timed stroke, and the demon shrieked afresh as glowing steel split one huge eye. The maimed head jerked back and away, and then Bahzell was under it once more, and his sword spat blue fire as it sheared through the monster's other foreleg.

Brandark Brandarkson crouched on his knees, fighting to believe his own eyes, as the demon crashed half on its side under the fury of Bahzell's attack. It clawed back up, scattering mud and leaves and the splintered limbs of trees, and Bahzell's sword crashed down again. Split scales spat shards of horn, blood spouted, and the demon screamed yet again—this time with a high, squealing note of panic—and scrabbled away from its tiny foe.

But Bahzell followed it, wading into its stench and

fury, hurling blow after blow into its teeth. It clawed and bit, but it was half-blind, half-crippled by the damage to its limbs. Flailing wings kept it upright, yet it had lost its lizard-quick sureness. It floundered and beat at him, and he staggered under its massive blows, but he kept his footing, and his blade howled in his hands. He was too close for the demon's fangs to get a clear stroke at him, and he was a thing of steel and wires, not flesh and bone. Tireless and implacable, absorbing the frantic blows he couldn't avoid and striking again and again and again.

The demon slipped and half fell once more, then lunged up, wings beating madly, but that terrible blue sword smashed into its left wing. It sheared through gristle and muscle and bone, and the monster's wordless bellow of agony filled the world. It turned on Bahzell with renewed fury, yet now it was the fury of desperation, and Bahzell howled Tomanak's name yet again and flung himself bodily upon it.

A boot lashed out, driving its toe into the spouting wound in the demon's wing. A leg straightened, and Brandark stared in disbelief as Bahzell vaulted up onto the monster's back. The creature shook itself, frantic to throw him off, but he flung his blade back over his shoulder, and even through the demon's bellows, Brandark heard his grunt as he brought the sword down.

Five feet of razored steel—and that glittering blue nimbus—exploded across a sinuous, armored neck with an ear-shattering *CRACK*! It ripped through half-inch scale like tissue, bit deep into unnatural flesh, and the demon stiffened with a whip-crack jerk of agony. For one instant it stood, fanged mouth open in a terrible, soundless shriek, and then it crashed down, toppling in dreadful slow motion—a mountain of horn and scale crumbling in on itself—and took Bahzell with it in its ruin.

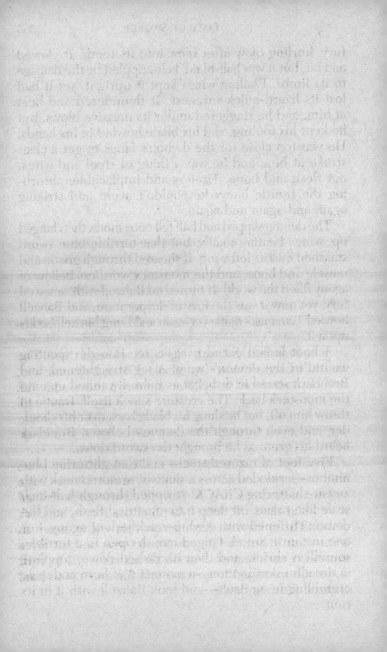

# CHAPTER THIRTY-TWO

The hurricane died, and quiet fell like a hammer, broken only by a soft, fitful patter—the sound of the last broken branches, falling as the wind released them. The invisible barrier which had blocked Brandark vanished, and he floundered to his feet and down the muddy hill to the mountainous, crumpled heap of the demon, still twitching with the last flicker of its unnatural vitality while Bahzell lay facedown, half buried under one outthrust limb.

Brandark flung himself to his knees, and his hand trembled with more than the aftermath of the Rage as he touched the side of Bahzell's neck, then gasped in relief at the slow, strong throb of the Horse Stealer's pulse. The spiderlike limb across him was massive as a tree trunk, but the Bloody Sword wrapped his arms around it and heaved. It took all his strength to shift it, yet he managed to move it just far enough to haul Bahzell from under it.

He dragged his friend clear, circling round upwind of the fallen demon to get out of the worst of its stench, and arranged him on his back. Bahzell was bruised, battered, and filthy with foul-smelling blood, and huge streaks of steel plates had been ripped from his scale mail, but Brandark heaved an even deeper sigh of relief as he examined him. Hradani tended to survive anything that didn't kill them outright, and, impossible as it seemed, Bahzell didn't even seem to have any broken bones. The Bloody Sword slumped down on his heels in disbelief. He'd seen it with his own eyes, and it didn't help. He *still* didn't believe it.

The eerie blackness faded into the more natural dimness of evening, and Brandark shook himself. He thrust himself back upright with the stiffness of an old, old man and picked his way back down to the demon. It took him several minutes to spot Bahzell's sword—it was hidden almost to the hilt under the demon's body—and even longer to summon the courage to touch it. Brandark knew that blade as well as his own, but the crackling blue corona that had turned it into a weapon out of legend left him off balance and unsure. No trace of that eldritch glare remained, yet he had to draw a deep breath and clench his jaw before he gripped the hilt. Nothing happened, and he pulled it from under the monster and carried it gingerly back up the slope just as Bahzell groaned and began to stir.

The Horse Stealer groaned again and shoved himself up to sit on the muddy hillside. He blinked his eyes, as if they didn't want to focus, then scrubbed at them with one hand. It was as filthy as the rest of him, smearing more mud and blood across his face, but it seemed to help, and he turned his head as Brandark went to his knees at his side and laid the sword beside him.

"I trust—" it cost Brandark a great deal of effort to put the right drawl into his voice "—that you don't plan to do that again anytime soon?"

"Ah?" Bahzell blinked again, owlishly, and shook his head. It was a tentative gesture, as if he were assuring himself it was still attached, but he managed a lopsided grin. "No," he said after a moment. "No, I'm not thinking as how that's something a man wants to be doing too often. Best save it up for times when life goes all boring on him."

"Boring," Brandark repeated dryly. "I see." Bahzell started to stand, and the Bloody Sword pushed him back down. "Just sit there and feel bored a bit longer while you get your breath back," he advised testily.

"Hush, now!" Bahzell brushed the restraining hand aside and rose. "I've a notion someone dropped a tree on me when I wasn't watching, but I'm in one piece yet, Brandark!"

He stretched his arms enormously, then put his hands on his hips and tried a few limbering up exercises and smiled more naturally at his friend as various joints and muscles worked. Brandark still looked dubious, but in truth, Bahzell felt far better than he knew he had any right feeling. Bruised, battered, and exhausted, perhaps, yet that was a preposterously light price for his survival. He rubbed a particularly tender bruise on his jaw, and his smile turned into a frown as he looked down at the Bloody Sword.

"Indeed, I'm thinking I should be feeling a sight worse than I am. Where's—"

He turned, and his voice died as he saw the outstretched demon. The light was almost gone, hiding the creature's more hideous details, but he could see enough, and his hand stopped moving along his jaw. He stood motionless, gazing at the enormous carcass, and then slowly, slowly lowered his hand. He turned to look at Brandark with his mouth slightly open and his ears half-flattened, and the Bloody Sword shrugged.

"Don't ask me. I *saw* you kill it, and I still don't know how you did it. All I know is that you started shouting

Tomanāk's name, lit up like Wencit's sword, and charged straight at it like a maniac. Of course," Brandark stood and slapped him on the shoulder with a grin, "you never have been noted for imaginative tactics, but still—!"

"Tactics, is it?" Bahzell closed his mouth with an effort and tried to summon up a glare.

"No, not tactics; the *absence* of them," Brandark corrected. "Still, it seems to've worked, and—"

"Indeed it did," an earthquake voice rumbled suddenly behind them.

Both hradani spun, and it was Brandark's turn to drop his jaw as he saw the huge shape on the crest of the hill. Blue light, like a gentle shadow of the glare which had engulfed Bahzell, shone from it, and the Bloody Sword felt himself slip to one knee in automatic response.

Bahzell didn't. His head went up, and his shoulders straightened, but he kept his feet and met Tomanāk's eyes steadily. The god cocked his head for a moment, then nodded in approval.

"You did well, Bahzell." His impossibly deep voice was quiet, yet a fanfare of trumpets seemed to sound in its depths.

"Aye, well, as to that, I've a notion *you* had something to do with it, as well."

"I told you I strengthen my champions."

"Do you, now?" Bahzell cocked his ears, and his voice was thoughtful. "I'm thinking it might be you were doing just a mite more than that this time."

"Not a great deal," Tomanāk said, and shook his head at Bahzell's skeptical look. "Oh, I lent your sword a bit of my power, but that would have meant little without your heart and purpose behind it, Bahzell."

"Mine?" Bahzell sounded surprised, and Tomanāk nodded, then lowered his eyes to include Brandark in his gaze.

"Yours and no one else's. The Rage is your people's

curse, but it need not be one forever. That's one reason I wanted you as my champion."

Bahzell looked a question at him, and the War God sighed.

"Bahzell, Brandark, what was done to your people went deeper than even the wizards behind it dreamed. Their purpose was simply to goad and control you, to create a weapon, but the consequences of a spell may go far beyond what the wizard intended."

The hradani stared at him, listening intently, and Tomanāk folded his arms across his immense chest.

"Wizardry is power—nothing more, and nothing less. As Wencit told you, it's energy which can be applied to specific tasks. Some of those tasks are straightforward; others are complex and subtle, especially when they pertain to living creatures. Inanimate objects can be altered, transformed, even destroyed with relative impunity and without changing their fundamental natures. Blast a boulder to gravel, and it remains the same stone; you've simply broken it into fragments."

He raised an eyebrow, as if to ask if they followed him, and they nodded silently.

"But changes in living creatures are more complex. Life is ongoing, eternally changing and becoming, and when the dark wizards made your people fodder for their armies, they forced a change even more profound than they realized. They changed your basic matrix, the factors which control your heredity. That's why the Rage has bred true among hradani . . . but it's no longer the Rage they intended you to have."

He fell silent, and Bahzell scratched the tip of one ear and frowned. He glanced at Brandark, who looked as puzzled as he felt, then back at Tomanāk.

"Begging your pardon, but I'm not understanding."

"I know." Tomanāk gazed down at the Horse Stealer, then raised one hand to gesture at the demon's carcass.

"The dark wizards intended you and your people to be no more than that demon was: ravening beasts with an unstoppable lust to kill. And, for a time—a very long one, as mortals reckon it—that was what the Rage made you. What it still makes some of you. But what happens when you *give* yourself to the Rage, Bahzell?"

The Horse Stealer flushed, recalling the shameful seduction of the Rage's power and focused passion, but Tomanāk shook his head.

"No, Bahzell," he said gently. "I know what you *think* happens, but the Rage doesn't make you a killer when you embrace it . . . because it isn't really 'the Rage' at all."

Bahzell blinked, and Brandark jerked upright beside him.

"Not—?" the Horse Stealer began, and Tomanāk shook his head once more.

"No. It's *similar* to the Rage, and it springs from the same changes wizardry wrought in you, but it's quite different. Perhaps your people will think of another name for it in years to come, as you learn more about it and yourselves. You see, the Rage controls those it strikes without warning, but *you* control *it* when you summon it to you. It becomes a tool, something you can use at need, not something that uses *you*."

Bahzell stiffened in shock, and Tomanāk nodded, but there was a warning note in his voice when he continued.

"Don't mistake me. Even when you control it, the Rage remains a deadly danger. Just as wizardry, it's the use to which it's put which makes it 'good' or 'evil.' A man who knowingly summons the Rage to aid him in a crime is no less a criminal—indeed, he becomes a worse criminal than one whom the Rage maddens against his will—and the old Rage, the one the wizards intended, is far from dead among your people. It's dying. In time, it will be no more than a memory, but that time lies many years

from now, and there will always be those, like Churnazh
and Harnak, who glory in destruction and use it to that
end. But for the rest of your people, as you learn to control and use it—as *you* used it today, Bahzell—the Rage
will become a gift, as well."

Bahzell inhaled deeply. What Tomanāk had said seemed
impossible. For as long as hradani could remember, the
Rage had been their darkest shame, their most bitter
curse. How could something which had cost them so
much, made them monsters to be shunned by the other
Races of Man, possibly be a *gift*?

Yet even as he thought that, his mind spun back over
the handful of times he'd summoned the Rage, and the first,
faint ghost of belief touched him. He'd never really thought
about it, he realized. He'd been too ashamed, too frightened by it . . . and he'd never summoned it except in battle.
It was too powerful a demon to be unchained unless his
very survival left him no choice, and he'd always locked the
chains back about it as quickly as he could.

And because he had, he'd never realized it wasn't the
*destruction* of the Rage that tempted him at all. It was
the exaltation, the focus, the sense that in its grip he
became all that he could possibly be. He'd simply never
considered using that power and focus for anything other
than warfare, and he sucked in a deep breath of total
shock as he realized that he could. That it didn't *have* to
be used for destruction.

That his people held in their own hands the power to
free themselves of their ancient curse at last.

"I—" He stopped and drew another breath. "I'm thinking I'll need time, and not a little of it, to be understanding
all you've said," he said, and his voice was unwontedly
hesitant. "Yet if it's true . . ."

He trailed off, and Tomanāk nodded once more.

"It's true, Bahzell, and it will be one of your tasks to
teach your people that. Yes, and to remind them that

swords have two edges, that they must evolve new laws to govern the use of the Rage and punish those who abuse it. As Ottovar once taught wizards to restrain their power, so your people must learn to restrain theirs, and the learning won't be easy."

"No," Bahzell said softly. "No, I can be seeing that."

"I know," Tomanāk said gently. "It was one reason I chose you—and hoped you would choose me, in turn. And now," the god's voice turned brisker, "since it seems you *have* chosen me, are you prepared to swear Sword Oath to me, Bahzell Bahnakson?"

The sudden question wrenched the Horse Stealer's mind from the stunning revelation Tomanāk had just made, and he shook himself as he gazed up at the god. A corner of his mind still yammered in panic at the thought of "destinies" and gods-given "tasks," yet it was only a tiny voice, overwhelmed by that terrible moment of clarity when he'd first seen the demon clearly, recognized all it represented, and realized what he'd been born to fight. And even if that memory had not been etched imperishably into his heart and mind, he had no choice. He'd already given himself to the War God's service, accepted Tomanāk's aid in battle, and as he'd told the god that first night, when Bahzell Bahnakson gave his word, it meant something.

And so he gazed at the glowing shape before him, and nodded.

"Aye. I am that," he said softly, and Tomanāk smiled and reached up over his shoulder and drew his own sword.

It was a plain, utilitarian weapon, its hilt devoid of gold or gems, its blade unmarked by inlay work, yet it needed none of those things. It was tall as Bahzell himself, and it turned every sword he'd ever seen into flawed, imperfect copies, as if its forging had included every essential element of the very concept of "sword"—and excluded every *non*essential. It was no prince's plaything, no sword of state. It was a weapon, borne by a warrior and a leader of warriors.

Tomanak's nimbus glowed higher, licking out to touch the trunks and branches of the trees about the hill as he held the mirror-bright blade in his hands. He extended the hilt to Bahzell, and the hradani licked his lips and steeled himself to lay his own hands upon that plain, wire-bound pommel. Something crackled under his fingers, like a living heart of electricity, a leashed echo of the raw power he'd felt from his own blade as he charged the demon, and a patina of the god's own light flickered about him as Tomanāk looked gravely down at him.

"Do you, Bahzell Bahnakson, swear fealty to me?"

"I do." Bahzell said, and Brandark swallowed beside him, for his friend's voice was a firm, quiet echo of the god's subterranean rumble. There was a kinship between them, almost a fusion, and Brandark felt both awed and humbled and strangely excluded as he watched and listened.

"Will you honor and keep my Code? Will you bear true service to the Powers of Light, heeding the commands of your own heart and mind and striving always against the Dark as they require, even unto death?"

"I will."

"Do you swear by my Sword and your own to render compassion to those in need, justice to those you may be set to command, loyalty to those you choose to serve, and punishment to those who knowingly serve the Dark?"

"I do."

"Then I accept your oath, Bahzell Bahnakson, and bid you take up your blade once more. Bear it well in the cause to which you have been called."

The wind died. All movement ceased, and silence hovered, like a pause in the heartbeat of eternity, and then Tomanāk smiled down upon his newest champion.

He withdrew his sword from Bahzell's hands, and the hradani blinked as if waking from sleep. He stood a moment, then smiled back up at the god who had become *his* deity, and stooped to pick up the sword Brandark had recovered from under the demon's corpse. He lifted it easily, then paused with an arrested expression and looked down at it, for it felt different in his hands.

He raised the blade to examine it, and his ears pricked in surprise. It was the same weapon it had always been, yet it weighed more lightly in his hands. The blade which had been forged of good, serviceable steel glittered with a new, richer shine in the War God's light, and Tomanāk's crossed sword and mace were etched deep into it, just below the quillons. He felt no quiver of power, no sudden surge of strength, yet somehow it had been touched by the same elemental perfection that imbued the god's own sword, and he raised wondering eyes to Tomanāk's.

"My champion bears my Sword, as well as his own, Bahzell, so I've made a few changes in it."

"Changes?" An echo of a hradani's instinctive distrust of all things arcane echoed in Bahzell's voice, and Tomanāk smiled wryly.

"Nothing I think you'll object to," he soothed, and Bahzell's ears tilted back. He frowned, and the god laughed out loud. "Oh, Bahzell, Bahzell! Not even single combat with a demon can change you, can it?"

"I'm sure I wouldn't be knowing about such as that," Bahzell said politely, but a gleam of amusement lit his own eyes, and he flicked his ears impudently. "But you were saying as how you'd made some 'changes' in my blade?"

"Indeed. First, of course, it bears my sign now, so that others may recognize it as a champion's blade and know you for what you claim to be."

"*Claim* to be, is it?" Bahzell stiffened his spine and cocked his head. "I'm thinking I'm not so pleased to be needing proof of my own word!"

"Bahzell," Tomanak replied, "you're a *hradani*. The *first* hradani to become my champion in over twelve hundred years. It may seem unfair to you, but don't you think a certain amount of, ah, skepticism is inevitable?"

Bahzell made a sound deep in his throat, and Tomanak sighed.

"Will it make you feel any better to know that *all* of my champions' swords bear my sign? Or do you want to stand here and argue about it all night?"

Bahzell flushed and twitched his ears, and Tomanak grinned.

"Thank you. Now, about the other changes. For one thing, this blade is now unbreakable. For another, you'll never drop it or lose it in battle—and no one else can wield it. In fact, no one else can even pick it up unless you choose to hand it to them. I trust you find none of that objectionable?"

The god asked the question with a sort of teasing humor, and Bahzell managed a smile in reply as he shook his head.

"Good, because that's about all I did to it—aside from one other tiny thing most champions' swords don't do, of course."

"Other thing?" Bahzell's ears cocked once more, and Tomanak grinned.

"Yes. You see, it comes when you call it."

"It *what?*" Bahzell peered up like someone awaiting the joke's punchline, and Tomanak's grin grew broader.

"It comes when you call it," he repeated. "It *is* the symbol of what you've become, Bahzell, and while I value my champions' independence, it can make them a bit ... fractious, shall we say? As a hradani, you may need to prove your status to your fellows a bit more often and conclusively than most, so I've given you a means to do just that by summoning your blade to you."

Bahzell blinked once more, and Tomanāk's grin became a smile that looked oddly gentle and yet not out of place on that stern, warrior's face.

"And with that, Bahzell, I bid you good night," he said, and vanished like a wind-snuffed candle.

# CHAPTER THIRTY-THREE

Crown Prince Harnak stood by the rail and wrapped his cloak more tightly about him as wind whipped across the steel-gray Spear River. The air was chill, if far warmer than it would have been at home in Navahk, and the deck still felt alien and threatening underfoot, yet it was infinitely better than the icy journey across the Ghoul Moor and Troll Garth had been.

He shivered, and not with cold, at the memory of that nightmare ride. His father had made no more than a token protest at his choice of routes. Indeed, Harnak suspected Churnazh would shed no tears if his firstborn son failed to return—so long as no one could blame *him* for it— but Harnak's retainers had been another matter. They knew the perils of his proposed path as well as he did, and they'd lacked any promise of safety from Sharnā.

He'd been less than reassured by that promise himself and understood why men he couldn't even tell about it had been terrified, but understanding hadn't made him patient. He'd taken out his own fear on them, lashing them with his contempt, reminding them of their oaths, driving them with such fury that they'd feared him more than the journey, and it had worked. They'd been surly and frightened as their horses forged through the snow, but none had dared protest, and his stature with them had grown as no attacks came. There'd been a night or two on the Ghoul Moor when they'd huddled in their blankets like terrified children, refusing to look at the things moving in the icy moonlight beyond their campfires, yet the Scorpion's promise had held, and the journey to Krelik had been accomplished without incident.

Harnak had been in two minds about that. His relief upon reaching Krelik to find the promised ship waiting had been enormous, but the trip had given him too much time to brood over his mission.

The ceremony which bound the demon to its task had been all he'd dreamed of. The sacrifice had been even stronger than Tharnatus had hoped. Her shrieks had become gurgling, animal sounds of torment long before the end, yet she'd survived it all, right up to the moment the demon appeared to rip out her still-living heart. The sense of power, the echoes of his own hunger which had washed over him from the rest of the congregation, amplified by his own awe and terror at the raw might they'd summoned, had filled him with a towering confidence that their purpose must succeed.

And there'd been another moment, almost sweeter yet, when Tharnatus presented the consecrated blade to him, charged with the sacrifice's very soul. Harnak hadn't known exactly how Tharnatus meant to prepare the sword for its task, yet he'd expected it to be an anticlimax. Surely nothing could equal the towering power of seeing that monstrous demon bow to their command!

He'd been wrong. The demon had devoured the sacrifice's life energy as the price of its service, but Harnak knew now that there was more than simple energy to life, for Tharnatus had trapped their victim's very soul. Snatched it up before it could flee, and bound it into the cold, hard-edged steel soaked in her life's blood. Harnak had *felt* her soul shriek in terror and agony worse even than the torture of her body as something else—a tendril of Sharnā's very essence—reached out like gloating quicksand to suck her into its embrace. He'd sensed the terrible instant when that soul broke and shattered, smashed into slivers of raw torment in the brief, endless moment before it became something else.

A key. A . . . doorway into another place and the path to an unspeakable well of power. The power, he'd realized shakenly, of Sharnā Himself. The Scorpion's own presence had filled the blade, and he'd felt it tremble at his side, alive and humming with voracity, as Tharnatus solemnly belted it about his waist. He'd touched the hilt and sensed the weapon's yearning, its implacable purpose. It was impatient, that blade, eager to drink Bahzell's blood and soul, whispering promises of invincibility to him, and the shadow of its power had descended upon him like dark, impenetrable armor.

Yet there'd been a colder, frightening side to it, as well, for the Church had mustered all this might to insure Bahzell's destruction, and whatever his other faults, Harnak wasn't stupid enough to believe it would have done so if there'd been no need. He'd *seen* the demon, felt the raw destruction that filled the very air about it. No mortal warrior could stand against it, yet the Church had forged the blade he bore, as well. Just in case, Tharnatus had said, but the sword's very existence said the Church was unsure the demon could bring Bahzell down. And if that uncertainty was justified, if Bahzell could, indeed, withstand the very spawn of Sharnā, would even the power of Harnak's blade be enough?

He stood on the deck and listened to wind whine in the rigging, the slap and wash of water along the hull.

They were lonely sounds, cold ones that strengthened the chill about his heart, yet he had no choice. He'd set himself to this task, knowingly or not, the first time he entered Sharnā's temple, accepted the Scorpion's protection and power. Should Harnak fail Him in return, he would envy the maiden who'd died upon the altar, and he knew it.

He shivered again, then shook himself. This was no time for brooding. They were four days out of South Hold; all too soon it would be time to unload their horses and set out on Bahzell's trail once more . . . if the demon hadn't already slain him.

Harnak of Navahk closed his eyes, longing to pray for the demon's success. But only one god would hear him now, and that god had already done all it might to bring that success about. And so he drew a deep, chill breath, squared his shoulders, and went below once more, to wait.

South Hold was a fortress city, built in the angle between the Spear and Darkwater rivers. Its walls towered over the water, gray and cold against a sky of winter-blue steel as Harnak's vessel entered the crowded anchorage where tall, square-rigged ships lay to their buoys or nuzzled the quays. Those ships flew the banners of Purple Lord trading houses, for South Hold might be the major port of the Empire of the Spear, but the Purple Lords refused passage up the Spear to seagoing vessels of any other land. They used their lucrative stranglehold on the river to monopolize the Spearmen's carrying trade, and they cared not at all for the festering resentment that roused.

Harnak's river schooner edged in among them, and he stood on the foredeck, gawking at the size of the city and the strength of its defenses. South Hold made Navahk look like the wretched knot of misery it was, and he felt a sudden, fresh chill at the thought of how the city might react to the arrival of two score northern hradani.

But that was a concern which never arose, for Harnak's taciturn skipper knew his job. Harnak had never learned what the human truly was—a smuggler, at the least, though it seemed likely from the brutality of his crew that he dabbled in more violent trades when opportunity arose— but clearly the Church had briefed him well for his mission. He guided his vessel across the main basin without stopping, then slipped it deftly into the channel of the Darkwater and alongside a run-down wharf on the river's southern bank. The warehouses beyond it were as ramshackle as the wharf itself, and they were more than a mile outside South Hold's walls. That was a clear enough indication of the sort of trade they served; the surly, heavily armed "watchmen" who glowered suspiciously at the schooner simply confirmed it.

The schooner's master wasted no time. Hardly had his sails been furled and his mooring made fast than he was hustling his passengers ashore. His determination to complete his mission and be gone was evident, but Harnak had little time to resent it, for someone awaited him at dockside.

The prince beckoned his chief guardsman to him and jerked his chin at the confusion of men and horses beginning to froth awkwardly ashore.

"Get those fools straightened out, Gharnash. We don't want any attention we can avoid."

"Yes, Highness." Gharnash looked as if he wanted— again—to ask what was truly happening. The guardsman was hard and brutal, a clanless man, outlawed by his own tribe and taken into Harnak's service precisely because he had nowhere else to turn, no other refuge or countervailing loyalty, yet he was no fool. He'd served Harnak for over six years, and he knew the prince too well to accept Harnak's surface explanation for this journey. That

Harnak hated Bahzell and wanted him dead, yes; that much Gharnash readily believed, but he also knew the prince *feared* the Horse Stealer. That made his feverish insistence on personally hunting Bahzell down most unlike him, and there was something . . . odd about Harnak's new sword.

Yet Gharnash said nothing. His prince had secrets he didn't know—and didn't *want* to know—and instinct and reason alike told him this was one of them.

Harnak gazed into Gharnash's eyes, reading the man's thoughts more clearly than Gharnash knew, then snorted and turned away. He stepped to the dock with an arrogant confidence he was far from feeling, and a small, red-cloaked human bowed to him.

"Greetings, Your Highness. Our master welcomes you."

Harnak returned the greeting with a shallower bow of his own, and his heart sank. If all had gone well, the demon should already have slain Bahzell, yet there was no exultation on his greeter's face. The man straightened from his bow and let his cloak slip open to reveal a gemmed amulet, and Harnak inhaled sharply. This man was an archpriest, senior even to Tharnatus, and he was suddenly acutely aware of the lack of respect his own bow had implied.

The archpriest met his eyes, and a faint, amused smile curled his lips as he read the quick prickle of Harnak's panic. But he forbore to comment upon it, and gestured to a nearby warehouse.

"Come, Your Highness. Let us discuss our business less publicly."

"Ah, of course," Harnak agreed, and followed the priest through a door one of his attendants held open. The attendant closed the door behind them and stood guarding their privacy, and Harnak licked his lips.

"Please excuse any seeming disrespect," he began stiffly, "but—"

"Don't disturb yourself, Your Highness," the archpriest said smoothly. "We both serve the Scorpion; let His service make us brothers."

Harnak nodded stiff thanks, and the priest smiled again. There was no humor in that smile, and the prince felt his belly tighten.

"I know your mission here, of course," the archpriest told him, "and I have information for you."

"Information?" Harnak's voice was sharper than he'd intended. There was only one piece of "information" he wanted to hear, and the priest's tone told him he wouldn't.

"Yes. I regret to inform you—" the man's smile vanished into an expression of bleak hatred "—that the greater servant failed in its task."

"It *failed?!*" Harnak goggled at the other in disbelief—and fear. "How? I *saw* the servant—*nothing* could have withstood it!"

"The evidence, alas, suggests you're in error." The priest's eyes glittered in the dim warehouse. "I don't know precisely how it happened, but the servant was destroyed, and Bahzell . . . wasn't." He shrugged and glanced significantly at the blade at Harnak's side. "Surely you were told it might fail, Your Highness. If not, why are you here?"

"Well, of course I knew it was *possible*," Harnak muttered, "but I didn't think— That is, I found it difficult to believe the Scorpion's sting could actually miss its mark."

"But it hasn't, Your Highness. Not yet, for you are His true sting, are you not?"

Harnak nodded curtly, unable to trust his tongue, and the archpriest donned his smile again.

"Be of sound heart, Your Highness. The Scorpion will guide you to him you seek, and the blade you bear will not fail. He will fight at your very side through it, and no mortal can prevail against Him when He Himself takes the field. Yet I fear you must be on your way soon if you're to overtake the Horse Stealer."

"You know where he is?"

"No, but I know where he's bound, which is almost as good."

"Well?" Harnak pressed.

"For a time, Your Highness, he was in the company of certain enemies of Carnadosa. They didn't tell us who those enemies were, but we have our own sources, including certain dog brothers who met them and survived, and they need not concern you, anyway, for Bahzell is no longer with them. The Carnadosans have returned to their own concerns, leaving us to deal with ours, but we feel confident that Bahzell will shortly seek to reach Alfroma."

"Alfroma? Where's that, and why should Bahzell go there?"

"It lies in the Duchy of Jashân, Your Highness, and why he wishes to go there need not concern you, either. If he reaches it, however, your chance to slay him will vanish . . . and the Scorpion will be, ah, *displeased*."

Harnak swallowed and nodded.

"Excellent," the archpriest said benignly. "Now, Bahzell was just inside the northern edge of the Shipwood when the servant intercepted him and was destroyed. That was two days ago. Given his desire to reach Alfroma, it seems certain he'll proceed south through the forest. If he reaches the Darkwater, he can travel upriver by boat to his destination, but crossing the Shipwood should slow him and give you your chance to overtake him."

"But how will I find him?" Harnak tried to hide his secret hope that there was no way to do that, but the priest only gestured to his sword.

"The Scorpion will guide you. I fear the dog brothers have lost so heavily in their attempts upon him that they've called off the active hunt for him, but two of them will guide you as far as Sindark on the Darkwater. If Bahzell knows the land and his own whereabouts well enough, he'll no doubt head for Sindark himself, as the most likely place to find passage upriver, but you can travel by the highroads while he picks his way through the forest. You may well intercept him there; if not, you should be west of him, between him and his destination, and you can take ship down the river until you meet him. The lesser servants still find him difficult to locate in the wilderness, but the sword you bear is no lesser servant. Once you come within ten leagues of him, it will lead you directly to him."

The archpriest shrugged, and a chill touched Harnak's heart as the human smiled once more.

"From there, Your Highness," he said softly, "the task will be yours."

# CHAPTER THIRTY-FOUR

"Well there's a fine thing," Bahzell sighed. He gazed out over the swift-flowing river and sank down on his heels, still holding the packhorse's lead. The animal looked about for something to browse upon but found only dead leaves and winter-browned moss and blew heavily in resignation.

"As a navigator, you make a fine champion of Tomanāk."

Brandark stood beside his friend, rubbing his horse's forehead, and one of the mules nudged him hopefully. Unlike the horses which had fled, both mules—smart enough to remember the hradani were a source of grain—had returned the morning after the demon's death, and the hopeful one nudged the Bloody Sword again, harder, then shook its head and lipped at the grain sack across its companion's pack saddle.

"Now isn't that just like you," Bahzell replied. "If you're thinking you can do better, why then, lead the way, little man."

"Me? I'm the city boy, remember? You're the Horse Stealer."

"Aye, and no Horse Stealer with his wits about him would be wandering about these godsforsaken woods in winter, either," Bahzell growled back.

"Which explains *your* presence, but what am *I* doing here?"

Bahzell snorted and pondered the water before him. It was too broad to be anything except the Darkwater, but he'd expected to hit the river almost two days ago. That meant he was well and truly off the course he'd tried to hold, but had he strayed east or west?

He eased down to sit on a tree root and stretched his legs before him. His boots were sadly worn, which was a worrisome thing, for boots his size were hard come by. He could feel the sharp edges of rocks and the lumpy hardness of roots and fallen branches through their thinning soles, yet if the truth be known, he was more aware of his legs' weariness. Iron-thewed Horse Stealer that he was, this journey was telling upon him, and he was only grateful they'd moved far enough south to find warmer weather.

He flipped a stone into the river and watched it splash, then peered up at the sky and tried to estimate the time. About the second hour of the afternoon, he decided finally. That gave them another three or four hours of light, and he had no intention of sitting here on his arse wondering where he was while they sped past.

"Well," he said finally, "I'm thinking we've borne too far east or west, and whichever it may be, we've little choice but to follow the river till we find a way across it. So, since you've come all over sarcastic about my guidance, why don't you be suggesting which way we should be going?"

"That's right, dump it all on me." Brandark glanced

up at the sky in turn, then shrugged. "Given the Dark-water's general course and how much longer than expected it's taken us to get here, I'd say we've fallen off to the east. That being the case, I vote we go upstream."

"Ah, the wit of the man!" Bahzell marveled. "Were you truly after figuring that all out on your very own?"

Brandark made a rude gesture, and the Horse Stealer laughed.

"Well, I'll not be surprised if you've the right of it after all, and either way is better than none, so we'd best be going."

He heaved himself back to his feet, settled his sword once more on his back, and led the way northwest along the riverbank.

The sun had sunk low before them when they came to a spot where the banks had been logged back for over a mile on each side. A small, palisaded village crouched on the southern bank, and a broad-beamed ferry was drawn up at a rough dock near it. Thick guide ropes stretched across the stream, running over crude but efficient pulleys, and Brandark groaned in resignation as he and Bahzell headed for them.

The Horse Stealer ignored him and gripped the guide rope, then grunted as he threw his weight upon it. A ferry that size had never been meant for one man to move unaided, but Bahzell's mighty heave urged it into the stream. It curtsied clumsily on the current, and Brandark leaned his own weight on the rope beside him. The craft moved a bit more quickly, yet the river was broad, and it took them the better part of fifteen panting, heaving minutes to work it across to their side.

Bahzell gasped in relief when the square bow nudged the mud at his feet, yet his brow furrowed in puzzle-ment as he wiped sweat from it. He could see at least a score of people standing about the village gate, and half a dozen horsemen sat their mounts facing them, yet it seemed none of them had as much as looked up as their ferryboat moved away from them. That indicated a certain lack of caution to Bahzell. The village was small enough to offer easy pickings to any band of brigands (assuming any such ever came this way), and *someone* should have been keeping an eye on the boat.

He shrugged the thought away and helped Brandark lead their animals onto the ferry. It was a tight fit—they never would have made it with the horses they'd lost—and the Bloody Sword stood in the bow while Bahzell took the stern. The rope was chest-high for most humans, though considerably lower for Bahzell, and they leaned on it once more to work their way back across the stream.

"I wonder what they do for a living around here," Brandark panted as they neared midstream. "I don't see any sign of farmland."

"Woodsmen, I'm thinking," Bahzell replied. "Oh, be still, you nag!" He broke off to kick one of the mules on the haunch as it stamped uneasily towards the side. The mule flattened its ears and glared at him, but it also stopped moving, and he grunted in satisfaction.

"You think they float timber downstream to South Hold?"

"Well, they are calling it the 'Shipwood.'" Bahzell flicked his ears at the logged-off swath along the river. "They never used all that wood to build yon miserable village, but there's no cause they should be floating it just to South Hold. There's Bortalik Bay to the south, and no question the Purple Lords need timber enough for their shipping."

"You're probably right," Brandark grunted, heaving on the rope.

"Aye," Bahzell agreed as they neared the southern bank, but his eyes were on the people clustered around the palisade gate, and he frowned. Brandark looked up at the absent note in his voice, then followed his glance back to the village, and his ears pricked.

"Trouble, you think?" he asked casually.

"As to that, I've no way of knowing, but those folk seem all-fired interested in something besides us, my lad."

"Well, we'll know soon enough," Brandark replied philosophically, and Bahzell nodded as the ferry grounded once more. No one came down to help them disembark, and Bahzell's curiosity flared higher as they urged their animals onto the dock. Ignoring the departure of their ferryboat was one thing; ignoring its return with two large, unknown, and heavily armed warriors was something else again, and he gave Brandark a speculative glance.

"Are you thinking we should be wandering over to see what's caught them all up so?"

"Actually, no," Brandark said. "Whatever it is, it's their business, and we're a pair of hradani a long, long way from home."

"And you the lad who said you wanted adventure!"

"I spoke from the enthusiasm of ignorance—and you shouldn't rub my nose in it."

"Ah, but it's after being such a long, lovely nose," Bahzell chuckled. "Still and all, you may have the right of it. We've no cause to be mixing in other folk's affairs, and—"

He broke off, ears pricking, as a sudden, loud wailing rose from the village. His eyes narrowed, and he peered intently at the horsemen at the gate. One of them, much more richly dressed than the others, sat his saddle with an air of supreme arrogance, one fist on his hip, holding a riding crop, while the other hand held his reins, and two drably dressed villagers had gone to their knees before him. They were too distant for Bahzell to make out words, but he recognized pleading when he saw it, and his ears went flat to his skull as the richly dressed horseman leaned from the saddle and his long crop flashed. The lash on its end exploded across the cheek of one of the kneeling men, knocking him over, and Bahzell snarled.

"Now that, I'm thinking, changes things a mite," he grated as a louder keen of despair went up. A woman dashed from the village and crouched over the fallen man. She screamed something at the man with the crop, and it flashed again. She got her arm up just in time to block it short of her own face, and Bahzell snarled again and started forward.

"Ah, Bahzell?" Brandark's voice stopped him, and he turned to glower at his friend.

"What?" he said flatly.

"I just wanted to mention that we *are* strangers here-abouts. A certain, um, caution might be indicated."

"Caution, is it? And what about that whoreson with the whip?"

"Goodness, and there's not even blood on your knuckles!" Brandark murmured. An unwilling grin twitched Bahzell's lips, but there was no give in his expression, and the Bloody Sword sighed. "All right. All right! I suppose it's all that new champion nobility rushing to your head. But if it's all the same to you, can we at least try talking to them?"

"And what were you thinking I meant to do? Just walk up and have two or three heads off their shoulders?"

"Well, you *can* be a bit direct at times," Brandark pointed out, but he was grinning as he said it, and he swung back up onto his horse. "All right," he repeated. "If we're going to poke our noses in, let's get to it."

He touched a heel to his horse and trotted forward at Bahzell's side as the Horse Stealer stalked over to the group by the gate. Two more women had emerged from it, and though he still couldn't make out the words, he heard their imploring tones. The richly dressed man shook his head and nodded to one of the men with him, and the setting sun flashed on a drawn sword as the retainer walked his horse forward.

The villagers backed away in terror, and Bahzell's lips tightened. He picked up his pace a bit, and the rearmost horseman suddenly looked over his shoulder. He stiffened and leaned forward, poking one of his companions and gesturing, and the richly dressed man's head snapped around. The man with the sword stopped and turned his head in turn, and then all the horsemen were shifting position, drawing their mounts around to face the newcomers while their hands rested near their sword hilts.

Bahzell crossed the last few feet of muddy ground and paused, arms folded and hands well away from his own weapons, to survey them. The villagers peered at him from frightened eyes set in faces of despair, but his attention was on the richly dressed man—a half-elf, from his features and coloring—and the armed and mailed horsemen at his side.

"What d'*you* want?" the half-elf demanded in Spearman, and not even his atrocious accent could hide his imperious disdain as he gazed at the travel-worn hradani.

"As to that, we're but passing through," Bahzell replied in a voice which was far calmer than he felt.

"Then keep right on passing," the Purple Lord sniffed. "There's no place here for such as you."

"Such as us, is it?" Bahzell cocked his ears and tilted his head to study the other with cold eyes. "And could you be telling me just who you are to be saying that?"

"I own this village," the Purple Lord shot back, "and you're trespassing. Just like *these* scum." He jabbed his crop contemptuously at the peasants and spat on the ground.

"Now that's a strange thing," Bahzell replied, "for I'm thinking they've the look of the folk who built this village in the first place."

"And what's that to you?" the half-elf demanded, with the arrogance Purple Lords were famous for. "I own the land under it, and I own the trees they've cut."

"And they did it all without your even knowing, did they?" Bahzell marveled.

"Of course not, you fool!"

"Friend," Bahzell said gently, "I'd not use words like 'fool' so free if I were you."

The Purple Lord started to spit something back, then paused and gave the towering hradani a measuring look. He frowned, then shrugged.

"I don't really care what *you*'d do. This is none of your affair. These lazy bastards owe me the next quarter's rent, but they can't pay, and I've no use for idlers!"

Bahzell glanced at the villagers, and his eyes lingered on work-worn clothing and calloused hands, then moved slowly back to the Purple Lord's soft palms and manicured nails. The half-elf flushed angrily under the contempt in those eyes, but Bahzell only looked back at the villagers.

"Is that the right of it?" he asked, and fearful expressions looked back at him. Eyes shifted uneasily to the Purple Lord and his armed men, and Bahzell sighed. "Don't you be minding old Windy Guts," he said gently. "It's a champion of Tomanāk I am," he felt ridiculous as he claimed the title for the first time, "so just tell me true."

The man whose face bore the crop's bleeding welt stared at him, eyes wide at the unexpected announcement, and the Purple Lord cracked a scornful laugh.

"*You?* A champion of Tomanāk?! You're a poor liar, hradani!"

"Don't be making me prove you wrong," Bahzell advised him, "for you'll not like the way I do it."

His deep voice was level, but the Purple Lord blanched at something in it and edged his horse back a stride. Bahzell held his eyes for a moment, then looked back at the villager, and the man swallowed.

"Are . . . are ye truly what ye say, sir?" he asked timidly.

"I am that, though I'll not blame you for wondering."

Bahzell glanced down at his tattered, stained self and grinned wryly. "Still and all, it's not clothes make the man, or Puff Guts yonder would be a king!"

Someone guffawed nervously, and the Purple Lord flushed.

"So tell me the truth of what's happening here," Bahzell urged.

"Well, sir." The villager darted an anxious look at the Purple Lord, then drew a deep breath. "The truth is, it's been a mortal hard year," he said in a rush. "The price of timber, well, it's been less'n half what it us'ly is, an' after Milord took his tithe of it, there's nigh nothin' left. We . . . we paid half our rent, sir, 'deed we did, an' if Milord'd only wait till spring, we'd pay it all, no question. But—"

He shrugged helplessly, and Bahzell swiveled his eyes back to the landlord. The Purple Lord flushed even darker, but his lip curled.

"They've always got some excuse, but there are plenty of others who'll jump at the chance to take their places—yes, and pay their rent on time, too!"

"So you're after turning them out in the teeth of winter, is it? And them with half their rent for the *next* quarter already paid?"

"And what business is it of yours?" the Purple Lord snapped. "I'm within my rights!"

"Are you, now? And no doubt you've some bit of paper to prove it?"

"*Prove* it?!" The landlord gasped incredulously, then shook himself. "Hirahim! Why am I even wasting time with the likes of you? Be on your way, hradani, and be glad I let you go!"

"As to that, it's happy I'll be to move on," Bahzell said calmly. "As soon as you've returned the rent these folk *did* pay, that is."

"*What?*" The Purple Lord gawked at him. "You're mad!"

"That's as may be, but if you're after putting them out, then I'm thinking they're not after owing rent for the time they won't be here. Aye," Bahzell's eyes narrowed, "and I've a shrewd notion that precious paper of yours would be saying the same thing, wouldn't it?"

"'Deed, sir," a woman's voice said nervously, "it does, and 'twas that we asked him for when he come to put us out, but he said—"

"Hold your tongue, bitch!" the Purple Lord spat furiously. The woman who'd spoken cowered back, and he glared at her. "It's none of this bastard's affair! One more word, and I'll have the whip to you!"

"Now that's where you're wrong," Bahzell said flatly, and the landlord quivered with rage as he glared at the ragged, muddy figure before him. His mouth worked, and he jerked around to his seven guardsmen.

"Kill these swine!" he barked.

His men had more than half-expected the command, and they drew their swords instantly. Bahzell's blade was still sheathed as they spurred forward, grinning at the sport fate had dropped in their way, but none of them realized what they faced. Hradani were rarely seen in these lands, and never so far east, and they were totally unprepared for how quickly Bahzell's hands moved. Five feet of glittering steel hissed free and came down overhand in the same motion, and the guard captain screamed as it bit deep into his armored chest.

His corpse toppled from its horse, and one of his men shouted a shocked, incredulous oath and came straight at the hradani. His sword flashed, but he was more accustomed to terrorizing tenants than facing trained warriors, and Bahzell's blade licked out almost contemptuously. The guardsman grunted, staring stupidly down at the two feet of steel buried in his guts, then shrieked as Bahzell plucked him from the saddle like a speared salmon.

Two more men charged the Horse Stealer, but one of them veered aside, face etched with sudden panic as Brandark spurred to meet him. The guardsman got his blade up in time to block a straight-armed cut, but the force of the blow drove his sword to the side, and a lightning backhand took out his throat. He fell with a bubbling gurgle, and Bahzell put his armored shoulder into the barrel of his companion's rearing horse.

The horse went down squealing, and Bahzell cut yet another guardsman from his saddle while the fallen man fought to scramble free of his mount. He managed it—and rose just in time to meet Brandark's sword. He crashed back with a split skull, and the two surviving guards were no longer smiling as they flung themselves desperately at the hradani.

They lasted no longer than their fellows, and the Purple Lord gaped in terror as Bahzell and Brandark cut his men apart with polished efficiency. His horse reared as he spurred it, but he was trapped between the palisade and Bahzell. He stared desperately around, and his hand darted to his ornamented, gold-crusted sword hilt.

"Don't be stupid, man!" Bahzell snapped, but the half-elf was too panicked to heed the warning. He slammed his spurs home once more, and his sword swung wildly as the beast squealed and bolted forward.

Bahzell ducked the clumsy stroke easily, and his own blade hissed back around in a dreadful, economic riposte. He didn't even think about it; he simply reacted, and the Purple Lord was flung from his saddle without a sound. He hit the mud with a sodden thump, the villagers gasped in horror as he fell, and then there was only stillness, and eight dead men sprawled on the churned up ground.

Bahzell lowered his sword slowly and muttered an oath as he surveyed the carnage. He'd never dreamed the man might be daft enough to try something like this, and his heart sank as he recognized the trouble to come. He turned his head to meet Brandark's eyes, and his friend sighed.

"Well," he said wryly, "no one ever said hradani were smart."

# CHAPTER THIRTY-FIVE

"No, no, *no*, Malith!" Bahzell sighed and shook his head while the village headman looked at him, shrewd old eyes stubborn. "You just be telling whoever asks exactly what I've told you to say."

"But the army, Milord," Malith protested. "They'll not be happy, and it's not right they should be chasing you when—"

"Oh, hush, man! The Phrobus-spawned army can be looking after itself, and right this moment it's *your* necks I'm thinking of. So just tell me if you've all the details straight."

"But it's not *right*, Milord! 'Twas *our* trouble, and—"

"*Malith!*" The villager winced at the volume of Bahzell's exasperation and scrubbed his calloused hands together, then swallowed.

"Yes, Milord. I understand," he said meekly.

"Good!" Bahzell looked up as Malith's wife scurried off to hide the last of the money they'd found on the

421

dead landlord's person. Two more women were busy stuffing the hradani's pack saddles with food under Brandark's supervision, and the Horse Stealer nodded in satisfaction. He'd been looking forward to a night or two under a roof, but that was before he landed himself and Brandark ın this fresh fix. Fiendark seize it, that pompous lackwit *would* be related to the local governor!

Brandark buckled the saddle tight and wiggled his ears outrageously at the two young women, then kissed each of them firmly. Both of them giggled and blushed, but one of them laughed out loud and seized his right ear to drag his head down and give him a daring kiss in reply before they darted back inside the palisade.

Bahzell grunted, shoved himself to his feet, and crossed to Brandark. It was time and past time to be out of here, he thought, though precisely where he and Brandark could go now was something of a delicate question. The only thing of which he was certain was that they couldn't take their fresh trouble to Jashân and drop it on Zarantha and her family. Relations between the Spearmen and the Purple Lords were always bitter, for the Empire hated and resented the half-elves' monopolistic control of its foreign trade. But that very control made them a force not even the most powerful Spearman noble could challenge with impunity, and they were only too likely to choose to make an example of Duke Caswal if he tried to shield two hradani who'd "murdered" the son of a powerful family. They'd done it before, using their grip on the Spear River and its shipping to blockade the trade of nobles who'd irritated them as a way to remind their fellows of who held the Empire's leash.

"This," Brandark remarked as Bahzell reached him, "is probably the worst idea you've had yet. You know that, don't you?"

"D'you have a better one?"

"No, not really," the Bloody Sword admitted.

"Well, then." Bahzell rubbed his chin for a moment and frowned at the eight new horses they'd added to their string. They were well-bred animals, no doubt worth a pretty price somewhere, but they were going to be a handful for two people to manage, and none of them were up to a hradani's weight. On the other hand, they couldn't exactly leave them behind, now could they?

He sighed, then clapped Brandark on the shoulder.

"Well, climb up, little man. Climb up! We've some ground to cover before sunrise!"

"No doubt." Brandark swung up into the saddle and twitched his ears at his friend. "Just once, Bahzell—just *once!*—I'd like to leave someplace with you and *not* have someone on our trail. Is that too much to ask?"

"Oh, be still with you!" Bahzell was already jogging south down the rough trail that served the village as a road, and Brandark urged his horse to a canter at his heels. The other animals lurched into motion on their leads, and the Horse Stealer's voice carried through the wet squelch of hooves in mud. "You've more complaints than a little old lady in a brothel! Why, the way you're after carrying on, folk might think you weren't enjoying yourself at all, at all."

"*Enjoying* myself! Listen, you overgrown lump of gristle, I—"

Their cheerful bickering faded into the darkness, and the villagers shook their heads at one another in disbelief.

Major Rathan No'hai Taihar was a lean, dangerous man. He was also a very well-born Purple Lord, and it showed—both in the arrogant tilt of his head and the rage in his eyes as he gazed down at the body of his cousin Yithar and listened to the illiterate headman of this miserable collection of hovels.

" . . . an' then Milord Yithar come t'collect th' rest of next quarter's rent, Milord," Malith said anxiously, hands wringing a shapeless cap before him. "We was expectin' him, of course, for he'd said as how he'd be here, an' he'd just come up th' track when we heard it."

"Heard what?" Rathan demanded, waving a scented handkerchief under his nose against the muddy woodland stink. He knew there was money in the timber business, but what had possessed Yithar to buy up this wretched village was more than he—

"We heard 'em comin' out of th' woods, Milord." Rathan's eyes snapped back from the body to Malith's face, and the villager swallowed. "Hradani they was, Milord. Must'a been at least a half-score of 'em—maybe more—an' I think they was layin' for Milord Yithar, like they knew he was collectin', y'see."

"Hradani?" Rathan repeated incredulously.

"Aye, Milord. Hradani. Y'can see their tracks yourself, out yonder where they come from, an' again where they headed south with Milord Yithar's horses . . . after."

Rathan glared at him, and Malith swallowed again, strangling his cap.

"And none of you did a thing to help him, hey?" Rathan's voice was silk-wrapped ice, and Malith paled.

"Milord . . . Milord Yithar don't allow no weapons 'mongst his people—not but a boar spear or a huntin' bow or two—an' we're not trained with 'em no how. 'Twas all we could do to get the gates closed and save our ownselves, 'deed it was, Milord!"

Rathan growled. The fingers of his right hand twitched towards his sword, yet the inability of these patchwork peasants to defend even themselves was disgustingly evident. Singing tension held for a long, still moment, and then he growled again and took his hand away with a grimace of contempt.

"So you just watched these bastard hradani murder

Lord Yithar and his men," he sneered instead, and Malith stared at the ground and bobbed his head.

"We did, Milord. 'Tweren't no good thinkin' we could'a done elsewise, for we couldn't. 'Deed, we couldn't even a held th' gate, if they'd thought to attack us when they was done."

"Attack *you?*" Rathan gave a crack of scornful laughter. "Why in Hirahim's name should anyone attack *this?*" His gesture of disdain took in the village, and Malith looked up earnestly.

"Why, Milord, they would'a done it in a minute, 'deed they would'a, if they'd'a known."

"Known *what*, you fool?"

"Why, known as how we'd saved up Milord Yithar's rent money, Milord. Every copper of it." The headman reached out as if to grasp the major's arm before he remembered himself and snatched his hand back, but his pathetic eagerness was plain to see. "They was so busy lootin' him an' his men, they must not'a realized Milord Yithar was a'comin' here, not leavin', Milord, an' we been downright afeared they'd come back an' take th' rent, as well!"

Rathan blinked, for he'd assumed the villagers were going to claim the brigands *had* stolen the rent payment. No one could have proven otherwise, and it was a rare peasant who wouldn't do his betters gleefully out of their legitimate earnings.

"You mean they *didn't* take the rent?"

"No, Milord, 'tis what I'm a'sayin'. They didn't know as 'twas here, an' we'd be thankful if you'd take it with you when you goes. 'Tisn't much for Milord Yithar's family, an' all, but we feel it sharp that we couldn't'a done somethin' to save him. He . . . he could be a mite short if the dibs was out'a tune, Milord Yithar could, meanin' no disrespect, but if you'd see as how his family gets th' rent we're owin' . . . ?"

The headman's voice trailed off, and Rathan shook

himself. He turned away from the village, gazing down
at the countless tracks which marked the muddy field
where his cousin had died—the tracks, had he but known,
which the villagers themselves had made under Bahzell's
direction—and then back at Malith. His expression was
just as arrogant, but a faint hint of approval, like a master's
for a trained dog's cleverness, tinged his smile.

"Of course, Headman Malith. Give it to my clerk—
he'll count it and give you a receipt, and I'll personally
see that Lord Yithar's family receives it. Yes," his smile
vanished into a glare as his eyes turned back to the south,
"and all the other money he'd collected, when we run
these bastards to earth!"

He stood for a moment longer, glaring into the falling twilight, then inhaled sharply and beckoned to his
second in command.

"Get Tregar over here to take charge of these yokels'
rent payment, Halith," he said shortly. "Keep an eye on
him while he counts it, and then get the men ready to
move out."

"Tonight, sir?" Halith said, and Rathan snarled.

"In the morning, idiot! We need light to track by. But
get a couple of couriers off immediately to alert the border posts. These bastards may try to double back to the
north. Even if they don't, I want patrols out sweeping
southward with daylight. We'll teach these scum what it
means to murder Purple Lords!"

"Yes, sir!" his subordinate barked, and jogged back to
the remainder of the men while Rathan returned his
attention to Malith.

"From all I can see, there was little your people could
have done, after all," he conceded, "and you did well to
protect the rent you owed Lord Yithar. I'll see that my
report reflects that."

"Thank you, Milord!" Malith bobbed servilely, still
wringing his cap.

"In the meantime, we'll be camping here tonight before we go after them," Rathan went on. "We'll need fodder for our mounts. And have your women see to some sort of supper for my men."

"At once, Milord!"

"Good." Rathan strode away, and, as the major turned his back, he failed to note the most unservile satisfaction—and concern for the village's benefactors—that flickered in Malith's shrewd old eyes.

Bahzell and Brandark sat on their bedrolls in their fireless camp, eating as twilight settled. They'd put in a good, hard night and a day of travel, and it was unlikely anyone was even on their heels yet, but that was no reason to get careless and show a light.

"Well," Brandark leaned back finally, fingering silent chords on his balalaika, "how soon d'you think they'll come after us?"

"As to that," Bahzell returned, drawing off his boots and wiggling his toes in relief, "I've no way of knowing for certain, but if Malith was after being right about how soon that Yithar bastard would be missed, it's likely enough they'll be on our trail by morning."

He drew out the roll of cured leather Malith had given him and unrolled it. He set his feet on it and leaned forward to scribe round them with the tip of a small knife, then went to work cutting the leather to pad the insoles of his worn-out boots.

"You take that mighty calmly, I must say," Brandark observed.

"There's naught at all, at all, I could be doing about it by taking it otherwise," Bahzell replied. "And taken all in all, it's better they be chasing after the likes of us than taking it out on Malith's folk."

"Well, that tale you primed Malith with should certainly see to it that they do," Brandark said dryly.

"Aye, and that's a shrewd man yonder. I've little doubt he told it well," Bahzell agreed with a chuckle.

"Aren't you afraid one of the other villagers may tell them the truth in hopes of some reward from the authorities?"

"That lot?" Bahzell laughed out loud. "Brandark, there's not a man or woman in that village as isn't related to Malith one way or another, and villages like that know a thing or two about loyalty! Oh, no, my lad. When folk are pushed down as far as these Purple Lords are after pushing Malith's lot, they'll jump at the chance to get a bit of their own back. That's something Churnazh had best be remembering, when all's said."

"True," Brandark acknowledged, then grinned. "And, come to think of it, knowing they've got a good two years' rent hidden away should be a bit of an incentive, as well!"

"That's as may be, but it wasn't why I was after leaving it to them. We've kept enough and more for our own needs, but those folk . . . they've worked mortal hard for the little they have. If old Yithar could be paying them back a bit of all he's squeezed from 'em, why, it was our bounden duty to let him be doing it."

"Maybe, but—"

Brandark's sentence died, and both hradani jerked their heads up as a huge figure abruptly materialized. The horses and mules stood quietly, oblivious to the sudden arrival, but Bahzell scrambled up to his stocking feet as Tomanāk folded his arms across his chest and gazed down at him.

Silence stretched out, and Brandark set his balalaika aside and rose beside his friend. Still the silence lingered, until, at length, Bahzell cleared his throat.

"I'm thinking you've more things to be doing than dropping in to pass the time of day regular like," he said to the god. "Especially with it being as hard as you say to be communicating with mortals and all."

"You think correctly," Tomanāk rumbled, and shook his head. "That was a fair piece of work you did at that village, Bahzell, but only fair. Chopping miscreants up may be an excellent way to relieve your tensions, but sometimes it's better to settle things without swords."

"As to that, it was after being *his* idea, not mine," Bahzell shot back. "I was only after seeing justice done."

"True enough," Tomanāk agreed, "and I can't fault you—or you, Brandark—" the Bloody Sword twitched as the War God shot him a glance "—for defending yourselves. You *were* just a bit hasty when you cut Yithar himself down, Bahzell. He was hardly a fit opponent for one of my champions, and you probably could have disarmed him instead. But, again, I'll grant ample provocation, and things like that happen when instincts take over in a fight. No, I don't fault you there, but this story you gave Malith to tell—!"

The god frowned, and Bahzell cocked his ears in surprise.

"Why, I was thinking it a neat enough tale," he said after a moment, "and they were needing *something* to keep the noose out from around their own necks for what we did."

"But you told him to *lie.*"

"And a good thing I did, too!" Bahzell shot back.

Tomanāk blinked. A look very much like bafflement crossed his features, and he unfolded his arms to plant his fists on his hips and lean forward over the Horse Stealer.

"Bahzell," he said almost plaintively, "I'm the god of justice, as well as war. My champions can't go around *lying* to people!"

"No more I did," Bahzell said virtuously. Tomanāk's frown deepened, and the Horse Stealer shrugged. "Every word I was after telling Malith and his folk was true as death," he pointed out, "and I've not said a word about it to another soul—excepting yourself and Brandark, that is—so how could I be lying to anyone about it?"

"But you told *Malith* to lie. In fact, you made the entire lie up and *coached* him in it! A secondhand lie is still a lie, Bahzell."

"Now that's plain foolishness," the Horse Stealer replied. "The truth would only have been landing them in a mortal lot of trouble."

"Perhaps it would, and I'm not saying *they* weren't justified. But you can't just go about making up lies whenever you find yourself in trouble."

"Find myself in trouble, is it?" It was Bahzell's turn to snort, and he did so with panache. "Sure, and would you be so very kind as to be telling me just how Malith's tale will be getting me *out* of trouble? Lying for profit, now, I can be seeing why that should be upsetting you, but this—?"

He raised his hands, palms up, and Tomanak rocked back on his heels. Half a dozen thoughts seemed to chase themselves across his face, but then he sighed and shook his head.

"All right, Bahzell. All right!" He smiled wryly and shook his head again. "You're new to this, and it's been a long time since I last had a hradani champion. You don't seem to have quite the, ah, normal mindset of the job." Bahzell only snorted once more, and the god's smile became a grin. "No, I don't suppose you do, at that," he murmured, then straightened and waved a finger at the Horse Stealer.

"Very well, Bahzell. We'll let it pass, this time—and you were probably right. But mind you, no lies that *will* profit you!" he admonished, and faded once more into the gathering night before his unrepentant champion could reply.

# CHAPTER THIRTY-SIX

Prince Harnak drew rein and dabbed irritably at the sweat on his brow. The clothing he'd brought with him suited a northern winter, not the unnatural heat of this southern warm spell, and he muttered a sour curse on the hot, clammy woolens under his chain mail as he glowered at the terrain.

He'd never been good with maps, and his notion of his whereabouts had become uncomfortably vague. In fact, the only things he was sure of was that he was far south of Sindark, floundering about in an unknown land where every hand was potentially hostile . . . and that Bahzell was somewhere ahead of him still.

His survey of the countryside told him nothing. It was more of the gentle, sparsely wooded hills that stretched from the Shipwood to Bortalik Bay, without a village in sight. That was good—they'd nearly collided with some local lordling's retainers when they strayed too near a small town three nights ago—but the lack of any road or guidepost made him uneasy.

Not that he was without *any* guides. He touched his sword hilt once more, almost against his will, and felt the pull that had first drawn him south, away from Sindark. There, he thought—to the southeast again. The hatred of the cursed blade sought the Horse Stealer like a lodestone . . . and it was growing stronger. Ten leagues, the archpriest had said; that was the range at which the sword could sense Bahzell. Judging by how fierce its pull had become, they were getting close, and Harnak spat on the ground as he released the hilt. The oppressive alienness of this land—his sense that he was far, far from home and riding further with every hour—made him edgy, and fear of what would happen when he and Bahzell finally met gnawed his belly like a worm of acid. Yet for all that, impatience goaded him on. His own hatred warred with his fear . . . and at least *some* of his troubles would be resolved, whatever happened, when he ran the Horse Stealer to ground at last.

He settled himself in the saddle again, nodded irritably to Gharnash, and pushed his horse back up to a weary trot.

"Are you sure it's really winter?" Brandark asked plaintively as he wiped his streaming face.

"Aye—or what passes for it in these parts. And a fine one *you* are to be complaining, you with your horse under your arse!" Bahzell snorted.

"I didn't complain; I only asked a question," Brandark said with dignity, and turned to gaze behind them. "Think they're still back there?"

"As to that, you've as good a notion as I—but if they're not behind still, they've at least sent word ahead. You can lay to that, my lad."

Brandark grunted unhappily, although both of them were aware they'd actually done very well . . . so far. There'd been one close call two days after Tomanāk's last visit when a mounted patrol thudded urgently past their hide in a handy coppice. The patrol hadn't been following their tracks, yet neither of them had doubted what brought it this way. The Lands of the Purple Lords were a hotbed of semi-independent city-states, locked in bitter competition (mercantile and otherwise) despite their nominal allegiance to the Conclave of Lords at Bortalik. Population was sparse, for half-elves were less fertile than most of the Races of Man, and villages of their mostly human peasants tended to cluster around the larger cities, while vast, still unclaimed areas—luckily for fugitives—lay outside any petty prince's holding. The Conclave Army was charged with policing those areas but spent most of its time on the frontiers, and few things would bring thirty-five of its mounted troopers this far south. For that matter, most of the local lordlings would have fits if the army intruded upon their private domains . . . unless, of course, the officer commanding the intrusion had a good reason for his presence.

"Where are we, anyway?" Brandark asked after a moment.

"By my reckoning, we've come maybe a hundred fifty leagues from the Darkwater," Bahzell replied. "If that's so, we're naught but fifty leagues or so from the coast."

"That close?" Brandark frowned and pulled on his nose. "What happens once we *reach* the coast, if you don't mind my asking? As you say, they must have sent word ahead of us to the ports. That means ships are out, and since I still can't swim and *you* can't walk on water, it might be time to consider what we're going to do next."

Bahzell snorted in agreement and paused in the welcome shade of a small stand of trees. He mopped at his own face, then shrugged.

"I'm thinking it's likely we *have* lost whoever was actually on our trail," he said finally. "We've not set so hard a pace we'd not have seen *something* of them by now else, and that rain the other day was hard enough to be taking out our tracks. If that's the way of it, then all we really need do is play least in sight and keep clear of roads."

"And?"

"From the map, there's precious few coast towns west of Bortalik. I'm minded to make it clean to the sea if we can, then turn west along the shore."

"To where?"

"As to that, we'll have to be making up our minds when we get there. We might strike for the Marfang Channel, find a way across, and take ship from Marfang itself. Or we might try northwest, amongst the Wild Wash Hradani, or cut north through the Leaf Dance Forest back up into the Empire of the Spear."

"D'you have any idea how *far* that is?" Brandark demanded.

"Aye, I do that—a better one than you, I'm thinking." Bahzell raised a foot and grimaced at the holes in the sole of his boot. "But if you've a better notion, it's pleased I'll be to hear it."

"No, no. Far be it from me to interfere when you've done such a fine job of planning our excursion. What's a few hundred more leagues when we're having such fun?"

"Well?" Rathan's voice was sharp as the scout trotted up to him. The major's elegant appearance had become sadly bedraggled over the last week of hard riding and frequent rain, but the toughness that elegance had cloaked had become more evident as it frayed, and the scout shifted uneasily. The major had been less than pleased when they lost the trail of his cousin's killers. His order to spread out and find it again had been curt, but the need to sweep every fold of rolling ground had slowed them badly, and he'd begun taking his frustration out on anyone who *hadn't* found the tracks he wanted.

"I'm . . . not certain, sir," the scout said now.

"Not certain?" Rathan repeated in a dangerous tone, and the scout swallowed.

"Well, I've found *a* trail, Major. I'm just not certain it's the one we've been following."

"Show me!" Rathan snapped.

"Yes, sir."

The scout turned his horse and led the way. He almost wished he'd kept his mouth shut, but if he hadn't reported it and someone else *had*, the consequences would have been even worse, he thought gloomily.

Twenty minutes brought them to his find, and he dismounted beside the ashes of a fire.

"Here, Major," he said.

Rathan dismounted in turn, propped his hands on his hips, and turned in a complete circle. The camp was clearly recent, but the hradani they were tracking were trailwise and canny. Their fires, when they made them at all, were smaller than this one, their camps selected with an eye to concealment, and they did a far better job than this of hiding the signs of their presence when they moved on.

"And what," he asked with ominous quiet, "makes you think *this* was the bastards we want?"

"I never said it was, sir," the scout said quickly, "but you wanted to know about *any* tracks we found, and we are hunting hradani."

"So?" Rathan demanded.

"This, sir." The scout pulled a bronze buckle from his belt pouch. "I found it when I first searched the camp."

The major turned the buckle in his fingers and frowned at the jagged characters etched into the metal.

"What is this?" he asked after a moment, his voice less irritated and more intent, and the scout hid his relief as he tapped the marks with a finger.

"Those're hradani runes, sir. I've seen ones like them on captured Wild Wash equipment."

Rathan's head jerked up, and he stared around the camp once more. There'd been more horses here, and heavier ones, than they'd been trailing, and the tracks slanted into the campsite from the wrong direction, which meant—

"They've joined up with the rest of their filthy band!" he snapped, and twisted round to his second in command. "Halith!"

"Sir!"

"Get couriers out. Call in all the scouts, then send riders to the closest regular army posts. There are more of them than we thought, and I'll want every man when we catch up with them. Go on, man! Get moving!"

"Yes, sir!" Halith wheeled his horse, already calling out the names of his chosen messengers, and Rathan laughed. It wasn't a pleasant laugh, and his eyes glittered as he stared off to the southeast along the plainly marked tracks leading from the camp.

"I've got you now, you murdering bastards!" he whispered, and dropped the buckle. It landed rune-side up, and as he turned to remount his horse, his heel came down on the sigil of Crown Prince Harnak's personal guard.

The sun lay heavy on the western horizon when Bahzell called a halt. A stream flowed at the bottom of a deep, tree-lined ravine, and the grass along its banks was still green. The horses and mules would like that, and Bahzell liked the concealment the ravine offered.

Brandark dismounted to lead his horse down the gully's steep northern face. The slope was acute enough to make getting their animals down it difficult, but the southern side was far lower, and the Bloody Sword nodded in appreciation. Bahzell had far better instincts for this sort of thing than he did—no doubt from the time he'd spent on the Wind Plain—but Brandark approved. If anyone stumbled over them, they'd probably come from the north, and the steepness on that side would slow them while the hradani broke south.

"I see you've shown your usual fine eye for selecting first-class accommodations," he said. "What do you think about a fire?"

"Best not," Bahzell replied. "It's warm enough without, and those who can't see flames can still smell smoke if the wind's wrong."

"Um." Brandark pulled at his nose, then nodded. "You're probably right. Of course, by now we both stink enough they can probably smell us *without* smoke if they get within a league."

"Well, yon stream's deep enough. Once we've the horses picketed, I'll be taking the first watch, if you've a mind to soak your delicate skin."

"Done!" Brandark sighed. "Gods! Even *cold* water'll feel good by now!"

Harnak cursed as his horse stumbled. All of their mounts were weary, and his men were straggling once more as the sun began to slip below the horizon, but the prince never considered stopping. He no longer even had to touch the hilt to feel his sword's hard, hating pull. That fiery hunger had bled into his own blood. It dragged him on despite exhausted horses and failing light, simmering in his soul until he hovered on the very brink of the Rage. He was here. The whoreson bastard was *here*, so close Harnak could smell him, and he snarled and struck his mount with his spurs.

The horse squealed in surprised hurt, lunging so hard it almost unseated him. Exhaustion or no, there was no withstanding the goad of roweled steel, and it bounded ahead while Harnak's guardsmen swore under their breath and fought to match their prince's pace.

Some of them couldn't, however they tried, and they

tried hard. They'd feared this journey from the moment they heard of it, and, like Harnak himself, they felt adrift and lost in this strange, too warm place where anyone they met was likely to see them as brigands or invaders. They dreaded the thought of facing a roused and angry land so far from home, yet they'd begun to harbor even more fearful suspicions about their leader and the sword he wore. Harnak surrounded himself with hard and brutal men, and some of the cursed weapon's ravening hunger spilled over into them. It touched the dark spots in their own blood-stained souls like seductive black fire, hazing their thoughts, and when they realized what was happening, they were terrified.

But it was growing harder for them to recognize the influence. It was becoming part of them, like a pale shadow of the furnace it had lit deep at Harnak's heart. It gripped them like a drug, blending with their fear of losing the column in this alien land, and goaded them on as Harnak's spurs goaded his horse. Yet try as they might, their weary mounts were unequal to their demands. More of them fell back, stringing out in a long, ragged line as the darkness came down.

Harnak knew it was happening, and a corner of his mind demanded he slow, let the others catch up, bring them all in together to overwhelm Bahzell and Brandark when he found them. Yet it was only a corner, lost in the roiling blood taste, and he ignored it and drove on into the falling shadows.

Rathan turned his head to glare at the western horizon as the last crimson rim of sun fumed amid the clouds. They were close to the bastards now. He knew it—he could *feel* it. Hradani needed big, heavy horses which could never match the pace and endurance of his men's lighter mounts, and enough detachments had come in to double his company's original hundred-man strength. He had men enough to deal with any band of brigands; all he needed was another two hours of daylight, and he didn't have them.

He clenched his jaw and fought his own impatience. It didn't matter, he told himself. The sun would rise again, and, indeed, it might be wiser to wait until it did. A night battle was always confusing, at best; at worst, it could turn into disaster as friend turned on friend and the enemy escaped.

He was just opening his mouth to order a halt when his lead scouts crested a low slope several hundred yards ahead of him. The last light burned like sullen blood on their helmets, and then, suddenly, they were snatching at slung bows and he heard the first shrill screams.

Harnak jerked around in the saddle as a horse shrieked like a tortured woman. There was still light enough for him to see one of his rearmost men go down as a mortally wounded mount plunged head over crupper. The guardsman hit hard and lay still, and shouts of alarm and terror mixed with fresh cries of pain as arrows pelted his straggling rearguard.

The prince stared in disbelief, and a flicker of motion even further behind him caught his eye. Dark, indistinct figures, blurry but gilded with sparks of sunset from helmets and chain mail, swirled on a low crest beyond his men, shooting as fast as they could pull their bows. The light was so bad they were firing almost blind, yet blind fire was as deadly as aimed when there was enough of it, and another of his men pitched from his saddle.

Harnak had no idea who they were, but their abrupt, murderous appearance filled the tiny corner of his soul that still belonged to him with panic. He didn't know how many enemies were back there, but his men were too spread out for a fight, and their horses were too weary for flight. He knew, suddenly and beyond question, that he would never see Navahk again, that the Scorpion had sent him to his death after all, and terror mixed with the wild, overmastering hunger of the sword he bore—the hunger that had come to dominate all he was—and flashed over into the Rage.

He howled like a mad animal, and a livid green glare flashed like poisoned lightning as he ripped his sword from its sheath. His men heard him, recognized his Rage and felt their own respond, and the wild, shrill scream of hradani fury rose, filling the newborn night as the last embers died on the horizon and Harnak's column came apart.

Most of his men wheeled on their attackers, blazing with the need to rend and kill until they themselves were slain, but those closest to Harnak didn't. The instant their prince drew the cursed blade, its power reached out to them. The dark secrets of their own hearts made them easy prey, and it seized them by the throat, wrenching them back to the south with Harnak, for the one creature in all the world it had been forged to slay lay ahead, not behind. It hurled them onward while their fellows turned at bay, and they thundered blindly into the night behind their howling prince.

"What in the names of all the gods—?!"

Major Rathan blanched as the shrieks rose like demons. Darkness fell with deadly speed, washing away vision, but not before he saw the first huge figures explode into his scouts. The horse archers tried to scatter, but they'd never expected their enemies to wheel into the teeth of their fire, and the hradani's weary mounts had caught their riders' fury, burning out their last strength in a frantic surge of speed there was no time to evade. Most of the archers got their swords out before the charge smashed home, but it didn't matter. They went down like scythed wheat as their quarry turned upon them.

"Form up! *Form up!*" Rathan shouted, and bugles blared as his stunned men responded. There was no time to dress ranks properly, and unit organization went by the board as the troopers struggled to form front. It was all a mad swirl, a crazed delirium of plunging horses and shouts in the darkness, but somehow they formed a line.

"Lances!" Rathan bellowed. The last light was gone, drowning the hills in darkness that would make any semblance of control impossible, but he dared not let his men be taken at a stand by charging enemies, and at least the hradani's shrieks of Rage told him roughly where they were.

"*Charge!*" he screamed, and two hundred mounted men thundered forward into the night.

Bahzell Bahnakson jerked to his feet as the first screams came out of the north. He stood among the trees for just a second, peering into the darkness, and knew he'd heard those sounds before—*made* them before. It wasn't possible. Not this far south! Yet there could be no mistake, and then he heard bugles ringing over the hills and knew there was no time to waste on confusion or wonder.

He slithered down into the ravine like an out-of-control boulder. He almost fell a dozen times, but somehow he kept his feet and staggered into the camp just as a soaking wet, stark naked Brandark erupted from the stream.

"What—?!"

"No time, man! No time! They'll be on us in minutes!" Bahzell shouted back, and Brandark strangled his questions and dashed for the heap of his clothes and armor, ignoring shirt and trousers to drag on his arming doublet while Bahzell leapt to the picket line. He grabbed a pack saddle and pushed his way in among the stamping, suddenly panicked animals, but the cacophony of screams raced nearer like some huge, malevolent beast, and it was headed straight for them.

He spun away from the horses and reached for his sword as he realized there wasn't even time to saddle up. Brandark was still struggling with his haubergeon, and Bahzell backpedaled away from their mounts, putting himself between his friend and the lip of the ravine, as mounted men thundered into the woods above them with insane speed.

Horses went down, shrieking as legs broke or they speared themselves on unseen branches, but a few of them somehow threaded the obstacle and hurtled down the slope with howling demons on their backs, and crimson-shot green fire blazed from Harnak's sword as he took his mount into the ravine like a madman. His horse squatted back on its haunches, sliding and slithering, screaming in fear as the ground fell away before it, but somehow it held its feet, and the prince's eyes were pits of madness.

"*Bahzell!*" he shrieked, and charged.

Bahzell's head twisted round at the sound of his name, and blue flame snapped down his own blade as the sword in Harnak's hand hurled the prince at him. There was no more time for confusion—there was only the instant answer of his own Rage, and he leapt to meet his enemy.

"*Tomanāk!*" His bull-throated war cry battered through the high, mad shriek of Harnak's hatred, and his sword streamed blue fire as it hissed forward. A blaze of bloody green steel answered, and the blades met in a terrible explosion of fury, bleaching the ravine with a glare of hate that blasted up like sheet lightning. The cursed sword howled like a living soul, and the shock of impact hurled Harnak from the saddle.

The prince hit on his shoulder, yet the power bound into his blade possessed him, and he rolled back to his feet with deadly speed. His plunging mount blocked

Bahzell just long enough for him to surge upright before the Horse Stealer could reach him, and he flung himself at Bahzell with elemental madness.

Steel crashed and belled like the hammers of enraged giants, wrapped in hissing sheets of light that blazed hotter with every stroke. Bahzell felt the power of Harnak's weapon, sensed its hatred and implacable purpose fueling the Navahkan's Rage, and staggered back one stride, then another, as Harnak hewed at him. A livid emerald corona rose about the shrieking Navahkan, a vague shape that swirled and fought to take the shape of a huge, green scorpion. Its pincers spread wide, groping for Bahzell, and the Horse Stealer fell back again as a deadly stinger stabbed at him. Reeking steam hissed upward where that stinger's poison spattered like deadly rain, but there was a presence behind Bahzell, as well. He sensed a vast shape rising about him, flickering with an azure glory to match Harnak's poisonous green, and knew this was no longer a matter of Horse Stealer against Navahkan.

A corner of his mind gibbered in panic—not of Harnak, but of what Tomanāk had said about the dangers when god met god in combat—as a warring confrontation of power seethed and frothed. It filled the ravine like a flood, spilling outward in the roil and flash of lightning, and he and Harnak stood at its heart, its focus and its avatars— the vessels that gave it purchase in the world of mortals. He heard more steel clash as Brandark fought for his life, but he dared not take his attention from Harnak. It wasn't the prince he fought; it was the unspeakable foulness reaching for him from the prince's blade, and that blade was shorter than his own, quicker and handier in close combat. He knew—somehow, he knew—the slightest wound would be death and worse than death, and it whistled in again and again, keening its hate.

He blocked another deadly stroke and twisted his wrists, guiding it to the side. He spun on his left foot, pivoting as the force of Harnak's blow carried him past, and his right foot lashed up into the prince's spine so hard Harnak screamed in pain despite his Rage, but he didn't fall. He staggered forward a dozen steps and whirled, bringing his sword around just in time, and fresh fire fountained up out of the ravine as steel met steel once more.

Major Rathan swallowed as lightning flashed and glared somewhere ahead of him. It was silent with distance, yet its heat seemed to burn across the miles like bitter summer sun. What in all of Krahana's hells had he and his men stumbled *into*? His charge had come apart in the darkness, just as he'd feared, and a hurricane of combat raged across the night-struck hills. A dozen hradani, possibly more, had died on his men's lances without breaking through, but others had carried on into sword range, and no Purple Lord trooper was a fit match for a hradani in the grip of the Rage. Screams and shrieks and curses and the clash of steel and gurgle of dying men filled the darkness, but Rathan's cavalry had the edge in numbers. Sections of three fought to stay together and engage each hradani, horses went down, taking their riders with them, and then a howling, dismounted hradani, streaming blood from a dozen wounds, came straight at him like a shape from a nightmare, and Rathan had no time to worry about lights on the horizon.

Bahzell blocked another blow and brought his hilt up. His pommel crashed into Harnak's face, and the prince screamed as his jaw shattered. He staggered back, cutting the air before him in a frenzy while the scorpion shape shrieked its own fury, and Bahzell stepped into him. His blade came down, ripping through chain mail, and blue-lit steel cut into Harnak's upper arm, but the Navahkan twisted aside at the last moment and slashed out wildly. Bahzell leapt away from him again, and the prince lunged after him, yet for all its fury, his attack was wild and uncoordinated.

Bahzell recognized the danger he faced, knew the driving power the Rage would have given Harnak even without whatever demon filled the blade he bore, yet Harnak fought with unthinking fury, and Bahzell's mind was cold and clear. The Rage ruled Harnak, but Bahzell ruled the Rage, and he reached out to it, using it as he never had before, willing its power into his arms and shoulders. He waded into Harnak's assault, smashing the Navahkan back step by frothing step, driving him now. The prince stumbled and almost fell, then staggered back again. He recovered his balance and charged once more, but this time he was just too slow.

Bahzell's dropped point flashed out in a deadly lunge, splitting chain mail like rotten cloth, and the crown prince of Navahk convulsed in agony as his own charge impaled him. A foot of gory steel stood out of his back, and blood sprayed from his mouth as he stared down at the sword in his guts.

The light of that sword flared up into his misshapen face, etching it in a dreadful blue glare, and his arms fell to his sides. The tip of his own sword hissed as it touched the ground, and his scorpion shroud of light screamed. It writhed and twisted, still fighting to reach Bahzell, but its avatar had failed it. Harnak took one hand from his hilt and reached out, as if to pluck at the impaling steel, and then he raised his head. His eyes met Bahzell's, filled with madness and the Rage but touched with the awareness of his own death, and the Horse Stealer stepped back. He yanked his sword free, and Harnak's hand clutched weakly, uselessly, at the terrible, spouting wound in his belly, but his eyes never left Bahzell's.

He was still staring into the Horse Stealer's eyes when Bahzell's flaming sword swept in once more and struck his head from his shoulders.

✦  ✦  ✦

Rathan wrenched his sweating horse aside, and impact exploded up his arm as his sword bit into a neck. The charging hradani went down, and he whirled, looking for fresh foes, but the sound of battle was fading. Here and there hooves pounded as some, at least, of the hradani broke through their enemies and fled. Some of his men galloped in pursuit, others knelt over writhing, wounded fellows, and Rathan swallowed bile as he realized how many of his troopers were down.

He turned his head once more, staring into the south, but light no longer flashed on the horizon. He tried desperately to imagine what it might have been, and part of him urged him to go find out. It must have been connected to his own battle, whatever it had been, and terrifying as the unknown was, he knew it must be investigated.

But not now, he told himself. His command was harrowed and riven, its men scattered in pursuit of an unknown number of surviving hradani. Whatever that light had been, he had to reorganize and see to his wounded first.

Bahzell spun away from Harnak's corpse. There were three other bodies on the ravine floor, and Brandark was backed up against the picket line, fighting desperately as a fourth Navahkan pressed in upon him. The Bloody Sword's left arm hung straight and useless from the shoulder, and there was blood on his face. He was weakening fast, and Bahzell leapt to his aid.

Too late. Brandark went down as steel slammed into his thigh, and his attacker howled in triumph and raised his sword in both hands. It started down in the killing stroke, and then Bahzell's blade smashed across his spine. He fell away, and Bahzell spun once more, straddling Brandark's helpless body, as Harnak's last two guardsmen came at him.

One of them was a little in advance of the other, and his charge ended in the thud of dead meat as he ran headlong into Bahzell's two-handed stroke. His companion got through, and Bahzell grunted as steel crashed into his side. His mail blunted the blow, but blood welled down his ribs, and his left arm flashed out. It snaked around his opponent's sword arm and through his armpit, and Bahzell's hand licked up behind the other's shoulder. He heaved, and the Navahkan lost footing and sword alike. He smashed into the ground face-first, and Bahzell's knee came down on his spine.

The Horse Stealer dropped his own sword. His right hand darted down, found his enemy's chin, cupped hard, and he straightened his back explosively.

The crunching *crack!* of vertebrae filled the ravine, and suddenly the night was still and dark once more.

# CHAPTER THIRTY-SEVEN

Bahzell finished making camp, such as it was, and let himself slide down beside Brandark's bedroll with a groan of weary pain. Broken ribs throbbed dully under the rough, blood-stiff dressing on his left side, yet he was in far better shape than Brandark. The Bloody Sword was barely conscious, and Bahzell tasted the bitterness of guilt as he uncapped his water bottle.

Brandark had faced no less than four Rage-maddened opponents—and killed three of them—while Bahzell dueled with Harnak. It was the sort of fight that made legends, but it had cost him the tip of his right ear and the last two fingers of his left hand, and those were the least of his hurts. The ugly cut in his left biceps had bled badly until Bahzell's rough and ready stitches closed it, yet the wound in his right leg was far worse. Steel had cut to the bone, severing muscle and tendons; it would have crippled him for life . . . except that Bahzell knew enough field medicine to recognize the stench of gangrene.

His friend was going to die, and it was Bahzell's fault. He knew Brandark would disagree, that he'd say—truthfully—that he'd chosen to come despite Bahzell's warnings, yet it was Bahzell who'd brought Harnak after them, and it was Bahzell's insistence on aiding Malith's villagers which had doomed Brandark. The Purple Lord cavalry would cut his throat instantly, not tend his wounds, if Bahzell left him behind, but dragging him along was only prolonging his torment, and Bahzell knew it.

He held the water bottle to Brandark's lips, and the Bloody Sword swallowed thirstily. He drank half the bottle, and his eyes slid open. They were cloudy with pain and fever, but he managed to smile.

"Still with you, you see," he husked in a parody of his usual tenor, and Bahzell soaked a rag in water and mopped his face.

"Aye, so I do," he replied, and somehow he kept his own voice steady as Brandark closed his eyes once more.

He lay silent, breathing raggedly, and Bahzell cursed his powerlessness. He'd managed to stop the bleeding and get Brandark onto one of their horses, then thrown a pack saddle onto one of the mules and driven the other animals away before he broke south once more. He'd hoped the patrol which must have attacked Harnak's men would decide the "brigands" had scattered and split up to chase riderless horses, and it seemed to have worked. No one had come straight after them, at any rate, but they were still hunting, and some of them, at least, were ahead of the hradani. He'd lain on the crest of a hill and watched a score of troopers sweep a shallow valley he and Brandark had yet to cross, and he knew they wouldn't give up. Not after the losses they must have taken against Harnak's guardsmen. It was only a matter of time until one of those patrols caught up with them, and when it did—

"You know you've . . . got to leave me behind, don't you?"

Brandark whispered, and Bahzell looked down quickly. He opened his mouth, but Brandark shook his head with another of those tight smiles. "D'you think . . . I don't know I'm dying?"

"Hush, little man! There's no need to talk of dying yet."

"Give me . . . a couple of days . . . and I won't *have* to 'talk' about it." Fever left Brandark's weak voice hoarse and frayed, but it still held a trace of his usual tartness. "I know you're . . . an idiot, but don't . . . *prove* it. 'Thout me . . . to slow you, you might break through yet."

"And what sort of champion of Tomanāk goes about abandoning his friends, then?" Bahzell shot back, wiping the Bloody Sword's face once more. "A fine way to act that'd be!"

"Oh . . . hog turds." Brandark's strength was ebbing quickly, but he shook his head again. "Don' han' . . . me that," he muttered. "Nev'r wanted . . . be a champion 'n th' firs' place, you . . . idio' . . . ."

He trailed off in incoherent mumbles, and Bahzell stared out into the night and bit his lip. He'd never felt so helpless, so useless. He rested one hand lightly on Brandark's right shoulder for a long, silent moment, then rose and stumped across the fireless camp to the one pack of rations he'd hung on to. He started to open it, then stopped, and his ears flattened as he glared down at a long, cloth-wrapped bundle.

It was Harnak's sword, shrouded in the dead prince's bloodstained cloak. Its fire had faded when Harnak died, yet Bahzell had sensed the power and hatred lying quiescent in it, waiting only for a hand to lift it once more. He'd dared not leave it behind—gods only knew what it would do to anyone mad enough to touch it!—but what was he supposed to do with it now?

He straightened his aching spine and growled in bleak, exhausted bitterness. He hadn't dared touch the thing with his bare hand, but he'd held it in a fold of Harnak's cloak to examine it and found the scorpion etched into its guard. He would have liked to think that simply marked it as an assassin's blade, but what he'd seen—and felt— it do in battle made that nonsense. No, he knew why it bore Sharnā's symbol . . . and that it proved things were even worse in Navahk than he'd believed. Gods! Did Churnazh even suspect what was using him as its opening wedge? It seemed impossible. Crude and brutal Churnazh was, but surely he had cunning enough to know what would happen if any of his neighbors came to suspect him of trafficking with Sharnā! Yet if Sharnā's church could reach as high as Navahk's crown prince, who knew who *else* it had reached? Or where?

Bahzell scrubbed his face with his palms, feeling sick and exhausted and used up. He was the only one with proof of how far evil had reached into Navahk. That made it his job to do something about it, but he was so tired. So very, very tired and sick at heart.

"So," he muttered bitterly into his palms, "why not be telling me what I should do *now*, Tomanāk?"

"Do you really want to ask me that?"

Bahzell snatched his hands down and stared around in shock, but the night was still and quiet, free of apparitions, and he swallowed, then drew a breath.

"As to that," he told the darkness, "it's new at this championing I am. I've no real notion what it is I can or can't be asking of you."

"You may ask anything you wish of me," that deep voice murmured within him. "What I can give you, I will."

"Will you, now? And what of *him?*" Bahzell cried in despair. "It was me brought him to this, and not a thing at all can I do for him now!"

"I think we had this conversation once before," Tomanāk said quietly, "and I told you then that I can heal through my champions." Bahzell stiffened and sensed an unseen smile. "You've destroyed a nest of black wizards, rescued a mage, slain a demon, saved an entire village's homes, and bested a servant of Sharná armed with a cursed blade far more powerful than you've guessed even yet, Bahzell. After all that, is it so hard to believe I'd help your friend if you asked it of me?"

"You can heal him?" Bahzell demanded, disregarding the catalog of his own accomplishments.

"*We* can heal him," Tomanák corrected, "if you serve as my channel, but it won't be an instantaneous process. That would require too direct an intrusion on my part."

"I'm not caring about 'instant,' " Bahzell shot back. "Just you be telling me what to do and how to go about it!"

"You have a unique mode of prayer," Tomanák said so dryly Bahzell blushed, but then the god chuckled in his brain. "No matter. It's the way you are, and difficult as you can be, I wouldn't change you if I could."

Bahzell's face burned still hotter, but Tomanák only chuckled again and said, "Draw your sword, Bahzell. Hold it in one hand and lay the other on Brandark, then just concentrate on your friend. Think of him as you remember him and see him that way once more."

"And is that all there is to it?" Bahzell asked incredulously.

"You may find it a bit more difficult than you assume, my friend," Tomanák told him. "And don't get too confident. How much we accomplish will be up to you as much as to me. Are you ready?"

Bahzell hesitated in sudden, acute nervousness. It was one thing to fight demons and cursed blades. Fighting, at least, was something he understood; this notion of *healing* was something else again, and the idea that *he* could do it was . . . disconcerting. And, he admitted, frightening. Another step into whatever future he'd embraced when he entered the War God's service, yes, but an uncanny one that would make his acceptance of that future more explicit and inescapable. He stood motionless for a few seconds longer, then sighed and drew his sword. He held it in his right hand and knelt beside his friend, then laid a tentative hand on Brandark's wounded arm.

"Ahem!" Bahzell's ears flicked as a throat cleared itself soundlessly in his brain. "You'll have to do a bit better than that," Tomanāk informed him.

"Better?"

"Bahzell, we're not going to *hurt* him, but how well this works will depend in no small part on how thoroughly you enter into it. Now stop being afraid he's going to break—or that *you're* going to turn into a purple toad— and do it!"

Bahzell blushed more brightly than ever, but his mouth twitched in a small smile at the asperity in the god's mental voice. He drew a deep breath, closed his eyes, and fastened one huge hand on Brandark's slack shoulder. No one had told him to, but he bent his head, resting his forehead against the quillons of the sword in his other hand, and tried to empty his mind of Brandark as he now was. It was hard—far harder than he'd anticipated— for the image of his dying friend haunted him, and something deep inside jeered at the thought that *he* could do anything to change that. This wasn't the sort of battle Bahzell Bahnakson had ever trained to fight. It wasn't one where size or strength mattered, and he didn't know the moves or counters, but he clenched his jaw and threw every scrap of will and energy into it.

Sweat beaded his brow, and his fingers ached about his sword, but slowly—*so* slowly!—he forced his mental picture of Brandark to change. He drove back the slack-faced, gray-skinned reality, fighting it like some living enemy, and a new picture replaced it. Brandark lounging back on the deck of the ferryboat leaving Riverside in his dandy's lace shirt and flowered waistcoat, smiling down into the deck house at Zarantha and Rekah, ears aquiver and eyes alight as he sang his maddening *Lay of Bahzell Bloody-Hand* to them. The spritely notes of the balalaika, the smile on Brandark's face, the sense of energy and deviltry which were so much a part of him—Bahzell brought them all together, welding them into what Brandark ought to be. What he *was*, Bahzell told himself fiercely—and what he would be again!

Sweat rolled down his cheeks, and then, suddenly, his mind snapped into focus. It was like the release of an arbalest bolt, an abrupt, breathless flash of vision, and in that instant he truly heard the music, Brandark's voice, the slap and gurgle of water under the ferry's bow. It was as if he could reach out, touch that moment once more. And then, in some strange fashion he knew he would never be able to describe, he *did* touch it, and became a bridge, a connection between the image and this wretched, fireless camp. Something crossed that bridge, flowed through him, burned in his veins like agony, and something else came with it—something fierce with war cries and the clash of steel, terrifying with the thunder of heavy cavalry, grim with purpose and glorious with the bright, defiant sound of bugles. His closed eyes couldn't see the brilliant blue light that flashed briefly from his blade, licked up his body, darted down his arm to Brandark, but he felt it. Felt it like the strike of lightning, cauterizing him, consuming him, and his own strength poured out to meld with it and flood down, down, down into Brandark's faltering body.

It was the most draining, glorious thing he'd ever experienced, and it was far too intense to sustain. He felt that torrent of power snap into Brandark, felt his friend's heart spasm under its lash, and then he was shrugged aside. The energy was too potent, too wild and fierce to constrain, and Bahzell cried out as it flung him away. His eyes popped open, and then he gazed down at Brandark, chest heaving as he sucked in huge lungfuls of air, and the world went very, very still.

His friend's cropped ear and fingers were healed over, no longer raw and crusted but clean, smooth tissue.

Bahzell reached out and touched that wounded ear. It was cool, no longer hot with fever, and suddenly Bahzell was fumbling with the dressing on Brandark's arm. He ripped it aside, and his eyes went huge when he saw the cut. It was less completely healed than the Bloody Sword's ear or fingers, but the wound looked at least two weeks old, and Bahzell's hands shook as he drew his dagger and cut away the bandages on Brandark's thigh.

He hesitated as he bared the inmost layer, clotted and thick with oozing suppuration, then drew them aside and gasped. The terrible wound remained, but it was clean and healthy. He touched it lightly, then pressed harder, felt the solid, meaty strength of intact muscle and sinew, and drew a deep, hacking breath of joy.

"Well done!" a deep, echoing voice cried within him. "Well done, indeed, Bahzell Bahnakson!"

"Thank you," Bahzell whispered, and it was not for the compliment. He closed his eyes again, recalling how he'd thrown the uselessness of uncaring gods into Tomanāk's teeth, and someone else laughed deep inside him. It was a laugh of welcome, a war leader's slap of congratulation on the shoulder of a warrior who'd fought well and hard in his first battle, and he smiled.

"Thank you," he repeated more normally.

"I told you it would take us both," Tomanāk said, "and it's not every one of my champions who can fight as hard to heal a friend as to slay a foe, Bahzell." Bahzell inhaled once more, treasuring the deep, joyous holiness of that moment—the knowledge that he held life in his hands, not death—and someone else's huge, gentle hand seemed to rest lightly upon his head for a single endless moment. But then it withdrew, and he straightened as he sensed the War God's change of mood.

"Brandark will recover fully, in time," Tomanāk told

him. "He'll need care, and it will be some weeks still before that leg is fit to bear his weight, but he'll recover. Without the tip of his ear or the fingers, I fear, but fully in every other sense. And with that behind us, perhaps its time to turn to the question you originally asked."

"Which question?"

"The one about what to do with Harnak's sword," Tomanāk said dryly.

"Ah, *that* one!" Bahzell shook himself and settled back on his heels, sword across his thighs. "I'll not deny I'd dearly like that answered, yet it's but one. What's to be done about old Demon Breath's doings in Navahk?"

"One thing at a time, Bahzell. One thing at a time. My champions are only mortal, and I expect them to remember that."

"Well, there's a relief!" Bahzell chuckled.

"I'm glad you think so. First, the sword. You were right not to leave it behind. It's failed in its original purpose, but that only makes it more dangerous, in a way. It was forged as a gate, Bahzell—an opening to Sharnā's realm so that he himself might strike at you through Harnak." Bahzell swallowed, but the god continued calmly. "That constituted an unusual risk, even for him, and when you and I defeated him, it cost the Dark Gods more access here than you can guess. I'm sure his fellows will have something to say to him about it, but despite his failure in *this* instance, it remains a gate keyed to him, a path to reach anyone unfortunate enough to pick it up. There are few ways to neutralize something this powerful short of destroying it, and that, unfortunately, would liberate all its energy at once—and kill whoever destroyed it. Under the circumstances, the wisest course is to bury it at sea. Somewhere nice and deep, where my brother Korthrala can keep it safe."

"At sea, is it? And how am I to be getting there with the ports no doubt closed against me?"

"That, Bahzell, is up to you. I'm sure you'll think of something."

The Horse Stealer growled under his breath, yet there was an odd lack of power to the growl, and he felt the flicker of Tomanāk's tart amusement.

"As for Navahk," the god went on after a moment, "I think we can leave that for later. There are other forces at work, and I don't expect you to deal with all of Norfressa's problems on your own. Send word to your father and let him alert his allies. The Dark Gods work best *in* the dark; expose them to the light of day, and half the battle is won. In the meantime, you and Brandark have enough problems to deal with. Just try to get both of you out of this in one piece, Bahzell. Brandark is one of my sister's favorites—and *I've* put a great deal of effort into *you*."

Bahzell started to shoot something back, but there was a sudden stillness in his mind, and he knew Tomanāk had gone.

"Well," he murmured instead, gazing down at Brandark's relaxed face and listening to his even, sleeping breath, "now *there's* a thing!"

# CHAPTER THIRTY-EIGHT

Wind whipped out of the south, rough coated and sinewy, carrying a deep, rhythmic crash of sound and the high, fierce cry of gulls. The world was awash with energy and life, dancing on Bahzell's skin like electricity as he waded through waist-high grass, topped the crumbly sand of a high-crested dune, and saw the sea at last.

It froze him, that sight. It held him like a fist, staring out over the endless blue and flashing white, lungs aching with the smell of salt. Surf boomed and spurted against the tan-colored beach in explosions of foam, and his braid whipped like a kite's tail as the ocean's breath plucked at his worn and tattered clothing. He'd never seen, never imagined, the like of this moment, and a vast, inarticulate longing seized him. He didn't know what it was he suddenly wanted, yet he felt it calling to him in the surge of deep water and the shrill voice of sea birds, and his heart leapt in answer.

"Phrobus," a tenor voice said softly, half lost in the tumult about them. "It's *big*, isn't it?"

"Aye, it is that," Bahzell replied, equally quietly, and turned his head.

Brandark sat his horse with unwonted awkwardness, eyes huge in wonder. His bandage-wrapped right leg still gave him considerable pain, and it was all he could do to hobble about on it dismounted, for his body had yet to complete its healing. Yet a literal glow of health seemed to follow him about, and his reaction when he woke clearheaded and hungry for the first time in days had been all Bahzell could have desired. For once, even Brandark had been stunned into silence by the change in his condition, and when he learned how that change had come about—!

It had been too good to last, of course, and in his heart of hearts, Bahzell was glad of it. Refreshing it might have been to have Brandark deferring to him every time he turned around, but it had also been profoundly unnatural, and he'd felt nothing but relief the first time the word "idiot" escaped Brandark's lips once more. By now, things were almost back to normal, and the Bloody Sword shook himself.

"Well," he said dryly, "this is all very impressive, I'm sure, but what do you plan for your next trick?"

"'Next trick,' is it now?"

"Indeed. You said something about heading west along the shore, I believe, but that was when we still had all our supplies. Now—" Brandark waved at the single sparsely filled pack on the mule beside his horse and shrugged.

"D'you know, I've been giving that very thing some thought my own self," Bahzell rumbled, "and I'm thinking what we need is a ship."

"A *ship?*" Brandark looked at him in disbelief. "And just how, pray tell, do you propose to manage that? Those bastards hunting us are still back there somewhere," he jabbed a thumb over his shoulder, "and correct me if I'm wrong, but hadn't we decided they must have sent word ahead?"

"Ah, the pessimism of the man!" Bahzell shook his head mournfully. "Here he is, with a champion of Tomanāk to see him safe home, and all he can be thinking of is wee little things to carp over!"

"If you think half an army of cavalry is a 'wee little thing,' then Harnak must've hit you on the head with that thing." Brandark kicked the cloak-wrapped sword with his left foot.

"Nonsense! Now don't you be worrying about a thing, a thing, for I've a plan, little man."

"Gods preserve us, *he's* got a plan!" Brandark groaned, and Bahzell threw back his head and laughed. He couldn't help it. A strange, deep bubble of joy had filled him since the night he'd healed Brandark—or helped Tomanāk heal him, or whatever had happened—and the wild, restless vitality of the sea flowed into him. It was like a moment of rebirth, a strange, unshakable confidence and zesty delight impossible to resist, and he roared with laughter. He saw Brandark staring at him for a moment, and then his friend began to laugh, as well. They stood there on the dune, laughing like fools, drunk on the sheer joy of living, and Bahzell slapped Brandark on the shoulder.

"Aye, it's a plan I have, so come along with you, now! We've things to do before I set it in motion and dazzle you with my wit!"

"Ah, now! There's what we want," Bahzell said in satisfied tones. The sun was slanting back into the west once more as they stood on a firm-packed beach, waves washing about the hocks of Brandark's horse and Bahzell's calves, and looked out across a hundred yards of sea at a small island. It wasn't much of an island—just a bare, lumpy heap of sand, sea grass, and stunted scrub, no more than a hundred yards across at its widest point—and Brandark gazed at the Horse Stealer in patent disbelief.

"*That's* what we want?"

"Aye, the very thing. And unless I'm much mistaken, the tide's gone out, as well," Bahzell observed with even deeper satisfaction.

"And what, if I may ask, do *you* know about tides?"

"Not so very much," Bahzell conceded cheerfully, "but look yonder." He pointed up the beach, where the sand turned crumbly and a tangled necklace of driftwood marked the tide line. "I'm thinking that's where the water's coming to at *high* tide, so, as it's down where we are just this minute—" He shrugged, and Brandark sighed.

"I hate it when you go all deductive on me. But even allowing that you're right about the tide, what difference does it make?"

"It's part of the plan," Bahzell said smugly, and started wading out into the sea.

"Hey! Where d'you think you're going?!"

"Follow and see," Bahzell shot back, never turning his head, and Brandark muttered under his breath. He hesitated another moment, but Bahzell was already waist-deep in surging water and showed no sign of stopping, so he closed his mouth with a snap and urged his mount into the waves.

The horse didn't want to go, and the mule was even more recalcitrant. Brandark had his hands full getting them started, but Bahzell only grinned back over his shoulder at him as he cursed them with fervent artistry. The mule laid back its ears and bared its teeth, but a firm yank on its lead rein started it moving once more, and both animals churned forward at last.

They never quite had to swim, but it was close before they reached the island and scrambled ashore once more. By the time Brandark led the soaked, indignant mule ashore, Bahzell was standing on the southern side of the island, hands on his hips, and gazing out to sea with obvious delight.

"Will you *please* tell me what you think we're doing?"

"Eh?" Bahzell turned to face him, and the Bloody Sword waved an exasperated hand.

"What're we *doing* out here?!"

"As to that, we're about to make camp," Bahzell said, and grinned again as Brandark swelled with frustration. "Now, now! Think on it a minute. We've kept below the tide line since lunch. What d'you think will be happening to our tracks when it comes back in?"

Brandark paused, eyebrows arched, and rubbed his truncated right ear.

"All right," he said after a moment, "I can see that. But they'll know that's what we did and just cast up and down the shore from where the trail disappeared."

"So they will, but they'll not be finding us unless they search every islet they come across, now will they?"

Brandark rubbed his ear harder, then nodded.

"All right," he conceded. "As long as we don't do anything to call attention to ourselves, they'll probably assume we kept on going. Gods know only a lunatic *wouldn't* keep running! But we're short on provisions, Bahzell, and I don't see any sign of fresh water. We can't stay here long."

"No more will we have to. Give me another few hours, and I'll be off with the dark to fetch back a ship for us."

Brandark's jaw dropped. He stared at his friend without speaking for over a minute, then shook his head slowly.

"The man's mad. Stark, staring mad! Where d'you think you're going to find a ship, you idiot?"

"Why, as to that, I'm thinking there's ships and to spare down to Bortalik Bay," Bahzell said cheerfully, "and we've still that nice, fat purse Yithar was after leaving us. With that, all I need do is nip down and, ah, *hire* one of them."

Bahzell dumped the last armload of driftwood on the heap and regarded it with a proprietary air. He'd chosen the site for the bonfire-to-be with care, then spent over an hour heaping sand into a high wall to improve it. The island's low spine and his piled barrier would prevent anyone ashore from seeing it, but once lit, it should be visible for miles from seaward.

Brandark had sat propped against his saddle, strumming experimentally on his balalaika while he worked. The Bloody Sword's maimed left hand made chording difficult, and he seemed to be concentrating on that to the exclusion of all else—until Bahzell dusted his palms with an air of finality.

"You do realize just how stupid this is, don't you?" he said then, never looking up from the bridge of his instrument.

"Well, no one was ever after calling me smart." Bahzell crossed to the tethered mule and horse to free their leads from the picket lines and grinned at Brandark's caustic snort. "And stupid or no, I've yet to hear a better idea from *you*."

"I've done my part by trying to talk you out of this. I don't have the energy to think up better ideas on top of that."

"And here I thought you such a clever lad!" Bahzell gathered the animals' reins and headed down the beach into the wash of the surf. Water filled his worn, leaky boots instantly, but he ignored it. He was still damp from wading out to the island in the first place, and it was no part of his plan to leave visible tracks along any of the islet's shoreline.

"You'll never be able to do it—not alone," Brandark said more seriously.

"I'm thinking you're wrong, and wrong or no, it's a notion worth trying. We've little chance of outrunning them all afoot, and they'll not be expecting such as this."

"Maybe that just indicates how much smarter than

you they are!" Brandark growled, eyes still fixed on his balalaika.

"It may that," Bahzell agreed, listening to the grumbling breath of the sea, "but smarter or no, it's time I was gone. Don't you go drifting off to sleep, now!"

"Don't worry about *me*, you lunatic. Just watch your own backside, and—" Brandark looked up at last, his eyes unwontedly serious in the twilight "—good luck."

Bahzell nodded, raised one hand in a half wave, and waded further out into the surf.

It had been dead low water when they crossed to the island; by the time Bahzell reached the mainland once more, the flood tide was sending hissing waves high up the beach. A newly risen moon spilled silver light over the sand, and he looked back over his shoulder in satisfaction as he led the unsaddled horse and mule clear of the water. His and Brandark's earlier tracks had already been eaten by the tide, leaving no sign that anyone had detoured to the island, and he moved rapidly along between the surf and the high-tide mark for the better part of a mile before he climbed higher up on the beach. If any tracker did cast along the shoreline for his trail, they should find exactly what he wanted them to: the same prints of one pair of boots, one horse, and one mule, with nothing to suggest that at least one of their quarry was no longer in front of them. He hoped no one would ever see those tracks at all, but if they did, he'd at least gotten Brandark safely out of it, and he'd left all their remaining provisions with the Bloody Sword. They should last him for a week or so, if he was careful with his water. By then, any pursuit should have moved on to other areas and his leg should be recovered enough to give him an excellent chance of making it back to the Empire of the Spear on his own.

Not, Bahzell reminded himself, that there would be

any reason for Brandark to do any such thing . . . assuming, of course, that his plan worked.

He urged the animals up the beach into the lee of the high dunes to avoid silhouetting himself against the moon-silvered sea and jogged eastward.

Bahzell had gone perhaps a league when his head jerked up, and he frowned. His ears pricked, trying to identify the sound which had cut even through the grumble of the surf, and then he blinked in disbelief. The high, fierce cry of a hunting falcon came yet again, and he wheeled away from the sea as a black shape swept across the star-strewn sky.

An instant of cold panic touched his heart, yet there was too little time to feel it fully. There was no way a falcon should be on the wing so late at night, and even less reason for the bird to launch itself towards him like a lodestone to steel. Instinct screamed warning at the unnaturalness of its appearance, but another instinct brought his right arm flashing up to guard his face as the fierce-beaked predator shot straight into it. His muscles tensed against the rending attack of powerful talons, but it never came. Instead, those lethal claws struck his wrist and closed with impossible gentleness.

Bahzell's breath hissed out of him in a deep, shuddering gasp, but his relief was far from total. He lowered his arm slowly, cautiously, extending it well away from him, and the bird mantled as it shifted its weight to balance on his wrist. It cocked its head, small, round eyes bright with reflected moonlight, and Bahzell swallowed. He wore no falconer's gauntlet, but the bird still gripped with those gentle talons, and then its beak opened.

"Hello, Bahzell." The Horse Stealer twitched again, muscles tensing to jump back. His ears flattened, but then he made himself stand very still, for he recognized the voice issuing from that dangerous, hooked beak. It was Zarantha's! He stared at the falcon and licked his lips, aware that he must look like a total idiot, then opened his mouth to reply, but the falcon spoke again before he could.

"I asked Wencit for a favor," Zarantha's voice went on, "and Father agreed to give up his prize falcon for it. Wencit promises it will find you, but I'm afraid not even he can guarantee it will ever come home again afterward. Father was a bit upset by that, but I guess he thinks getting his daughter back is worth a few sacrifices."

Despite himself, Bahzell grinned as he heard the familiar, laughing wickedness in Zarantha's voice. It was even more welcome—and precious—as he recalled her wan, wounded look on the morning they parted, and the falcon flapped its wings again, shifting from foot to foot as if it shared her laughter.

"At any rate, Wencit got me safely home, dear friend," Zarantha went on more seriously. "He tells me his gramerhain suggests that you and Brandark won't be able to visit us after all—this time, at least—so I wanted you to know you don't have to worry about me anymore. I've heard from Tothas, as well. He and Rekah are indeed well, and they should be home within a few weeks, too. Thank you, my friend. Thank you from the bottom of my heart. If we never meet again, know that I will never forget all you and Brandark did for us."

The voice paused for a moment, then changed. It was no longer Zarantha's, but a man's, deep and measured.

"I know little of sorcery, Bahzell Bahnakson and Brandark Brandarkson, but if Wencit is correct and you ever hear this message, know that Caswal of Jashân stands eternally in your debt. I repeat my daughter's invitation, and beg you to visit us here, if ever it should be possible, and I name you Bahzell and Brandark of Jashân, sept to Jashân. If ever I, or any man of Jashân may serve you or yours, send word. And if the gods decree we shall never meet, know that wherever you may go, you are blood of our blood and bone of our bone, my friends."

Duke Jashân's voice ceased, and the bird stood silent for another moment while Bahzell stared at it. Then Zarantha spoke a final time, and her voice was soft.

"And so our journey ends at last, dearest of friends and now my brothers. My life and the lives of those dear to me were your gift, and I give you now the only gift I can across the miles between us: my love. May it go with you always, and may the Gods of Light keep and guard you both as you kept and guarded me. Farewell, Bahzell Bahnakson, Prince of Hurgrum. Farewell Brandark. Remember us."

Bahzell blinked eyes that burned with sudden, unexpected tears. The falcon lingered on his wrist, gaze still fixed upon him, and he drew a deep breath.

"Farewell, Zarantha of Jashân," he whispered, and the bird threw back its head with another high, fierce cry. And then, suddenly, it launched itself like an arrow from the string and vanished into the stars, and only the sigh of the wind and the rumble of the surf breathed in the night.

The trip took longer than Bahzell had expected, but it was without further incident, for there were few decent anchorages between Falan Bay and Bortalik, and the merchant princes who ruled the city of Bortalik protected their position. No other ports were permitted along their coastline. Even fishing villages were almost unheard of and existed only on sufferance. Bortalik tolerated them within a few leagues of the city itself, where the city's customs agents could police them, but none were allowed to dabble in trade. More than one fishing port had been burned out—by landing parties from merchantmen, as well as warships—if the city merchants so much as suspected it of smuggling. And so, ironically in a land whose enormous wealth depended upon its control of seaborne trade, this entire vast sweep of coast was almost empty.

Almost, but not quite. The moon was well into the west when Bahzell rounded a headland and found himself abruptly facing a good-sized village at last. There were few lights, ashore or afloat, and he frowned at the fishing boats drawn up on the beach or nestled alongside the rickety-looking wharves.

The animals blew gratefully as he squatted on his heels, gazing at the boats and pondering his options. It was tempting, but, after several moments' consideration, he shook his head. He was no seaman, yet those vessels looked too flimsy to his landsman's eye. Most of them were little more than glorified rowboats or small, single-masted craft. No, he needed something bigger and better suited to deep water . . . but that didn't mean the village was useless to him.

He led the horse and mule inland, eyes sweeping the dark. This might be a fishing village, but somewhere there had to be a—

Ah! He grinned to himself as he found the small, stone-walled pasture. It held perhaps a dozen cattle and runty horses, and he made his way around to a gate in the low wall. The night was undisturbed by so much as a barking dog as he eased the gate open and turned his own animals quietly into the pasture. They stood for a moment, gazing back at him curiously, then shook their heads and trotted over to the pasture's other inhabitants, and Bahzell chuckled as he closed the gate behind them.

Unless he missed his guess, the owner of that pasture was unlikely to mention the sudden arrival of two big, strong, healthy, and expensive animals to anyone. Indeed, he might go to some lengths to hide his unexpected gifts, which would suit Bahzell fine. Even if he did report them to the authorities, Bahzell should be long gone by the time those authorities figured out where they'd come from, and he felt better leaving them to someone's care. They'd served him and Brandark well, and the thought of simply abandoning them hadn't set well with him.

He started off once more, and, divested of the animals, he made better time. He jogged past two more villages—their existence welcome signs that he was nearing his destination—and the moon was still well above the horizon when he finally spied the dull glint of high walls before him.

Bortalik dozed under the moon. Bahzell made his way out onto a rocky point and leaned back against a boulder, catching his breath while he gazed across a wide arm of Bortalik Bay at the sleeping city. Watch lights dotted the curtain wall and crowned the countless towers that ribbed its length, and more lights were smears of brightness along the wharves that lined its foot. There was activity at dockside even this late at night, and masts and rigging rose in a black lace forest against the light. Other vessels dotted the bay, lying to anchors or buoys, and, despite himself, Bahzell felt a trace of wonder at the sheer size of the port.

The northern hradani tribes knew little more about the Purple Lords than the Purple Lords knew about them, but even they had heard of Bortalik Bay, and Zarantha and Tothas had told him far more. Bortalik was the undisputed queen of the southern coast and determined to remain so. The enormous bay was not simply a superb natural anchorage; it also controlled the entire delta of the mighty Spear River and, with it, all trade that moved up the Spear or any of its tributaries. It was an advantage the Purple Lords used ruthlessly, and the power it gave them was obvious as Bahzell looked out upon their city.

He shook himself after a moment and turned his eyes away from the city walls and back out over the bay, searching for what he needed. Not too small, he thought, but not too big, either, and well away from the docks. Surely, among all that shipping, there must be—

His eyes settled on a single vessel, and he rubbed his chin. The twin-masted schooner was further from shore than he'd hoped, but aside from that it seemed perfect. The anchor light on its foredeck burned like a lonely star, for there was nothing else within a hundred yards of it, and even in the uncertain moonlight it looked low, sleek, and fast. Best of all, it was little larger than one of Kilthan's riverboats, which suggested a reasonably small crew.

He studied it a moment longer, then nodded once.

There was no surf within the confines of the sheltered bay, but water washed and surged rhythmically as Bahzell laid aside his baldric and unbuckled his weapon harness. He'd left his arbalest and scale mail with Brandark, for he'd known this moment was coming, but he felt exposed and vulnerable as he methodically stripped to the skin. He belted his dagger and a fat, jingling purse back about his naked waist, then laid his sheathed sword atop his discarded boots and clothing with a final pat he hoped looked less dubious than it felt. Part of him wanted to ask Tomanāk if this whole notion was truly a good idea, but the rest of him dug in stubborn toes and refused the temptation. A man couldn't just go about asking "May I?" every time he had to make a decision, he told himself. Of course, he *was* relying heavily on what Tomanāk had told him about his sword, but even so—

He snorted and shook himself, ears half-flattened in amusement. Either it worked, or it didn't, and standing here thinking of excuses to delay the inevitable wouldn't change the final outcome! He grinned crookedly at the thought and waded out into the bay.

The bottom dropped off more sharply than he'd expected. It was going to be a longer swim than he'd planned, but a broken, drifting spar bumped up against him, as if to compensate, and he seized it gratefully. He was no fish, and the spar's added buoyancy was welcome as he kicked his way across the bay. There was enough noise in the night to hide most sounds, yet there was no point taking chances, and he tried—not entirely successfully—to avoid splashes. It was a long, tiring swim; the bay was colder than he'd anticipated when he was only wading through the surf; and he was acutely aware that he was a land animal. He sensed the empty water between him and the bottom, how easily it could suck him under, and found himself thinking about sharks. Or octopuses— they ate people, too, didn't they? And even if they didn't, the gods only knew what *else* might be hiding just under the water, circling him, waiting . . . .

He pushed the thought firmly away. People swam in the sea all the time, and they'd hardly do that if something pounced on anyone who tried! Of course, that didn't mean nothing *ever* pounced, and—

He looked up and inhaled in deep, heartfelt relief as he saw his destination close ahead. He kicked more strongly, and his ears twitched in amusement at his own eagerness to reach it. For all he knew, that vessel's entire crew had seen him coming and was lined up behind the bulwark to knock him on the head, but it didn't matter. The company of his thoughts on the swim out left him impatient to confront them even so.

He reached the schooner's side and swam along it as quietly as he could. It was flush-decked, with a low sheer and a freeboard of no more than six or seven feet, yet that was high enough to make things difficult for a man in the water. He was confident that he could lunge high enough to get his fingers over the rail, but not without an appalling amount of noise, and he continued forward until he reached the flared bow. The bowsprit was a long, graceful lance, reaching out above his head, but the anchor cable plunged into the water beside him, and he laid a hand on the thick hawser. He craned his neck, peering up to where it curved over the anchor bits. It looked far more promising than trying to heave himself bodily over the side, and he nodded in satisfaction and shoved the broken spar away.

He got a grip on the hawser and hauled himself cautiously up it. A cathead thrust out above him, and he hooked an elbow around it, then curled his body up to get his knees over it. He crouched there a moment, catching his breath, listening to the trickling splash as water dribbled back into the bay from his skin, then shoved his head cautiously over the rail.

There was no one in sight, but he heard a fiddle and what sounded like an accordion, and what he'd thought was just an anchor light was also the gleam of light from the scuttles of a low, midships deckhouse. More light glowed from an open companion, and his ears flattened at the realization that some, at least, of the crew was awake. He had no special desire to harm anyone if he could help it, but they wouldn't have any way of knowing he sought peaceable conversation, now would they? That was why he'd hoped to surprise them asleep in their berths, but it seemed he was going to have to do things the hard way.

He sighed and stood, balancing on the cathead, then stepped across to the deck. His bare feet made no sound, and he started towards the companion. If he could come down it and block access to the deck, then—

"Here, now! What're you doing creeping about my ship?"

The sharp, crisp voice was behind him, and he spun like a cat, one hand going to his dagger.

"Ah, now! None of that!" the voice said even more sharply, and Bahzell swallowed an oath. There *had* been men on deck; he simply hadn't seen them because they were so small they'd been hidden behind the deckhouse. Now five halflings stood facing him, and each of them held a drawn shortsword as if he knew what to do with it.

He stepped back against the rail, taking his hand carefully from his dagger, and his eyes narrowed. He'd seen several halflings since leaving Navahk, but none as big as these fellows. They might be little more than half his own height, but they were a good foot or more taller than the only other ones he'd met, and there was nothing hesitant about them. They seemed confident of their ability to deal with him, and the one who'd spoken cocked his head, then spat over the side.

"Ha!" The spokesman wore the golden trident badge of a worshiper of Korthrala. Now he surveyed the towering, naked, soaking wet intruder on his foredeck and tweaked a handlebar mustache with such superb panache Bahzell's lips twitched despite himself. "You've picked the wrong ship tonight, friend," the halfling said with obvious satisfaction. "I think we'll just feed you back to the fishes and be done with it."

"Now, now. Let's not be doing anything hasty," Bahzell rumbled back.

"Oh, *we* won't be hasty, friend!" The halfling smiled unpleasantly and nodded to his fellows, who split up into pairs to come at Bahzell from both sides. "But *you* might want to nip back over the side right sharp."

"And here was I, thinking as how halflings were such cautious folk, and all," Bahzell replied, still keeping his hand away from his dagger.

"Not Marfang Island halflings." The spokesman kept his eyes fixed on Bahzell, but his lip curled. "*We* can get downright nasty, so if I were you, I'd be back over that rail double quick."

"Marfang Island, is it?" Bahzell murmured, and his ears cocked. He'd heard of Marfang Island halflings.

They were said to be a breed apart from their fellows—taller, stronger, and noted for a personal courage that verged all too often on rashness. Even the Wild Wash hradani who lived across the channel from their island home had learned to treat them with cautious respect, despite their size advantage. More to the point this night, the Marfang Islanders were also the finest seamen Norfressa bred, despite their small stature, and they hated the Purple Lords with a passion for their interference with free trade.

"Aye, it is," the halfling agreed. "And the rail's still waiting for you," he added pointedly.

"You've guts enough for five wee, tiny fellows with knives, I'll grant that," Bahzell said easily, and the halfling gave a crack of laughter.

"Maybe so, but there *are* four of us, and you've naught but a knife yourself, longshanks!"

"Do I now?" Bahzell murmured, and raised his empty right hand with a brief, silent prayer that he'd understood Tomanāk correctly that night in the Shipwood. The halflings stopped, suddenly wary, and he drew a deep breath.

"Come!" he bellowed, and the halflings jumped back in surprise at the sheer volume of his shout—then jumped back again, with unseemly haste, as five feet of gleaming steel snapped into existence in his hand and an empty scabbard thumped the deck at his feet.

"Well now! It *did* work," Bahzell observed. He put both hands on his hilt but lowered the tip of the blade to touch the deck unthreateningly and smiled at the spokesman. "I'm thinking I've a bit more than a knife now, friend," he pointed out genially, and the halfling swallowed.

"How . . . how did—?" He stopped and shook himself, then cleared his throat. "Who in Korthrala's name *are* you, and what d'you want?" he demanded.

"As to that, my name is Bahzell Bahnakson, Prince of Hurgrum, and I've need of your ship."

"Prince of—?" the halfling began incredulously, only to stop with a bark of laughter. "Aye, of course you're a prince! What else could you be?" He ran his eyes back over the naked hradani and tweaked his mustache once more. Bahzell's ears flicked in amusement at his tone, but there was no more give in his eyes than in the halfling's, and he nodded.

"That I am, friend, and a champion of Tomanāk." All five halflings looked at one another in disbelief, and Bahzell's voice hardened. "I'd not be laughing at *that*, were I you, for I'm not in the mood." He raised the tip of his sword slightly, and the spokesman held out a restraining hand as his fellows bristled in instant response.

"Not yet, lads," he said, his eyes still locked with Bahzell's. More feet scampered up the companion as his crew belowdecks realized something was happening, but neither he nor Bahzell turned their heads. They faced each other in the darkness, and then the halfling looked pointedly at Bahzell's sword and raised an eyebrow. The Horse Stealer turned it slightly, letting the light catch the symbols of Tomanāk etched deep into the steel, and the halfling nodded and lowered his own blade.

"Well, then, Bahzell Bahnakson," he said dryly, "my name's Evark, and I'm master of this ship. If you need her, I'm the man you have to talk to about it, so suppose you tell me why I should waste time listening?"

"I've no mind to be rude," Bahzell replied politely, "but I'm thinking this—" he twitched his sword "—might be one reason."

"It might," Evark allowed. "You might even be able to carve us all up into fish food with it, though I doubt Tomanāk would approve. But that would still leave you a little problem, friend—unless you've got a spare crew tucked away?"

Bahzell chuckled and leaned back, propping his weight on his sword.

"You've a way about you, Evark, indeed you do. Very well, then, if it's a reason you're wanting, d'you think we could be keeping our swords out of each other long enough for me to give you one?" He twitched his heavy purse so that it jingled, and added, "You've my word you'll not lose by listening."

"Oh, I suppose we might." Evark beckoned his crewmen back and sat on the roof of the deckhouse, his own sword across his thighs, and grinned at Bahzell. "Assuming, of course, that you understand we'll still chop you into dog meat if it's not a reason we like."

Brandark sat huddled in a blanket beside the piled heap of driftwood and stared morosely out to sea. The night lay in ashes about him, a hint of gray tinged the eastern horizon, and he chewed the inside of his lip.

Bahzell should have been back by now, assuming his lunatic plan had worked, and worry gnawed at the Bloody Sword. The whole idea was crazy, and he was bitterly aware why Bahzell had hatched it. He touched his bandaged leg and swore. The sheer joy of realizing it was going to heal after all had been so great he'd almost been able to forget what his continuing incapacity implied, but he could no longer pretend. Without him to look after, Bahzell could have played catch-as-catch-can with the cavalry patrols; with someone who could barely ride, much less walk, that was impossible. Which was why Bahzell had hit upon the notion of somehow hiring—or stealing—a ship. The idea had a sort of elegant simplicity, but only an idiot would think a hunted fugitive could sneak into the Purple Lords' very capital, get aboard a ship, and—

His thoughts broke off as something flashed in the darkness. It blinked again, then burned steadily—a tiny pinprick of light, spilling reflections of itself across the sea. Brandark stared at it incredulously, unable to believe in it, and then he was fumbling madly for his tinderbox.

A brilliant arm of sun heaved itself drippingly out of the sea just as the launch came gliding in. There was something strange about the boat, and it had taken Brandark several seconds to realize what it was. That enormous shape in the bows had to be Bahzell, but the oarsmen looked like children beside him, and the Bloody Sword shook his head in fresh disbelief as he saw the glint of ivory horns and realized they were halflings.

The boat slid up on the beach, and Bahzell—wearing sword and dagger but otherwise naked as the day he was born—leapt over the side and heaved it higher on the sand.

"I see there's some benefits to bringing along some-one your size after all!" a voice called from the stern sheets, and Bahzell grinned.

"You've a sharp tongue for so small a fellow, Evark!" he replied. The fiercely mustachioed halfling laughed, and then Bahzell was bounding through the surf to clasp Brandark on both shoulders. "And you, little man! Don't be telling me you weren't feeling just a *mite* anxious."

"Me? Anxious?" Brandark heard the huskiness in his own voice and cleared his throat. "Nonsense!" he said more strongly. "Everyone knows Horse Stealers are born to be hanged. What could have happened to you on a simple little job like this?"

He waved at the boat as Evark jumped onto the beach and stumped up to them. The halfling captain propped his hands on his hips and peered up at the two hradani, then shook his head.

"Hanged, is it? Well, he came near enough to it, I suppose. But what's a man to do when an idiot with more sword than brain climbs over the side of his ship in the middle of the night?"

"Here, now! It's hard enough when *one* of you is after calling me names!"

Evark ignored Bahzell and thrust out a hand to Brandark. "So, you're the bard, are you?" he said gruffly.

"Ah, no." Brandark grasped the proffered hand with a smile. "I'd like to be one, but I've been told I lack the voice for it."

"Do you, now? Well, never mind. From what your friend tells me, the two of you managed to piss off half the Purple Lord army, and that's recommendation enough to anyone who's ever had to deal with 'em! Besides, Korthrala wouldn't like me anymore if I left one of Scale Balancer's lot to fend for himself, and if Tomanāk's crazy enough to take on a hradani champion, who am I to argue with him?"

"Ah, the tongue of him!" Bahzell mourned, then laid a hand on the captain's shoulder. "Brandark, be known to Evark of Marfang Island, master of the *Wind Dancer*, who's after being kind enough to offer us a ride."

"But I'll not change my schedule for you, mind!" Evark said gruffly. "I'm bound straight to Belhadan with a cargo of Wakūo dates. They won't keep long, so it's to Belhadan you'll go if you ship along with me. Aye, and you'll pull your weight aboard, too!"

"Belhadan?" Brandark laughed. "D'you know, I suddenly have an absolutely *overwhelming* desire to see Belhadan. Where is it?"

"You'll find out, my lad," Evark assured him. Several more of his men swarmed ashore and began gathering up the hradani's sparse gear, and the captain made a shooing gesture at the launch. "Get aboard, get aboard! Your friend's been freezing his arse long enough—we'd best get him back to *Wind Dancer* and into some clothes before something he'll miss freezes off!"

"Aye, I'll be going along with that." Bahzell grinned at Evark and slipped an arm around Brandark to help him hobble to the boat. "It's a terrible temper he has for such a wee little fellow," he told the Bloody Sword, "but he's a head on his shoulders for all that."

"And a good thing, too," Evark snorted, chivvying his passengers across the beach. "Korthrala knows the pair of you need looking after if even *half* of what you've told me is true, longshanks! Damn me for a Purple Lord if I know which of you's the bigger idiot—you, for getting yourself into this, or this other fathom of fish bait for following you!"

"Oh, it's Bahzell, hands down," Brandark assured him as the Horse Stealer half-lifted him over the gunwale and settled him on a thwart. One of Evark's men handed him his balalaika with a grin, the other halflings scrambled back aboard, and Bahzell heaved the launch off the beach and crawled over the stem as they backed oars to slide away from the island.

The bonfire still burned, pale and smoky in the growing, golden light, and Brandark gazed back at it and shook his head again at the breakneck speed with which everything had changed. They were going to live after all.

"So, I'm the bigger idiot, am I?" Bahzell growled as the launch curtsied across the water. "And where would you be without me, hey?"

"Snug in bed in Navahk—and hating every minute of it," Brandark said, and Evark snorted behind him.

"Well, you're a long way from Navahk—wherever it is—" the captain observed, putting the tiller over to steer for his ship "—and I can hardly wait till I put the two of you ashore in Belhadan! Korthrala, the Axemen will have a fit! Still," he squinted into the sun, his voice more thoughtful, "I doubt you'd've made it this far if you couldn't land on your feet."

"Oh, we'll be fine," Brandark said, turning on the thwart to sit facing him. "Assuming, of course, that Bahzell doesn't find something else to come all over noble about."

"Noble, is he? *Him?*" Evark gave a crack of laughter. "Now somehow I don't think that's the very word *I'd* use to describe him!"

"Oh, but he is!" Brandark assured the captain. "Nobler than you could possibly guess."

"Here! That's enough of that!" Bahzell protested while the entire boat's crew chortled.

"Don't let his modesty fool you," Brandark said earnestly, a wicked gleam in his eye. "He's too shy to brag on himself, but *I* know. In fact, why don't I just entertain you with a song on the way back to your ship, Captain?"

"Oh, no, you don't!" Bahzell made a grab for the balalaika, but he couldn't reach far enough past the oarsmen, and Brandark settled the instrument in his lap with a seraphic smile.

"It's just a little thing I'm still working on," he told a grinning Evark while Bahzell sputtered behind him. "I call it *The Lay of Bahzell Bloody-Hand*, and it goes like this—"

# APPENDIX

# THE GODS OF NORFRESSA

## THE GODS OF LIGHT

*Orr All-Father*: Often called "The Creator" or "The Establisher," Orr is considered the creator of the universe and the king and judge of gods. He is the father or creator of all but one of the Gods of Light and the most powerful of all the gods, whether of Light or Dark. His symbol is a blue starburst.

*Kontifrio*: "The Mother of Women" is Orr's wife and the goddess of home, family, and the harvest. According to Norfressan theology, Kontifrio was Orr's second creation (after Orfressa, the rest of the universe), and she is the most nurturing of the gods and the mother of all Orr's children except Orfressa herself. Her hatred for Shīgū is implacable. Her symbol is a sheaf of wheat tied with a grape vine.

*Chemalka Orfressa*: "The Lady of the Storm" is the sixth child of Orr and Kontifrio. She is the goddess of weather, good and bad, and has little to do with mortals. Her symbol is the sun seen through clouds.

*Chesmirsa Orfressa*: "The Singer of Light" is the fourth child of Orr and Kontifrio and the younger twin sister of Tomanak, the War God. Chesmirsa is the goddess of bards, poetry, music and art. She is very fond of mortals and has a mischievous sense of humor. Her symbol is the harp.

*Hirahim Lightfoot*: Known as "The Laughing God" and "The Great Seducer," Hirahim is something of a rogue element among the Gods of Light. He is the only one of them who is not related to Orr (no one seems certain where he came from, though he acknowledges Orr's authority . . . as much as he does anyone's) and he is the true prankster of the gods. He is the god of merchants, thieves, and dancers, but he is also known as the god of seductions, as he has a terrible weakness for attractive female mortals (or goddesses). His symbol is a silver flute.

*Isvaria Orfressa*: "The Lady of Remembrance" (also called "The Slayer") is the first child of Orr and Kontifrio. She is the goddess of needful death and the completion of life and rules the House of the Dead, where she keeps the Scroll of the Dead. Somewhat to her mother's dismay, she is also Hirahim's lover. The third most powerful of the Gods of Light, she is the special enemy of Krahana, and her symbol is a scroll with skull winding knobs.

*Khalifrio Orfressa*: "The Lady of the Lightning" is Orr and Kontifrio's second child and the goddess of elemental destruction. She is considered a Goddess of Light despite her penchant for destructiveness, but she has very little to do with mortals (and mortals are just as happy about it, thank you). Her symbol is a forked lightning bolt.

*Korthrala Orfro*: Called "Sea Spume" and "Foam Beard," Korthrala is the fifth child of Orr and Kontifrio.

He is the god of the sea but also of love, hate, and passion. He is a very powerful god, if not over-blessed with wisdom, and is very fond of mortals. His symbol is the net and trident.

*Lillinara Orfressa*: Known as "Friend of Women" and "The Silver Lady," Lillinara is Orr and Kontifrio's eleventh child, the goddess of the moon and women. She is one of the more complex deities and extremely focused. She is appealed to by young women and maidens in her persona as the Maid and by mature women and mothers in her persona as the Mother. As avenger, she manifests as the Crone, who also comforts the dying. She dislikes Hirahim Lightfoot intensely, but she hates Shigu (as the essential perversion of all womankind) with every fiber of her being. Her symbol is the moon.

*Norfram Orfro*: The "Lord of Chance" is Orr and Kontifrio's ninth child and the god of fortune, good and bad. His symbol is the infinity sign.

*Orfressa:* According to Norfressan theology, Orfressa is not a god but the universe herself, created by Orr even before Kontifrio, and she is not truly "awake." Or, rather, she is seldom aware of anything as ephemeral as mortals. On the very rare occasions when she does take notice of mortal affairs, terrible things tend to happen, and even Orr can restrain her wrath only with difficulty.

*Semkirk Orfro*: Known as "The Watcher," Semkirk is the tenth child of Orr and Kontifrio. He is the god of wisdom and mental and physical discipline and, before the Fall of Kontovar, was the god of white wizardry. Since the Fall, he has become the special patron of the psionic magi, who conduct a merciless war against evil wizards.

He is a particularly deadly enemy of Carnadosa, the goddess of black wizardry. His symbol is a golden scepter.

*Silendros Orfressa*: The fourteenth and final child of Orr and Kontifrio, Silendros (called "Jewel of the Heavens") is the goddess of stars and the night. She is greatly reverenced by jewel smiths, who see their art as an attempt to capture the beauty of her heavens in the work of their hands, but generally has little to do with mortals. Her symbol is a silver star.

*Sorbus Kontifra*: Known as "Iron Bender," Sorbus is the smith of the gods. He is also the product of history's greatest seduction (that of Kontifrio by Hirahim—a "prank" Kontifrio has never quite forgiven), yet he is the most stolid and dependable of all the gods, and Orr accepts him as his own son. His symbol is an anvil.

*Tolomos Orfro*: "The Torch Bearer" is the twelfth child of Orr and Kontifrio. He is the god of light and the sun and the patron of all those who work with heat. His symbol is a golden flame.

*Tomanak Orfro*: Tomanak, the third child of Orr and Kontifrio, is Chesmirsa's older twin brother and second only to Orr himself in power. He is known by many names—"Sword of Light," "Scale Balancer," "Lord of Battle," and "Judge of Princes" to list but four—and has been entrusted by his father with the task of overseeing the balance of the Scales of Orr. He is also captain general of the Gods of Light and the foremost enemy of all the Dark Gods (indeed, it was he who cast Phrobus down when Phrobus first rebelled against his father). His symbols are a sword and/or a spiked mace.

*Torframos Orfro*: Known as "Stone Beard" and "Lord of Earthquakes," Torframos is the eighth child of Orr and Kontifrio. He is the lord of the Earth, the keeper of the deep places and special patron of engineers and those who delve, and is especially revered by dwarves. His symbol is the miner's pick.

*Toragan Orfro*: "The Huntsman," also called "Woodhelm," is the thirteenth child of Orr and Kontifrio and the god of nature. Forests are especially sacred to him, and he has a reputation for punishing those who hunt needlessly or cruelly. His symbol is an oak tree.

## THE DARK GODS

*Phrobus Orfro*: Called "Father of Evil" and "Lord of Deceit," Phrobus is the seventh child of Orr and Kontifrio, which explains why seven is considered *the* unlucky number in Norfressa. No one recalls his original name; "Phrobus" ("Truth Bender") was given to him by Tomanāk when he cast Phrobus down for his treacherous attempt to wrest rulership from Orr. Following that defeat, Phrobus turned openly to the dark and became, in fact, the opening wedge by which evil first entered Orfressa. He is the most powerful of the gods of Light or Dark after Tomanāk, and the hatred between him and Tomanāk is unthinkably bitter, but Phrobus fears his brother worse than death itself. His symbol is a flame-eyed skull.

*Shīgū*: Called "The Twisted One," "Queen of Hell," and "Mother of Madness," Shīgū is the wife of Phrobus. No one knows exactly where she came from, but most believe she was, in fact, a powerful demoness raised to godhood by Phrobus when he sought a mate to breed his own pantheon to oppose that of his father. Her power is deep but subtle, her cruelty and malice are bottomless, and her favored weapon is madness. She is even more hated, loathed, and feared by mortals than Phrobus, and her worship is punishable by death in all Norfressan realms. Her symbol is a flaming spider.

*Carnadosa Phrofressa*: "The Lady of Wizardry" is the fifth child of Phrobus and Shigū. She has become the goddess of black wizardry, but she herself might be considered totally amoral rather than evil for evil's sake. She enshrines the concept of power sought by any means and at any cost to others. Her symbol is a wizard's wand.

*Fiendark Phrofro*: The firstborn child of Phrobus and Shigū, Fiendark is known as "Lord of the Furies." He is cast very much in his father's image (though, fortunately, he is considerably less powerful), and all evil creatures owe him allegiance as Phrobus' deputy. Unlike Phrobus, who seeks always to pervert or conquer, however, Fiendark also delights in destruction for destruction's sake. His symbols are a flaming sword or flame-shot cloud of smoke.

*Krahana Phrofressa*: "The Lady of the Damned" is the fourth child of Phrobus and Shigū and, in most ways, the most loathsome of them all. She is noted for her hideous beauty and holds dominion over the undead (which makes her Isvaria's most hated foe) and rules the hells in which the souls of those who have sold themselves to evil spend eternity. Her symbol is a splintered coffin.

*Krashnark Phrofro*: The second son of Phrobus and Shigū, Krashnark is something of a disappointment to his parents. The most powerful of Phrobus' children, Krashnark (known as "Devil Master") is the god of devils and ambitious war. He is ruthless, merciless, and cruel, but personally courageous and possessed of a strong, personal code of honor, which makes him the only Dark God Tomanāk actually respects. He is, unfortunately, loyal to his father, and his power and sense of honor have made him the "enforcer" of the Dark Gods. His symbol is a flaming steward's rod.

*Sharnā Phrofro*: Called "Demonspawn" and "Lord of the Scorpion," Sharnā is Krashnark's younger, identical twin (a fact which pleases neither of them). Sharnā is the god of demons and the patron of assassins, the personification of cunning and deception. He is substantially less powerful than Krashnark and a total coward, and the demons who owe him allegiance hate and fear Krashnark's more powerful devils almost as much as Sharnā hates and fears his brother. His symbols are the giant scorpion (which serves as his mount) and a bleeding heart in a mailed fist.

# DAVID WEBER

continued ☞

# PRAISE FOR
## LOIS MCMASTER BUJOLD

### What the critics say:

**The Warrior's Apprentice:** "Now here's a fun romp through the spaceways—not so much a space opera as space ballet. ... it has all the 'right stuff.' A lot of thought and thoughtfulness stand behind the all-too-human characters. Enjoy this one, and look forward to the next." —Dean Lambe, *SF Reviews*

"The pace is breathless, the characterization thoughtful and emotionally powerful, and the author's narrative technique and command of language compelling. Highly recommended."
—*Booklist*

**Brothers in Arms:** " ... she gives it a genuine depth of character, while reveling in the wild turnings of her tale. ... Bujold is as audacious as her favorite hero, and as brilliantly (if sneakily) successful." —*Locus*

"Miles Vorkosigan is such a great character that I'll read anything Lois wants to write about him. ... a book to re-read on cold rainy days." —Robert Coulson, *Comic Buyer's Guide*

**Borders of Infinity:** "Bujold's series hero Miles Vorkosigan may be a lord by birth and an admiral by rank, but a bone disease that has left him hobbled and in frequent pain has sensitized him to the suffering of outcasts in his very hierarchical era. ... Playing off Miles's reserve and cleverness, Bujold draws outrageous and outlandish foils to color her high-minded adventures." —*Publishers Weekly*

**Falling Free:** "In *Falling Free* Lois McMaster Bujold has written her fourth straight superb novel. ... How to break down a talent like Bujold's into analyzable components? Best not to try. Best to say: 'Read, or you will be missing something extraordinary.' " —Roland Green, *Chicago Sun-Times*

**The Vor Game:** "The chronicles of Miles Vorkosigan are far too witty to be literary junk food, but they rouse the kind of craving that makes popcorn magically vanish during a double feature." —Faren Miller, *Locus*

# MORE PRAISE FOR
# LOIS MCMASTER BUJOLD

## What the readers say:

"My copy of *Shards of Honor* is falling apart I've reread it so often. . . . I'll read whatever you write. You've certainly proved yourself a grand storyteller."
—Lisa Kolbe, Colorado Springs, CO

"I experience the stories of Miles Vorkosigan as almost viscerally uplifting. . . . But certainly, even the weightiest theme would have less impact than a cinder on snow were it not for a rousing good story, and good story-telling with it. This is the second thing I want to thank you for. . . . I suppose if you boiled down all I've said to its simplest expression, it would be that I immensely enjoy and admire your work. I submit that, as literature, your work raises the overall level of the science fiction genre, and spiritually, your work cannot avoid positively influencing all who read it."
—Glen Stonebraker, Gaithersburg, MD

" 'The Mountains of Mourning' [in *Borders of Infinity*] was one of the best-crafted, and simply best, works I'd ever read. When I finished it, I immediately turned back to the beginning and read it again, and I can't remember the last time I did that."
—Betsy Bizot, Lisle, IL

"I can only hope that you will continue to write, so that I can continue to read (and of course buy) your books, for they make me laugh and cry and think . . . rare indeed."
—Steven Knott, Major, USAF

# THE SHIP WHO SANG IS NOT ALONE!

*Anne McCaffrey, with Margaret Ball, Mercedes Lackey, S.M. Stirling, and Jody Lynn Nye, explores the universe she created with her ground-breaking novel,* The Ship Who Sang.

## PARTNERSHIP
### by Anne McCaffrey & Margaret Ball
"[*PartnerShip*] captures the spirit of *The Ship Who Sang* ... a single, solid plot full of creative nastiness and the sort of egocentric villains you love to hate."
—Carolyn Cushman, **Locus**

## THE SHIP WHO SEARCHED
### by Anne McCaffrey & Mercedes Lackey
Tia, a bright and spunky seven-year-old accompanying her exo-archaeologist parents on a dig, is afflicted by a paralyzing alien virus. Tia won't be satisfied to glide through life like a ghost in a machine. Like her predecessor Helva, *The Ship Who Sang*, she would rather strap on a spaceship!

## THE CITY WHO FOUGHT
### by Anne McCaffrey & S.M. Stirling
Simeon was the "brain" running a peaceful space station—but when the invaders arrived, his only hope of protecting his crew and himself was to become *The City Who Fought*.

## THE SHIP WHO WON
### by Anne McCaffrey & Jody Lynn Nye
"*Oodles of fun.*" —*Locus*
"*Fast, furious and fun.*" —*Chicago Sun-Times*

## If You See Me Coming You'd Better Run!

Bahzell gazed down at the pudgy, white-faced, sweating landlord, and folded his arms across his massive chest.

"Now don't you worry, friend," he soothed. "I've no doubt you've been told all manner of tales about my folk, and dreadful they must have been, but you've my word they weren't true. Why, we're almost as civilized as your own folk these days, and as one civilized man to another, I'd not harm a hair on your head. Still," his voice stayed just as soothing, but his eyes glittered, "I'm bound to admit there *are* things can cause any of us to backslide a mite. Like lies. Why, I've seen one of my folk rip both a man's arms off for a lie. Dreadful sorry he was for it afterward, but—"

He shrugged, and the landlord whimpered. Bahzell let him sweat for a long, frightened minute, then went on in a harder voice.

"There's a lass half-dead upstairs. That's bad enough, I'm thinking, but there's worse, for Lady Zarantha *isn't* upstairs. Now, it's possible she's dead, but there's no way I can know until I find her, and find her I will, one way or another. Alive or dead, I *will* find her, and if it should happen when I do that I'm after learning you *did* know something and kept it from me, or warned those as have her I was coming, I'll be back." The landlord looked up in dull terror, and Bahzell bared his teeth and spoke very, very softly.

"And if I *do* come back, you'd best be remembering every tale you ever heard about my folk, friend, because this I promise you. If Lady Zarantha dies, you'll wish you'd died with her—however it was—before you do."

# Baen Books by David Weber

*Honor Harrington Novels:*
**On Basilisk Station**
**The Honor of the Queen**
**The Short Victorious War**
**Field of Dishonor**
**Flag in Exile**
**Honor Among Enemies**
**In Enemy Hands**
**Echoes of Honor**

*Edited by David Weber:*
**More Than Honor**
**Worlds of Honor**

**Mutineer's Moon**
**The Armageddon Inheritance**
**Heirs of Empire**

**Path of the Fury**

**Oath of Swords**
**The War God's Own**

**The Apocalypse Troll**

*With Steve White:*
**Insurrection**
**Crusade**
**In Death Ground**